PUPPET

Also by Joy Fielding

Lost
Whispers and Lies
Grand Avenue
The First Time
Missing Pieces
Don't Cry Now
Tell Me No Secrets
See Jane Run
Good Intentions
The Deep End
Life Penalty
The Other Woman
Kiss Mommy Goodbye

PUPPET

JOY FIELDING

ATRIA BOOKS

New York   London   Toronto   Sydney

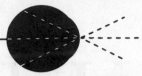

**This Large Print Book carries the
Seal of Approval of N.A.V.H.**

ATRIA BOOKS
1230 Avenue of the Americas
New York, NY 10020

ISBN: 0-7432-6966-7

First Atria Books large-print hardcover edition January 2005

10 9 8 7 6 5 4 3 2 1

ATRIA BOOKS is a trademark of Simon & Schuster, Inc.

Manufactured in the United States of America

For information regarding special discounts for bulk purchases, please contact Simon & Schuster Special Sales at 1-800-456-6798 or business@simonandschuster.com

To Warren, Shannon, and Annie.
My heart, my soul, and my salvation.

ACKNOWLEDGMENTS

A big thank-you to my two favorite cities in the world, Toronto and Palm Beach, and to the wonderful people in each. To Owen Laster, Larry Mirkin, and Beverley Slopen, my very own Three Musketeers, who keep me on the straight and narrow—or circuitous and flighty, as the case may be. To Aurora, who has been with our family for more than thirteen years, and for Rosie, who is always willing to help out. To Owen's former assistants Jonathan Peckarsky and Bill Kingsland, and to his current one, Susanna Schell, all unfailingly pleasant in the face of often peculiar and pesky requests. To Julia Noonan with the Metro West Detention Center and to Berthe Cano at the Toronto Reference Library, for generously sharing their time and answering my many questions. To lawyers David Bayliss and Larry Douglas, who taught me more than I really wanted to know about the Canadian justice system. To my sister Renee, and all my wonderfully supportive friends in both Canada and the U.S., for being, respectively, my sister and my wonderfully supportive friends. To my toy poodle, Casey, who never fails to make me smile. To Emily Bestler, Sarah Branham, Judith Curr, Louise Burke, Seale Ballenger, Thomas Semosh, and all the wonderful people at Atria and Pocket Books. To Maya Mavjee, John Neale, Brad Martin, Stephanie Gowan, Val Gow, and everyone at Doubleday Canada. To Corinne Assayag, who has done such a spectacular job designing and overseeing my website, and to my daughter, Shannon, for her advice, encouragement, and much-needed assistance with my email. To Warren, for reading the manuscript in its final stages, and to Annie, for finally getting around to reading my last book. To the hardworking booksellers and author escorts I've met during my various book tours. And once again, to my readers everywhere. Thank you. You never cease to amaze me.

PUPPET

ONE

Some of the things Amanda Travis likes: the color black; lunchtime spinning classes at the fitness center on Clematis Street in downtown Palm Beach; her all-white, one-bedroom, oceanfront condo in Jupiter; a compliant jury; men whose wives don't understand them.

Some of the things she doesn't: the color pink; when the temperature outside her condo's floor-to-ceiling windows falls below sixty-five degrees; clients who don't follow her advice; the color gray; being asked to show her ID when she goes to a bar; nicknames of any shape and size.

Something else she doesn't like: bite marks.

Especially bite marks that are deep and clearly defined, even after the passing of several days; bite marks that lie like a bright purple tattoo amidst a puddle of mustard-color bruises; bite marks that are all but smiling at her from the photographs on the defense table in front of her.

Amanda shakes blond, shoulder-length hair away from her thin face and slips the offending photographs beneath a pad of lined, yellow legal paper, then picks up a pencil and pretends to be jotting down something of importance, when what she actually writes is **Remember to buy toothpaste**. This gesture is for the jury's benefit, in case any of them is watching. Which is doubtful. Already this morning, she's caught one of the jurors, a middle-aged man with thinning Ronald Reagan–red hair, nodding off. She sighs, drops her pencil, sits back in her chair, and pushes her lips into a pout of disapproval. Not big. Just enough to let the jury know what she thinks of the testimony being given. Which she would like them to believe is not much.

"He was yelling about something," the young woman on the witness stand is saying, one hand absently reaching up to tug at her hair. She glances toward the defense table, pulls the platinum curls away from their black roots, and twists them around square, fake fingernails. "He's always yelling about something."

Again Amanda lifts the pencil into her right hand, adds **Stouffer's frozen macaroni and**

cheese to the impromptu list of groceries she is creating. And **orange juice,** she remembers, scribbling it across the page with exaggerated flourish, as if she has just remembered a key point of law. The action dislodges the pictures beneath the legal pad, so that once again the photographic impressions of her client's teeth against the witness's skin are winking up at her.

It's the bite marks that will do her in.

She might be able to fudge the facts, obfuscate the evidence, overwhelm the jury with irrelevant details and not always reasonable doubt, but there is simply no getting around those awful pictures. They will seal her client's fate and mar her perfect record, like a blemish on an otherwise flawless complexion, detracting from almost a year of sterling performances on behalf of the poor, the unlucky, and the overwhelmingly guilty.

Damn Derek Clemens anyway. Did he have to be so damn obvious?

Amanda reaches over and pats the hand of the man sitting beside her. Another salvo for the jury, although she wonders if any of them is really fooled. Surely they watch enough television to know the various tricks of the trade: the mock outrage, the sympathetic glances, the disbelieving shakes of the head. She withdraws her hand, surreptitiously rubs the touch of her client's skin onto her black linen skirt beneath the table. **Idiot,** she thinks behind her reassuring smile. **You couldn't have exercised even a modicum of self-control. You had to bite her too.**

The defendant smiles back at her, although thankfully, his lips remain closed. The jury will soon be seeing more than enough of Derek Clemens's teeth.

At twenty-eight years old and a wiry five feet ten inches tall, Derek Clemens is the same age and height as the woman selected to represent him. Even their hair is the same shade of delicate blond, their eyes variations of the same cool blue, although hers are darker, more opaque, his paler, sliding toward pastel. In other, more pleasant circumstances, Amanda Travis and Derek Clemens might be mistaken for brother and sister, perhaps even fraternal twins.

Amanda shrugs off the unpleasant thought, grateful, as always, for being an only child. She swivels around in her chair, looks toward the long expanse of windows at the back of the courtroom. Beyond those windows is a typical February day in south Florida—the sky turquoise, the air warm, the beach beckoning. She fights the urge to wander over to the windows, to lean her head against the tinted glass, and stare out past the Intracoastal Waterway to the ocean beyond. Only in Palm Beach does one find an ocean view from a courtroom to rival the view from the penthouse suite of a top hotel.

Perversely, Amanda would rather be here, in Courtroom 5C of the Palm Beach County Court House, sitting beside some lowlife accused of assaulting his live-in girlfriend—five counts, no less, including sexual assault and uttering death threats—than sunbathing on the cool sand next to some underdressed, overnourished snowbird. More than a few minutes of lying on her back with the surf washing over her bare toes is enough to send Amanda Travis screaming for the hot pavement.

"I'd like to retrace the events of the morning of August sixteenth, Miss Fletcher," the assistant district attorney is saying, the deep baritone of his voice drawing Amanda's attention back to the front of the courtroom as easily as a lover's seductive sigh.

Caroline Fletcher nods and continues playing with her overly bleached hair, her surgically amplified bosom straining against the buttons of her perversely conservative blue blouse. It helps the defendant's case that the woman Derek Clemens is accused of assaulting looks like a stripper, although in fact, she works in a hairdressing salon. Amanda smiles with the knowledge this is less important than the image being projected. In law, as in so much of life, appearance counts far more than substance. It is, after all, the **appearance** of justice, and not justice itself, that must be seen to be done.

"August the sixteenth?" The young woman uses her tongue to push the gum she's been surreptitiously chewing throughout her testimony to the side of her mouth.

"The day of the attack," the prosecutor reminds her, approaching the stand and hovering over his star witness. Tyrone King is almost six feet six inches tall with chocolate brown skin and a shiny bald head. When Amanda first joined the law firm of Beatty and Rowe just over a year ago, she heard rumors that the handsome assistant district attorney was a nephew of Martin Luther King's, but when she asked him about it, he laughed and said he suspected all black men in the South named King were rumored to be related to the assassinated leader. "You've testified that the accused came home from work in a foul mood."

"He was always in a foul mood."

Amanda rises halfway out of her chair, voices her objection to the generalization. The objection is sustained. The witness tugs harder on her hair.

"How did this mood manifest itself?"

The witness looks confused.

"Did he raise his voice? Was he yelling?"

"His boss yelled at him, so he came home and yelled at me."

"Objection."

"Sustained."

"What was he yelling about, Miss Fletcher?"

The witness rolls her eyes toward the high ceiling. "He said the place was a mess and that there was never anything to eat, and he was sick of working the midnight shift only to come home to a messy apartment and nothing for breakfast."

"And what did you do?"

"I told him I didn't have time to listen to his complaints, that I had to go to work. And then he said there was no way I was going out and leaving him with the baby all day, that he needed his sleep, and I told him that I couldn't very well take the baby with me to a hairdressing salon, and it just went on from there."

"Can you tell us what happened exactly?"

The witness shrugs, her tongue pushing the gum in her mouth nervously from one cheek to the other. "I don't know **exactly**."

"To the best of your recollection."

"We started screaming at each other. He said I didn't do nothing around the apartment, that I just sat around on my bony ass all day, and that if I wasn't going to do any cooking or cleaning, then the least I could do was get down on my knees and give him a . . ." Caroline Fletcher stops, straightens her shoulders, and looks imploringly at the jury. "You know."

"He demanded oral sex?"

The witness nods. "They're never too tired for that."

The seven women on the jury chuckle knowingly, as does Amanda, who hides her smile inside the palm of her hand and decides against objecting.

"What happened then?" the prosecutor asks.

"He started pulling me toward the bedroom. I kept telling him no, I didn't have time, but he wasn't listening. Then I remembered this movie I saw on TV where the girl, I think it was Jennifer Lopez, I can't remember for sure, but anyway, this guy was attacking her, and she realized that the more she struggled, the more turned on he got, and the worse things got for her, so she stopped struggling, and that kind of threw him off guard, and she was able to escape. So I decided to try that."

"You stopped struggling?"

Again Caroline Fletcher nods. "I kind of went all weak, like I was giving in, and then, as soon as we got to the bedroom door, I pushed him out of the way, ran inside the room, and locked the door."

"And what did Derek Clemens do then?"

"He was so mad. He started banging on the door, yelling that he was going to kill my ass."

"And how did you interpret that?"

"That he was going to kill my ass," Caroline Fletcher explains.

Amanda stares directly at the jury. Surely, her eyes are saying, they can't consider this outburst a serious death threat. She grabs her pencil, adds **bran flakes** to her makeshift list of groceries.

"Go on, Miss Fletcher."

"Well, he was banging on the door and screaming, and so, of course, Tiffany woke up and started crying."

"Tiffany?"

"Our daughter. She's fifteen months old."

"Where was Tiffany during all this?"

"In her crib. In the living room. That's

where we keep it. The apartment only has one bedroom, and Derek says he needs his privacy."

"So his yelling woke up the baby."

"His yelling woke up the whole damn building."

"Objection."

"Sustained."

"And then what?"

"Well, I realized that if I didn't open the door, he was just gonna break it down, so I told him I'd open the door, but only if he promised to calm down first. And he promised, and then it got real quiet, except for the baby crying, so I opened the door, and next thing I knew, he was all over me, punching me and ripping at my dress."

"Is this the dress?" The assistant district attorney maneuvers the distance from the witness stand to the prosecutor's table in two quick strides, retrieving a shapeless, gray jersey dress that has obviously seen better days. He shows it to the witness before offering it up for the jury's inspection.

"Yes, sir. That's it."

Amanda leans back in her chair, as if to indicate her lack of concern. She hopes the jury will be as unimpressed as she is by the two tiny rips to the bottom of the dress's side

seams, fissures that could just as easily have re-
sulted from Caroline Fletcher pulling the dress
down over her hips, as from Derek Clemens
pulling it up.

"What happened after he ripped your dress?"

"He threw me down on the bed, on my
stomach, and bit me."

The incriminating photographs appear, as if
by magic, in the hands of the assistant district
attorney. They are quickly introduced into evidence and distributed to the jury. Amanda
watches the jurors as they examine the impressions of Derek Clemens's teeth branded into
the middle of Caroline Fletcher's back, disgust
flickering across their faces like flames from a
campfire as they struggle to maintain the ve-
neer of impartiality.

As always, the jurors are a decidedly mixed
lot—an old Jewish retiree squeezed between
two middle-aged black women; a clean-shaven
Hispanic man in a suit and tie next to a pony-
tailed young man in a T-shirt and jeans; a
black woman with white hair behind a white
woman with black hair; the heavyset, the lean,
the eager, the blasé. All with one thing in common—the contempt in their eyes as they
glance from the photographs to the defendant.

"What happened after he bit you?"

Caroline Fletcher hesitates, looks toward her feet. "He flipped me over on my back and had sex with me."

"He raped you?" the prosecutor asks, carefully rephrasing her answer.

"Yes, sir. He raped me."

"He raped you," Tyrone King repeats. "And then what?"

"After he was finished, I called the salon to tell them I'd be late for work, and he grabbed the phone out of my hands and threw it at my head."

Resulting in the charge of assault with a deadly weapon, Amanda thinks, adding a legitimate question to her list of groceries. **You called the salon and not the police?**

"He threw the phone at your head," the prosecutor repeats, in what is fast becoming a tiresome habit.

"Yes, sir. It hit the side of my head, then fell to the floor and broke apart."

"What happened next?"

"I changed my clothes and went to work. He ripped my dress," she reminds the jury. "So I had to change."

"And did you report what happened to the police?"

"Yes, sir."

"When was that?"

"A couple of days later. He started hitting me again, and I told him if he didn't stop, I'd go to the police, and he didn't stop, so I did."

"What did you tell the police?"

Caroline Fletcher looks confused. "Well, what the officer already told you." She is alluding to Sergeant Dan Peterson, the previous witness, a man so nearsighted his face virtually vanished inside his notes for most of his testimony.

"You told him about the rape?"

"I told him that me and Derek had been fighting, that Derek was always slapping me around and stuff, and then he took some pictures."

Tyrone King lifts long, elegant fingers into the air, signaling for his witness to pause while he locates several more photographs and shows them to Caroline Fletcher. "Are these the pictures the police officer took?"

Caroline winces as she looks over the various pictures. A nice touch, Amanda thinks, wondering if she's been coached. **Don't be afraid to show some emotion,** she can almost hear Tyrone King whisper in his seductive baritone. **It's crucial that you appear sympathetic to the jury.**

Amanda looks toward her lap, tries picturing the photographs through the jury's eyes. Not too damning really. A few scratches on the woman's cheek that could easily be the result of her daughter's groping fingers, a slight red mark on her chin, a fading purple blotch on her upper right arm, either of which could have come from almost anything. Hardly the stuff of a major assault. Nothing to directly implicate her client.

"And that's when I told him about Derek biting me," Caroline continues, unprompted. "And so he took pictures of my back, and then he asked me if Derek had sexually assaulted me, and I said I wasn't sure."

"You weren't sure?"

"Well, we've been together for three years. We have a baby. I wasn't sure about my rights until Sergeant Peterson told me."

"And that's when you decided to press charges against Derek Clemens?"

"Yes, sir. So I pressed charges, and the police drove me back to my apartment, and they arrested Derek."

A phone rings, disturbing the natural rhythms of the room. A tune emerges. **Camptown ladies sing dis song—Doo-dah! Doo-dah**. And then again. **Camptown ladies sing dis song . . .**

Amanda glances toward her purse on the floor by her feet. Surely she hasn't left her phone on, she hopes, reaching inside her purse, as do several women on the jury. The Hispanic man reaches for his jacket pocket. The prosecuting attorney looks accusingly at the woman who is his second chair, but she shakes her head and widens her eyes, as if to say, Not me.

Camptown ladies sing dis song—Doo-dah! doo-dah.

"Oh, my God," the witness suddenly exclaims, the color disappearing from her already pale face as she grabs her enormous canvas bag from the floor beside her and rummages around inside it, the tune growing louder, more insistent.

Camptown ladies sing dis song . . .

"I'm so sorry," she apologizes to the judge, who peers at her disapprovingly over the top of a pair of wire-rimmed reading glasses as she switches her portable phone off and flings it back in her purse. "I told people not to call me," she offers by way of explanation.

"Kindly leave your phone at home this afternoon," the judge says curtly, taking the opportunity to break for lunch. "And your gum," he adds, before telling everyone to be back at two o'clock.

"So where we going for lunch?" Derek Clemens asks casually, his arm brushing against Amanda's as they rise to their feet.

"I don't do lunch." Amanda gathers her papers into her briefcase. "I suggest you grab a bite in the cafeteria." Instantly she regrets her choice of words. "I'll meet you back here in an hour."

"Where you going?" she hears him ask, but she is already halfway down the center aisle of the courtroom, the ocean roaring in the distance as she steps into the hallway and runs toward the bank of elevators to her right. One opens just as she approaches, which she takes as a good omen, and she checks her watch as she steps inside. If she moves fast enough, she can just make it to the club for the start of her spinning class.

She checks her phone for messages as she runs south along Olive toward Clematis. There are three. Two are from Janet Berg, who lives in the apartment directly below hers, and with whose husband Amanda had a brief, and unnoteworthy, fling several months earlier. Is it possible Janet found out about the affair? Amanda quickly erases both messages, then listens to the third, which is mercifully from her secretary, Kelly Jamieson. Amanda inherited the relentlessly perky young woman with spiky red hair from her predecessor at Beatty and Rowe, a woman who'd apparently grown disillusioned with being a grossly overworked and woefully underpaid associate in the busiest criminal legal firm in town and left to become the trophy wife of an aging lothario.

Nothing wrong with that, Amanda thinks, nearing the corner of Olive and Clematis. She considers trophy wife a noble profession.

Having been one herself.

She calls her office, begins speaking even before her secretary has time to say hello. "Kelly, what's up?" She crosses the street as the light is changing from amber to red.

"Gerald Rayner called to see if you'd agree to another postponement on the Buford case; Maxine Fisher wants to know if she can come in next Wednesday at eleven instead of Thursday at ten; Ellie called to remind you about lunch tomorrow; Ron says he needs you at the meeting on Friday; and a Ben Myers called from Toronto. He wants you to call him, says it's urgent. He left his number."

Amanda stops dead in the middle of the street. "What did you say?"

"Ben Myers called from Toronto," her secretary repeats. "You're from Toronto originally, aren't you?"

Amanda licks at a fresh bead of perspiration forming on her upper lip.

A horn begins honking, followed by another. Amanda tries to put one foot in front of the other, but it is only when she notices several cars impatiently nudging toward her that her legs agree to move.

Puppet! she hears distant voices cry as she weaves her way through the moving line of cars to the other side of the street.

"Amanda? Amanda, are you there?"

"I'll talk to you later." Amanda clicks off the phone and drops it back inside her purse. She stands for several seconds on the sidewalk, taking deep breaths, and exhaling all reminders of the past. By the time she reaches the glass door of the fitness center, she has almost succeeded in erasing the conversation with her secretary from her mind.

Something else Amanda Travis doesn't like: memories.

Two

By the time Amanda changes out of her work clothes, finishes securing her hair into a ponytail and lacing up her sneakers, the spinning class is already under way, and every bike is taken. "Dammit," she mutters, slapping at her black leotards and realizing she is surprisingly, perilously close to tears. They really should get more bicycles in here, she thinks, deciding that eight bicycles are hardly enough for such a popular class. She toys briefly with the idea of pushing one of the other women off her seat, trying to choose between the well-toned teenager showing off in the front row or the breathless fifty-something-year-old struggling in the back. She settles on the latter, thinking it would probably be an act of mercy to dislodge her. The poor woman will give herself a heart attack, if she's not careful. Doesn't she know that spinning classes are for those who don't really need them?

Amanda stands in the doorway for several seconds, enviously monitoring the class, hoping that one of the participants will eventually read the desperation in her eyes and relinquish her seat. Don't they understand she only has so much time? That unlike most of them, she has an actual job she has to return to, that she is due back in court in just over an hour, and that she needs these forty-five minutes of torturous cycling to burn off some morning steam and gather her resources for this afternoon?

"Okay, everybody, up off your tush," the male instructor barks over the steady assault of rock music. The women, sweat already dripping into glazed eyes and open mouths, promptly lift their rear ends obligingly into the air, pedaling harder, faster, harder, faster, trying to keep up with their leader, while Blondie sings from nearby speakers.

The conversation with her secretary suddenly sneaks up on Amanda, whispering in her ear. **And a Ben Myers called from Toronto,** her secretary says. **He wants you to call him. Says it's urgent.**

Amanda quickly retreats to the main room and jumps on the first empty treadmill in front of the second-floor windows overlooking the street, ratcheting up the speed until she is running. Three television sets look down at her from strategic positions around the room. The sound on all three is turned off, although the closed captioning is unavoidable. It competes with the flow of headline news that scrolls relentlessly across the bottoms of the screens. Amanda feels a headache hovering behind her eyes and turns away as the news announcer begins reporting important, late-breaking news from the Middle East.

He says it's urgent.

"Dammit." Amanda adjusts the incline on the treadmill to its steepest level.

"Shouldn't do that," a man says, stopping by her side.

Amanda feels the man's breath warm on her bare arm. "Shouldn't do what?" she asks without looking at him. His voice is unfamiliar, and she tries to imagine what he looks like. Thirtyish, she decides. Dark hair, brown eyes. Good biceps, strong thighs.

"You're just asking for an injury when you make the incline so steep. I speak from experience," he adds when she ignores his warning. "I tore my adductor muscle last year. Took me six months to recover."

Amanda glances in his direction without breaking stride, gratified that he is much as she pictured, except he's probably closer to forty than thirty, and his eyes are green, not brown. Handsome in an overly groomed sort of way. Never too far from his blow-dryer. She's seen him here before and knows this isn't the first time she's caught his eye. She presses a button, feels the machine's incline decrease beneath her feet. "Better?"

"Actually it would be better if you didn't use the incline at all. You're already running against pressure. The incline just puts added strain on the groin muscles."

"Wouldn't want to strain those." Amanda returns the incline to zero. "Thank you." She wonders how long it's going to take the man to introduce himself.

"Carter Reese," he says before she's completed the thought.

"Amanda Travis." She swallows him in a glance as he steps onto the treadmill beside her: the broad shoulders, the muscular legs, the thick neck. Probably played football in college. Now he plays golf and works out. Most likely an investment counselor. Newly divorced or recently separated, judging by his lack of a wedding band. A couple of kids. Not interested in anything serious. She gives him three minutes before he suggests meeting later for a drink.

"People call you Mandy?"

"Never."

"Okay, then. Amanda it is. So, you come here often?" he says only half-jokingly.

Amanda smiles. She likes a man who's comfortable with clichés. "As often as I can."

"I usually see you on those crazy bicycles."

"Unfortunately, I got here a little late today. They were all taken."

"You live around here?"

"I live in Jupiter. You?"

"West Palm. Don't tell me you came all the way from Jupiter just to exercise."

"No. I came from work."

"What is it you do?"

"I'm a lawyer."

"Really? I'm impressed."

Amanda smiles. "You are?" She wonders if he's mocking her.

"Lawyers with great legs impress me," he continues.

Amanda's smile freezes. She should have known. Two minutes, she thinks.

"And you?"

"Investment counselor."

"Now I'm the one who's impressed," she offers, silently congratulating herself on her intuitive powers, and hoping she doesn't sound too insincere.

But if he suspects her compliment is anything less than genuine, he gives no such indication. "So, what sort of law do you practice?"

"Criminal."

Carter Reese laughs out loud.

"I'm sorry. Did I say something funny?"

He shakes his head. "You just don't strike me as the criminal lawyer type."

"And what type is that?"

"Rough, tough, beer belly." He makes an obvious show of looking her up and down, then smiles appreciatively, as if her flat stomach were sculpted for his benefit. "I'm not seeing any beer belly."

"What you see isn't always what you get," Amanda warns playfully.

"I'd like to see more."

One minute.

"What time do you finish work?" he asks.

"I should be through about five."

"About?"

"More or less."

"About?" he repeats, except this time he pronounces it **aboot.** "Do I detect traces of a Canadian accent?"

You're from Toronto originally, aren't you?

Amanda bristles. She's worked hard to eliminate all such traces from her voice. "So, are you going to ask me out for a drink later or what?"

A slight pause, a grin in his voice. "I was thinking about it."

"Think faster. I have to be back in court in less than an hour."

He smiles. "A woman who doesn't believe in beating around the bush. I like that."

"The Monkey Bar?" she suggests. "Six o'clock? That'll give me time to check in with my office."

"I have a better idea."

This doesn't surprise Amanda, who is used to the better ideas of men like Carter Reese.

"I know this great little spot up in your neck of the woods. We could meet there for drinks, maybe have some dinner . . ."

"Sounds good." Amanda watches the grin in his voice spread across the square set of his jaw. He's feeling terribly pleased with himself, she thinks, feeling pretty pleased herself. After all, when it comes to relieving stress, sex is almost as good as spinning.

* * *

"Did you have sex with the defendant after the incident on August the sixteenth?" Amanda asks the witness at the start of her cross-examination. She rises from her chair as she is speaking, buttoning the top button of her tailored black jacket, and walking briskly toward Caroline Fletcher, who looks imploringly at the prosecutor.

"Objection," he offers obligingly.

"On what grounds?" Amanda scoffs.

"Relevance." Tyrone King approaches the judge. "Your Honor, the issue here is what happened on the morning in question, not what might have happened later."

"On the contrary," Amanda argues. "My client is facing some very serious charges. The witness claims that on the morning of August sixteenth, she was raped; Derek Clemens insists the sex was consensual and offers as evidence the fact that they made love again later that same day. If this is true, it's not only relevant, it goes to the witness's credibility."

"The objection is overruled," the judge agrees, directing the witness to answer the question.

"Did you and the defendant make love again after the incident on August the sixteenth?" Amanda repeats when the witness hesitates.

"We had sex, yes," Caroline Fletcher answers.

"That same night?"

"When I got home from work."

Amanda turns toward the jury, carefully plucked eyebrows lifting in well-rehearsed confusion. "Why?" she asks simply.

"I don't understand."

"Frankly, neither do I. I mean, you claim Derek Clemens raped you earlier in the day. Why would you willingly consent to have sex with him only hours later?"

"He said he was sorry," Caroline replies earnestly.

"He said he was sorry?"

"He can be very persuasive when he wants to be."

"I see. So this isn't the first time this sort of thing has happened."

"**What** sort of thing?"

"I'll rephrase." Amanda takes a deep breath. "How would you characterize your relationship with the defendant, Miss Fletcher?"

"I'm not sure."

"Would you say it was stormy?"

"I guess."

"You fought a lot?"

"He was always yelling about something."

"Did you yell back?"

"Sometimes."

"And had these fights ever gotten physical before the morning of August the sixteenth?"

"Sometimes he'd hit me."

"Ever hit him back?"

"Just to protect myself."

"So, the answer is yes, you sometimes hit him back?"

The witness glares at Amanda. "He's a lot stronger than I am."

"Okay. Just to be clear: you and Derek Clemens had a very stormy relationship, you fought often, and those fights sometimes got physical. Is that correct?"

"Yes," Caroline agrees reluctantly.

"Did these fights often end with sex?"

The witness fidgets in her chair. "Sometimes."

"So isn't it possible that Derek Clemens thought it was simply business as usual on the morning of August the sixteenth?"

Caroline Fletcher crosses her arms stubbornly across her inflated chest. "He knew exactly what he was doing."

Amanda pauses, checks the notes in her hands, although she already has them committed to memory. "Miss Fletcher, when Mr. King questioned you about what happened that morning, you said that Derek Clemens threw you on the bed, flipped you over onto your back, and had sex with you."

"I said he raped me."

"Yes, but your original words were that he had sex with you. And you admitted it wasn't until after you spoke to the police that you decided you'd been raped."

"Like I said, I wasn't sure about my rights until Sergeant Peterson told me."

"You needed someone to tell you you'd been raped?"

"Objection."

"Sustained," the judge says. "Move on, Ms. Travis."

Again Amanda glances unnecessarily at her notes. "And after the alleged assault, you called the hairdressing salon where you worked."

"To tell them I'd be late."

"You didn't call the police," Amanda states.

"No."

"In fact, you didn't contact the police until two days later."

Caroline Fletcher scowls.

"So, at the time Derek Clemens said he was going to 'kill your ass,' you didn't feel seriously threatened, did you, Miss Fletcher?"

"I felt threatened."

"You recognized it was just a figure of speech, didn't you?"

"I felt seriously threatened," the witness insists.

"So threatened you returned home right after work?"

"I had a baby to take care of."

"A baby you had no problem leaving alone with a man you claim beat and raped you. Not to mention threatened your life."

"Derek wouldn't hurt the baby."

"Oh, I'm quite certain of that," Amanda agrees heartily, smiling toward the defendant. "In fact, Derek Clemens is a wonderful father, is he not?"

"He's a good father," the witness admits with obvious reluctance.

"He's Tiffany's primary caregiver, isn't that right?"

"Well, he was the one home during the day."

"And now?"

"Now?"

"Now that you and Derek Clemens are no longer together, who takes care of Tiffany?"

"We both do."

"Isn't it true that she lives with her father?"

"Most of the time."

"And you're now living with another man?"

Amanda checks her notes. "One Adam Johnson?"

"Not anymore."

"You broke up? Why is that?"

The assistant district attorney is instantly on his feet. "Objection, Your Honor. I don't see how this line of questioning is relevant to the proceedings at hand."

"I believe I can show relevance with my next question, Your Honor."

"Proceed."

"Is it true Adam Johnson has a restraining order out against you, Miss Fletcher?"

"Objection."

"Overruled."

"Why did Adam Johnson take out a restraining order, Miss Fletcher?"

The witness shakes her head, begins nervously chipping at the polish on the middle finger of her left hand. "Adam Johnson is a liar. He just wants to make trouble for me."

"I see. It has nothing to do with the fact you attacked him with a pair of scissors?"

"They were just manicure scissors," Caroline Fletcher protests weakly.

"I have no more questions of this witness." Amanda returns to her seat at the defense table and tries not to smile.

* * *

The phone is ringing as Amanda walks by her secretary into her small office. "I'm not here," she says in passing, closing the door behind her, and flipping through the stack of messages on her desk. She takes off her jacket, kicks off the black canvas pumps that have been pinching her toes all afternoon, and falls into her black leather chair. She's tempted to stretch her legs across the top of her desk in triumph, the way men do in movies when they're feeling especially smug, but it's a little premature. The trial is far from over just because the prosecutor's star witness delivered a less than stellar performance. There's still the matter of those gruesome bite marks on Caroline Fletcher's back. Will Derek Clemens really be able to persuade the jury to overlook the evidence of their own eyes?

Another reason Amanda is reluctant to put her feet up: there's no room. She needs more space. Her eyes skip from the blank computer screen in the middle of her desk to the various files and papers piled high along either side. Dozens of black, felt-tipped pens are strewn among a haphazard collection of paperweights and miniature pieces of crystal—a small poodle, an open book, a gold-plated quill in a tiny inkwell. Strange purchases for someone who normally disdains clutter, she thinks absently, looking toward the window of her third-floor office and wincing, as she always does, at the sight of the bright, bubble-gum-pink building across the street. Not that she is in any position to throw decorative stones, she decides, having failed in her attempt to persuade the powers that be at Beatty and Rowe to repaint their canary-yellow building a more palatable white.

The door opens after a gentle knock, and Amanda's secretary peeks her head inside. Underneath the shock of orange-red hair, Kelly Jamieson is vaguely cross-eyed, despite corrective surgery and heavy glasses. A long, thin nose sits in the middle of a moon-shaped face; her chest is flat; her legs are short and slightly bowed. Curiously, these flawed parts make for an oddly endearing whole. "That was Ben Myers again," she announces, her voice crackling like logs in an open fire.

Amanda lifts a file from her desk, pretends to be reading.

"I told him you weren't back from court yet. He left his home number, said you can phone him as late as you want."

Amanda drops the file to the desk, plays with the corner of another. "It's late now," she says. "Why don't you call it a night?"

Kelly hovers in the doorway. "Can I ask you a question?"

Amanda lifts her eyes to her secretary, finds herself holding her breath.

"Who is this guy?"

Amanda conjures up half a dozen lies in the space of several seconds, abandons them just as fast. "He's my ex-husband."

"Your ex-husband?" There's no disguising the surprise in her secretary's voice. Her eyes squeeze against the bridge of her nose. "I thought Sean Travis was your ex-husband."

"Him too."

"You have two ex-husbands?"

Amanda hears the silent addendum—**And you're only twenty-eight!**

"What can I say? I'm a very good lawyer and a very bad wife."

Amanda waits for Kelly to protest—**Oh, no. I'm sure you were a wonderful wife**—but no such protest is forthcoming. "What do you think he wants?"

"I have no idea."

"He said it was really important."

Amanda nods, feels her body tense.

"Are you going to call him later?"

"No."

Silence. Her secretary sways from one foot to

the other. "Okay, well, I guess I'll go home now."

Amanda nods her approval, even as Kelly remains rooted to the spot. "Is there something else?" Amanda ventures warily.

Kelly approaches, extends a small piece of paper toward her boss. "His home phone number," she says, depositing the pink memo slip carefully on Amanda's desk. "In case you change your mind."

THREE

Three reasons why Amanda knows Carter Reese is married even before he admits it: number one, the little out-of-the-way spot he has chosen for dinner is **so** little and out-of-the-way that Amanda, who knows the area well, drives twice through the nondescript strip mall in which it is located before finally spotting it cramped between a pet store and a discount shoe outlet; number two, it is so dark inside the windowless space that she can barely see what she is eating, although she notices her companion glances nervously toward the front door every time he hears it open; number three, he is constantly touching the ring finger of his left hand, as if to make sure he remembered to remove his wedding band, a nervous habit and dead giveaway.

"It's okay," she tells him finally, finishing the last of her mussels and deciding to put him out of his misery. "I have no problem with your being married."

"What?" Even in the dim light, the shock is clearly visible on his face.

"It doesn't bother me that you're married," Amanda says earnestly. "In fact, it makes things easier."

"What?" Carter Reese says again.

"I'm not looking for a serious relationship; I have a very demanding career; I've got a million things on my plate at the moment; and it's much less complicated this way. So you can relax. You don't have to lie to me. Most of the time, anyway," she adds with a smile.

There is a moment's silence while Carter Reese tries to decide if this is one of those times. The candle in the middle of the table flickers precariously as he exhales. "Is this some kind of test?"

Amanda laughs. "I'm just saying it's not important, that's all."

Carter leans back in his chair, shakes his head, folds his muscular arms across his chest, stares off into the darkness.

"Is there a problem?" Amanda asks.

"To be honest, I'm not quite sure how to take this."

"What do you mean?"

He laughs self-consciously. "Well, truth-fully, I don't know whether to be ecstatic or in-sulted."

Amanda reaches across the table for his hand. "It was certainly never my intention to insult you."

Another deep exhalation. "Okay, then." A smile that wavers precariously between **I must be the luckiest guy on earth** and **There's got to be a catch here somewhere.** "Okay, then," he repeats, squeezing her fingers. "Ec-stasy it is."

Amanda laughs. "Good. Now that that's out of the way, maybe we can order dessert." She looks around for their waiter, but sees only vague shapes moving in the background.

"Is there anything you'd like to know?" Carter asks.

"About what?"

"About my marriage."

Amanda gives the question a moment's thought. Clearly he feels he owes her some sort of explanation, but truthfully, there is nothing about his marriage she wants to know. She senses, however, that he will be hurt if she says this, so she settles for the obvious: "How long have you been married?"

"Fifteen years. Two kids. A boy, Jason, he's

thirteen, and a girl, Rochelle, who'll be eleven in March. Sandy's an artist," he continues un-prompted, as if his wife were standing at his side, waiting to be introduced. "She paints. She's very talented."

Amanda does her best to look interested. She hopes he isn't a purger, one of those men so relieved to have been found out that they spend the entire evening regurgitating all their guilty little secrets.

"She's really a very nice woman."

"I'm sure she's lovely."

"There's nothing wrong with my marriage. Just that, you know . . ."

"You've grown apart," Amanda volunteers. She's seen this script before. She knows every-body's lines.

"It's nobody's fault. It's just, well, you know."

Amanda slides her hands away from his and adjusts the plunging neckline of her black sweater, hoping to distract him.

"The kids take up a lot of her time and en-ergy," Carter continues, seemingly oblivious to Amanda's impressive cleavage. "She's not very interested in sex anymore. Says she's too tired. You know."

Amanda nods, although she can't imagine ever being too tired to have sex. She finishes what's left of the wine in her glass in a single gulp.

"So," he says, sensing perhaps it's time to move on. "Tell me more about you. How did such a beautiful woman end up in such an ugly profession?"

Amanda shrugs. "I thought it would be fun."

"Fun?"

"Interesting," she amends, although **fun** is the more accurate description.

"And is it?"

"Sometimes."

"Depends on the criminal, I guess," Carter offers.

"No," Amanda counters. "Generally speaking, criminals themselves are a pretty dull lot. They're amazingly similar. Most of them aren't very bright or imaginative. It's only their crimes that make them interesting. And the fact that none of them ever thinks he's going to get caught."

"He?"

"Usually. Especially in crimes of violence."

"Women aren't violent?"

"I didn't say that," she said, thinking of Caroline Fletcher.

"Sandy once threw an omelet at my head."

Amanda blanches at the casual reference to Carter's wife. For a woman who didn't even exist a few moments ago, she is suddenly very much a force to be reckoned with. "An omelet?"

"She was making breakfast and I mentioned that I thought she'd put on a few pounds recently. Next thing I knew this omelet came flying across the room, caught me smack in the middle of the forehead."

Assault with a deadly egg, Amanda thinks. Aloud she says, "Probably wasn't the best thing to tell her first thing in the morning."

Carter chuckles at the memory. "Is there ever a good time?"

"I doubt it."

"You ever been married?"

"No," Amanda lies, deciding it's easier this way. Two ex-husbands would be too much of a distraction for Carter Reese, who is having enough trouble trying to figure out what to do with his wife. Besides, she has no interest in re-hashing the boring details of why each marriage fell apart. Simply put, the first time she was too young; the second time he was too old. Well, maybe not quite so simple as that, but what difference does it make? She doubts Carter Reese will be around long enough for it to matter. Surprise me, she finds herself thinking, smiling at the man across the table, silently urging him to deviate from the script. I will if you will, her eyes try to tell him. He pats her hand and looks anxiously toward the door.

The waiter suddenly materializes at the side of their table, startling Amanda, who didn't see him approach. "How was everything?" he asks, clearing away the dishes.

"Delicious."

"Thank you." He says this as if he has cooked the meal himself. "Dessert for anyone? We make a mean key lime tart."

"Sounds good."

"Decaf cappuccino," Carter tells the waiter. "And an extra fork."

Amanda stiffens. She's always hated sharing her food, dislikes another person's hand reaching into her plate.

"So, what brought you to Florida?" Carter asks.

Amanda suddenly becomes aware of how quiet it has become, as if everybody in the room has stopped talking and is waiting for her answer. She peers through the dim light at the several other people in the restaurant, but all are busy eating and seem reassuringly unconcerned with her presence. "I came here on a holiday eight years ago," she tells him. "Liked what I saw, decided to stay."

At what point does a half-truth become a lie? she wonders, thinking of the oath all witnesses are obliged to take in court. **Do you swear to tell the truth, the** whole **truth . . . ?**

Does anyone ever tell the whole truth?

I came here on a holiday eight years ago (to escape my first husband), **liked what I saw** (saw my second), **decided to stay.**

"So you went to law school here?"

"Went to law school." **Got married again.** "Got my citizenship." **Got divorced again.** "Practiced for a year with this small firm in Jupiter before being asked to join Beatty and Rowe."

"And your family? Where are they?"

"My mother's up in Toronto. My dad died eleven years ago."

"I lost my mother last year." Carter says this as if he merely misplaced her and that if he looks hard enough, she may just turn up again. "Cancer."

Amanda nods sympathetically. "It's hard. . . ."

"Not for my father. He got married again two months later. The girl next door," Carter adds bitterly, a sneer tugging at the sides of his full lips.

Amanda finds the combination of sneer and bitterness almost unbearably attractive. They add character to an otherwise bland voice and generically handsome features. She's sorry now she ordered dessert. The sooner they get away from all these unwanted relatives the better. "You know I have a cappuccino maker at my condo," she says seductively.

Carter Reese is instantly on his feet. "Waiter," he barks at the darkness, either unmindful or uncaring that he is now the center of everyone's attention. "Check, please."

Amanda meets up with Carter Reese outside the elegant marble and glass lobby of her condominium on North Ocean Boulevard. They have parked their cars—she in her designated spot underground, he in guest parking out front. "Good evening, Joe," she greets the elderly doorman, ushering Carter toward the elevators at the back of the lobby.

Carter rarely lifts his eyes from his black, tassled loafers as they wait for an elevator to arrive. Clearly he is uncomfortable with the lobby's harsh lights, with the image of himself as eager adulterer that reflects endlessly back at him from the mirrors lining the walls. "Slow elevators," he comments under his breath, although they haven't been waiting long.

A few more seconds and the elevator finally arrives, the door opening to disgorge an attractive middle-aged woman whose large white poodle is straining against his leash. The dog barks when he sees Carter, lunges toward him. "Pussycat!" the woman admonishes, tugging on the dog's rhinestone collar. "Sorry. He doesn't like strangers."

"This one's safe," Amanda assures both the woman and her dog, following Carter into the empty elevator, and pressing the button for the fifteenth floor. "Or maybe not," she says with a laugh, as his hands reach out to encircle her waist even before the elevator doors are fully closed. He pulls her to him, their lips barely an inch apart when the doors suddenly lurch to a stop and then reopen.

"Oh," says the woman who steps inside.

Carter's hands drop instantly to his sides. His eyes return to the floor.

"Janet," Amanda says as the woman pointedly looks toward the front of the elevator. Guess now isn't the best time to ask her what those two phone calls to my office were about, Amanda decides, as an attractive man in his

midthirties, wearing a Hawaiian shirt and a
deep scowl, enters the elevator. "Victor," she
acknowledges, as Janet glares toward her husband. Amanda quickly scans the woman's face
for signs of her rumored brow lift.

No one says another word until the couple
disembark on the fourteenth floor.

"Friendly people," Carter says, slipping his
arms back around her, nuzzling the side of her
neck.

The phone is ringing as they approach the
door to her apartment.

"Don't answer it," Carter says as they step
inside.

"I have no intention of answering it." She
throws her purse on the white tile floor, burrows in against him as the phone continues its
insistent ring.

He kisses her neck, his tongue playing with
the folds of her ear.

She takes his hand, leads him past the
moonlit-bathed, all-white living room toward
the all-white master bedroom, the phone's
shrill ring pursuing them.

It stops after four rings, signaling that voice
mail has picked it up. "So, what do you think
of my view?"

"Spectacular," he says, ignoring the impressive panorama of surf and sky visible from the bedroom's floor-to-ceiling windows to plant a row of kisses on the side of her face.

She laughs as he reaches underneath her sweater and swallows her bare breasts in the palms of his hands. "Full moon," she remarks.

"Brings out the beast." He brings her hands to the front of his pants, kisses her hard on the mouth.

The phone rings.

"Persistent little devil," Carter says, glancing toward the phone on the bedside table.

"Ignore it."

"You're sure?"

Amanda's response is to pull her sweater up over her head, toss it to the floor.

"God, you're beautiful," Carter whispers as the phone stops ringing.

She tugs at the buckle of his belt, slides his pants down over his hips, stumbles with him toward the bed in the center of the room. Within seconds, they are on top of the white duvet and fumbling with the remainder of their clothes. A few more seconds and they are both naked, his hands roughly caressing her body, his tongue seeking hers. Just what the doctor ordered, she thinks as he raises himself to his knees and enters her sharply, his body pounding into hers, blocking out the sound of the ocean waves, the hum of the air-conditioning unit, the renewed ringing of the telephone.

Carter's head turns toward the sound. "Look, maybe it's an emergency."

In response, Amanda grabs his buttocks, pushes him deeper inside her. She reaches between his legs, silently directing him to pick up the speed of his thrusts. Luckily, he requires no further encouragement, and the next twenty minutes pass pleasantly in a variety of frenzied positions.

"Wow," he enthuses afterward. "That was something else."

Amanda is tempted to ask, What else? Instead she says, "You up for an encore?" She is reaching for him just as the phone resumes its painful ring.

"Why don't you just answer the damn thing? Whoever it is obviously isn't going away."

Amanda nods, knowing Carter Reese is right. She's only postponing the inevitable, prolonging the torture, by refusing to answer the phone. She grabs it off the night table, pulls the cord across Carter's chest. "Hello?" she snaps into the receiver.

"Finally wore you down, did I?" says the once-familiar voice.

Amanda takes a deep breath, trying to still the angry pounding of her heart. "This better be good."

"It's about your mother," Ben Myers says.

Amanda tries picturing her former husband, but it's hard to imagine him as anything other than the dangerously handsome young rebel in the scruffy black leather jacket he was at the time of their first encounter. She wonders if the years since she last saw him have added any weight to his skinny frame, if his dark hair has thinned, if time has hardened the soft brown of his eyes. His cheeks probably still crinkle when he smiles, she thinks, although the smile was always wary, slow in coming. Amanda pushes her hair roughly away from her face and leans back against the headboard. "My mother," she repeats dully. "Is she dead?"

"No."

"Sick?"

"No. Mandy—"

"Don't call me that. Was she in some kind of accident?"

"She's in trouble."

"Really? Who'd she kill?"

Carter Reese's forehead disappears into a se-

ries of deep furrows. **Who'd she kill?** the furrows repeat.

"Ben?"

The silence that follows lasts perhaps a beat
too long. "A man by the name of John
Mallins."

"What!"

"Ring any bells?"

"What are you talking about?"

"Yesterday at around four o'clock in the afternoon, your mother shot and killed a man by
the name of John Mallins in the lobby of the
Four Seasons hotel."

Amanda feels her whole body flush hot with
rage. "What kind of sick joke is this?"

"Trust me. It's no joke."

"You're seriously trying to tell me that yesterday afternoon my mother shot and killed
someone in the lobby of the Four Seasons
hotel?"

"Your mother shot someone?" asks Carter
Reese.

"A man named John Mallins," Ben tells
Amanda.

"Who the hell is John Mallins?"

"You have no idea?"

"How would I know? I haven't spoken to
my mother since before our divorce."

Carter's eyes narrow. **You told me you'd never been married,** the eyes accuse.

"What does my mother say?"

"She's not saying anything."

"Why doesn't that surprise me?"

"You need to come home, Amanda."

"What? No way."

"Your mother's in jail. She's been arrested for murder."

"My mother's in jail. She's been arrested for murder," Amanda repeats, thinking she must be in the middle of some postcoital nightmare.

Carter begins inching out of the bed, searching through the folds of the duvet for his pants.

"Look, there's obviously been some mistake."

"There's no mistake, Puppet. I'm sorry."

"What?"

"Your mother shot a man three times in front of at least twenty witnesses. She's already confessed."

"You have no right to call me that."

"Look, I don't think you're hearing me."

"Oh, I heard you. Believe me, I heard you."

"Then you understand you have to come home as soon as possible."

"I can't do that. I'm in the middle of an important case. I can't just walk out."

"You can get a postponement."

"Impossible. I'm sure you can handle things there."

"Impossible," he says, throwing the word back at her.

"I can't come home, Ben."

"She's your mother."

"Tell **her** that." Amanda hangs up the phone, then angrily pulls the cord from the wall before racing into the kitchen and disabling the phone there. Then she marches into the living room and pulls open the sliding glass doors, stepping onto her large wraparound patio, and gulping in the cool ocean air, trying to draw moisture into her parched lungs.

Puppet, the waves beckon from below. **Puppet. Puppet.**

Amanda quickly retreats inside her apartment. "Carter," she calls out, pulling the doors closed, desperately trying to block out the unwanted voice. She looks anxiously toward the bedroom. "Carter, get that gorgeous ass of yours in here. The night is young."

But the moon illuminates an empty apartment, and the silence tells her Carter Reese is gone.

FOUR

Do you swear to tell the truth, the whole truth, and nothing but the truth?" the clerk intones solemnly as Derek Clemens lays his left hand across the Bible and raises his right.

"I do."

Amanda studies her client as he states and spells his name, then gives the court his address. Although he is wearing a clean white shirt and pressed black pants, as per Amanda's instructions, his appearance is vaguely slovenly. His open collar rests too loosely around his neck; the suede belt at his waist is scratched and frayed; his blond hair, parted down the middle and pulled into a ponytail, looks stringy and unwashed.

("I washed it this morning," he assured her testily.)

Amanda rises to her feet, unbuttoning the buttons of her black jacket, the same jacket she was wearing yesterday, as well as the same black skirt, and the same black shoes that are still pinching her toes. Only her white blouse is different, although it is a duplicate of the one she was wearing yesterday. She goes over the basic facts of the defendant's former relationship with Caroline Fletcher, their prior living arrangement, their frequent squabbles, their habit of fierce fighting and making up. "Suppose you give us your version of what happened on the morning of August sixteenth," she says, her eyes scanning the jury to make sure everyone is paying proper attention, gratified to find all eyes open and fixed upon the witness. No one nodding off just yet.

Of course they probably all had a good night's sleep, she thinks enviously, recalling the frustrating hours between midnight and 6 a.m. that she spent tossing and turning and cursing all things Canadian. How dare Ben call her after all these years. How dare he make such outrageous demands. How dare he call her Puppet.

She is nobody's puppet anymore.

You have to come home as soon as possible.

I can't do that.

What do you mean, you can't do that?
I'm in the middle of an important case.

"I mean, I work all night," Derek Clemens is saying, and Amanda wonders how much of his testimony she has missed. "I don't think it's asking too much for her to at least make sure there's some milk in the apartment, so I can have a bowl of cereal when I come home."

"So, you'd been working all night, and you were tired and hungry."

"I work from eleven o'clock at night until seven in the morning . . ."

Roughly the same hours she spent tossing and turning in her bed, Amanda thinks, nodding in genuine sympathy.

". . . so, yeah, I was tired and hungry. The apartment's a pigsty. And there she is getting ready to go out. Putting on perfume. Not so much as a 'Hi, how are you?' So I go into the kitchen and I pour myself a bowl of Special K, which I'm not crazy about anyway, but that's all we ever have, 'cause Caroline's always on a diet. And we're out of milk. I mean, what kind of mother is she, she doesn't make sure there's milk for the baby?"

She's your mother.
Tell her that.

"And that made you angry?" Amanda asks,

shaking the intrusive voices away with a toss of her head.

"Damn right it made me angry."

"What did you do?"

"I told her that since she was sticking me with the kid all day, the least she could do was pick up a quart of milk and bring it home before she went to work. And she says she doesn't have time. I said, what do you mean you don't have time? It's not even eight o'clock, the salon doesn't open for another hour. She says she wants to get there early because Jessica promised to cut her hair before everybody arrives. Then Tiffany wakes up and starts screaming, and I'm exhausted, man, I just want to get some sleep. So I ask her to take the baby with her. She says, absolutely not. And then she tries to push me out of the way, 'cause I'm standing in front of the door. So I grab her arm, and that's when she slaps me."

"**She** slapped **you**?"

"Yeah. Caroline's got a mean temper. It doesn't take much to set her off."

"Objection." Tyrone King rises partway to his feet as the judge sustains his objection.

"Just answer the question, Mr. Clemens," the judge directs.

"Sorry, Your Honor."

"What happened after she slapped you?" Amanda asks.

"I don't remember the exact sequence of events." Derek's careful choice of words sounds like a foreign language on his tongue. "But I **do** remember trying to shield my face. I wait tables on weekends and it doesn't look good for me to come in looking all beat up."

"So you're saying she hit you more than once?"

"Oh, yeah. She got in at least three or four shots before I had enough."

Your mother shot a man three times in front of at least twenty witnesses.

"And what did you do then?" Amanda asks, her voice louder than she intends.

"I grabbed her, pushed her out of the way, told her to get the hell out, that I'd had enough of her crap, and I was going to bed."

"And what did she do?"

"She followed me into the bedroom, scream-ing and pounding on my back. I warned her to leave me alone, but she was like a crazy woman."

"You didn't demand oral sex?"

"Are you kidding? The last thing I was

gonna do was trust my dick in her mouth. Sorry, Your Honor," Derek Clemens says over the muffled laughter of some of the jurors.

"Perhaps you could be a little less colorful in your descriptions," the judge says, although the bemused twinkle in his eyes tells Amanda he rather enjoyed the outburst.

"And yet you did end up having sex with her," Amanda reminds the witness.

"Yeah." He shakes his head in disbelief. "That was pretty much our pattern. One minute we're trading punches, the next minute we're naked and going at it like rabbits."

"Did you rip her dress?"

He shakes his head. "Those seams rip every time you look at them. Caroline was always complaining about it."

"Did you force her to have sex?"

"No way."

You need to come home, Amanda.

What? No way.

Amanda takes a deep breath. "How do you explain the bite marks, Mr. Clemens?"

Derek Clemens has the good sense to look genuinely embarrassed. He too takes a deep breath, then turns to face the jury, tells his story directly to them. "After we finished having sex, Caroline started getting all upset again. She said I made her late, and now Jessica wouldn't have time to cut her hair, and it was all my fault. I told her to shut up and let me get some sleep, and she starts pounding me again. I managed to get out of bed and get behind her, and I'm reaching around her for her hands, trying to keep them from swinging at me, when suddenly, she grabs my hair. My hair's pretty long." He shakes his ponytail from side to side by way of illustration. "And she gets a pretty good grip on it and starts tugging at it. I swear I thought she was gonna pull it right out of my head, and I'm yelling at her to let go. So, of course, what does she do? She pulls harder, that's what. It hurt like hell, and I didn't know how to get her to stop. So, I bit her. She still wouldn't let go. So I bit her again. Harder the second time. That's when she let go of my hair."

"You're saying you bit her in self-defense?"

"I just wanted her to stop pulling my hair," he says plaintively.

"And then what happened?"

"Then she grabbed the phone and threw it at me. I caught it and threw it right back. It was a reflex action. I didn't mean to hit her with it."

"Did you confine her in the apartment against her will?"

"Hell, no. At that point, I was begging her to get the hell out."

"What did you mean when you threatened to 'kill her ass'?"

Derek Clemens shrugs. "It's just an expression. If anybody was afraid for their ass, it was me."

"How tall are you, Mr. Clemens?"

"Five feet eleven inches."

"And how much do you weigh?"

"A hundred and sixty-five pounds."

"And you're trying to tell us that even though you're five inches taller and approximately forty pounds heavier than Caroline Fletcher," Amanda continues, knowing if she doesn't ask this question, the prosecutor will, "that you were the one afraid for your life?"

"Hey," Derek replies with a self-effacing smile. "It's not the size of the **gun** that's gonna kill you. It's those nasty little bullets."

The jury is still chuckling as Amanda rests her case.

"So, how long do you think the jury will be out?" Ellie Townshend is asking between nibbles on her Cobb salad. Ellie Townshend is Amanda's closest friend, although they rarely see each other more than once a month. Not

even that, since Ellie and Michael got en-
gaged.

"Depends how smart they are," Amanda answers, wondering if any of the jurors will be
clever enough to realize that Derek's story
couldn't possibly have gone down the way he
described. All they'd have to do is reenact the
sequence of events as described by the defendant to realize that if Derek Clemens had indeed been standing behind Caroline Fletcher,
and she was pulling on his hair in the manner
he claimed, his mouth wouldn't have been able
to reach much below her shoulders, let alone
all the way down to **the middle of her back**.
Such an act was simply impossible unless he
was directly on top of her.

Of course Amanda wasn't about to challenge
her own witness.

"So, have you found a dress for the wedding?" Ellie is asking. Eager hazel eyes open
wide with expectation. Soft amber waves frame
round, dimpled cheeks.

"Not yet." Amanda looks down the busy
main street. They are sitting in the open front
window of the Big City Tavern on Clematis
watching a desultory parade of tourists stroll
by. A soft breeze plays lazily with the ends of
the paper tablecloths. The temperature sits on

the welcome side of eighty. Another perfect day in south Florida, Amanda thinks, feeling vaguely guilty for not enjoying it more.

"What do you mean, not yet? What are you waiting for?"

"The wedding isn't till June," Amanda reminds her friend gently.

"Which is practically around the corner. Oh, my God. Don't turn around."

Instinctively Amanda swivels around in her seat. "Shit," she mutters under her breath, watching Sean Travis approach, his arm draped protectively around his new wife. Shit, shit, shit, she thinks, groaning audibly as he spots her. What are the odds? Two ex-husbands in as many days. Did her secretary forget to remind her it was National Ex-Husbands Week?

"Amanda," Sean acknowledges, his arm tightening around his young wife.

"Sean, how are you?"

"Well. And you?"

"Well," she replies. "You remember Ellie."

"Of course. How are you?"

"Well."

Well, well, well, Amanda thinks. "You must be Jennifer." She studies her former husband and his new wife dispassionately, finding the woman's black hair and gray eyes a nice compliment to Sean's graying hair and black eyes.

The new wife shakes Amanda's hand, then rests it on the slight bulge of her stomach.

"We're due in July," Sean says proudly, noticing the direction of Amanda's gaze.

"Congratulations," she offers sincerely.

"We can't wait," Jennifer trills.

"Well, nice seeing you," Sean tells Amanda, sounding as if he means it. "Enjoy your lunch."

"Good luck," Amanda calls after them.

"Bastard," Ellie bristles. "Rubbing her pregnancy in your face like that."

"I don't think he meant to do that."

Ellie shrugs. The shrug says she isn't convinced.

"I'm the one who didn't want children, Ellie."

"Which I'll never understand. You'd be a great mom."

"Yeah, right. I had such a good example." Amanda pictures her mother sitting in a Toronto jail cell, then immediately banishes the unwanted image. Stubborn traces of the woman cling to the periphery of her mind's eye as she debates whether to tell Ellie about Ben's phone call. When Amanda finally opens her mouth to speak, she realizes Ellie is already midsentence. "I'm sorry, what?"

"I said, how did it feel, seeing Sean again?"

Amanda shrugs the last vestige of her mother aside. "A little strange, I guess. It's weird to think you have nothing to say to someone you once thought you'd spend the rest of your life with."

"Any regrets?"

"Lots of them," Amanda admits with a sigh. "I wasn't a very good wife."

"It just wasn't a very good match, that's all."

Amanda smiles warmly at her friend. "That was sweet. Thank you."

"It's the truth. Sean Travis may be a very nice man, but he was never the man for you."

Amanda sees Ben Myers lurking in the shadows of her vision and tries blinking him away.

"Are you all right?"

"I'm fine."

"You look like there's something you want to tell me."

"Tell you?" **Well, all right. Since you asked. I got a rather disturbing phone call last night, just after having totally meaningless sex with an almost total stranger. The call was from my ex-husband, not the man we just talked to, but a man you don't know even exists, my first ex-husband—**

I'm sorry, I don't know why I never told you about him, please forgive me. Anyway, he was calling to tell me that my mother has been arrested for shooting a man in the lobby of the Four Seasons hotel in Toronto. Amanda stabs at a piece of lettuce. Then she stuffs it inside her mouth before she can say these things out loud. "No," she says instead, offering her friend her most reassuring smile. "There's nothing."

After lunch, Amanda thinks of going back to her office, but decides against it, not feeling up to dealing with Kelly's questioning eyes. Nor can she go to the gym, she decides, in case Carter Reese is there. And there's no point in going back to court. It's way too early. It could be hours, even days, before the jury returns with its verdict.

On impulse, she hops on the old-fashioned green trolley that runs back and forth between Clematis Street and nearby City Place, a recently constructed mecca of shops and restaurants that occupies several city blocks. Maybe she'll go to a movie, she decides as she disembarks the trolley and makes her way through the slow-moving crowd toward the tall escalator. But everyone in Palm Beach seems to have had the same idea, and the line for the multiplex is long and unruly. Amanda returns to the glorified shopping mall below and spends several hours peering absently into the line of store windows, looking for a dress for Ellie's wedding. But even though she's tempted by a long black dress she sees hanging on the far wall in Betsey Johnson, she doesn't go inside. Instead she continues trancelike up one street and down another, then sits for a while on an empty bench beside the large decorative fountain in the middle of the busy square, watching as children duck in and around the adults eating on the outside patio of Bellagio, an Italian restaurant renowned more for the size of its portions than the quality of its food.

Seeing Sean with his new wife has upset her, she realizes, although she's not sure why. A touch of nostalgia maybe. He was a good man, a kind man, a man she'd literally run into while walking aimlessly down a crowded beach. They'd gone for drinks, then dinner. She'd found him easy to talk to. Or maybe she'd just felt like talking. And he'd obviously liked what he was hearing. At least in the beginning.

Beginnings are easy, Amanda thinks. I'm great at beginnings.

Endings too, she decides, jumping to her

feet and almost plowing into an elderly couple carefully trying to navigate their way along the uneven stone surface. It was her decision to end her marriage to Sean, just as it was her decision to walk out on her earlier marriage to Ben. None of that growing-old-together nonsense for her. None of that till-death-do-us-part crap. Love 'em and leave 'em. That's her motto. And it's always preferable to be the one who says good-bye.

Puppet, she hears someone shout. **Over here, Puppet. This way.**

Amanda's head snaps to her right. But all she sees is a group of children playing. "Over here, pea-brain," a young boy is shouting at his friend. "No, stupid. This way!"

Puppet! Puppet!

Amanda ducks into the nearest store to escape the sound, grabs several hangers of clothing off a rack, and heads for the dressing rooms at the back.

"Can I help you with that?" a salesgirl asks. She is maybe eighteen, the same age as Amanda when she married Ben.

Has he remarried? she wonders. "No, I am not doing this," Amanda says out loud, rubbing her forehead in an effort to erase Ben from her mind.

"I'm sorry?" the salesgirl asks. "You **don't** want to try these things on?"

"What? Yes, I do. Of course I do." Minutes later, she is standing in the cramped little space they called a dressing room, looking at herself in the long, narrow mirror, her mother's youthful reflection staring back.

Hello, Puppet, her mother says.

Amanda shudders. She was six years old when her mother put a curse on old Mr. Walsh, who lived next door, and who insisted on parking his car right in the middle of their shared driveway. Two months later, the hapless man was dead. Such was her mother's terrible power.

And now another man is dead, Amanda thinks. Shot three times at presumably close range. What's the matter, Mom? Curses not fast-acting enough for you these days?

Puppet! her mother calls from outside the door.

"I'm sorry. What?"

"I asked how you were doing in there," the salesgirl responds.

"Fine," Amanda says, although she has yet to try on a single item. "Thank you."

"Is that your phone ringing?" the salesgirl asks.

Amanda becomes aware of a phone ringing somewhere beside her. "Oh. Oh, yes." She reaches inside her black leather purse. "Hello?" she asks timidly.

Finally wore you down, did I?

"What?"

"They just called from court," her secretary informs her. "The jury's back."

FIVE

"On the charge of uttering death threats, how do you find?"

"We find the defendant not guilty."

"On the charge of forcible confinement, how do you find?"

"We find the defendant not guilty."

"On the charge of sexual assault, how do you find?"

"We find the defendant not guilty."

"On the charge of assault with a deadly weapon, how do you find?"

"We find the defendant not guilty."

"On the charge of assault and battery, how do you find?"

"We find the defendant guilty."

"Thank you," the judge says, dismissing the jury, and setting a date for sentencing.

"What just happened?" Derek Clemens's eyes flit between his lawyer and the buxom young woman he used to live with, who is quietly crying in the back of the courtroom.

"You were acquitted on four of the five charges."

"Then how come they found me guilty of the fifth?"

"Because you bit her, Derek," Amanda reminds him.

"I raped her too," he says. "They acquitted me of that."

Amanda shakes her head, partly in disgust, partly in disbelief. To think she'd almost talked herself into believing even some of his story. "See you back here for sentencing."

"You think I'll go to jail?"

"It's a first offense; you're Tiffany's primary caregiver. It's more likely you'll get probation."

"I swear I'll kill that bitch if I end up in jail."

"Fine. Just remember to get yourself another lawyer." Amanda slings her purse over her right shoulder and heads toward the back of the courtroom, Derek Clemens at her heels.

"Hey, wait up. I thought we could maybe grab a drink. To celebrate."

Amanda doesn't even bother slowing down.

The full moon follows her as she drives north along Congress. Beside her on the front seat of her three-year-old black Thunderbird convertible is a freshly purchased bottle of expensive red wine. The Thunderbird was a gift from Sean on their fourth, and as it turned out, last anniversary. The wine was a present to herself. After all, hadn't she helped make the world a safer place for nasty cannibals everywhere? "I did my job," she reminds herself, turning left on Forty-fifth and heading toward I-95.

It's not her fault Derek Clemens is such a convincing liar. It's not her fault Caroline Fletcher is her own worst enemy. The justice system is a crapshoot at the best of times, which is why a good lawyer is always preferable to a good cause. The innocent often suffer; the guilty regularly go free. And luckily, one face pretty much blurs into another over time, Amanda knows. By tomorrow morning she won't even remember what Caroline Fletcher looked like, crying in the back of the courtroom. With a little luck, that is, and enough celebratory glasses of wine. Amanda pats the bottle on the black leather seat beside her. The new day will bring a fresh batch of lowlife to her desk to be processed and prepped. Pay your money; take your chance. Head 'em out, move 'em on.

Amanda checks her rearview mirror as she

switches into the right-hand lane, sees her mother's eyes lurking behind her own. Some faces don't blur as easily as others, the eyes warn.

She takes the ramp a touch too quickly onto I-95, then cuts in front of a white Lexus SUV. The driver swerves and shakes his fist in fruitless indignation. Just where do you think you're going in such a damn hurry? the fist demands, as Amanda stares slack-jawed at the stagnant lines of traffic heading north.

The highway, as usual, is a clogged artery of cars. Weary commuters heading home from work, clueless tourists looking for the newest hot spot, barefoot teenagers with fake IDs heading for the hippest bar, seniors who should have had their driver's licenses revoked years ago, not sure where they are, let alone where they're headed. A typical Friday night in February. Probably an accident somewhere up ahead, judging by the volume of traffic and how slowly it's moving. Her own fault, she thinks, checking the clock on her car's dashboard. Almost seven. She shouldn't have stayed so long at the office after court. She shouldn't have spent so long in the liquor store choosing wine. She shouldn't have picked I-95 at seven o'clock on a Friday night in February. What was normally a twenty-minute drive from here to Jupiter, and she'd be lucky to be home by eight. Amanda leans her head back against her headrest. No point in getting all bent out of shape over something she can't control.

This philosophy works for about ten minutes before she's ready to explode. "Okay, enough of this. Let's get a move on, people." She glares at the creamy yellow moon overhead, as if the smiling face she sees carved into its side is somehow responsible for her predicament. Full moons are a dangerous time, she knows, glancing at the car beside her, seeing a woman in a matching pink sweater set talking on her phone.

I could call someone, she decides, reaching for her purse. Although she's not sure exactly whom to call. Ellie would think it strange to hear from her twice in one day, and she vaguely recalls Kelly having mentioned she'd be at her parents' house for dinner. "Ellie and Kelly," Amanda says out loud, the names rolling off her tongue. "Ellie and Kelly. Kelly and Ellie. Everything's swelly with Ellie and Kelly." Oh, great. Now I'm a total lunatic, she thinks, deciding to call her friend Vanessa. "Oh, sure. Call Vanessa. She hasn't heard from you in what? Two years?" Or how about Judy Knelman? You used to see her and her husband every few weeks when you were married to Sean. And that other woman, the one who married Sean's friend Bryce Hall? What was her name? Edna, Emma, Emily? "Oh, yeah, all Sean's friends are just dying to hear from you."

Why is she still thinking about Sean? Just because she ran into him at lunch? He's turned up unexpectedly before. Once, at the Kravits Center, a couple of years ago. He was still pretty bitter then, even though she'd asked for nothing in their divorce, but still he'd pretended not to see her, ducking into the men's room as she was walking over to say hello. She'd pushed the incident out of her mind, scarcely giving him another thought. When something was over, it was over and done. Out of sight, out of mind. Hadn't that always been her motto?

Of course Jennifer had yet to enter the picture. Jennifer with her peaches-and-cream complexion and long, shiny black hair. And swelling belly.

Swelling belly, swelling belly, swelling belly.

Is that what has her feeling so out of sorts?

That could have been me, she reminds herself. I'm the one who insisted I didn't want children. I'm the one who said I wasn't cut out to be a mother. **You'd be a great mother, Ellie** had told her at lunch. Sure thing. Just like my mother—a woman whose maternal instincts manifested themselves in two ways: indifference and rage. Strangely enough, she'd always preferred the rage.

Amanda glances back toward the woman in the pink sweater set, who smiles at her as she continues talking on the phone.

The last time Amanda saw her mother, her mother was wearing a blouse in almost that exact shade of pink. Her short, honey-blond hair was freshly washed and neatly coiffed, as always. Indeed, Amanda can't remember a time when her mother didn't look as if she'd just come from the beauty salon. Even if she was drunker than the proverbial skunk, and falling all over everything, her hair was always picture-perfect.

What's she done now?

Really, this doesn't concern me.

Who'd she kill?

This is not my problem.

She's your mother.

Not anymore.

Amanda pushes her mother's image aside with a swat of her hand, as if shooing away a pesky fly. "Can we please get this show on the road?" she begs the other drivers, and mercifully the cars in front of her begin to pick up their pace. "Thank you," she says to the smiling face in the moon.

Forty minutes later, she is home.

"Hi, Joe." She waves to the doorman.

"You get stuck in that mess on I-95?"

"I sure did."

"Radio said there was an accident at the exit to Riviera Beach."

"There were still police cars at the side of the road," Amanda tells him.

"Expecting company?" He nods toward the bottle of wine in her hand.

Amanda feels her spine stiffen. Is it curiosity she hears in his voice or judgment? "Not tonight."

He smiles. "Well, have a good one."

"You too."

He was just making idle conversation, she reassures herself in the elevator, grateful that the ride to the fifteenth floor is mercifully uneventful. No unnecessary stops. No former lovers. No suspicious wives. "Just me and my bottle," Amanda says to the empty hallway as the elevator doors open. She walks briskly to her unit on the southeast corner, almost tripping over a piece of ivory-trimmed red carpet that has come loose from the ivory-colored wall. She'll have to call the building manager in the morning, tell him to send someone up to repair it before anyone gets hurt. Wouldn't want some ambitious young litigator, such as herself, to sue.

Not that personal injury lawsuits are her area of expertise, Amanda thinks. No, her specialty is defending creeps who try to swallow their girlfriends. Not to mention those who beat up strangers in a bar or rob a 7-Eleven and shoot a few innocent bystanders. Of course if the creep who does the shooting is the son of a prominent local politician, or if one of the bystanders happens to be young and beautiful, and therefore likely to make the front page of the **Palm Beach Post,** then it becomes a case for Jackson Beatty or Stanley Rowe, who keep all the really good stuff for themselves.

"The good stuff," Amanda says out loud, wondering when she became so jaded. And what has her more upset—the fact Derek Clemens was acquitted on four charges or found guilty of one?

She stands for several seconds outside her apartment door, almost reluctant to go inside. How many messages from her former husband will she find waiting on her voice mail? Although, surprisingly, there were no further messages from him at work.

Nor are there any now. "Good," Amanda says, standing in the middle of her all-white kitchen and uncorking the bottle of red wine. "Good," she repeats, feeling curiously slighted. She fills a large wineglass almost to the top and takes a long sip, deciding she should probably eat something. She opens her fridge, finds nothing but a bottle of orange juice and a dozen containers of assorted fruit-flavored yogurt. She checks the best-before date of a strawberry-kiwi yogurt and sees that it expired five days ago. Which means all the other yogurts are likewise past their prime, since she bought them all at the same time. How long ago? When was the last time she went shopping for groceries? There isn't even any milk, for Pete's sake.

What kind of mother is she, she doesn't make sure there's any milk for the baby?

"Luckily, I don't have a baby," Amanda states, as if pleading her case. Carrying her wineglass in one hand and the bottle in the other, she walks into the living room. "See? No baby." She takes another sip of wine, kicks off her shoes, and flops down on her white canvas sofa, downing half the glass in one prolonged gulp, the way her mother used to do.

It's not really surprising that Ben hasn't

called, she decides. He was never one of those men who couldn't take a hint. He always knew when to stop, when to give up, when to cut his losses and run.

What is surprising is that he called her at all.

Amanda giggles. Of course the circumstances are rather unusual. It's not every day your mother commits murder.

Then again, who knows how many people her mother has killed over the years. John Mallins may be the first man she's dispatched so publicly, but Amanda is convinced there are bodies everywhere.

She downs the rest of her drink, then pours herself another, spilling a few drops on the white tile at her feet, and just missing the corner of her black-bordered white rug. She should really get a few more pieces of furniture for this room. Another chair to fill the empty space by the left wall, perhaps a coffee table, another lamp. Her apartment has always looked vaguely unfinished, as if someone were just preparing to move in. Or out.

Just the way I like it, she thinks, taking another swallow of her wine as she examines the bare white walls, feeling her shoulders finally starting to relax. "To the man in the moon," she says, nodding toward it, and taking a sip. "And to Ben, my first ex-husband." Another sip, longer this time. "And to Sean, my second." Another sip, and then another. "Hell, to all my ex-husbands, past and future." She tops up her glass, raises it in the air. "And to all my mother's unsuspecting victims: Old Mr. Walsh. John Mallins. My father," she whispers, struggling to her feet. "Oh, no. We are not going there. We are definitely not going anywhere near there."

The doorbell rings. Amanda stares at the door without moving. After several seconds, it rings again.

"Come on, open up," a woman's voice commands.

Amanda goes to the door and opens it without asking who it is. "Janet," she says to the woman whose light brown bangs all but swamp her forehead. What's the point of having your brow lifted, she wonders, if you're going to cover the whole thing up? She thinks of asking, To what do I owe the honor?—but decides she already knows. Instead she settles on, "Would you like a drink?"

"No, thank you."

Amanda smiles and pours what's left in the bottle into her glass.

"Can I come in?"

Amanda steps back to allow Janet entry, follows her into the living room, motions toward the sofa. "Please sit down."

"No, thank you. I won't be staying long."

Then why did you ask to come in? Amanda wonders, but decides not to ask. She is too busy staring at Janet's unnaturally swollen lips. What possesses attractive women like Janet to do such horrible things to themselves? she wonders, then stops herself because she knows the answer. The answer is women like herself. Amanda takes another sip of her drink.

"I'm sure you know why I'm here."

"I'm sorry. I've been meaning to return your call. It's just that I've been so busy—"

"You're not fooling anyone, you know."

"I think I better sit down." Amanda sinks down into her sofa, feels the room spinning around her.

"I know about you and my husband."

Amanda says nothing. She remembers something about the best defense being a good offense, but has neither the energy nor the willpower to engage in a debate.

"Victor told me all about your little affair."

Amanda shakes her head in bewilderment. What is it with men and their horrible need to confess? Again she knows the answer. Confession may be good for the soul, but it's even better for passing off the guilt.

Janet mistakes Amanda's bewilderment for denial. "You're trying to tell me you didn't have an affair with my husband?"

"I'd hardly call it an affair."

"Really? What would you call sleeping with somebody else's husband?"

Amanda is much too tired to mount a good rebuttal. "Thoughtless," she hears herself say. "And stupid. Very stupid."

"Well, at least you've got that right," Janet agrees, looking distinctly uneasy, as if she'd come prepared for a good fight and wasn't ready to accept victory so easily. She glares at the wineglass in Amanda's hand.

"Are you sure you wouldn't like something to drink?" Amanda asks.

"What's the matter, Mandy? No married men left to drink with?"

"Please don't call me Mandy."

"Oh, sorry. Do only the men you sleep with get to call you that?"

Amanda struggles to stand up, when all she really wants to do is lie down. "Maybe you should go now."

"Not till I've said what I came here to say."

"I'm sorry. I thought you'd already . . . said."

"This is all a game to you, isn't it? Playing with people's lives. It doesn't bother you that people get hurt? That one night of mindless fun for you might equal a lifetime of pain for others? That my marriage might never recover?"

"I really think you're making way too much of this. It was just one night. It didn't mean anything to either of us."

"It meant something to me," Janet says simply.

A flush of shame washes across Amanda's face. "I'm sorry."

"Just stay away from my husband." Janet walks quickly to the door, slams it behind her.

The vibration from the door zaps through Amanda's body like an electrical charge. This would probably be a good time to get out of town, she thinks, then throws up all over her white living room rug.

When Amanda wakes up on the living room floor, it is almost 2 a.m. "Oh, shit," she mutters, the smell of vomit still alarmingly fresh. She stares at the huge red stain in the middle of her carpet. It looks like blood, she thinks, knowing that no amount of soap and water is going to wash the stain away. "Shit," she says again, her head pounding as relentlessly as the surf beneath her windows. She touches her hair, feels it sticky and covered with bile.

"You're disgusting," she says, stepping into her shower fully clothed, and standing under the gush of hot water that shoots from the oversize showerhead. She's ruining her suit, she knows. Just as she's ruined the rug. Not to mention her whole life, she decides melodramatically, pouring almost a full bottle of shampoo over her hair and digging her long nails into her scalp.

Oh, well. Like mother, like daughter.

Although she doesn't remember her mother ever actually throwing up after one of her many binges. She'd drink herself into oblivion, and there she'd stay—aloof and unavailable, her physical presence defined by her emotional absence.

After her shower, Amanda strips off her wet clothes, scrapes her body raw with a large white towel, then crawls into bed. She'll deal with the rug in the morning, although what can she do with it really, except roll it up and throw it away? Even with repeated professional cleanings, a shapeless puddle of blush will always be visible beneath the surface. She won-

ders what the manager of the Four Seasons
hotel in Toronto has done with the rug in his
lobby. Three bullets make for a lot of spilled
blood. "Maybe I should call and ask him how
he handled the situation." Amanda reaches for
the phone beside her bed, presses in the number she hadn't realized she's already committed
to memory.

"Hello?" the sleepy voice on the other end
responds.

"What did they do with the rug?"

"Amanda?"

She pictures Ben scrambling to sit up, sees
him brush several loose strands of hair from
half-open eyes. "I'm assuming there was a lot
of blood," she continues. "I just wondered what
they did with the rug."

"I don't know," he answers, as if this were
the most natural of conversations for them to
be having at this hour of the morning.

"Who the hell is John Mallins?" she asks.

"We don't have a lot of details."

"What **do** you have?"

"We know he's from England. That he was
here on vacation with his wife and kids."

"What's his connection to my mother?"

"As far as the police can determine, there is
none."

"You're saying that my mother shot and killed a total stranger?"

"Apparently."

Amanda leans back against her headboard. This was excessive, even for her mother. "Was she drunk?"

"No," Ben says. "You really need to come home, Amanda."

Amanda hangs up the phone without saying good-bye. She walks to her window and stares out at the moon.

Six

The plane from Palm Beach to Toronto takes off almost an hour late.

Amanda breathes a sigh of relief that they are finally taxiing down the runway, grateful that she no longer has the opportunity to run screaming down the aisle, hollering, "I've changed my mind. Let me out of here," which she would surely have done had she not found herself at the very back of the crowded 737, squished between a gum-chewing teenage girl and a middle-aged businessman so engrossed in his spy thriller, he hadn't even bothered looking up when she was climbing all over him to get to her seat.

More of the things Amanda hates: middle seats on airplanes; teenage girls who chew their gum loudly and crack it even louder, all the while flipping long, straight hair over their shoulders into her face; the shapeless black wool coat she's wearing for the first time in eight years, a coat she should have thrown out years ago.

Why hadn't she? Whatever style it once possessed is long gone, and it feels scratchy against her bare forearms. She thinks of taking it off, but there's hardly enough room in the tiny space allotted her to exhale properly, let alone to start shedding layers of clothing. Serves me right, she thinks, as several strands of her neighbor's hair flick toward her cheek. Should have taken off my coat before I sat down. Should have thrown the stupid thing out when I left Toronto.

"Should never have gotten on this damn plane in the first place, is what I should have done," she says out loud, then glances around self-consciously. But the teenage girl in the window seat is now cracking her gum to the sound of rock music leaking from her head-phones, and the face of the man on the aisle is buried even deeper inside his book, so apparently neither has noticed her outburst.

Why didn't I think of bringing a book? she wonders, trying to remember the last time she had the luxury of curling up with a good novel. A mystery thriller like the one the man beside her is so engrossed in, something that would help her pass the two and a half hours she'll be spending in the air, something that would help her forget where she's going. And why.

Amanda can't remember at what point she actually made the decision to go to Toronto. After talking to Ben, she'd drifted into an uneasy sleep, only to dream about being chased down the middle of I-95 by a pregnant Jennifer Travis, an angry Janet Berg, and a sobbing Caroline Fletcher. Somewhere in the middle of this pursuit, she stopped to buy a painting from Carter Reese's wife, Sandy, then awoke in a pool of sweat, thinking it was definitely time to get out of Dodge.

At barely 6 a.m., she called the airlines and was able to secure the last available seat on the nonstop flight that left Palm Beach for Toronto at two thirty in the afternoon. Then she called her secretary at home, forgetting that the poor young woman might actually have preferred sleeping in a little later on a Saturday morning, and told her that she might not be in the office Monday.

"Any particular reason I can give people?" Kelly asked, her voice alarmingly perky despite the early-morning hour.

"No."

"Will you be back Tuesday?"

"I'm not sure."

A pause. Amanda could almost hear the wheels in Kelly's head spinning, knew she was desperate to ask if this sudden change in plans had anything to do with the phone calls from Ben Myers.

"I'll call you as soon as I know my plans," Amanda said before hanging up. Then she threw a pair of black pants and a black turtleneck sweater into an overnight bag, along with her makeup bag and several changes of underwear, phoned Ben and told him she'd be arriving in Toronto at around five o'clock that afternoon, and took a cab to the airport, where she ate a slice of pepperoni pizza and gulped down a large Coke for breakfast, picked up her boarding pass, passed unchallenged through security, and fell into a mercifully dreamless sleep in the departure lounge while waiting to board her plane.

Luckily—or unluckily, she thinks now—someone saw her sleeping and shook her awake in time to make her flight. She bounded onto the plane just as the doors were about to close, squeezing her overnight bag into the already full overhead compartment before similarly squeezing herself into the middle seat in the second-to-last row of the plane. She was reminding herself about beggars not being choosers when the pilot announced they were experiencing a slight mechanical problem, and there would be a ten-minute delay. Ten minutes stretched into twenty, then thirty, and eventually fifty, as Amanda grew increasingly hot and restive inside her black wool coat. And now they were finally making their way down the runway, whatever problem they'd been having apparently solved.

"And away we go," Amanda whispers as the plane lifts into the air. She grips the armrests, tries hard not to panic. It's been eight years since her last plane trip. Even her honeymoon with Sean involved boats, not planes. A Caribbean cruise, she recalls wistfully, remembering that she and Ben never had a honeymoon at all.

She shakes the image of Ben from her head. She'll be seeing him soon enough. "Book me a room at the scene of the crime," she instructed him over the phone this morning. "I'll call you as soon as I'm settled in."

The girl in the window seat beside Amanda cracks her gum loudly several times in rapid succession, so that it sounds as if someone were firing a small pistol. What kind of gun had her mother used to murder this mysterious stranger? Amanda wonders, feeling her body grow clammy underneath her heavy coat.

An old image appears, the unexpected memory taking root and growing, like a weed, before Amanda has the chance to pull it out. She sees herself as a child, going through the closet in her mother's bedroom, looking for a pair of fancy shoes, something with high heels and pointy toes, preferably in silver or gold, something suitable for playing a fairy princess, but finding only a succession of sensible low-heeled shoes in black and brown lined along the floor. And then looking up, seeing a shoe box on the high shelf above where her mother's clothes were hanging, and thinking this must be where she keeps her special shoes, the ones a fairy princess would wear. She ran to the kitchen, retrieved the small stepladder that leaned against the side of the counter, returned with it to her mother's bedroom, and climbed to its third and final step, stretching her arms toward the shoe box, her fingertips repeatedly grazing its side, unable to make full contact, until finally she succeeded in dislodging it. The box fell to the floor, narrowly missing her head, and bouncing awkwardly along the carpet, the lid opening, disgorging its contents at her feet.

A gun, Amanda remembers now with a gasp, as she must have gasped then. Small and black, and surprisingly heavy.

She watches the child Amanda lift the strange object into her hands, sees her turn it over, then lift it to her nose to inhale its cold, metallic scent. And suddenly her mother is in the doorway, crying and yelling and waving her arms like a deranged puppet, wresting the gun from Amanda's fingers. The child flees the room in terror. Later, when Amanda goes to her mother's room to try to explain, her mother stares through her as if she doesn't exist.

The shoe box wasn't there the next time Amanda snuck into her mother's bedroom for a peek in her closet. Nor was its contents ever alluded to again. The question remained unasked throughout the years: What was her mother doing with a gun?

And now an addendum: Was it the same gun she used to murder John Mallins?

"Who the hell is John Mallins?" Amanda asks out loud.

"I'm sorry. Are you talking to me?" The man beside her stares at her with warm brown eyes.

"What? Oh, no. Sorry. I was just talking to myself. I didn't mean to disturb you."

"No problem. I do it all the time." His eyes return to his book.

Amanda finds herself staring at his face in profile. It's a pleasant face, she decides. Not particularly handsome. Although not **un**handsome. Long nose, high cheekbones, full lips, strong jaw. Kind eyes, she thinks, wishing he would focus them on her again. "Is that a good book?"

"What?"

"You seem very engrossed in your book."

"It's all right."

"Just all right?" Why is she badgering the poor man? Clearly he's not interested in prolonged conversation. He has no need to be distracted and entertained. **His** mother didn't shoot a stranger in the lobby of the Four Seasons hotel.

"It's pretty good so far." He lays the open book across his lap. "But I'm prepared to be disappointed."

"Why is that?"

"I read a lot of mysteries, and most of them start out okay, but then they kind of fall apart."

Amanda nods as if she agrees, although she hasn't read many mysteries. Life is confusing enough, she thinks. "And how does one prepare to be disappointed?"

The man smiles, takes several seconds to

ponder the question. "One thinks about the past," he says finally.

A line of perspiration immediately breaks out along Amanda's upper lip. She feels her cheeks grow pink and moist, as if she has just leaned over an open fire.

"Are you all right?" the man asks, brown eyes narrowing with concern.

"It's this coat," she lies. "I'm about ready to scream."

"Here," he offers. "Let me help you." He tugs the coat from her shoulders, holds it as she extricates her arms from its bulky sleeves, her right hand shooting out to narrowly miss the jaw of the girl beside her.

"Sorry about that," Amanda says.

A loud crack of gum tells Amanda her apology has been accepted.

"Would you like me to put this up top?" The man motions toward the compartment above their heads.

"Thank you."

"Feeling more comfortable now?"

Amanda pats the deep V of her white T-shirt, takes a deep breath. "Much. Thank you."

His eyes follow the motion of her hands. "Would you like a glass of water? I can ring for the stewardess."

"No, that's fine. Thanks again."

He smiles, extends his hand. "Jerrod Sugar."

It takes Amanda several seconds to realize this is his name and not some exotic beverage. "Amanda," she says, shaking his hand. "Amanda Travis."

"Heading home, Amanda?" Jerrod Sugar asks.

"No, actually. Florida's my home."

"Really? I thought I detected a trace of an accent. **Aboot**," he says with a chuckle.

Amanda stiffens. "No. Florida native. What about you?"

"I'm from Milwaukee, originally. Moved to Abacoa last year."

Amanda pictures the small, spanking new city that is being built between Palm Beach Gardens and Jupiter. Despite being only partially populated, it already boasts its own stadium, golf course, and full-fledged university. She also pictures a wife and three little Sugar cubes. "Why Abacoa?"

"I'm a professor," he says. "Got an offer I couldn't refuse."

"And what is it you profess exactly?"

He laughs. Amanda decides she likes the sound. She leans closer, her left breast brushing up against the side of his arm. "Economics,"

Jerrod Sugar says, reaching into his pocket to retrieve a business card, careful that his arm doesn't lose contact with her breast.

She makes a show of examining the card. "I'm afraid I know absolutely nothing about economics."

"I suspect you know a good deal. About a lot of things."

It was Amanda's turn to chuckle. "So why are you going to Toronto?"

"Convention. You?"

"Vacation," she says, the first word that pops into her mind.

"Vacation? Who vacations in Toronto in February?"

Amanda shrugs. He's right after all.

"Come on, fess up." This time he's the one who leans toward her, his eyes falling into the V of her T-shirt.

Amanda isn't sure if it's the obviousness of his gaze or the "fess up" that does it, but she suddenly hears herself say, "Actually, my ex-husband called to tell me my mother's been arrested for murder. He thought it might be a good idea for me to pay her a visit."

A smile cracks Jerrod's face almost in two. "You're joking, right?"

"I'm joking," Amanda confirms instantly.

He laughs, but the sound has a nervous consistency that wasn't there before. He turns away. Moments later, his nose is buried back inside his book.

Amanda was fourteen when she lost her virginity.

It happened at someone's cottage in Haliburton. The someone was Perry Singleton, whose sister, Claire, was in the same homeroom with Amanda at school, and whose parents invited Amanda to the cottage one weekend in July. The Singletons had obviously hoped the invitation might spark a friendship between their shy, introverted daughter and her more outgoing classmate, but the only thing it sparked was a fire between the legs of Claire's older brother.

At sixteen, Perry Singleton was already the guy your mother warned you about—good-looking, cocky, wild. Amanda had seen him swaggering down the halls of Jarvis Collegiate, heard the whispers of his sexual prowess and the rumors he kept a detailed chart of his various conquests, complete with an elaborate ratings system involving a combination of red ink, asterisks, and gold stars, and knew he wasn't above sharing this information with his friends. She often heard newly discarded girls crying in the washrooms, each having nursed the delusion she was different, the one to change him, to bring him to his senses and his knees.

Amanda had no such illusions, even at fourteen. She had no expectation of changing the roguish frog that was Perry Singleton into some boring prince, nor did she want to. What she aspired to—**all** she aspired to, in fact—was to be the highest-rated notch on his well-worn belt. She wanted the red ink, the asterisk, **and** the gold star.

And so when he came up behind her at the cottage and put his hand down the back of her shorts, she hadn't slapped it aside or acted shocked or played hard to get. Instead she'd turned around and placed her own hand firmly on the front of his jeans, then told him she'd sneak into his room after Claire fell asleep, to be ready for her.

He wasn't big on foreplay, which suited Amanda fine, since she found his hurried groping more annoying than exciting. She didn't feel much of anything the first time he entered her. It hurt, but not too much, probably because the whole thing was over within less than a minute. He didn't seem to notice that it was her first time. Or maybe he noticed, but didn't care, which was also okay with Amanda. It didn't take her long to discover what Perry liked, which was almost anything that involved his penis, and she'd seen enough movies to know the proper moves to make, and when to make them. It didn't matter that she herself received little satisfaction from the act. Personal satisfaction wasn't going to get her any asterisks or gold stars.

Suffice it to say, Perry Singleton was devastated when, two months later, she dropped him.

She quickly moved on to Ronnie Leighton, followed in rapid succession by Fred Coons, Norman McAuliff, Billy Kravitz, and Spenser Watt. All before her sixteenth birthday.

Ken Urbach, Jeremy Walberg, Ian Fitzhenry, Brian Castleman, Larry Burton, Stuart Magilny, at least half a dozen more, followed before she turned seventeen.

And then she finally met her match.

Amanda arches her back, looks past the teenage girl now dozing in the seat beside her, her jaw remaining strangely active, chewing even in her sleep. She sees Ben Myers reflected in the glass of the small window of the plane. His eyes are the color of bitter chocolate and his cheeks are rough with stubble. He is wearing the tightest, scruffiest jeans she has ever seen, and his long, black hair smells of beer and marijuana cigarettes. He wants nothing from no one, he asserts to all who will listen. People are hypocrites; success sucks; stability is for sissies. Except he doesn't say **sissies.** He says **pussies,** and Amanda finds herself thrilled by the sound.

Is it any wonder they discover one another? That they are pulled toward each other like opposite sides of a magnet? That they crash headlong into each other's arms?

"My parents are such losers," he confides one night. "They have no idea what I'm about."

"Mine don't even know I'm there," she confides in return, thinking it is preferable to be misunderstood than unnoticed.

"I'm bad news," he tells her.

"I'm worse."

The captain comes on the loudspeaker to announce their descent into Toronto. Amanda feels a painful popping in her ears, thinks of asking the girl beside her for a stick of gum, but is afraid the girl might simply reach into her mouth and break off a piece, so she grimaces and says nothing.

"Something wrong?" Jerrod Sugar asks.

Amanda points to her ears.

"Try swallowing."

Amanda tries not to hear anything sexual in his advice and swallows several times in quick succession, but she feels only a modicum of relief. Suddenly remembering that the most dangerous times for flying are during takeoff and landing, she grips tightly to the armrests.

"I wouldn't have pegged you for a white-knuckler," Jerrod Sugar says with a smile.

"I'm just full of surprises."

"I'll just bet you are." This time he doesn't look away.

Amanda senses he is about to suggest that they share a limo or perhaps meet later for a drink, but he says nothing, and this time it is Amanda who looks away. Again she glances toward the window, watches as the surrounding clouds are gradually absorbed by the snow-covered landscape below.

"It looks like another planet," she mutters, thinking that's exactly what it is.

The teenage girl beside her suddenly spins around in her seat. "I am so excited," she announces to Amanda, as if the two are long-lost friends. "I haven't seen my boyfriend in six months. We're both going to different colleges, and this is the first time we'll be in the same city at the same time. Do I look all right?" She smooths her hair, stares expectantly at Amanda, her jaw grinding ferociously.

"Maybe you could lose the gum," Amanda offers.

Immediately, the girl spits the mangled pink wad into her hand. "I forgot I had it in my mouth." She giggles. "Yuck. It's pretty stale." She drops it inside the airsickness bag. "Better?"

"Much."

"Thanks. I'm so nervous. I think I have to pee." She unfastens her seat belt, struggles to stand up.

"I think you're supposed to stay in your seat while we're making our descent." Amanda points to the **Fasten Seat Belt** sign overhead.

"Shoot," the girl says, sitting back down.

Immediately Amanda thinks of her mother.

As soon as they land, Jerrod Sugar retrieves Amanda's overnight bag from the overhead bin, then helps her on with her coat, his hands lingering a second longer than necessary on her shoulders.

"I'll be at the Metro Convention Center until Thursday," he tells her. "If you have any free time, why don't you give me a call."

SEVEN

The walk from the plane to Canadian customs is endless. Amanda proceeds slowly down the long corridor, the strap of her bulky, black leather overnight bag weighing heavily on her right shoulder, thinking that she should have bought one of those clever suitcases with wheels she sees everyone else pulling easily behind them. Except what would be the point? Wheels mean speed, and speed means getting to her destination quicker, when what she really wants is not to get there at all.

She steps onto a long escalator, begins yet another descent. At the bottom, she joins hundreds of other people waiting in at least a dozen long lines to clear Canadian customs. She hears a woman complain that two jumbo jets have landed at the same time, disgorging their passengers simultaneously, which means it will likely take an hour to get to the front of the line. Amanda shrugs, probably the only person in the crowded area who welcomes this bit of unpleasant news. She looks around for Jerrod Sugar, thinks she sees him several rows away, talking to an attractive woman closer to his own age, but when she looks the other way, she sees him again, this time talking animatedly into his cell phone. It occurs to Amanda, as she moves several baby steps forward in line, that Jerrod Sugar has one of those faces that always look familiar. It also occurs to her that despite sitting next to the man for much of the afternoon, and actively flirting with him through part of it, she really has no idea what he looks like at all, and that she probably won't recognize him should she decide to take him up on his offer and call him at his hotel.

Despite the volume of people and the dire predictions, the process moves along at a relatively brisk pace, and within half an hour Amanda finds herself near the front of the line. "Purpose of your visit?" she hears the customs officer bark at the couple in front of her.

"Business," says the husband.

"Pleasure," says his wife.

Well, which is it? Amanda wants to ask, glancing at the customs form in her hand, scoffing out loud when she sees she's checked off **Pleasure**. There should be a box for **Duty**, she thinks. Or **Guilted into It**. How about one for **Mother Is a Murderer?**

"Miss?" a voice is saying from somewhere beside her.

She feels a tap on her shoulder. "You're up," the man behind her says, motioning ahead.

Amanda nods, her heart racing as if she were an illegal immigrant trying to sneak into the country as she hands her passport and declaration form to the waiting official.

"Where are you from?" he asks, although he has all the information in front of him.

"Florida." She wonders if the data on his computer is telling him otherwise, that she was, in fact, born right here in Toronto, and that as a consequence of her hedging the truth, she will be handcuffed and put on a return flight to the U.S. immediately.

"And what brings you to Toronto at this time of year?" the man asks pleasantly.

Amanda notes that the customs official is young and anemically attractive, his skin pale, and his light brown hair already thinning, although his voice is surprisingly deep. "I'm here to see my mother," she says, almost choking on the last word.

Surely he has sensed her hesitation. Surely

he will press her for details. **Who is your mother?** he will demand. **How long has it been since you've seen her? Why the long estrangement? Why the need to see her now? Who are you? Who are you** really?

"How long will you be staying?" he asks instead.

"Just a few days."

"Are you bringing any gifts?"

Amanda almost laughs. When was the last time she and her mother exchanged gifts? Had they ever? "No. No gifts."

"Any cigarettes or alcohol?"

She feels last night's wine claw at her throat. "No."

"Enjoy your visit." The officer stamps her declaration form, returns it to her along with her passport, and signals for the next person in line.

"Thank you." Reluctantly, Amanda leaves his side and follows the flow of traffic into the baggage claim area. Luckily, she has no baggage to claim, and so she proceeds to the exit, where yet another official is waiting to check her declaration form.

"Fine," he tells her, taking the form from her hand and sparing her the indignity of some stranger rifling through her bag, although all such a search would reveal is her makeup kit, black pants, and a matching turtleneck sweater, and several unexciting changes of cotton underwear. Amanda pushes her feet toward the exit, as if she were slogging through thick globs of freshly poured concrete, her eyes passing over the eager faces of those waiting to greet their loved ones. All around her are the happy sounds of people being reunited—**Hi, sweetheart. Did you have a good flight?; Look at you! You're so big, I almost didn't recognize you!; Welcome home, Daddy!** She catches sight of her teenage seatmate as the girl flings herself into her boyfriend's open arms with joyous abandon and feels a slight rip in the vicinity of her heart. When was the last time she literally flew into someone's arms? When was the last time someone was waiting to catch her?

"Where do they keep the goddamn taxis?" she mutters without moving her lips. Already she feels the bitter cold February air sliding along the floor toward her legs, like a deadly snake. She'll probably have to buy a pair of boots, she thinks, irritated already, and she hasn't even left the airport. "Damn this weather," she says out loud.

"Talking to yourself again?" a voice asks,

and Amanda freezes on the spot, refusing to look around. "You always did like talking to yourself."

Amanda's heart rushes into her ears, deafening her to everything except the pulse of her own anxiety. "You didn't have to come all the way out here," an alarmingly calm voice responds from somewhere far away. "I said I'd call you as soon as I got settled in."

"I thought you might appreciate a friendly face."

"Is it friendly?" she hears herself ask.

"Why don't you turn around, see for yourself?"

Slowly, Amanda shifts her position, turns toward the voice. Reluctantly, she lifts her eyes, absorbs the man standing before her, the details of his face sinking into her consciousness, like water into a sponge.

Ben Myers looks exactly like the man she ran away from eight years ago, and yet nothing like him at all. He is still tall and lanky, handsome in the casually disheveled way that used to drive her wild, but his brown eyes are now more wary than wounded, and his posture is more purposefully erect, quiet confidence having replaced noisy bravado. The heavy, black leather jacket he wears is utilitarian rather than rebellious. Amanda understands that her bad boy has become a man. And a good one, at that.

"Ben," she says, as her ears begin to clear and her heartbeat returns to something approaching normal.

"Amanda," he acknowledges. "You look wonderful."

"Thank you. So do you."

He takes the overnight bag from her shoulder, tosses it easily over his own. "Is this everything?"

"Yes."

"Not planning on staying around very long, I gather."

"I thought a day or two would be . . ." She breaks off, decides against finishing the thought. Besides, he is already walking away from her, and she has to scamper to keep pace with his long strides.

"Car's this way," he says over his shoulder, walking toward the elevator. "Button up," he advises as the elevator stops at the fifth floor. "It's cold out."

The arctic air hits her, like a glass of ice water tossed in her face, as soon as she steps off the elevator and into the parking garage. Except that water would freeze before it reached her, she thinks, clasping the collar of her coat tightly to her throat, silently berating herself for not thinking to bring a scarf. Or a pair of gloves. What the hell am I doing here? she wonders. What am I doing in this frozen wasteland, trailing after a man who used to be my husband, who's about to drive me to the hotel where my mother, whom I haven't talked to in years, shot and killed a man I've never even heard of?

"This way," Ben says.

"The Mercedes?"

"Not exactly." He points toward an old, white Corvette.

"My God. You still have it."

"You know me. I have a hard time letting go of things."

Amanda ignores the implication, rubbing her hands together in a futile effort to generate some heat as he unlocks the car doors and throws her overnight bag in the small area that passes for a backseat. She touches the side of the old car, warm memories dulling the sting of its frigid surface.

A decade ago, she'd watched Ben, a cocky kid in skinny black jeans and a ratty black leather jacket, emerge from the pristine, white sports car and bound up the steps to her front door. She'd rushed outside to meet him, hoping to see her mother's disapproving stare from her bedroom window as she defiantly thrust her hand inside his. But when she looked up, she saw that the drapes to her mother's bedroom were closed, as usual, and that no one was watching. Just as there was no one waiting up to berate her when she snuck in the next morning at almost 4 a.m.

So much for warm memories, Amanda thinks now as she climbs into the car.

The car should have told her what kind of man Ben really was. He'd paid for the the damn thing himself, working every weekend and summer since he'd turned fourteen, and putting aside every penny earned to purchase the secondhand car of his dreams. This should have told her something about his drive, his determination, his will to succeed. But all she could see was the black leather jacket and the white Corvette. She may have understood the surly cock of his head, but she'd missed entirely the steel of his backbone. She'd listened to the defiance in his voice as he railed against authority without hearing the authority in his own voice as he railed.

She knew she wasn't the first woman to be seduced by an image, to be betrayed by the projection of her own needs on someone with needs of his own. What she wanted was style; what she got was substance. What she wanted was her mother's worst nightmare; what she got was a man to make any mother proud. Which was the last thing she wanted.

"You really didn't have to come all the way out here to pick me up," she tells him now, as he pays the parking lot attendant and waves away the receipt.

"Maybe I was afraid you'd chicken out when you got here, hop on the first plane back."

"The thought occurred to me."

"I thought it might." He smiles, as if he still knows her after all these years, as if he ever knew her at all.

"So, how is she?" Amanda doesn't say whom, and he doesn't ask, for which she is grateful. They both know whom she's talking about.

"Holding up surprisingly well."

"She's not the one who took three bullets at close range."

"True enough."

"Are you going to tell me what happened?"

"I've already told you."

"My mother shot and killed a total stranger in the lobby of the Four Seasons hotel," Amanda reiterates. No matter how many times she says it, it makes no sense. In fact, if anything, the words make less sense with each repetition. Like clothes that fade through repeated washings, the words lose their luster and grow pale. She might as well be speaking a foreign language. "What else?"

"Nothing else."

"Ben, I didn't come all this way for nothing else."

"Don't you think if I knew anything else, I'd tell you?"

"So tell me again everything you **do** know."

He pauses, gulps air like water, then releases it slowly, his warm breath spreading across the car's front window like a slow stain. "It's my understanding that your mother was sitting in a corner of the lobby of the Four Seasons when one of the registered guests, a man by the name of John Mallins, approached the front desk. According to numerous witnesses, your mother calmly got up from her chair and cut across the lobby, withdrawing a gun from her purse and shooting John Mallins three times, whereupon she returned the gun to her purse, reclaimed her seat, and quietly waited for the police to arrive."

"You're saying she did this without provocation of any kind?"

"Apparently."

"She never said anything to him?"

"Nothing anyone heard."

"He never said anything to her?"

"He didn't get the chance."

"She just walked over and shot him," Amanda states.

"Apparently," Ben says, as he said earlier.

Why does he keep saying that? Amanda wonders. Nothing about any of this is even remotely apparent.

"According to a hotel clerk, she'd been sitting in the lobby all day," Ben continues, unprompted.

"What are you saying? That she was waiting to ambush him?"

"It would seem so."

Amanda tries to imagine her mother sitting in a corner of a hotel lobby, patiently waiting to pounce on some unsuspecting stranger. "What's this guy look like anyway?"

"Average height, a little stocky, dark hair, a mustache."

"How old is he? **Was** he?" she corrects immediately.

"Late forties."

"Late forties," Amanda repeats, trying to draw a picture of him in her mind. "I don't get it. Who is this man?"

"Amanda . . . ," Ben says patiently.

"Ben," she interrupts, "my mother might be a nutcase, but she's not crazy enough to sit in a hotel lobby all day waiting to murder a total stranger. Obviously, she knew the man. She knew he was in town, and she knew where he was staying. That means there has to be a connection between them."

"If there is, your mother isn't sharing it with the rest of us."

"She's saying she randomly selected—"

"She isn't saying anything," he says.

Amanda stares at the foot of snow carpeting the flat landscape along Highway 401, shaking her head in growing frustration. "Is it possible she's in the middle of some sort of menopausal breakdown?"

"She's a little old for that sort of thing, isn't she?"

Amanda regards him quizzically. She's always regarded her mother as a relatively young woman, even though she was thirty-four when Amanda was born. Which would make her almost sixty-two now, Amanda calculates. Definitely past the age for menopausal breakdowns. Although when had her mother ever followed anybody's schedule but her own?

"You think it could be Alzheimer's?"

"I guess that's a possibility."

"But you don't think that's it?"

"I don't think that's it," he admits.

"Why?"

"She just seems very . . ."

"Very what?"

"Very sane," he says after a long pause.

"My mother seems very sane," Amanda repeats. "Now I know she's nuts."

Ben laughs, and Amanda realizes how nice a sound his laughter makes, and how rarely she has heard it.

"Has she been seen by a psychiatrist?"

"**Seen** being the operative word," Ben says, "since she refused to talk to him. She's not making this any easier on herself."

"And that surprises you because . . . ?"

He laughs again, although this time the sound is strangled, as if a rope is being slowly twisted around his throat. "Maybe she'll talk to you."

Amanda closes her eyes, tries remembering the last time she and her mother talked. She hears voices raised in anger, accusations tossed carelessly, like a rubber ball, back and forth between them. **Well, with a daughter like you, no wonder your father had a heart attack!**

"When can I see her?"

"I thought we'd drive up tomorrow around one o'clock."

"Where is she?"

"Metro West Detention Center."

"What's that like?"

"It's not the Four Seasons."

"Well, then, maybe she won't kill anybody else." Amanda shakes her head, as if to ask, Can this really be happening? Are we actually having this conversation? "Will there be any problem getting me in?"

Ben shakes his head. "I'll tell them you're my assistant."

Amanda ignores the playful twinkle in his eyes. "Does she know I'm here?"

"No."

"You think that's a good idea? She's not big on surprises."

"I didn't want to say anything in case . . ."

"I didn't show up?"

"Something like that."

She glances back out the window, sees the words **Second Skin** printed large across the side of a low brick building. What a good idea, she thinks, shivering inside her black coat. I could use a second skin right now.

"Still cold?" Ben adjusts the heater. A fresh gust of hot air blows against her feet.

"I guess I forgot how cold it gets here at this time of year."

"Some years are worse than others."

Amanda nods, studying him in profile. His nose is longer than she remembers, his cheekbones more defined. A handsome man by any standards, she thinks, feeling an old twinge, willing herself to look away. "So, how've you been?" she asks after a pause of several seconds.

"I'm fine."

"You like being a lawyer?"

"I do. And you?"

"I do." She laughs. "We sound like we're getting married."

He smiles weakly. "I think once was enough, don't you?"

She nods. "You haven't remarried?" His hands are hidden inside massive black leather gloves, but she doesn't recall noticing a wedding ring in the airport. She wonders what he did with his old wedding band, if it was easier to let go of than his old Corvette.

He shakes his head no.

"Girlfriend?"

"A friend," he admits after a pause, clearly reluctant to share the details of his personal life with her.

"A friend who's a girl," she teases, although she finds herself curiously annoyed at the idea he might be involved with someone else. Why? she wonders, surprised by this almost visceral reaction. She's been through dozens of men in the years since she left, including another marriage and divorce. Did she seriously think he'd been pining for her all these years, just waiting for her to come to her senses and return home? Is she even remotely interested in rekindling the fragile spark that obviously still exists between them? She scoffs out loud, pushes the troubling thought from her brain.

"Something wrong?"

"What does your girlfriend do?" Amanda asks, ignoring the question and deciding that while it might be nice to sleep with Ben, for old times' sake, she certainly isn't in the market for anything more. Been there, she reminds herself. Done that.

"She's a lawyer."

"She isn't."

"With the Crown Attorney's Office."

The crown attorney was the Canadian equivalent of the U.S. district attorney. "So you've been sleeping with the enemy."

Ben says nothing. Amanda notices the sharp creases around the knuckles of his black leather gloves as his fingers tighten their grip on the steering wheel.

Who'd have thought? she thinks, then repeats out loud, "Who'd have thought?"

"What?"

"Everything."

He nods. "Who'd have thought?" he agrees.

EIGHT

Traffic along the highway is mercifully light, although everything slows to a crawl once they reach the Allen Expressway. Somewhere between Lawrence Avenue and Eglinton, Amanda closes her eyes and pretends to be dozing. She has no desire to see the changes to the city time has wrought, and even less desire to pursue the conversation. Amazingly, the ruse drifts into reality, and Amanda awakens just as Ben is pulling into the driveway of the beautiful midtown hotel.

"I fell asleep?"

"Snores and all," Ben confirms.

"I snored?"

"I guess some things never change."

Amanda feels her cheeks grow warm despite the cold blast of air that hits her face as the uniformed doorman pulls open the car door. "Women don't snore," she tells Ben testily, grabbing the doorman's hand and pulling herself up and out of the car. "I don't snore." She can't decide if she's angry at him for his casual—and somewhat proprietary—reference to their shared past, or at herself for falling asleep, as if, by doing so, she has exposed her vulnerability and thereby allowed him the upper hand. The upper hand at what? she wonders, reaching into the backseat for her overnight bag, feeling the leather fingers of Ben's gloves brush against her bare knuckles. "I can do that," she tells him, as he lifts the bag from the backseat and carries it toward the lobby. "You don't have to come in." But he is already inside the revolving door, and by the time she pushes her way through, he is only steps away from the reception desk.

Amanda stops abruptly, feeling the whoosh of the glass door as it continues revolving behind her. So, this is where it happened, she thinks, sniffing at the perfumed air for the merest whiff of blood. This is where my mother shot and killed a man.

She stares at the large, rectangular, floral-print rug that cuts across the middle of the large, well-lit lobby, searching for maroon-colored stains anywhere along its dark wool surface, but she finds none, which means it's undoubtedly a replacement. Can't very well let a large pool of blood be the first sight that greets unwary travelers. Not exactly the stuff of good first impressions.

A glorious arrangement of real flowers sits in the middle of a mahogany table in the center of the rug. Coppery brown marble covers the walls and floor. Mirrored-glass columns stretch toward the high ceiling. A bank of ornate elevators line the far wall, the reception desk to their right. A lobby bar is on the left, as are several comfortable seating areas, each with a sofa and two chairs in complementary shades of beige. This is where my mother sat all day, waiting to murder one of the guests, Amanda realizes, trying to guess exactly which chair her mother might have chosen.

"Amanda," Ben calls from the reception desk. "They need some identification."

Amanda pushes herself toward him, although it seems she's lost all sensation in her legs. She feels her knees about to give way, and she stumbles. Instantly Ben is at her side, his hand on her elbow, guiding her forward.

"Are you all right?"

"They cleaned things up pretty quick," she

mutters, brushing aside his concern with an impatient toss of her head, and proffering her passport to the clerk.

"Good evening, Ms. Travis." The young man's smile reveals at least a dozen more teeth than necessary. "Nice to have you with us. I see you'll be staying here for seven nights."

"No," Amanda corrects sharply.

The desk clerk visibly blanches, his teeth disappearing behind the thin line of his lips.

"Two nights will be more than enough." Amanda glares at her former husband, as if to say, What on earth would make you think I might consider staying a full week?

Ben says nothing. The desk clerk pushes a form across the desk, indicates the place for her signature.

"Don't you need an imprint of my credit card?" Amanda asks when the clerk fails to request it.

"The gentleman has already taken care of that."

Amanda smiles tightly and hands the clerk her own credit card, whispering under her breath to Ben, "What do you think you're doing?"

"Just trying to expedite things."

"I can take care of myself."

"I know that." He refrains from stating the obvious—"You always have"—but she hears it anyway.

What was John Mallins doing at the reception desk when her mother shot him? she wonders. Was this the same clerk he'd been talking to at the time?

"You're on the sixteenth floor," the young man tells her, looking altogether too cheery to have recently witnessed a cold-blooded killing. He hands her a small envelope containing her key card, then lowers his voice, as if he is about to impart some news of great importance. "Room 1612. If you have any questions, please don't hesitate to call. Do you need help with your bags?"

"We're fine," Ben informs him, slipping the overnight bag back over his shoulder and heading for the bank of elevators.

Amanda is about to stop him, tell him she can handle things from here on out, that it isn't necessary for him to accompany her to her room, that just because her mother shot and killed a man in the lobby of this very hotel, she doesn't need tucking in and looking after, that she isn't the damsel in distress he thought he'd rescued when he married her, that he should know better by now.

Unless of course, he's in the mood for a conciliatory quickie, she decides. A brief reminder of the impulsiveness of their youth, an acknowledgment of the chemistry still stalking them, something to get out of their systems once and for all, a let's-just-satisfy-our-curiosity-and-get-this-over-with kind of onetime thing they could enjoy and then forget ever happened. She might be up for that, she is thinking, as he lowers her bag to the marble floor.

"I'll let you find your way from here," he tells her.

Amanda tries not to look either surprised or disappointed. It's better this way, she decides, wondering if he's going to suggest having dinner after she settles in. She's hungry. She hasn't eaten anything all day.

"I'll pick you up around one o'clock tomorrow," he says instead.

"Fine." Room service it is, she thinks, retrieving her bag from the floor as a set of elevator doors opens to her left. She steps inside and presses the button for the sixteenth floor.

"Oh, I almost forgot." Ben unzips his jacket and pulls out a large manila envelope, thrusting it toward her just as a middle-aged couple enter the elevator, snow sparkling on the shoulders of the woman's black mink coat.

"What's this?" Amanda asks.

"Something you might want to look at later."

The envelope weighs heavily in Amanda's hands, as the woman in the black mink coat presses the button for the twenty-eighth floor, and the elevator doors draw to a close.

Amanda throws her overnight bag across the queen-size bed and walks to the window, stares down at the street. It's very dark, and only a few people are out walking, their faces buried against the raised collars of their winter coats, their backs hunched against the wind, snow falling like confetti on their heads. "What the hell am I doing here?" she asks the silent room. Just last night I was staring out the window at the ocean. "Last night you were puking your guts out," she amends, exchanging the envelope in her hand for the room-service menu lying on the desk. She grabs the remote-control unit from the top of a nearby cabinet and flips on the television. "Get some noise in here," she says, glancing back at the envelope on the desk, and deciding not to open it until after she's had something to eat. She already has a pretty good idea what's inside it. She should eat something first. Shore up her strength.

It takes less than a minute to unpack the few items in her bag, five more minutes to decide what she wants for dinner. "I'll have the carrot soup and the roast chicken," she tells room service, as a television announcer excitedly reminds her to stay tuned for **Hockey Night in Canada**.

"That'll be one hour," room service says.

"An hour?"

"We're very busy."

Amanda hangs up the phone and plops down on the edge of the bed, her eyes moving restlessly between the salmon-colored walls and the beige carpet at her feet. She leans back, kicks off her black, ankle-high boots, and dangles her now bare feet in the air, as if she were sitting at the end of a dock. "What am I going to do for an hour?" she asks the floral print on the wall above the bed.

She could watch television. Except she doesn't understand a thing about hockey, and two complete cycles with the remote-control unit reveal there is absolutely nothing on TV she wants to see. Even the porn available—among the offerings, something called **The Fuller Bush Girl**—fails to tempt her.

She could take a walk, explore the neighborhood, with its trendy boutiques and hip night-clubs. Except that it's cold and it's wet, the shops are all closed, and even the thought of alcohol makes her stomach lurch.

Damn that ex-husband of hers anyway. Where was he rushing off to in such a hurry? Hot date with the comely assistant crown attorney? "Well, it **is** Saturday night," she reminds herself out loud, falling back against the pillows and wondering why she is thinking about Ben at all. She's barely thought of him in years.

Although that's not exactly true, she admits silently, covering her eyes with her right forearm, trying to block out the image of him standing in the airport, her first sight of him in over eight years. And there he was, looking as good as he had on the day she'd told him she was leaving.

"I don't understand why you're doing this," he'd said simply, then, even more simply, "Do you?"

Amanda sits up abruptly. "I will not do this." She reaches for the phone. "No way am I going through that again." She calls the operator. "Can you get me the hotel at the Metro Convention Center, please?" A minute later, she is talking to a woman who greets her in both English and French. "Jerrod Sugar's room, please. Thank you."

"Mr. Sugar isn't answering," the woman informs her after half a dozen rings. "Would you like to leave a message on his voice mail?"

"No, thank you. I'll call back." Missed your chance, big guy, Amanda thinks as she hangs up the phone. "Okay, I give up. **Hockey Night in Canada** it is!" She flips to the proper channel, spends ten minutes trying to follow the action. "What the hell is an 'offside'?" she demands of the announcer, pushing herself off the bed and deciding to take a bath. She turns on the tap, strips out of her clothes, and stands naked in the middle of the bathroom, waiting for the tub to fill.

The phone rings.

"Ben," she says, turning off the tap, and reaching for the phone beside the toilet. She lets it ring a second time before picking it up. No point in appearing too eager. "Hello?" **No, I think I'm too tired for dinner. Thanks anyway. I'm just going to climb into a hot bath and get a good night's sleep. I'll see you tomorrow.**

"Ms. Travis," an unfamiliar voice says, "this

is room service. We forgot to ask what kind of potatoes you'd like with your chicken."

A sharp stab of disappointment pushes its way between Amanda's breasts. "What are my choices?"

"We have french fries, mashed, baked, or au gratin."

She shrugs. "Baked."

"Butter, sour cream, chives, bacon?"

What the hell? "All of the above."

"Thank you. We'll get that to you as soon as possible."

Amanda returns the receiver to its carriage, turns the hot-water tap back on, and watches until the tub is full almost to the very top. Steam is rising from its surface as she steps gingerly inside, the water quickly turning her skin an alarming shade of pink as she settles in and closes her eyes. "What's the matter with you?" she asks, water sneaking between her barely parted lips. Are you upset because your mother murdered a man in cold blood, or because your ex-husband didn't ask you out to dinner?

She flips onto her side, causing water to splash over the edge of the tub and onto the floor. Don't be ridiculous, she castigates herself. I have no interest in Ben Myers. He is part of a past I couldn't wait to escape, a past I **did** escape, a past he has somehow managed to drag me back into. **That** is what I'm so upset about, why I'm feeling at such loose ends. It has nothing to do with him. Nothing at all.

Except did he have to show up at the airport, looking so goddamn knight-in-shining-armorish? Did he have to look so damn good?

Amanda feels the sudden threat of tears and sits up abruptly, once again sending spasms through the water and causing it to slosh over the side of the tub. Ripping the paper cover off the small bar of soap, she begins furiously scrubbing at her arms and legs, rolling the sweet-smelling soap across her breasts and stomach, trying to ignore the tears now falling down her cheeks, to pretend that they are merely errant drops of bathwater. She swipes at them with the back of her hand, feels the acid-like sting of soap in her eyes. Good, she thinks. Something real to cry about.

She pushes a washcloth against her eyes, presses it against her closed lids until she sees small squares of gray, like a crossword puzzle. And then the puzzle explodes into a series of images: Ben following her out of the club she'd been tossed from because the bartender wasn't buying her fake ID, then kissing her full on the mouth before he even told her his name; Ben's hair falling into his eyes as he thrust himself repeatedly inside her, his entire body glistening with sweat; Ben's naked body as he lay sleeping beside her, his sly smile when he awoke and reached for her again.

They were so good together.

Before he started mistaking sex for love.

"No!" Amanda cries now, shaking her head, water spraying from her hair like water from a dog's back. "I am not doing this."

Except she has always done **exactly** this, she thinks, wrapping herself in a thick white towel and emerging from the tub. She has always used sex—as a weapon, as a panacea, as a way of keeping her distance, of maintaining control. She laughs. Intimacy as a substitute for intimacy. Hadn't Sean accused her of that very thing?

Amanda wraps herself in the long, white terry-cloth robe the hotel provides, towel-drying her hair as she returns to the bedroom. Outside her window, snow continues to fall. Inside, burly young men continue skating across the television screen. An announcer yells, "Icing!"—whatever that means. Only a minute away from her still-steaming bath, and already

Amanda feels cold. She checks the clock beside her bed. Almost half an hour before dinner is scheduled to arrive. Reluctantly, she grabs the manila envelope from the desk and carries it to the bed, where she pulls down the floral bedspread and sticks her feet beneath crisp white sheets. "Might as well get this over with."

She tears at the envelope before she realizes it isn't sealed, pulls out a series of newspaper reports. **WOMAN SHOOTS MAN IN CROWDED HOTEL LOBBY,** one headline screams. **MURDER AT THE FOUR SEASONS HOTEL,** announces another. And still another: **WOMAN TARGETS TOURIST.**

"Great." Amanda stares hard at the grainy, black-and-white photograph of the man identified as John Mallins, finding him much as Ben described—a middle-aged man with a mustache. Ordinary in every respect but one—he'd been shot and killed by the woman in the photograph next to his.

Amanda delays looking at the picture of her mother for as long as she can, choosing to concentrate on the text below it. **Gwen Price,** it reads, **age 61, is seen being led from the lobby of the Four Seasons hotel by two policemen, after a man vacationing at the** hotel was gunned down at point-blank range.

Amanda gasps as she raises her eyes to the photograph of her mother being led from the hotel in handcuffs. Who is this person? she wonders, trying to reconcile the frail, fair-haired woman she sees with the raging harridan of her childhood and the glassy-eyed automaton of her youth. Another photograph is more familiar. It is a close-up of her mother sitting in the backseat of the police car, staring out the side window, her gaze blank, bordering on indifference, although her jaw is relaxed, and her lips are actually hinting at a smile. "What the hell are you smiling about?"

The papers are frustratingly vague about the actual attack, the police unwilling to speculate on a motive for the shooting. **"At this point, your guess is as good as mine,"** someone named Detective Billingsly is quoted as saying.

"Who are you, John Mallins?" Amanda skims the various articles for any pertinent information, but finds only details she already knows. **John Mallins . . . 47 years old . . . a businessman from England . . . vacationing in Toronto with his wife and two children . . .** She stops reading, her gaze returning to the man's picture. "Who vacations in Toronto in February?" she asks out loud, echoing Jerrod Sugar's earlier query. "You came here to see somebody, didn't you?" Was it my mother?

There is a knock on the door. "Room service," a voice announces before Amanda has time to ask who it is.

"You're early," Amanda tells the young man gratefully, leading him into the center of the room. He is short and slender in his maroon uniform, his pale skin scarred by acne. He looks barely out of his teens. "You can set it up over here." She motions to the foot of the bed.

The waiter awkwardly adjusts the sides of the tray table, smooths the white tablecloth, lifts the lid off the carrot soup for her inspection, then does the same thing with the main course. "Roast chicken, asparagus, and a baked potato with butter, sour cream, bacon, and chives."

"It smells wonderful." She signs the chit, leaves a generous tip. "Thank you." He doesn't move, and for a second Amanda wonders if she's left enough. She follows his gaze to the bed, the newspaper clippings lying like squares on a quilt across the bedspread. "Terrible thing," she ventures. "Were you here at the time?"

"I was in the hotel, yeah. But not in the lobby. I didn't see anything."

"I bet you've heard plenty, though."

He shrugs. "A bit."

"Like what?"

"We're not supposed to talk about it." The young man shifts uneasily from one foot to the other, eyeing the clippings suspiciously. "Are you a reporter?"

"A reporter? God, no. I was just curious." Amanda leans forward to sniff at the carrot soup, allows the front of her robe to gape slightly. "Is his family still here?"

The boy's eyes glom on to her partially exposed breasts. "Yeah," he mutters distractedly. "Actually, I just took the kids up some hamburgers."

"They're not on this floor, are they?" She tries to make the question sound as casual as possible, but a slight catch in her voice threatens to betray her. "I mean, it freaks me out a little to think I might be staying on the same floor as some poor guy who got shot."

"Don't worry. They're on the twenty-fourth floor, other side of the hotel."

Amanda smiles, gathers the sides of her robe together.

"I probably shouldn't have told you that."

"Told me what?" Amanda smiles, and the waiter nods gratefully before backing out of the room. "Other side of the hotel," Amanda repeats as she plops down on the bed, and lifts the lid from her carrot soup, wondering what, if anything, she plans to do with this information. "Twenty-fourth floor."

NINE

Surprisingly, she sleeps well, having dozed off sometime during the third period of the hockey game, and waking up only when a knock on her door announces room service is waiting with her breakfast. She throws on her robe and stumbles groggily toward the door, sleep clinging to her neck and shoulders, like a too needy lover. She vaguely remembers having filled out the breakfast menu and hanging it outside her door last night when she wheeled her dinner tray into the hall, but she can't remember what items she selected. "Smells good," she says, the wondrous scent of Canadian bacon bringing her fully awake as she ushers the pretty Filipino waitress inside. The young woman sets up the tray table at the foot of the bed. "Were you here when that man was shot?" Amanda asks casually, as the woman hands over the bill for her signature. What the hell? It doesn't hurt to try.

The waitress shakes her head, her dark pony-tail waving adamantly from side to side. "It was my day off."

"Terrible thing."

"Yes, miss. Very terrible."

"Did you ever meet Mr. Mallins?"

Again, a vigorous shake of her head.

"I understand his family is staying on the twenty-fourth floor."

"I don't know, miss," the waitress replies, cutting Amanda off before she can say any-thing else. She motions toward the tray table. "Here you have orange juice, coffee, bacon and eggs, whole-wheat toast, and morning newspa-per. Can I get you anything else?"

"No, nothing. Thank you."

"Have a nice day."

"You too." Amanda pours herself a cup of coffee and carries it to the window, stares down at the street. There isn't a lot of traffic, which isn't surprising since it's early Sunday morning and the snow has been falling steadily all night. What was she doing badgering the poor waitress? Does she really think the kitchen staff will know anything of value? Even if she can persuade one of them to tell her what room the dead man's family is staying in, even if she is foolhardy enough to go up there, it doesn't necessarily follow that Mrs. Mallins will know anything about why her husband was shot. And even if she did, does Amanda seriously think she'd consider sharing that information with the daughter of the woman who shot him?

Still, seeing her, talking to her, might provide at least a clue.

Or maybe not.

When had she ever had a clue about anything where her mother was concerned?

Amanda returns to the tray table, glances down at the morning paper. The front page is filled with news about the growing probability of America going to war with Iraq. There is nothing on the front page, or indeed, anywhere in the first section, at all about the murder. Only in the section called GTA, which she assumes stands for Greater Toronto Area, does she find any mention of the crime, and it's basically a recap of everything she's already read. **Mystery Still Surrounds Murder of Tourist,** the small headline states, the ensuing article barely mentioning Mrs. Mallins at all.

"Somebody has to know something," Amanda mutters, unwrapping the cellophane from the top of the glass of freshly squeezed orange juice, and swallowing the juice in one long gulp. She looks at the clock. Eight thirty. Four and a half hours before she's supposed to meet Ben in the lobby. What's she supposed to do till then?

"I can't even go shopping," she pouts, knowing that the stores don't open until noon. She flips on the television set, browsing so quickly through the channels that the remote seizes up, its fading batteries unable to keep time with the speed of her thumb. Eventually, she succeeds in shutting the damn thing off and tosses the now useless remote to the floor, finishing her breakfast in silence. She then brushes and flosses her teeth until her gums are sore and stands under a long, hot shower, scrubbing mercilessly at whatever skin she has left after last night's bath. It takes her almost forty minutes to dry and style her hair so that it looks as if she hasn't styled it at all, and almost as long to apply her makeup so that it looks as if she isn't wearing any. Then she tugs her black turtleneck sweater so roughly over her head she practically has to start the whole process all over again. "What the hell am I doing?" she asks her reflection in the mirror, seriously considering packing up her overnight bag and catching the first plane out of town.

There is a knock on the door. Ben? Amanda wonders, hearing a noise in the hall. Is it possible the man at the reception desk slipped Ben a key card? That he would use it? "Ben?" Amanda asks, coming out of the bathroom as the door to her room opens.

"Oh, I'm so sorry," a woman in a neat blue uniform exclaims. "I didn't think anyone was here. I'll come back later to make up the bed."

"No, that's okay. You can do it now." Amanda steps back, allows the woman from housekeeping entry. "I'm leaving in a few minutes." She is? Where is she going?

The woman props her supply table against the open door. She is in her mid to late thirties, small and round, and her skin shines like rich black satin against the pale blue cotton of her uniform. "You sleep well?" she asks, scooping the remote-control unit off the floor.

"Very well, thank you. No dreams." No ex-husbands chasing her through snow-encrusted streets, no mothers waiting in opulent lobbies to ambush her with a gun.

"You saving these?" The housekeeper holds up the crumpled newspaper clippings littered among the sheets.

"No. You can throw them out." What's the point in saving them? She's read them so many times she can almost recite them by heart.

"Nasty business." The housekeeper shakes her head as she tosses the papers into a plastic garbage bag.

"Were you here when it happened?" Again Amanda tries to sound casual, as if she's merely making polite conversation.

"No. I was finished for the day. But one of my friends, she was just coming in for her shift, and she saw the whole thing."

"She did? What did she see?"

The woman from housekeeping leans in, whispers conspiratorially, "She saw this older, well-dressed woman walk across the lobby and shoot poor Mr. Mallins."

"Poor Mr. Mallins," Amanda repeats. "You sound like you knew him."

"I cleaned his suite a couple of times."

"He was staying in a suite?"

"I think he was pretty flush. Dressed real nice. Rumor has it he was wearing a two-thousand-dollar suit when he was shot."

Amanda absorbs this latest bit of information. The only men she's ever heard of who wear two-thousand-dollar suits are gangsters.

Is it possible her mother has some connection to organized crime?

"Besides, his wife and kids were with him," the housekeeper continues, oblivious to Amanda's inner musings. "They needed two rooms."

"Yes, I hear they're still at the hotel."

"Guess they have to wait until after the autopsy to take the body back to England. Such nice people. Kids are so well-behaved."

"What's Mrs. Mallins like?"

"Quiet. Doesn't say much. Just real polite." The housekeeper rolls the bedsheets into a giant ball, looks contrite. "The management says we shouldn't discuss what happened, but it's hard not to, you know. Everybody wants to talk about it."

"Of course."

"It's funny. People are always worrying about young black men causing trouble, when it's the old white women you gotta watch out for." She laughs.

Amanda tries to join in, but the laugh catches in her throat. "I better go, let you do your work." She grabs her purse and coat from the closet, throws both across her shoulders.

"Have a nice day," the housekeeper calls after her.

*   *   *

The elevator is empty when Amanda steps inside, but it stops on the fourteenth floor to admit a middle-aged man lugging a heavy suitcase, and again at the tenth floor for a woman and her two young children.

"Mommy," the little girl whines as the elevator doors draw to a close. "Tyler's stepping on my toes."

"Am not," her tow-haired brother responds, deliberately pushing against his younger sister.

"He's pushing me."

"Am not."

"Tyler, that's enough."

"I'm not doing anything."

"Well, stop it anyway." His exasperated mother smiles wanly at Amanda.

Attractive woman, Amanda thinks, although she already looks exhausted, and the day has barely begun. Amanda returns the woman's smile, silently congratulating herself for her decision not to procreate.

"Where's Daddy?" the little girl demands, tugging at her mother's skirt. "I want Daddy."

It suddenly occurs to Amanda that she is standing in the elevator with Mrs. Mallins and her two children. A million questions instantly fill her brain: What was your husband doing in Toronto? Did he come specifically to see my mother? What was the relationship between them? Is there anything, anything at all, you can tell me, that will make sense of all this craziness? "Mrs. Mallins," she begins softly, the name a whisper.

The woman turns toward her. "I'm sorry. Did you say something?"

The elevator door opens at the lobby, and the man with the heavy suitcase barrels his way out first. "I'm sorry to bother you," Amanda begins, hanging back.

"Daddy!" the little girl shouts, flying into her father's waiting arms.

"Daddy!" Tyler shouts louder, throwing himself against the man's legs.

"Yes?" The woman in the elevator looks expectantly at Amanda.

Amanda feels instantly foolish. "I'm sorry. My mistake. I thought you were someone else."

"What took you so long?" the woman's husband asks, as he guides his family toward the exit.

"Tyler had to go to the bathroom, and then Candace said she had a tummy ache."

"It's okay now," Candace assures her father, leaning into the revolving door. "Mommy, Tyler's pushing me."

Amanda watches them disappear into a

waiting taxi. What's the matter with you? she asks herself impatiently. Are you going to spend the next few days imagining every woman with two children that you see is Mrs. Mallins? It's not like you to jump to such ridiculous conclusions. You have to get a grip. "This is **so** not like you," she whispers into the collar of her coat.

She walks toward the sitting area to the left of the hotel entrance, stands for several minutes staring at the empty seats. **This is where my mother sat, a gun in her purse, waiting to kill a man.** Amanda lowers herself into one of the chairs, sinks back, tries to imagine her mother's arms resting where hers are now, her legs crossed in the same careless fashion. What was she thinking as she sat here, waiting? Was her gaze directed at the elevators or the door? Was John Mallins returning from a day of sightseeing or was he on his way out? Was his family with him? Had her mother been so heartless as to shoot him down in front of his wife and children?

Amanda jumps to her feet, startling a woman who has just sat down on the nearby sofa. This is silly. You're making yourself nuts. The papers didn't say anything about her mother killing John Mallins in front of his family. Although, yes, her mother **is** that heartless. Amanda laughs out loud. The woman on the sofa immediately gets up and moves to the bar.

Amanda takes a deep breath to calm herself down and approaches the reception desk. An attractive young woman with dark olive skin and a soft Indian accent smiles up at her. "Can I help you?" she asks, absently tucking her chin-length black hair behind her left ear.

"I wanted to inquire about your suites," Amanda hears herself say, wondering what the hell she's doing now. "Can you give me some information?"

"Certainly. We have three hundred and eighty guest rooms in the hotel, and nearly half of them are suites." The clerk slides a white piece of paper across the top of the desk. "This is our price list."

Amanda scans the Daily Tariff list, noting the list of options: Moderate Queen; Superior Room; Deluxe Room; Premium King; Four Seasons Executive Suite; Deluxe Four Seasons Executive Suite; Two-Bedroom Suite. "The two-bedroom suite," she says, seeing that the price is $795 a night.

"We have two kinds of two-bedroom suites," the clerk tells her. "One with a king-size bed in each room, and one with a king-size bed in one room and twin beds in the other."

Amanda feels her pulse quicken. "That's the one I'd be interested in." Surely there can't be too many such suites. "Some friends are coming to Toronto next month. I said I'd try to get some information for them."

"Perhaps this will help." The young woman produces a small brochure. "This tells you a little bit about the hotel and—"

"The two-bedroom suite," Amanda interrupts. "Does it have a nice view?"

"Oh, yes. Our suites start on the twenty-third floor and face south, so there's a lovely view of the city all the way down to the lake."

"And how many two-bedroom suites are there on each floor?"

"Just one."

Amanda smiles, drops the brochure into her purse, then pushes herself away from the desk. "Thank you."

"My pleasure. Have a nice day."

Amanda walks toward the exit, feeling inordinately self-satisfied. A gust of bitterly cold wind hits her square in the face as she steps outside, slapping her quickly back to reality.

So, big deal, the wind taunts her. So you wormed some information out of an eager-to-please receptionist. So you figured out how to find Mrs. Mallins. You're a lawyer, aren't you? You've been trained to ask the right questions. The more important question is, What are you going to do now?

The doorman signals for a taxi, and Amanda climbs inside. "Where to, miss?"

Amanda leans back against the cracked brown vinyl of the seat, catches a hint of stale body odor emanating from its surface. She hesitates, changing her mind several times before she finally speaks. "Mount Pleasant Cemetery," she says.

"Can you wait for me a few minutes?" she asks the driver, whose identification card on the back of the front seat gives his name as Abdul Jahib.

"Meter's running," he tells her with a shrug.

"I won't be long." She directs him along the winding road that cuts through the cemetery, an enormous property that sits smack in the middle of the city, bordered on the north and south by Davisville and St. Clair, and on the east and west by Mount Pleasant and Yonge. It's a beautiful space, even in the snow, with its rolling hills and wide variety of trees. Everything you could ask for in a final resting place. Peaceful. Quiet. Close to everything. A great view. **People are just dying to get in here,** she hears someone say, then looks skittishly over her shoulder, as if checking for ghosts. "Turn here," she directs the driver. Then: "Turn right." Seconds later: "Down this way."

Abdul Jahib pulls the car to a stop in front of a small gray monument, guarded over by a large stone angel. Amanda gets out of the car, casually absorbing the information inscribed across the monument's surface as she walks by. VERA TRUFFAUT, 1912–1998. Which made Vera eighty-six years old when she died, Amanda calculates. A perfectly respectable age to die.

She continues down the row of graves, wet snow dusting the tops of her decidedly non-winterized boots. Already she feels water seeping through the soft leather to settle uncomfortably between her toes, although she suspects this sensation is more imaginary than real. Still, it won't be long. These boots are more decorative than practical. They weren't designed for trudging through snow-covered cemeteries in the dead of winter.

STEPHEN MOLONEY, 1895–1978, she reads. Dead at eighty-three. Right next to MARTHA MOLONEY, 1897–1952. Dead at fifty-five. "Somebody got the raw end of that deal," Amanda comments, picking up her pace and almost slipping on a patch of black ice. JACK STANDFORD, 1912–1975. "Sixty-three." ARLENE HILL, 1916–1981. "Sixty-five."

She comes to an abrupt halt in front of a rose-colored granite tombstone. EDWARD PRICE. 1933–1992. LOVING HUSBAND AND FATHER. "Dead at fifty-nine," Amanda whispers, feeling her mother sneak up behind her, scream in her ear.

Well, with a daughter like you, no wonder your father had a heart attack!

IN OUR HEARTS YOU LIVE FOREVER.

"Hi, Daddy," Amanda says, tears filling her eyes, freezing on her cheeks.

Hi, Puppet, she hears him say.

It's been a long time, she continues silently.

Not so long really.

Eleven years.

That's not so long.

I've been away. I live in Florida now. I'm a lawyer. Did you know that?

Of course. I know everything about you. And I'm so proud of you.

Really? Why? You never showed much interest in me when you were alive.

You have to understand that your mother was going through a very rough time. She was drinking. She was depressed. She needed my attention, my support.

I needed you too.

You were always so strong and independent. Your mother—

My mother is a crazy woman. She was crazy then, and she's even crazier now.

She needs you.

Amanda laughs despite her tears. When has her mother ever needed her? "I'm not licensed to practice law in Canada, Daddy. Besides, she already has a good lawyer. I'm sure you remember Ben. Mom said he was the final nail in your coffin."

She didn't mean that.

You once said there were things you needed to tell me, things that would explain everything, that when I was old enough to understand, when the time was right . . . Amanda wipes the tears from her eyes. The time was never right, was it, Daddy?

EDWARD PRICE. 1933–1992.
LOVING HUSBAND AND
    FATHER.
IN OUR HEARTS YOU LIVE
    FOREVER.

Time runs out, and people die, Amanda thinks, walking back to the waiting cab. It's guilt that lives forever.

TEN

"S orry I'm late," Amanda apologizes, settling into the passenger seat of Ben's white Corvette. "I decided to buy some winter boots, and the stores didn't open until twelve." He seems a little distracted, so she doesn't tell him about her impromptu visit to the cemetery. Instead she stretches her long legs out in front of her, proudly displaying the new leather boots that cover her black pants up to her knees. "They're even lined."

"Very nice," he says without looking. "I hope you've eaten. We don't have time to stop for lunch."

"I had a big breakfast. Bacon, eggs, toast. The works. It should hold me till dinner." She wonders if he's annoyed with her for being late, and if that's the reason he avoids looking at her. "Is everything all right? I mean, my mother . . . Nothing's happened, has it?"

"Nothing's happened."

"Okay." She pauses, stares out the side window as they pull out of the hotel driveway and turn south onto Avenue Road. "I read the clippings you gave me. They were pretty vague."

"The picture of John Mallins didn't ring any bells?"

"I've never seen him before in my life."

Ben shrugs, nods without turning his head. He says nothing, the silence continuing as Avenue Road morphs into University Avenue. They speed past the Royal Ontario Museum and what used to be the Planetarium, then continue around the circle at Queen's Park, past the Parliament Buildings and the downtown campus of the University of Toronto.

"So, how was your date last night?"

"Fine."

"What'd you do?"

"Dinner at a friend's house."

"Really? Anyone I know?"

"I doubt it."

"No friends from the old days?" she asks playfully, despite the tone in his voice telling her to back off.

"You were my only friend," Ben reminds her, stopping at the red light at College Street, and swiveling around in his seat, looking at her for the first time since he pulled into the hotel driveway.

"Not a very good one," Amanda is forced to admit.

He shrugs again, the motion bringing his black leather jacket up around his ears. "Water under the bridge."

"We were very young."

"We still are."

Amanda nods, although she doesn't feel very young these days, hasn't in some time. "You think we could be friends again?" she ventures. "I mean, it's not for very long. After I leave, you can go back to hating me again."

"I don't hate you, Amanda."

"You should." The light changes to green, and the Corvette instantly takes off, zipping past the mirrored Hydro building and the row of hospitals that line both sides of the wide street. The car hugs the road, the vibrations from the various potholes and crevices traveling back and forth between Amanda's toes and the base of her neck. "I'd forgotten how you feel every bump in the road with this thing."

"Every bump in the road," he agrees. "There's the courthouse, incidentally." He motions to his left. "Your mother's bail hearing is on Tuesday."

Amanda blanches. "It's very strange to hear the words **mother** and **bail hearing** in the same sentence."

"I'm sure it is."

"Anyway, I doubt I'll still be here."

He shrugs, although this time his shoulders barely move.

"You think she'll make bail?"

"I think she'd stand a better chance if you were around to vouch for her."

"You're kidding, right?" Is he really asking her to speak on her mother's behalf?

"On the contrary, I'm very serious."

"You're asking me to perjure myself?"

"I hardly think that will be necessary."

"Not if I'm not here, it won't."

"She's your mother, Amanda," he reminds her again.

"If I have to testify as to my mother's character, they'll string her up on the spot."

He shakes his head. "We don't hang people in this country anymore, Amanda."

"Trust me, you'll resume the practice."

"Will you at least think about it?"

"I will, **at most,** think about it."

He sighs, and the silence returns, although the tension between them has dissipated.

"So, are you going to tell me all about your

dinner last night?" Amanda asks as the Metro Convention Center pops into view. She thinks of Jerrod Sugar and wonders fleetingly what he's doing.

"No, I am not going to tell you about my dinner."

"You're no fun. Will you at least tell me what was served?"

Ben laughs in spite of himself. "I will, **at most,** tell you what was served."

Amanda smiles, feeling the muscles in her neck and shoulders start to relax. "Okay, let's hear it."

"Well, let's see. There was a pear and endive salad to start, followed by rack of lamb, baby potatoes, and asparagus."

"I had asparagus too. And roast chicken."

"Really? Where'd you go?"

"Room service."

"Ah, my favorite. Was it good?"

"Delicious. What'd you have for dessert?"

"Chocolate cake and coffee. You?"

"I skipped dessert. Went to sleep early. What time did you go to bed?"

"Around midnight."

"Your place or hers?"

"Amanda . . ."

"Just making polite conversation."

"Uh-huh."

"Where do you live anyway?" she asks.

"I have a condo at Harborside. Overlooking the water."

"Get out. You do not."

"Floor-to-ceiling windows in every room."

"I can't believe it. Sounds just like my place in Florida."

"And that surprises you?"

"Well, you have to admit, it's kind of strange."

"What is?"

"How much we have in common."

"We always did," he states simply. "Isn't that why you left?"

The rhetorical question slams against Amanda's brain as Ben turns the car onto the Gardiner Expressway, heading west toward the 401. What the hell are you talking about? she wants to shout. "So, what's your girlfriend's name?" she asks instead.

He hesitates. "Jennifer."

"Why are they always named Jennifer?" she asks, picturing Sean's new wife.

"What?"

"So what exactly is the story with you and this Jennifer?" she recovers quickly.

"It's exactly none of your business."

"Aw, come on. Tell me."

"There's nothing to tell. We've only been dating a few months."

"That's long enough to tell."

"What about you?" Ben asks, suddenly switching gears, going on the offensive, as any attorney worth his salt would do. "Involved with anyone special since your most recent divorce?"

"Ouch. No. How'd you know about that anyway?"

He shrugs. "No great mystery. I ran into sombody who ran into you in Florida. Keith Halpern, I think it was."

"Oh, yes. Good old Keith." The first time she'd slept with Keith Halpern, she was sixteen years old. The last time was two years ago, after literally bumping into the now-successful stockbroker at the Palm Beach Grill. He was in Florida on holiday, he'd explained. His wife was visiting her parents in Boca for a few days; maybe they could get together for a drink? Her divorce had just been finalized; she was feeling more than a little vulnerable; she'd probably told him more than he needed to know. Clearly, he'd been only too happy to share that information with his former classmate.

The conversation drifts to a halt. Ben turns

on the radio, switches from one channel to another before anything has time to register on Amanda's consciousness. The flat line of the highway stretches out endlessly before her. There is nothing remotely interesting on either side of the road. "How far away is this place?" she asks as Ben exits onto Highway 427.

"We're almost there."

"We're back at the airport, for heaven's sake."

Ben turns right at Dixon and continues to the first traffic light, then turns left on Carlingview Road, heading north. "Just a few more minutes."

Amanda swivels her head to look out the rear window, realizes the city has all but disappeared behind her. "Maybe this isn't such a good idea."

"Maybe not," he agrees.

"Did you speak to my mother this morning?"

"No."

"So she still doesn't know I'm here?"

"I'm hoping the shock of seeing you will loosen her tongue."

"I wouldn't count on anything."

"I never do."

They continue north to Disco Road, then proceed east about three hundred feet, turning into a long driveway on the south side of the street.

Doesn't exactly make you want to get the white suit out of storage and start dancing, Amanda thinks, staring at the ugly, squat, brown-brick building looming ominously in the middle of the strangely named street. "Could it be any more depressing?" She pictures the prisons in south Florida, with their pastel-colored facades surrounded by scenic moats and exotic vegetation. Not even palm trees waving in a warm breeze would help this architectural monstrosity, she decides as Ben searches for a parking space in the crowded lot.

"I can drop you off at the door, if you'd like. Then you won't have to trudge through the snow."

"No, that's okay. I'm in no rush to go inside. Besides, I have my new boots." Again, she stretches her legs out in front of her, offering her footwear for his perusal.

This time he obliges her with a glance. "Very nice." He pulls the sports car into a spot near the back of the lot, shuts off the engine, exhales a deep breath of air. "You ready?"

"Can we just sit here for a few minutes?"

"Amanda . . ."

"Just for a few minutes."

He nods.

"It's a big place," Amanda says, stalling for time. "I didn't realize Toronto was such a hotbed of crime where women are concerned."

"The men's prison is around back." He points to the side of the building. "You're seeing both buildings."

Amanda closes her eyes in an effort to see nothing at all. "How'd you get involved in this mess anyway? Did my mother call you?"

"No. I read about her arrest in the morning paper, and I volunteered my services."

"Why on earth would you do that?"

"I don't know. I guess I felt a certain sense of obligation."

"Obligation? She was barely civil to you when we were married."

"Maybe that's why I did it."

"Because she was barely civil?"

"Because we used to be married."

Amanda brings her arms around her body, hugs herself with her hands. "You're saying you did it for me?"

"I'm saying I did it because I thought it was the right thing to do."

"Even though she's guilty?"

"Especially if she's guilty."

Amanda tries to laugh. "Don't tell me you

actually believe that nonsense about everyone being entitled to the best possible defense, regardless of guilt or innocence?"

"Don't you?"

"I guess," she acknowledges reluctantly, shivering inside her black wool coat. "It's getting harder though. I mean, occasionally, it would be nice to have a client who really **didn't** do it."

"Stranger things have happened."

"Like both of us ending up lawyers?"

"Like both of us ending up lawyers and then freezing to death in the parking lot of the Metro West Detention Center."

"You're saying it's time to go inside?"

"I'm saying it's time to go inside."

If anything, Amanda finds the interior of the Metro West Detention Center even uglier and more depressing than its outside. "What you see is definitely what you get," she mutters, as they step inside the first set of doors and wait to be admitted.

The guard sitting inside the thick glass booth beyond the second set of doors takes his time buzzing them in, then it's the usual routine of metal detectors and identification checks, of exposing the insides of purses and briefcases, and having personal belongings handled and scrutinized. "Sign in here," an officer instructs, pushing a clipboard across a low table, and regarding Amanda suspiciously.

Amanda stares at the man defiantly, silently daring him to detect a resemblance to her mother. In truth, she is an interesting combination and contradiction of both her parents. Her mother's full mouth resides inside her father's strong jaw; her father's soft eyes harbor her mother's fierce stare.

"This way," the officer says, leading them through dreary corridors leaking the odor of stale human flesh, a smell so unpleasantly pervasive that not even the stench of Javex can mask it.

"You come here often?" Amanda whispers to Ben, as the guard leads them into a small, windowless room.

"Too often," he replies, mistaking her attempt at humor for a legitimate question.

"The prisoner will be down shortly," the guard says, about to exit.

"Do you think we could get another chair in here?" Ben asks.

"I'll see what I can do."

Amanda listens to the officer's footsteps as they retreat down the corridor. She touches the back of one of two uncomfortable-looking, gray plastic chairs that sit on either side of a small, rectangular wood table. "Think all prisons use the same decorator?"

"Jails 'R Us," Ben quips.

Amanda paces back and forth between the table and the wall. She pushes her hair away from her face, unbuttons her coat, then buttons it up again.

"Why don't you sit down?" Ben says.

Amanda shakes her head. She needs to be standing when she sees her mother. Unconsciously she straightens her shoulders and pulls herself up to her full height, knowing it won't be long before her mother cuts her down to size.

"Are you all right?"

Amanda feels her mouth go dry, her breath grow labored. She fights the urge to burst into tears and run screaming from the room. "I'm not sure I can do this."

"You can do it."

"What if I don't **want** to do it?"

"Sometimes we have to do things we'd rather not."

"Since when did you become such a goddamn grown-up?" Amanda snaps, then looks guiltily at the floor.

Since you left, she hears him say, although he says nothing.

She watches his boots as he approaches, feels the warmth of his breath as he moves closer, his slight hesitation before taking her in his arms, hugging her close.

"It's okay," he whispers. "You're going to be fine."

"I don't feel fine." Although that's not entirely true, she realizes, her body relaxing against his, luxuriating in the strong familiarity of his touch. We were always such a perfect fit, she thinks, resting her cheek against the shoulder of his leather jacket.

Isn't that why you left? she hears him ask.

"She can't hurt you anymore, Mandy," Ben says softly.

Abruptly Amanda pulls out of his arms. "Don't call me that."

He moves quickly from her side, unzips his jacket, throws it over the back of one of the chairs, opens his briefcase, begins rifling through it. "Sorry."

"It's just that I hate nicknames."

"I know. Sorry. It won't happen again."

"I didn't mean to snap at you."

He says nothing further, although he doesn't have to. His posture, stiff to the point of rigid, says it all.

"I'm sorry," she offers.

"No problem." He flashes his best lawyer's smile. We'll keep this strictly business, the smile says.

Amanda hears footsteps in the hall, finds herself backing into a corner, and holding her breath as the door to the small room opens. A guard pokes his head inside. "They said you needed another chair?" He hands a chair to Ben without coming inside.

Amanda releases the breath in her lungs, wipes an errant tear from her eye, laughs out loud. What am I so damn nervous about? she wonders. My mother is in jail, for God's sake. There's no way she can hurt me anymore.

And then the door opens again, and Amanda finds herself face-to-face with the woman she's been running away from for most of her adult life.

ELEVEN

What Amanda sees: a small woman in an unflattering prison uniform, a dark green sweat suit trimmed in garish pink. The woman looks remarkably young for her almost sixty-two years, despite the total absence of makeup, her face calm, unmarked by worry, unscarred by remorse. Her hair is a circle of short blond curls. Her eyes are pale and blue, and they widen only slightly when they spot Amanda. A flash of longing passes through them, but it is so brief, Amanda isn't sure whether it was real or something she made up, a by-product of her own misplaced longing.

Her mother says nothing, causing Amanda to wonder if the woman even knows who she is. Is it possible she's suffering from dementia? Don't you recognize me, Mother? she wants to ask, but is unable to find her voice. Perhaps the same holds true for her mother. Perhaps she is so overwhelmed at seeing her only child after all this time that she can't speak, her normally harsh tongue lying flabby and inert at the bottom of her mouth, like a dying fish in a pail. Perhaps she is embarrassed, even ashamed, considering the circumstances that have brought them back together. More likely, she simply has nothing to say to the young woman she only fleetingly acknowledged to begin with. It would obviously take more effort than Amanda is worth.

"I called Amanda and told her what happened," Ben is explaining. "She flew in last night from Florida."

Her mother walks to the chair at the end of the table and sits down, says nothing.

What Amanda feels: fury.

She wants to throw herself at this woman and shake her until something—**anything**—registers in those malignantly placid blue eyes. **Say something,** she wants to scream, her mother's silence worse than any insult she could have hurled, her continuing indifference almost too much to bear. **I deserve an explanation. For why you murdered a man in cold blood. For why you treated me the way you did. For why you never loved me.**

What she says: "It's nice to see you too, Mother."

The last time Amanda saw her mother was just after her father's funeral. The funeral was a small affair, attended by family, a few business colleagues of her father's, and several of the neighbors. There were no friends to speak of because her parents had no friends. Her mother's wild mood swings and erratic behavior had seen to that. Not that Edward Price seemed to miss them; he'd devoted his life to looking after his unhappy wife. In the end, his reward had been a massive heart attack and a premature grave.

After the funeral, Amanda and Ben had accompanied her mother back home. Old Mrs. MacGiver, their neighbor from across the street, had sent over a homemade lemon cake, and Amanda was cutting it into slices while Ben busied himself making coffee. Her mother glared at them from her seat at the kitchen table, as if aware of their presence for the first time that day. "This isn't a party," she said, downing a large glass of vodka.

"Nobody said it was." Amanda bit down on her tongue to keep from saying more. "I just thought you might want to eat something." She deposited a piece of cake in front of her mother.

Her mother pushed it away. "You're wrong."

"Well, at least I'm consistent."

"Still with the mouth." Her mother's head shook with disapproval. "Always with the mouth."

"Would you like a cup of coffee, Mrs. Price?" Ben interrupted.

Gwen Price stared past him as if he weren't there. "You broke your father's heart," she said to Amanda.

"What are you talking about?"

"Amanda . . . ," Ben cautioned. Don't bite, his eyes warned. But it was too late. Amanda's mouth was already circling the bait, preparing to swallow the deadly hook.

"You think he didn't know his daughter was a slut?"

"Okay, Mrs. Price, I think you've said enough."

"Staying out all night, drinking, running off with some delinquent in a fancy sports car."

"Why, Mother, I didn't think you cared."

"He wanted so much for you. He had dreams about you becoming a lawyer. He always wanted to be a lawyer, you know, but his parents couldn't afford to send him to college. You didn't know that, did you?"

"How would I?" Amanda demanded, choking back tears. "He barely spoke to me."

"You were never around."

"That's bullshit."

"Amanda . . . ," Ben warned again.

"He never **tried** to speak to me. And the reason he never tried was that he was too damn busy looking after you. He gave up every-thing—his friends, his interests, his **daughter**—in order to make you happy. But you never were, were you, Mother? No. Be-cause how can anyone be happy when they're so consumed with rage over God only knows what? What is your problem, Mother? Tell me," Amanda demanded, biting off every word, so that each one became a sentence unto itself. "What. Is. Your. Problem?"

Her mother stared at her with eyes as cold as steel. "Well," she said, pouring herself another drink, "with a daughter like you, no wonder your father had a heart attack."

"How are you, Amanda?" her mother asks now, her voice so quiet, it takes Amanda sev-eral seconds to realize she's spoken at all.

"I'm fine," Amanda answers from her corner of the room, not sure how else to respond, her heart beating so wildly, it feels as if she is being pummeled from the inside out by an army of tiny fists.

"Ben," her mother says, acknowledging

him with an almost imperceptible nod of her head.

"How are you feeling today, Mrs. Price?"

"I'm well, Ben, thank you."

"You slept okay? Your cellmates not giving you any more problems?"

"What kind of problems?" Amanda asks.

"The first few nights your mother was here, one of the women in her cell was coming down off drugs, and she kept everyone up all night."

"Scrubbing and cleaning. You should have seen her. She couldn't sit still. She was up pacing and scouring the cell the whole night. It was quite unsettling."

"As opposed to killing a man in cold blood," Amanda says.

"But last night was better?" Ben asks, his eyes warning Amanda to back off.

"Yes, I slept very well."

"You slept very well," Amanda repeats incredulously, unable to restrain herself. "You're in jail, for God's sake. You shot a man. I would think that alone should be enough to keep you awake at night."

"Amanda, please," Ben cautions.

"It's all right," her mother says. "She's understandably upset."

Her mother's seeming serenity only serves to

increase Amanda's agitation. "Oh, good. The voice of reason."

"Maybe you should sit down," Ben advises.

"I don't want to sit down."

Ben turns his attention back to her mother. "Are they giving you your medication?"

"What medication?" Amanda asks.

Her mother shakes her head. "Just something for my osteoporosis. It's nothing to worry about."

"Who said I was worried?"

"Yes, they made sure I got my medication," Gwen Price answers, a slight twitch in the left corner of her mouth her only reaction to Amanda's sarcasm.

So her mother is mortal after all, Amanda thinks, with no small degree of satisfaction. Even a little ordinary. Like thousands of other women her age, she is suffering from a deterioration of her bones, a common and relatively mundane affliction. Amanda is surprised at the lack of drama. Don't the gods know whom they're dealing with?

"I'm sorry you had to fly all the way up here," her mother is saying.

"So am I," Amanda answers.

"It really wasn't necessary."

"You killed a man, Mother."

Gwen Price looks slowly around the room, although there is absolutely nothing to see. The gray walls are bare. No interesting rugs dot the concrete floor. "You don't have much of a tan for someone who lives in Florida," she says without looking at Amanda.

Amanda looks imploringly at Ben. What are we doing here? her eyes ask.

Humor her, his eyes respond. Go with the flow.

Amanda closes her eyes, sees her mother sitting on her living-room sofa, staring at the roaring fire in the fireplace, seemingly oblivious to the sparks spraying toward her feet. Okay, she decides, slowly reopening her eyes. I've questioned difficult witnesses before. Sometimes it's necessary to come in the back door, catch them off guard. "I'm not one for lying in the sun," she offers.

"A little bit of sun never hurt anyone."

"I guess." Not like three bullets to the heart.

"They say the sun is good for the soul, that people who are deprived of it for long periods of time can suffer from serious depression."

"Was that your problem?"

"Amanda . . . ," Ben cautions.

"I could never sit in the sun for very long," her mother continues. "With my pale skin, I burned to a crisp. But you have your father's complexion. I would have thought you'd tan rather nicely."

Amanda stares at her mother in amazement, thinking this is probably the longest conversation she has had with the woman in her entire life.

"So, who is this guy you shot, Mother?" she asks impatiently. So much for coming in the back door.

Her mother shakes her head. "I don't want to talk about it."

"What do you mean, you don't want to talk about it?"

"Mrs. Price," Ben begins, "we can't help you if you won't talk to us."

"I don't want your help."

Amanda throws up her arms in frustration. "Why doesn't that surprise me?"

"It's not that I'm not grateful."

"Grateful? Give me a break."

"I don't expect you to understand."

"You don't **want** me to understand."

"Just tell us what happened, Mrs. Price."

"I shot a man."

"We know that much," Amanda says. "What we don't know is **why** you shot him."

"It doesn't matter why."

"It **does** matter. You don't go around killing people for no reason. Even you, with your stupid curses, always had a reason. Who is this man?"

"I don't know."

"What was your relationship?"

"There was no relationship."

"You expect us to believe you shot and killed a total stranger, someone you'd never seen before in your life?"

"I don't expect you to believe anything."

"Good, because we **don't** believe you."

"That's fine."

"It's not fine. There are witnesses who say you'd been sitting in the lobby of that hotel all day."

"That's true."

"Why?"

"It's a very nice hotel. They have a lovely lobby."

"What!"

"Amanda," Ben warns. "Calm down."

"You're saying you were sitting in the hotel lobby because it's a nice place to sit?"

Her mother nods.

"And you just happened to have a loaded gun in your purse."

"I often carry it with me."

"You often walk around with a loaded gun in your purse?"

"Yes."

"Why?"

"The city is a dangerous place."

"Not if people don't walk around with guns."

Her mother almost smiles. "Ben, is this really necessary?"

"Is it necessary?" Amanda asks, her voice rising.

"I just don't see the relevance, considering . . ."

"Considering what?"

"Considering I'm going to plead guilty on Tuesday."

"You're going to plead her guilty?" Amanda demands of her former husband.

"I **am** guilty," her mother reminds her.

"Not if you're insane."

"You think I'm insane?"

"I think you're nuttier than a fruitcake in January."

"Amanda . . ."

"I assure you, I'm quite sane," her mother says calmly. "I knew exactly what I was doing when I shot that man, and I knew it was wrong. Isn't that the legal definition of sanity?"

"Sane people don't go around shooting total strangers."

"Maybe they do."

Amanda turns to Ben. "You can't seriously be planning to let her plead guilty."

"Believe me, it's not my choice."

"He has no choice," Gwen Price states. "And neither do you. I shot and killed a man, and I'm prepared to accept the consequences. It's really very simple."

"Nothing about you has ever been simple."

"Be that as it may," her mother replies. "It's still my decision."

"Who was John Mallins, Mother?"

"I have no idea."

"How did you know him?"

"I didn't."

"Then why were you waiting for him?"

"I wasn't."

"You just happened to be sitting in the hotel lobby with a loaded gun in your purse when he walked in," Amanda says for what feels like the hundredth time.

"That's right."

"And you got up from your chair, cut across the lobby, and shot him."

"Yes. Three times, I believe."

"For no reason."

"Yes."

"Because you felt like it."

"Yes."

"Why?"

"I don't know why. Maybe I didn't like his mustache."

"You didn't like his mustache!"

"It's as good a reason as any," her mother says.

"Don't mock me."

"I'm sorry, Puppet. That wasn't my intention."

"What?" Amanda stumbles backward, as if she's been struck.

"I didn't mean to mock you. It's just that—"

"Don't ever call me that."

Her mother looks genuinely chagrined. "I'm sorry."

"All right, look," Ben intervenes. "Let's get back on track, shall we?"

"There's only one track here," Gwen tells them. "And it leads directly to a prison cell. Now I understand your curiosity and I appreciate your wanting to help, but . . ."

"But what?" Amanda demands. "What about John Mallins's family, Mother? Don't you think his two children deserve an explanation for why you murdered their father? Don't you owe John Mallins's widow at least a hint of closure?"

"I'm very sorry for their pain," Gwen Price says, her eyes suddenly clouding over with tears.

What the hell is this? Amanda wonders, more terrified by her mother's unexpected tears than she ever was by her anger. Who is this woman? she thinks. What is she trying to pull now? "Who was John Mallins, Mother? Why did you shoot him?"

Her mother says nothing.

"The police will investigate, you know," Amanda tells her. "They'll get to the bottom of this."

A flicker of fear cuts across Gwen's face, then disappears. "They won't need to get to the bottom of anything once I plead guilty. They already have my confession, the murder weapon, and a lobbyful of eyewitnesses. Nobody cares why I shot the man as long as the prosecutors have their conviction."

"I care," Amanda says softly.

"I'm sorry," her mother says again.

Amanda rubs her forehead, looks toward the ceiling, takes a long, deep breath. "Okay, you win." She moves quickly to the door. "We're wasting our time here, Ben. Let's go."

"Mrs. Price, please," Ben urges.

"Let it go, Ben," Amanda snaps. "I refuse to play these stupid games. Her mind is obviously made up. She wants to rot in jail for the rest of her life. I say, let her." She pulls open the door.

"Amanda." Her mother's voice stops her cold.

Amanda swivels around, her hands clutching the door handle behind her back.

"I don't think I've ever told you how beautiful you are," her mother says.

Amanda doesn't know whether to laugh or cry. She runs from the room before she can do either.

Twelve

"Did you hear what she said?" Amanda bursts through the outside doors of the prison, begins angrily slogging her way through the slush-covered parking lot. "I can't believe she had the gall to say that to me."

"Amanda, slow down."

"The woman is a sadist. An amoral, card-carrying sadist."

"Amanda, where are you going?"

Amanda braces herself against the gusting wind, wet snowflakes pelting her cheeks and clinging to her eyes, like an extra layer of lashes. "What right does she have to say things like that? **I don't think I've ever told you how beautiful you are?!** What the hell is that? She knows damn well she's never told me I'm beautiful. 'Useless,' definitely. 'Worthless,' a million times. 'A blight on her existence,' more often than I can count. So, where does she get off? Tell me. Where does she get off?" Amanda spins around in helpless circles. "Where the hell is the fucking car?"

Ben points toward the far end of the lot.

"Well, who parked it way the hell over there anyway?" Amanda propels herself toward it.

"Amanda, be careful. It's icy underneath—"

Amanda hears his warning just as the heel of her boot connects with a hidden patch of ice. All at once she feels as if she is being simultaneously yanked back and pushed forward, as if invisible hands have grabbed onto the collar of her coat, while unseen feet are kicking her legs out from under her. Her body catapults into the air, and for an instant, she feels as if she is floating on a magic carpet. And then suddenly she is twisting in the frigid air, the magic carpet collapsing under her weight, and she falls to the pavement, like a puppet whose strings have been cruelly severed. **Puppet,** she hears her mother say as she hits the ground, and she bursts into a flood of bitter tears.

Ben is immediately at her side, solicitous hands on her arms, helping her to her feet. "Amanda, are you all right?"

"I'm fine." She brushes several clumps of wet snow from the side of her coat and refuses to look at him. "I'm fucking fine."

"Are you sure? That was some fall."

"I said I'm fine."

"Do you want to go back inside, sit down for a while?"

"Go back in there? Are you kidding me? I want to get away from this miserable place as fast as humanly possible."

"Okay." He takes her elbow, leads her gingerly toward the car. "Be careful."

"Goddamn boots."

He unlocks the car door, helps her inside. "You'll probably be pretty stiff later on. You might want to take a hot bath when you get back to the hotel."

Amanda nods without speaking, leans her head against the side window as Ben pulls the car out of the lot and onto Disco Road.

"Are you okay?"

"No."

"You think something might be broken?"

"No. And not my heart either, in case you're prone to thinking in clichés. Sorry," she apologizes immediately. "You didn't deserve that."

"You're angry. It's understandable."

"Really? And just what is it you understand?"

"You haven't seen your mother in years, and to see her now, under these circumstances . . ."

"She looks pretty damn good, don't you think? I mean, considering she's wearing the ugliest shade of green on the planet and she hasn't had her hair done in a couple of days. But hey, she's still slim and attractive and, let's not forget, she's **sleeping well**."

"You'd like to see her suffer more?"

"I'd like to see her burn in hell."

"Because she killed a man or because she said you look beautiful?"

Amanda's head snaps toward her former husband. "Oh, please."

"What has you so upset, Amanda?"

"Oh, I don't know. Could it be because my mother is in jail for murder?"

"Old news," Ben says dismissively. "Besides, I would have thought you'd relish the idea of your mother locked away in a cell somewhere. It might not be hellfire and brimstone, but it's pretty damn close."

"Did she look like she's suffering to you?" Amanda swipes at her running nose with the back of her hand. "Because she didn't look like she's suffering to me. And you know why?" she asks, not waiting for an answer. "Because she isn't. She's not remotely sorry for what she did. You can see it in her eyes, in her posture. Did you notice how still she sits? There's a calmness about her. A serenity. As if . . ."

"As if what?"

"I don't know." Amanda stares out the front window, following the arc of the windshield wipers as they swoop against the falling snow. "It's almost as if her demons have finally been stilled."

Ben glances toward her. "You're saying John Mallins was a demon?"

"I don't know what I'm saying."

"We'll try again tomorrow."

"What? You're kidding, right? No way I'm going back there." Amanda reaches down to massage her knee.

"Sore?"

"Furious," she responds, grateful when he laughs. "You're not really going to let her plead guilty on Tuesday, are you?"

"I'm not sure I can stop her."

Amanda shakes her head in frustration. "She's obviously insane."

"You heard the woman. She knew what she was doing, and she knew it was wrong."

"Temporary insanity then."

"Hard to plead temporary insanity when she was waiting for the man all afternoon with a gun. It bespeaks a certain measure of premeditation, don't you think?"

"Not guilty by reason of mental defect?"

"What defect?"

"That she's mental?" This time they both laugh. "You think the prosecution might be willing to cut a deal?"

"Why would they? They have an airtight case."

"They don't have a motive."

"They don't need one," he reminds her.

"What if I do?"

"Then I guess you'll just have to stick around a few more days and see what we can come up with."

"Shit." Amanda massages the back of her neck. Ben was right—already she's starting to stiffen up. "What the hell. Let her plead guilty, if that's what she wants. I don't care."

A faint ringing echoes through the car, ricochets off the windows. Ben reaches inside his leather jacket and pulls out his cell phone, answering it in the middle of its second ring. "Hello." He looks down, listens intently. "When did this happen?"

Amanda observes the intensity of his concentration as he listens, remembering such intensity was always one of his most attractive qualities. He had a way of making you feel as if you were the only person in the room who mattered, she thinks, hearing the faint echo of a woman's voice in the receiver, and experiencing a sharp stab of jealousy.

This is all her mother's fault, she decides. Seeing her mother for the first time in all these years, and under such extreme circumstances, has unsettled her, unearthed a veritable powder keg of long-buried memories and emotions.

She takes stock. What is she feeling exactly? Angry, no question. Helpless, definitely. Anxious, certainly. Confused, yes. Irritated, yes. Frustrated, you betcha.

What she isn't feeling: pity.

What she isn't feeling: compassion.

What she isn't feeling: tenderness.

No way.

I don't think I've ever told you how beautiful you are.

How dare you, Amanda thinks, kneading the muscles in her neck until her fingers start to ache. How dare you say something like that to me now? What are you trying to pull? What are you thinking? That just because I came back here, because I agreed to see you again, that all is forgiven? That I'm supposed to feel sorry for you because you're locked up in the ugliest damn building I've ever seen, wearing the ugliest damn sweat suit I've ever seen, and you look so frail inside all that thick cotton, and so, I don't know, so . . . human, for want of a better word.

But we all know that's not true, don't we, Mother?

Well, with a daughter like you, no wonder your father had a heart attack.

Yes, that's more like the woman we've come to know and loathe.

I don't think I've ever told you how beautiful you are.

No, you haven't. "And it's too goddamn late now."

"What is?" Ben asks, tucking the phone back inside his jacket.

"What?"

"What's too late?"

"What?" Amanda asks again, unable to say more.

"Are you all right?"

"Fine."

He smiles. "Fucking fine or just fine?"

She finds herself smiling in return. "Was that Jennifer who called?"

"It was."

"Checking on tonight's dinner plans?"

"She heard about something she thought might interest me."

"And did it?"

"Apparently another witness has come forward."

"In my mother's case?"

"Have you ever heard of a woman named Corinne Nash?"

"Corinne Nash?" Amanda chews the name silently in her mouth, pushing it across her tongue, trying to recognize the flavor. "No, I don't think so."

"She claims to be a friend of your mother's."

"Impossible. My mother doesn't have any friends."

"You've been away a long time, Amanda."

"Some things never change."

"And some things do. Shall we go talk to her?"

"You know where this woman lives?"

Ben turns the car onto the entrance ramp of the 401, waits for a break in the eastbound traffic. He offers nothing further.

Amanda smiles knowingly. Sometimes it pays to sleep with the enemy, she thinks.

The house on Whitmore Avenue is old and in obvious need of repair. Its mustard-yellow brick could use a good sandblasting, and the concrete stairs leading up to the tiny front porch, although shoveled clean of snow, are noticeably crumbling. A late-model Caprice sits in the driveway, too wide for the narrow garage attached to the house. Wooden shutters, whose white paint is chipping, frame small windows overlooking the street. A bronze knocker in the shape of a lion's head sits in the middle of an oak door, both in need of polishing. "Look familiar?" Ben asks, pulling up in front of the house.

"No."

He turns off the engine. "Let me do most of the talking," he cautions as Amanda climbs out of the car. "Amanda . . . ," he warns as she hurries up the steps.

"I won't say a word." She begins pounding on the door.

"Oh, that's good. She'll think it's the Gestapo."

"I'm not saying a thing."

"Who is it?" a woman's voice calls from inside the house.

"My name is Ben Myers," Ben says, his gloved hand reaching out to cover Amanda's mouth. "I'm representing Gwen Price, and I was wondering if I could talk to you for a few minutes."

The door opens immediately. Amanda shakes free of Ben's hand and steps aside, almost afraid to confront the woman face-on.

"You're Gwen's attorney?" The woman's voice is thin, almost girlish, and she's conservatively dressed in a brown skirt and beige sweater set. On her feet is a pair of fuzzy pink slippers. "Please come in. How is Gwen?"

"She's doing pretty well."

The aroma of freshly brewed coffee swirls around their heads as they step inside the small front foyer. Corinne Nash closes the door behind them. "If you wouldn't mind removing your boots . . ."

They immediately oblige, and Amanda takes the opportunity to sneak a look at her surroundings. The downstairs rooms are compact and neat—a living room to her left, a dining room to her right, a doorway open to the small kitchen at the back. A wooden staircase, covered by a runner of pale green carpeting, leads from the center hall to the rooms upstairs. Amanda pictures three bedrooms, the master bedroom only slightly larger than the other two, and probably only one bathroom. The walls throughout are an insipid shade of green that stops just short of institutional, and the carpets covering the wood floors in both the living and dining room are floral in pattern, as are the drapes.

"This is my assistant," Ben begins as Amanda finishes removing her boots and lifts her head.

"Oh, my God," Corinne Nash exclaims.

Amanda finds herself backing against the door as the woman walks toward her, one hand extended. Corinne Nash is tall, about five feet eight inches, with a huge bosom and ample hips, which make her little-girl voice all the more out of place, as if the voice were emanating from somewhere else in the room. Her chin-length hair is the same shade of golden brown as her eyes, and her lips are wide beneath a nose that is short and sculpted. In her youth, she was probably a force to be reckoned with, Amanda thinks, feeling the door handle at her back. "You're Amanda, aren't you?"

It takes Amanda a second to recover her voice. "You know me?"

"Of course I know you. Please, come in." Her arm sweeps across Amanda's shoulders as she guides her toward a living room bursting with furniture. "Let me take your coat. Please sit down." Her fingers flutter between the floral-print sofa in front of one window and the two cantaloupe-colored wing chairs in front of the other. An overstuffed, muted orange-and-green-striped armchair and matching ottoman sit in front of a fireplace at the far end of the room, and an antique Queen Anne chair upholstered in dark green needlepoint sits beside an old upright piano. On the wall above the piano is a painting of a naked woman reclining on a settee, the naked woman bearing an uncomfortable resemblance to the woman of the house. "Can I get you a cup of coffee? It's already made."

"Coffee would be great, thank you," Ben answers for both him and Amanda.

"How do you take it?"

"Cream and sugar," they answer together.

"Just like your mother," Corinne Nash says upon her return, depositing a tray with three mugs of steaming coffee and a plate of assorted cookies on the glass coffee table in front of them.

Amanda makes a mental note to start drinking her coffee black. "How do you know me?" she asks as the woman sits down in the closest of the two wing chairs.

"I've seen your picture many times."

"My picture? Which picture?"

Corinne Nash seems slightly taken aback. "Well, let's see. There's the one of you when you graduated from high school, and then there's another one of you just sitting staring out the window. One of those candid shots. Apparently your father took it when you didn't realize. That's your mother's favorite. And of course, all those pictures of you as a baby. It's amazing—you still have the same face. That's how I recognized you. Have you seen your mother? She's so proud of you. She must be so relieved you're here."

Amanda grabs her mug of coffee from the tray and raises it to her lips to keep from screaming, **What are you talking about? My mother never kept photographs of me. She was never proud.** She looks to Ben, her eyes appealing for help. But he looks as confused as she is.

"Mrs. Nash," he begins, "I understand you've talked to the police."

"Yes. I'm so sorry. I didn't know what to do. I didn't want to get your mother in any more trouble, that's why I waited a few days to come forward, but then I read that she had already confessed, and I wanted to do the right thing. I'm so sorry. I hope I haven't made things worse for her."

"What exactly did you tell the police, Mrs. Nash?"

"That I was with Gwen at the Four Seasons when she first saw that man."

"You were with her when she killed John Mallins?" Ben asks.

"No, not when she shot him. The day before."

"I don't understand," Amanda interrupts. "You're saying my mother was at the hotel the day before she shot him?"

"Yes. We'd gone to a movie, and then went for tea. They have a lovely bar in the lobby, and we often meet there for tea in the afternoon. They have these lovely biscuits." She offers the tray of cookies. "These aren't as good, of course."

Ben takes one. "Delicious. You made these?"

"Oh, my, no. I can't bake to save my life. Never could. My grandchildren complain about it whenever they visit. They say grandmothers are supposed to be able to bake cookies."

"How long have you known my mother?" Amanda asks, trying to give the woman context.

"About five years. We met at the movies. We were both alone, and we just sort of drifted into a conversation. Actually, I think I was the one who started talking to her. She was shier. At least at first. But I wore her down, I guess.

It turned out we had a lot in common. We were both widows and recovering alcoholics. Our children were grown. We both liked movies and the theater. So, we started meeting every couple of weeks, and then once a week, and after the movies, we'd sometimes go for tea."

"And that's when you saw John Mallins?" Ben asks, bringing them back to the matter at hand.

"Yes. Actually, we were just leaving the lobby bar when they came through the revolving door, laughing and holding hands on their way to the elevators. And I turned to Gwen and said something like 'Isn't that a lovely family?' Only Gwen looked like she'd just seen a ghost. She was shaking so hard I thought maybe she was having a seizure, so I sat her down and asked her if I should call an ambulance, but she insisted she was okay, even though you could see she wasn't herself. Then after a few minutes, we left. I called her later to check on how she was feeling, and she said she was fine."

"That was it?" Ben asks. "She never said anything to you about John Mallins?"

"Never mentioned him at all. In fact, it wasn't until I read about what happened in the papers and saw Gwen's picture next to that man's, that I put two and two together."

"And you're sure the man you saw that afternoon was John Mallins?" Amanda questions.

"The police asked me the same thing. I'm absolutely positive. I'm very good with faces. It was the same man all right."

"Think hard, Mrs. Nash. Had my mother ever mentioned John Mallins to you before?"

"Never. I still can't believe it."

"What?"

"That she shot that man. Like I told the police, your mother is the kindest, gentlest person I've ever known."

Amanda feels the coffee mug slip through her fingers. Before she can stop it, it bounces off her lap, spilling its contents across the floral-print rug. Like John Mallins's blood, Amanda thinks, watching as the stain reaches for her toes.

THIRTEEN

Did she really say my mother is the kindest, gentlest person she's ever known?" Amanda whispers as Corinne Nash rushes into the kitchen to retrieve some paper towels.

"That's what she said."

Amanda shakes her head in disbelief. "Who does she usually hang out with? Hitler?" She sinks back into the sofa, almost disappearing inside the cacophony of pink-and-green fabric flowers and vines.

"Have a cookie," Ben offers. "They're actually pretty good."

Amanda grabs a biscuit from the black enamel tray, swallowing it almost whole, as Corinne Nash scurries back into the room carrying a handful of paper towels. She drops to her knees, begins blotting up the stain.

"Oh, no," Amanda says, joining the older woman on the floor. "Please let me do that."

"Nonsense. It's done." Corinne proudly displays the now-wet paper towel. "Have another cookie," she instructs. "I'll get some more coffee."

"No, I'm fine," Amanda protests. "Really. I've put you to enough trouble already."

"I bet you haven't eaten anything all day, have you?" Corinne Nash shakes her head. "Just like your mother."

Amanda's smile is so tight, her cheeks feel as if they might split down the middle. When she speaks, her words rumble unsteadily from her throat, as if she is gargling. "I assure you, I'm nothing like my mother."

"Oh, really? I see all sorts of similarities," Corinne Nash says with a smile.

"I think maybe we should be going," Ben interjects quickly, guiding Amanda toward the front door. He keeps his arm wrapped tightly around her waist as she steps into her boots and gathers her coat around her.

"Wait," Amanda says as they are descending the front steps. "I just thought of something." She stops on the second-to-last step, takes a deep breath of late-afternoon air, turns back to Corinne Nash. "You wouldn't, by any chance, have a key to my mother's house, would you?" she asks, lowering her voice in an effort not to sound like her mother.

"As a matter of fact, I do," Corinne says with almost audible pride. "We exchanged keys a few months ago. We thought it would be a good idea. You know, in case of an emergency or something. I guess this qualifies. Would you like it?"

"Please," Ben says before Amanda can say otherwise. "Good thinking," he adds as Mrs. Nash disappears back into her house to find the key.

Amanda ignores the compliment. "I don't sound anything like my mother. How could she say that? You don't think I sound like my mother, do you?"

"Here it is," Mrs. Nash says upon her return, proudly offering the single silver key to Amanda. "Her plants probably need watering."

"We'll take care of it," Ben says, thanking the woman again.

Corinne Nash waves good-bye as they climb into the car. "Please tell your mother she's in my prayers."

"I'll be sure to do that," Amanda mutters. She is still muttering and Mrs. Nash is still waving as Ben throws the Corvette into gear and pulls away from the curb.

* * *

The two-story house on the west side of Palmerston is much like its owner—aging but proud, stately but eccentric. The bricks are a dull brown, the front door a bright yellow. Snow covers the sidewalk and outside steps, and no one has bothered to shovel the narrow driveway that is shared with the house next door. "A curse on you, Mr. Walsh," Amanda hears her mother yell as Ben pulls his car into the mutual driveway. "You'll be dead before the new year."

Sure enough, two months later, old Mr. Walsh was dead.

In the years that followed, several families moved in and out of the house next door. Amanda wonders who lives in it now, if they will be as incensed as her mother used to be at finding a car blocking the middle of the driveway. Not that her mother ever went anywhere, Amanda thinks, looking over at Ben, remembering how often this very car sat idling in this very position.

"You ready?" he asks.

"You're sure this isn't considered breaking and entering?"

In response, Ben holds up the key to the front door. "This was your idea, remember?"

"We aren't interfering with a police investigation?"

"Do you see any yellow tape?"

Amanda exhales a deep breath of air, watches it spread across the car's front window. He's right, of course. The police have no reason to search her mother's house. They already have the murder weapon. And even if they don't have a motive, they have something much better—a confession. Amanda releases another painful breath from her lungs and pushes open the car door.

"Careful on the ice," Ben warns as Amanda makes her way slowly to the walkway. She pretends not to see the arm he offers to help her up the snow-caked front stairs.

"Just what do you think we'll find in here?" she asks as the key twists in the lock.

"I have no idea."

In the second it takes for the key to release the lock, Amanda thinks of half a dozen reasons why they shouldn't be doing this: they are snooping where they don't belong; her mother will be furious when she finds out; this isn't her house, not anymore; she hasn't set foot in here since her father died; she vowed never to set foot in it again; just standing on the front porch is making her feel sick to her stomach.

To this list she adds one more reason: they might find something.

The door falls open. Ben steps confidently over the threshold. "Coming?"

"I'm not sure I can do this."

"Would you like to wait in the car?"

Amanda shakes her head, the only part of her body that seems capable of movement. Her limbs have frozen. She has the feeling that if she tries to force one leg in front of the other, it will snap off like an icicle.

A gust of cold air blows against the back of her coat, gently nudging her inside. She steps into the small front foyer, her eyes on the tiny gray-and-white squares of the linoleum floor. "Doesn't look like much has changed," she hears Ben say.

Slowly, reluctantly, Amanda lifts her eyes.

What Amanda sees: the ersatz gray-and-white mosaic tiles of the foyer disappearing into the dark wood floor of the narrow hallway, the gray-carpeted living room to her left, the wood-paneled study to her right, a stairway at the back, beside the kitchen, a sobbing child flying down those stairs and darting between rooms to escape her mother's wrath.

Amanda swallows, ignoring her mother's voice reminding her to wipe her feet on the frayed patch of gray carpet inside the front door. "Let's do this quickly, okay?"

"I'll take the main floor," Ben tells her. "Think you can handle the bedrooms?"

Amanda proceeds cautiously, as if half-expecting a deranged figure with a knife to come shrieking out of the shadows at the top of the stairs, as in **Psycho**. Already she can hear Ben rifling through the cabinets in the kitchen. What exactly is he looking for? she wonders, her boots leaving a wet trail as she climbs the steps. What are we doing here?

Her old bedroom is to the left of the landing. She stands in front of the door for several long seconds, her gaze traveling from the small twin bed against one pale pink wall, to the Renoir print of a girl standing on a swing that sits above the desk on the opposite side of the room, to the light wood dresser that fits just underneath the side window overlooking the mutual driveway. A perfect little girl's room, she thinks. Except that she was far from the perfect little girl.

Amanda steps into the room, spins slowly around, feels herself growing smaller with each spin, like Alice after that mysterious pill, until she is toddler-size. She hears laughter, feels strong female arms lifting her into the air, then dangling her from a great height, as her little legs kick happily at the air. "Who's my little puppet?" she hears a woman trill.

And then the laughter suddenly stops, freezing in the air, and raining down upon her head, like hail pellets. The toddler drops from the woman's arms, lies like a broken doll on the gray-carpeted floor, arms and legs splayed akimbo. Amanda sinks down onto the bed, wounded.

When she was a teenager, she begged her parents to let her make some changes to the decor. Her friends all had much cooler rooms, with queen-size beds and wallpaper that reflected their maturing, if questionable, tastes. She was tired of all the pink, she protested. Tired of all the girlish clutter. She'd long ago outgrown her collection of soap animals and glass paperweights. What she wanted were black walls, like Debbie Profumo. What she wanted was a state-of-the-art stereo system, like Andrea Argeris.

What she got was a warning to keep her voice down, her mother was resting.

In protest, she stopped hanging her clothes in the closet or tucking them neatly into drawers. She wallpapered her room with posters of Marilyn Manson and Sean Penn, listened to heavy-metal music, blasting her radio all night, until the time her father stormed into the room, tore it from the wall, and hurled it to the floor, damaging it beyond repair. "What's the matter with you?" he demanded, his eyes drifting to the packet of birth control pills she'd deliberately left on top of her desk. "You know your mother can't sleep with all that damn noise."

Her response had been to buy a new radio, play it even louder. Her response had been to stay out later and later, until she barely came home at all, and when she did, it was always with a resounding slam of the front door. Her response had been to sleep with every male who caught her eye, because she couldn't catch the eye of the one male who mattered most. Because his eye was elsewhere.

On her mother.

At least that's what Oprah would probably say, Amanda decides now, growing bored with all this amateur psychology and pushing herself off the bed, impatiently pulling open the various drawers of her dresser, looking for God only knows what.

What she finds: a few sweaters belonging to her mother, some old costume jewelry, a silk scarf bordered by a thick black line and decorated with colorful butterflies. Amanda crumples the delicate silk into the palms of her hands, raises the scarf to her nose, sniffs at its folds for traces of her mother, finds none. Absently she wraps the scarf around her neck, her attention shifting from the dresser to the desk. Restless hands sift through boxes of blank stationery and empty date books. In the bottom drawer, she finds a collection of old fashion magazines and thumbs lazily through them.

"Nothing here," she says aloud, returning the magazines to the bottom drawer, and walking back into the hall.

"Don't go," a small voice calls from behind her, and Amanda turns, even though she knows no one is there.

The second bedroom is only a few short steps away. It too is essentially as she remembers, its decor almost the same as the first, except that the bed that sits against the opposite wall is a double, and the walls are a subtler shade of pink. A desk is propped up against the window overlooking the street, a low dresser sits on the wall beside the closet. A Renoir print—this one of a field of flowers—hangs over the bed. Amanda can't remember anybody ever actually occupying this room. Her parents never had any guests. On impulse, she marches

over to the closet and pulls open the door, then
falls back, shields her eyes, as if blinded by a
sudden light.

The puppet stage sits on the floor of the
otherwise empty closet, two wooden dolls
folded neatly in the middle of the stage floor,
their bodies stretched across their legs as if ex-
ercising, their hands folded over the tops of
their feet, their eyes closed as if sleeping, their
strings spread out around them, as if they'd
stumbled into a spider's web.

Amanda gingerly carries the two-foot-high
stage into the center of the bedroom, lowering
it to the gray broadloom and sitting down,
cross-legged, beside it. With trembling fingers, she lifts the first puppet into her hands. It
is a boy with a big wooden head and a high
pompadour of painted-on black hair. Immediately the marionette's eyes pop open, revealing
orbs of bright neon green. His lips are thick,
his smile wide. He is wearing a cotton shirt
that is white and crisp, and blue sneakers peek
out from beneath a pair of stiff denim jeans.

Amanda dangles the puppet from its strings,
watching his awkward dance. Then she gathers
the second puppet, this one a red-cheeked girl
with huge blue eyes and waves of painted blond
hair, into her other hand and brings her around

to face her friend. Slowly she manipulates her fingers, watching as the girl puppet responds with a curtsy and the male puppet bows. In the next instant they are swirling gracefully around the stage.

"How are you doing up there?" Ben calls from downstairs.

The marionettes jerk up and apart, their hands rising into the air, as if someone is pointing a gun at their heads. "I'm fine," Amanda calls out, letting go of the dolls' strings, the puppets collapsing one on top of the other, as if they have, in fact, been shot.

"Find anything?" Ben asks from the bottom of the stairs.

"No. You?"

"Nothing so far. I'm heading for the basement."

"I should be through here soon," she calls after him, staring guiltily at the puppets. She carefully untangles the two sets of strings and returns the dolls to their former position in the center of the stage, their bodies folded neatly over at the waist, their eyes closed. "It's better that way," she tells them in a whisper, returning the stage to the closet and shutting the door.

She feels movement behind her and turns in

time to see her mother's face contorted with rage. "What are you doing in here?" her mother cries, grabbing her by the shoulders and shaking her as if she were nothing but a puppet herself.

"I was just playing," the child Amanda stammers, wiggling out of her mother's reach. "I'm sorry."

"Get out of here. Get out of here right now."

Amanda hurries out of the room, stops in the middle of the tiny hallway, tears filling her eyes and clinging to her mascara. "No," she says, resolutely patting the tears away. "You are through making me cry, Mother."

I don't think I've ever told you how beautiful you are.

"Fuck you."

"Did you say something?" Ben calls from two flights down.

The dull gray of the sky is slowly turning to slate as Amanda steps into her mother's bedroom. Soon it will be dark, she thinks, flipping on the overhead light and glancing toward her mother's queen-size bed. The floral bedspread that Amanda remembers from her youth has been replaced by a simple white duvet, not unlike the one in her own Florida bedroom, Amanda realizes with a shudder, but other than that, the room is essentially the same as it always was: the ubiquitous pink walls and gray broadloom, the assorted crystal knickknacks that are displayed in two raised alcoves on either side of the bed. Several photographs of Amanda's father sit on the dresser in front of the large side window, his forced smile at odds with the obvious worry in his eyes. Amanda lifts one of the pictures into her hands, runs a delicate finger across her father's handsome face, then returns the photograph to the dresser, placing it between two baby pictures of herself. On the nightstand beside her mother's bed, she sees the other photos Corinne Nash mentioned: her high school graduation picture, and a lovely candid shot of her staring out the living room window. When was that taken? she wonders, her body swaying toward it.

"What are you doing in here?" her father asks suddenly. "You know you shouldn't be in here."

"Sorry, Daddy," Amanda apologizes to his photograph. "I'll try to make this quick."

She rifles quickly through the drawers of her mother's dresser, her fingers floating across the assortment of bras and camisoles, nightgowns and pajamas. "Okay, don't go in there," she warns the little girl standing at the closet door.

"You know what happened the last time you opened that door." She rushes over to stop her, but the child has already succeeded in pulling open the door. Amanda stares openmouthed at the shoe box sitting on the top shelf of her mother's closet.

She wonders whether to call for Ben. Don't be silly, she assures herself. There's no gun there. "She already used it," Amanda says out loud, and almost laughs.

Amanda leans against her mother's clothes—a blue wool dress, tailored slacks in navy, black, and brown, a couple of pastel silk shirts, several A-line skirts, a brown corduroy jacket—as she stretches on her toes to reach the shoe box. The box feels empty as she brings it to her chest. Even still, Amanda hesitates to open it. "You're being really silly," she castigates herself, tearing off the top of the box and throwing it to the floor, peering inside.

She sees nothing in the box except a passbook for a long-standing savings account at the Toronto Dominion Bank. The remaining balance is an unimpressive $7.75. Clearly, not a bank her mother frequents often, Amanda thinks, hearing something drop from the box onto the floor. Her eyes scan the carpet, finally alighting on a small key. "Looks like a key to a safety-deposit box," she says, hearing Ben's footsteps on the stairs. Without further thought, she pockets both the passbook and the key.

"Find anything?" Ben asks, coming into the room.

Amanda displays the empty shoe box, says nothing.

"There's nothing downstairs either."

Amanda nods. "Oh, well. Can't say we didn't try."

They stare through the growing darkness at one another, her words bouncing off the walls and echoing in the still air of the late afternoon.

FOURTEEN

T ake a hot bath, order room service, and get some sleep," Ben instructs as they pull into the driveway of the Four Seasons hotel. "I'll call you in the morning."

Amanda forces her lips into a smile. She'd been just about to suggest they go somewhere nice for dinner. Her treat, she was about to say, when he beat her to the punch. So instead she flashes a knowing grin, says, "Say hi to Jennifer," then climbs out of the car, pushing against the revolving door into the lobby without so much as a backward glance. Seconds later, standing just inside the doors, pretending to be searching for her room key, her eyes drift sideways toward the glass door, and she sees that the white Corvette is already gone.

"A hot bath, room service, and a good night's sleep," she repeats with mounting irritation, stepping inside an empty elevator. "Good idea."

Her fingers hover over the button for the six-teenth floor for several seconds before pressing the one for the twenty-fourth floor instead.

This, on the other hand, is probably **not** such a good idea, she thinks as she exits the el-evator, following the corridor as it winds around to the south side of the building. "Now what?" She walks slowly down the long hall, stopping briefly in front of each set of doors, hoping to hear something from inside one of the rooms that might indicate which suite to choose. "Are you behind door number one or door number two?" she whispers at the cream-colored walls, but no answer is forthcoming.

Amanda knows she's being silly, that she has no business being up here, that Ben will be more than pissed when he finds out what she's done. It's not too late. She can still do as he in-structed: go back to her room, order room ser-vice, take a hot bath, and get a good night's sleep. She could even treat herself to a massage, she decides, about to turn around, do exactly that, when she sees the door to the room at the far end of the corridor open, and a man and a woman step into the hall, their arms around each other's waists.

She scratches suite 2420 from her invisible list and smiles at the couple as they pass by.

Which only leaves five more rooms to choose from. All she has to do is start knocking on doors. "You're out of your mind," she tells herself, but such admonishments come too late. Already she is standing in front of suite 2410; already her fist is raised and poised to strike. **Hello,** she hears herself say to the suite's curious occupant. **We don't know each other, but it seems my mother killed your husband, and I thought you might like to talk about it.**

No one answers her knock.

It's unlikely Mrs. Mallins and the kids are out sightseeing. "Another one down," Amanda mutters, moving on to the next room. Although she might have taken them out for dinner and a much needed change of scenery. "Doubtful," Amanda decides, knocking on the door to suite 2412.

"Who is it?" a woman calls from inside as Amanda holds her breath.

"Amanda Travis," Amanda answers truthfully, not sure how else to respond.

"Who?" the occupant of the room asks, but she opens the door anyway. Just a crack, but it's enough for Amanda to see that she's at least seventy years old and therefore not the woman she's looking for.

"Who is it, Bessie?" a gray-haired gentleman asks, coming up behind his wife.

"I'm sorry," Amanda apologizes. "I must have the wrong room."

The man shuts the door in Amanda's face. "What are you doing opening the door to strangers?" she hears the man lecturing his wife.

Amanda continues down the hall, gets no response from room 2414, and proceeds to room 2416, about to knock when she hears the high-pitched British accent of a young boy. "Mom, I think someone's knocking at the bedroom door."

The door to room 2416 opens before Amanda can decide what to do next. An attractive woman with dark, chin-length hair and piercing hazel eyes stands before her. She is several inches shorter than Amanda and wears no makeup save for a hint of lipstick. Her pale skin is noticeably splotchy from crying. Amanda quickly estimates the woman's age at around forty. She is wearing a black sweater and pants, much the same as what Amanda has on beneath her coat.

"Mrs. Mallins?"

"Yes."

"My name is Amanda Travis."

"Are you with the police?" the woman asks in the same soft lilt as her son.

"No. I'm a lawyer," Amanda stammers. "I was wondering if I could ask you a few questions."

Mrs. Mallins steps back to allow her entry. Amanda finds herself in the middle of the suite's spacious living area, beautifully appointed in shades of beige, red, and gold.

"Who is it, Mom?" A young girl enters the room from one of the bedrooms. She is in her early teens, tall and slender, with her mother's dark hair and piercing eyes.

"This is Amanda Travis," Mrs. Mallins says, introducing Amanda. "She's a lawyer with the Crown Attorney's Office."

Amanda is about to correct her when a boy of about ten or eleven comes bounding into the room. "What's going on?" he asks, eyeing Amanda suspiciously.

"Amanda Travis, these are my children, Hope and Spenser."

"Hello," Amanda says simply, almost afraid to say more.

"Can we go back to England now?" the boy asks. Long brown bangs fall into eyes that are lighter than either his mother's or his sister's, though no less intense.

"I'm afraid not just yet," Amanda tells him, watching the boy's round face cloud over with disappointment. She turns back to Mrs. Mallins, lowers her voice. "Do you think we might talk in private?"

"Of course."

"What about dinner?" Spenser demands.

"Your sister can take care of that," Mrs. Mallins says. "Can't you, love?"

"Of course," Hope replies in the same measured tones of her mother. She takes her brother's hand, leads him from the room. In the doorway, he pauses to look back, scowls at Amanda from over his shoulder.

Mrs. Mallins closes the door after them. "Can I take your coat?"

"No, thank you. I'm fine. Mrs. Mallins . . ."

"Please call me Hayley."

"Mrs. Mallins . . . ," Amanda repeats.

"Has there been any news? Do you have the results of the autopsy?" Mrs. Mallins grips the side of one of two red-and-gold wing chairs for support.

"No, I don't. Mrs. Mallins . . . Hayley . . . Listen, I'm really sorry. There's been a misunderstanding."

"What sort of misunderstanding?"

Amanda takes a deep breath, pushes the reluctant words from her mouth. "I'm not with the Crown Attorney's Office."

"You're not a lawyer?"

"I **am** a lawyer," Amanda corrects, silently debating how much information to divulge. "Just not with the Crown Attorney's Office." She pauses, waits for Hayley Mallins to demand just who the hell she **is** working for and what she's doing in her hotel room, but no such questions are forthcoming. "I'm working with Ben Myers."

"Ben Myers?"

"The lawyer representing Gwen Price."

The color drains from Hayley Mallins's face in one quick whoosh. She sinks into the chair she's been leaning against, her mouth opening and closing, although no words emerge. Probably not a good time to tell her I'm also the woman's daughter, Amanda decides, half-expecting Mrs. Mallins to jump up and order her from the room, as she perches on the end of the gold velvet sofa between the two wing chairs and waits for Mrs. Mallins to regain her voice.

"I don't see how I can help you," Hayley Mallins says after a long silence.

Amanda takes another deep breath. "We're trying to piece together exactly what happened that afternoon. If you have any information that might shed some light . . ."

"I don't see how I can help you," the woman repeats.

"Can you tell me what happened?" Amanda persists.

"I don't know what happened. Other than the obvious—my husband was shot and killed in the lobby of this hotel."

"You weren't with him at the time?"

She shakes her head. "The children and I were up here, waiting for him to come back."

"Come back from where?"

"What?"

"You said you were waiting for your husband to come back. I was wondering where he'd gone."

"Why? How is that relevant?"

"I'm just trying to get some background, Mrs. Mallins. I was wondering if it was something special that brought you to Toronto."

"We were here on holiday."

"What made you pick Toronto?"

"I don't understand."

"Seems like an odd choice at this time of year, that's all. Do you have friends here?"

"No." She hesitates. "My husband had some business to attend to."

"Really? What kind of business?"

"What difference does it make? Why are you asking me these questions?"

"I recognize you've been through a horrible ordeal, Mrs. Mallins. Hayley," Amanda corrects. "But I'm just trying to understand how this could have happened, if there was any connection at all between your husband and my . . . client." Amanda pushes her hair behind her ear, coughs into her hand.

"There was no connection," Hayley Mallins states emphatically.

"What sort of business was your husband in?"

"He ran a small shop. Cigarettes, candy, magazines. That sort of thing."

"In London?"

"No. In Sutton."

"Sutton?" Amanda tries hard to place it on the map of the British Isles currently unfolding in her mind. She silently curses herself for skipping all those geography classes in high school.

"It's a tiny little town north of Nottingham. North of London," Hayley continues, probably catching the blank look in Amanda's eyes.

"And this is the business that brought your husband to Toronto?"

"No," Hayley admits after a pause. "It was personal."

"Personal?"

"Family."

"He has family here?"

"Had," Hayley amends. "His mother. She died recently, and John came to settle her estate."

"His mother was Canadian?"

Hayley looks confused by the question. "I suppose."

"You don't know?"

"We'd never actually met."

"How long were you married?" Amanda asks, trying to keep the surprise out of her face and voice.

"Twenty-two years."

"You married very young."

"I suppose."

"So, your husband came to settle his mother's estate, and he brought his family with him," Amanda says.

"He didn't like leaving us."

"He took the kids out of school?"

Hayley shakes her head. "The kids are homeschooled."

"That isn't a lot of work for you?"

"No. I enjoy it."

Amanda nods understanding, although she has no understanding whatsoever of mothers who enjoy their children. "So, okay," she says, trying to piece together what few facts she has. "You and your children accompanied your husband to Toronto so that you could have a little holiday while he settled his mother's estate."

"That's right."

"Who was his contact?"

"His contact?"

"Do you know the name of the lawyer he was dealing with?"

"No."

"No one's been in touch with you since the shooting?"

Hayley shakes her head. A strand of silky black hair catches on the side of her prominent bottom lip and stays there. She makes no move to wipe it away.

"How long were you in the city before your husband was shot?"

"Just a few days."

"Did your husband have any visitors during that time?"

"No."

"Did he make any phone calls?"

"Not that I'm aware of."

"Did he ever mention a woman by the name of Gwen Price?"

The little color that had returned to Hayley's face immediately disappears. "No."

"He never mentioned her back in England?"

"No. Never."

"She wasn't someone from his past?"

"My husband had no past to speak of," Hayley insists, her voice more forceful than it's been since she opened the door. "His parents divorced when he was very young, and he moved with his father to England when he was four years old."

"He never came back to visit his mother?"

"No."

Amanda nods. That a child has no wish to visit his mother is finally something she understands. "And you're sure he never mentioned anyone by the name of Gwen Price?"

"Very sure."

"And yet she shot him."

"Yes."

"Can you think of any reason why?"

Hayley shakes her head, dislodging the stray hair from the side of her mouth. "Well, she's obviously crazy."

"You think she's delusional?"

"What other explanation is there? One doesn't just go around shooting complete strangers."

Exactly, Amanda thinks. "Where were you the day before your husband was killed, Mrs. Mallins?" she asks, suddenly switching gears.

"What?"

Amanda knows she's heard the question, that her "What?" is simply a way of biding her time while she decides how to answer it. "I asked if you and your family went anywhere the day before your husband was shot."

Hayley's eyes reflect her concentration. "We went to the CN Tower, and then to the museum. Spenser wanted to see the dinosaurs."

"And then you came back to the hotel?"

"Yes."

"Have the police told you that my . . . that Gwen Price was having tea in the lobby at the time of your return?"

"No. How do you know that? Is that what she told you?"

"No. Unfortunately my client is too upset to tell us much of anything."

Hayley Mallins shudders, her breath escaping her lungs in a series of jagged gasps.

Amanda wonders if she's about to have some sort of attack. "Are you all right, Mrs. Mallins? Would you like some water?"

"I'm fine," Hayley says, although clearly she is not. "So, what exactly is it you're getting at?"

Amanda takes several seconds to formulate a response. "According to an eyewitness who's just come forward, Gwen Price was having tea in the lobby bar when she saw you and your family enter the hotel. She became very agitated. The next morning she returned and waited in the lobby all day until she saw your husband. Then she pulled a gun from her purse, walked over, and shot him."

"Well, there's your answer," Hayley states, rising to her feet and pacing between the chair and the door. "She must have mistaken him for someone else."

Is it possible? Amanda wonders. Is it feasible her mother was confused, that she mistook John Mallins for another man? No, she decides, answering her own question. Her mother is many things, but confused definitely isn't one of them.

"She hasn't said anything to you?" Hayley asks. "About why she did it?"

"Nothing."

Hayley shakes her head. "Is that all then? Because I really should get back to my children." She glances at the closed bedroom door.

"How are they coping?" Amanda asks, stalling for time.

"They're all right, I guess. Obviously we're all in shock."

"If there's anything I can do . . ."

"If we could just go home . . ."

"It shouldn't be much longer."

"I don't understand why they need an autopsy at all." Hayley Mallins folds her arms across her chest, tucks her shaking hands inside her armpits, begins rocking back and forth on her heels. "It's obvious how my husband died. What do they need with an autopsy?"

"I'm sure it's just a matter of routine."

"Well, I think it's barbaric. Isn't it enough that my husband was shot? Do they have to cut him all up as well?" A deep sob escapes her throat.

Amanda quickly rises to her feet, walks toward Hayley Mallins, folds the smaller woman in her arms. "I'm very sorry for your loss," she says. You don't know how sorry, she thinks.

Hayley rests for several seconds against Amanda's shoulders, her plaintive cries disappearing into the black wool of Amanda's coat. Amanda catches several stray sounds, but it isn't until she's left the room and is standing in front of the elevators that those sounds form words, and she understands their meaning: "Dear God, what will become of us now?"

FIFTEEN

Amanda's head is spinning and her stomach is rumbling as she opens the door to her hotel room and propels herself toward the desk, pulling off her coat and tossing it on the bed as she reaches for the phone. "I have got to get something to eat," she announces to the empty room, dialing room service as she kicks off her boots and flips through the large leather-bound menu.

"Good evening, Ms. Travis," the voice answers. "How can we help you tonight?"

"I'll have the New York steak, medium rare, a baked potato with the works, and a Caesar salad. Extra dressing."

"Anything to drink?"

What the hell. "A glass of red wine."

"We'll try to have that to you within thirty minutes."

Amanda hangs up the phone and heads for

the bathroom, begins running the hot water for a bath. She has half an hour. Just enough time for a good soak. She strips off her clothes, wondering whether she should call Ben and tell him what she's done. "He's not going to be happy," she says to her reflection in the bathroom mirror. He'll tell her she had no business going to see Hayley Mallins without him. "Can't help it," she says defensively, feeling Ben's presence in the swirl of steam rising from the tub. "I've gotten used to doing things without you." Maybe if he hadn't been in such a damn hurry to see Jennifer . . .

And what did you learn from this ill-advised visit? she hears him interrupt.

"Not much," Amanda is forced to admit. She walks naked back into the main room, plops down on the edge of the bed, trying to gather her facts together to present them with the best possible spin. "I learned that poor Mrs. Mallins is as clueless as the rest of us. That she's never even heard of anyone named Gwen Price and has absolutely no idea why she killed her husband. How am I doing so far?" She jumps to her feet, begins pacing between the bed and the desk, in much the same fashion as Hayley Mallins had earlier.

The woman has a nice face, Amanda is

thinking. Under happier circumstances, and with a little bit of makeup, she might even be considered beautiful. No question her daughter will be a beauty. And the little boy, with those big, sad eyes. A future heartbreaker. Poor kids. Coming all the way from England, carefree tourists one day, grieving relatives the next. Some vacation.

Except they weren't really here on vacation, were they? No. John Mallins was here to settle his mother's estate.

Immediately Amanda is on her knees by the side of the bed, pulling the heavy Toronto phone book from the bottom drawer of the nightstand. Lowering her bare bottom to the plush carpet, she flips through the book's pages until she finds **M**, her eyes flitting quickly across Malcolm, Malia, and Malik, then Mallin, Malling, and Mallinos. "Mallins! Yes!" she shouts, counting a total of six.

Great. Now what?

"Think."

According to Hayley Mallins, other than his deceased mother, John Mallins had no family here. There was no reason to assume that any of the six Mallinses listed here were in any way related to the dead man.

Except that Mrs. Mallins had been somewhat less than forthcoming when it came to discussing why the family had chosen Toronto as a midwinter vacation spot, and it was only Amanda's stubborn prodding that had revealed the underlying reason for the trip. So maybe there was more Hayley Mallins wasn't telling.

Or more she didn't know.

One thing Amanda knows for sure: her mother shot John Mallins for a reason.

One just doesn't go around shooting complete strangers.

"There you have it," Amanda repeats in Hayley's elegant British tones. She stares at the list of names—Mallins, A.; Mallins, Harold; Mallins, L. . . . "Oh, my God, the bath!" A dense fog is already seeping into the hallway as Amanda slices her way through the steam to turn off the water that is cascading over the side of the tub. "No, don't do this," she implores, trying to soak up the water from the floor with all the towels at hand, seeing the clothes she discarded earlier serving as unwitting blotters. "Oh, great. This is just great."

It takes ten minutes to clean up the mess and wring the water from her sweater and pants. Amanda hangs them over the shower bar to dry out, but she suspects they're already ruined. Doesn't she deliberately buy clothes that specify **Dry Clean Only?**

She wraps herself in the white terry-cloth robe the hotel graciously provides and returns to the bedroom. The phone book lies open on the floor. "I don't have time for any fishing expeditions," she tells it, flipping it closed. "I'm leaving tomorrow." Or maybe Tuesday, she amends, inching the book back open, watching the pages fall one on top of the other, as columns of names blur into a shapeless, gray mass. Might as well stay until the mother of all mothers pleads guilty to murder and is locked away for the rest of her life.

C, H, L, M . . .

Malcolm, Malia, Mallinos . . .

One just doesn't go around shooting complete strangers.

Mallins.

Who the hell is John Mallins?

The police might not need to know the answer, Amanda thinks, but she does.

Mallins, A.; Mallins, Harold; Mallins, L. . . .

She picks up the phone, punches in the first number, wondering what on earth she's planning to say to Mallins, A.

"You have reached Alan and Marcy," the recorded message begins. "We're either working, walking the dog, or out eating. . . ."

Amanda hangs up the phone, calls the second number.

"You have reached the Mallins residence. We can't take your call at the moment, but if you'd leave your name, number, and a detailed message after the tone, we'll get back to you as soon as possible."

"Just how much detail would you like?" Amanda asks as she hangs up the phone, pressing in the numbers for Mallins, L.

"Hello," a voice answers on the third ring. The voice is young and male.

"Hello, my name is Amanda Travis, and I—"

"Hah, hah. Fooled you," the voice interrupts. "I'm Lenny Mallins, and this is a recording. If you have nothing better to do, leave your name and number after the tone."

Maybe there **is** something to be said for killing total strangers, Amanda decides, proceeding to the fourth name, listening to her fourth recorded message, this one coming at her first in English, then in fractured French. She wonders briefly where all the Mallinses are, if it's possible they're all together at some huge family gathering. Maybe at a wake for Mallins, John, she thinks, calling the fifth number on the list: Mallins, R.

"Hello," the woman says, picking up immediately.

Amanda says nothing for several seconds, half-expecting another burst of rude laughter. **Hah, hah. Fooled you.**

"Hello," the woman says again. Then, "Oh, fuck you."

The line goes dead in Amanda's hand. Quickly, she calls the number again. Again it's answered almost immediately.

"You got some sort of problem?" the woman says instead of hello.

"Mrs. Mallins?"

"Ms.," the woman corrects.

"My name is Amanda Travis."

"Yes?"

"I'm calling about John Mallins, the man who was—"

"Well, well, well."

"Excuse me?"

"I was wondering when you bozos would get around to calling me."

"You were?"

"It's taken you long enough."

"Yes, it has," Amanda agrees, deciding this is probably the simplest, and best, course to take. "I was wondering if I could come over and talk to you."

"Sure. But you'll have to get here pretty quick. I'm leaving for the Bahamas tomorrow morning and I've got a lot of packing to do."

"You're leaving town?"

"Just for a week. Hey, I booked this holiday six months ago, and I'm not canceling just because you guys suddenly woke up. You want to talk to me, you be here in half an hour." For the second time in as many minutes, the line goes dead in Amanda's hand.

The cab drops Amanda off in front of a tall, brick building that is virtually indistinguishable from the other tall, brick buildings in the area. "Welcome to Yonge and Eglinton," the cabdriver announces, as if he were auditioning for a job as a tour guide. "You know what they call this part of the city, don't you? Young and eligible," he answers with a chuckle when Amanda fails to respond.

Amanda pays the driver and gets out of the cab, checking her watch and noting that she has five minutes before her deadline is up. Pretty good, she thinks, pulling open the heavy glass door to the small front entrance, then scanning the long list of occupants' names on the wall to her left, searching for Mallins, R.

It took her five minutes to get dressed, another five minutes to fix her hair and makeup, four minutes to stand in front of the phone debating whether to call Ben, one minute to dial his number—**This is Ben Myers. I'm not home right now, but if you'll leave your name and number after the beep**—another minute to let loose a string of expletives, most of them unflattering epithets involving anyone named Jennifer, and five minutes to wolf down the dinner that arrived just as she was about to leave. (**God, what happened in here? I'll send someone from housekeeping up right away.**) Luckily, a lineup of cabs was waiting near the door to the hotel, and the driver assured her he could get her to her destination in no time flat.

"Ben's gonna kill me," she says now, pressing in the correct code.

"Come on up," a voice crackles over the speaker. "Apartment 1710."

A buzzer sounds to unlock the door, and Amanda walks through the old, sparsely furnished lobby toward the elevators. She waits what feels like an eternity for one of the elevator doors to open, then another eternity for the rickety, old elevator to grind to a halt at the seventeenth floor. It's now a minute past her half-hour deadline. She wonders if Mallins, R., will open her door.

I was wondering when you bozos were going to get around to calling me.

What does that mean?

Hey, I booked this holiday six months ago, and I'm not canceling just because you guys suddenly woke up.

Woke up to what?

"What the hell am I doing here?" Amanda whispers between barely parted lips. "Ben's gonna kill me." Providing R. Mallins doesn't kill me first, she thinks, and almost laughs.

The door opens. A middle-aged woman, short, round, with curly auburn hair, a pug nose sprinkled with tiny freckles, and an engaging smile, stands in the doorway, dimpled hands on wide hips. "You alone?" she asks, stretching her head into the hallway.

Amanda thinks about inventing a partner waiting for her downstairs, but one look into the woman's clear brown eyes tells her lying wouldn't be a good idea. "Yes," she answers truthfully. "I'm alone."

"Still not considered a very high priority, I take it." The woman, wearing an orange sweatshirt and a pair of faded jeans, ushers Amanda inside the small apartment, furnished in shades of blue and green. "Nice to see some things never change. Here, let me take your coat. You can leave your boots on, if you'd like."

Amanda wipes her soles on a remnant of blue carpet by the door and slips her coat off her shoulders, watching as Ms. Mallins hangs it in the sliver of space that passes for a hall closet. "I'm not sure I understand." She looks toward the long window that takes up most of the living room's north wall, sees the lights on in the apartment building across the street, and imagines people relaxing in front of roaring fireplaces, or settling in to watch their favorite shows on TV.

"Well, what would you know?" R. Mallins says with a shrug. "You were just a kid when all the shit went down."

Amanda finds herself holding her breath. "When what . . . shit . . . went down?"

The woman laughs, shakes her head. "What is it with you guys? Don't you ever talk to one another? I mean, I know the police are a pretty paranoid lot, but—"

"I'm not with the police," Amanda tells the clearly surprised woman.

"Oh?"

"I'm sorry if I gave you that impression."

The woman's arms fold across her expansive chest. "Exactly who the hell are you?"

"My name is Amanda Travis."

"Yes, so you said on the telephone. But you're not with the police?"

"No. I'm with the defense team representing Gwen Price, the woman—"

"—accused of shooting John Mallins."

"Yes."

"Well, isn't that rich." R. Mallins smiles her obvious satisfaction. She motions toward the green-and-blue-striped sofa that sits on the light parquet floor at right angles to a single dark blue chair. "Please sit down. Can I get you a drink?"

Amanda thinks of the glass of red wine she left untouched on the table in her hotel room and hopes that housekeeping doesn't take it away. She has the feeling she's going to need it when she gets back to her room. "Maybe some water."

"Water it is," the woman says with a chuckle, half a dozen steps all she needs to transport her into the vaguely dingy galley kitchen. She runs the tap, retrieves a glass from the cupboard over the sink, and fills it with water.

Amanda notes that a handle has fallen off one of the white cabinets and been replaced by a bright red knob, like a clown's nose. Ms.

Mallins returns to the living room, offering her the glass with one hand, as the other motions toward the sofa.

"Please," she says again. "Have a seat."

Amanda dutifully sinks into the green and blue stripes of the sofa, her boots resting lightly on a small oval of pale blue carpet. "Ms. Mallins . . ."

"Why don't you just call me Rachel." The woman lowers herself into the dark blue chair, looking at Amanda with a smile that says, This should be fun.

"Rachel," Amanda repeats.

"Amanda." A sly smile pulls at the woman's round cheeks.

"Exactly what . . . shit . . . went down?"

Rachel Mallins laughs. "You're cute," she says, as Amanda squirms, tries not to bristle, cute never having been a state she aspired to, or an adjective she coveted. "You don't know anything, do you, Amanda?"

"Not very much," Amanda admits.

"Yet you knew enough to find me."

"That was easy. I looked you up in the phone book."

"You looked me up in the phone book." Rachel Mallins laughs again. It's a pleasant, even raucous, sound. "May I ask why?"

"I interviewed Hayley Mallins, the murdered man's widow," Amanda begins, silently debating how much to tell Rachel Mallins, then deciding there was little to be gained at this point from keeping anything back. "She told me her husband's mother passed away recently, and that her husband was here to settle her estate, so . . ."

"So?" Rachel leans forward in her seat, tucks one hand inside the other, listening intently. Amanda notes the absence of any jewelry.

"So, even though Mrs. Mallins denies it, I thought it might be possible there were other Mallinses around who were related to the victim."

"Oh, you did, did you?"

"I did. Yes."

"And are there many of us?"

"What?"

"In the phone book."

"Oh. No. Not many. Six, actually."

"Actually," Rachel repeats, savoring the sound. "And you called us all?"

"You were number five on the list."

"Lucky me." Rachel Mallins laughs again. "Lucky you."

"You're saying you're related to John Mallins?"

"I am."

Amanda feels a breath catch in her throat. "Meaning?"

The slightest of pauses, a moment of indecision before Rachel's response. "Meaning he's my brother."

The glass of water almost slips from Amanda's hand. "Excuse me?"

"I'm John Mallins's sister." The smile slides from the woman's face. "Have a sip of water, Amanda. You're looking a little pale."

Amanda takes a sip of water, trying to focus her thoughts, prepare her next question. "I don't understand," she says finally, giving up.

"Of course. How could you?"

"You're saying Hayley Mallins lied when she told me her husband had no other relatives in Toronto?"

"Oh, I wouldn't know anything about that."

"You don't know whether she was lying or whether she honestly didn't know about you?" Amanda offers, trying to pin the woman down.

"I don't know anything about Hayley Mallins at all."

"You're saying you didn't know your brother was married?"

"My brother isn't married," the woman states emphatically. "You can be quite sure of that."

"I don't understand," Amanda says again, thinking she might as well be carrying a tape recording she can press in response to Rachel's every pronouncement. **I don't understand. I don't understand.**

"Well, obviously, the man who was murdered last week at the Four Seasons hotel was not my brother."

"I don't un—" Amanda bites down on her tongue and lowers her glass of water to the round glass table beside the sofa, rising slowly to her feet, and trying to contain her budding anger. "Okay, I don't know what kind of game you're playing, Rachel, but I really don't appreciate being toyed with. So if torturing lawyers is your idea of a fun way to spend an evening, you'll have to find yourself another attorney—"

"Oh, sit down. I thought you wanted to know about John Mallins."

Amanda remains on her feet. "I'm listening."

Rachel Mallins pushes herself out of her chair and walks over to the window. "You sound like Frasier Crane," she says with a chuckle. "On TV?"

"I don't watch much TV."

"You've never watched **Frasier?** It's a spin-off of **Cheers.** Surely you watched that."

"Can we get back to John Mallins?"

Rachel looks vaguely wounded. "You have to understand that this all happened a very long time ago. Twenty-five years ago, actually." She smiles, although this time the smile wobbles and threatens tears.

"What did?"

There is a pause before Rachel continues. "My brother and I were the product of what is now gently referred to as a 'dysfunctional family,' meaning our parents were both heavy drinkers, and my brother and I pretty much raised ourselves. And didn't do a very good job of it either." She shrugs. "I was married and divorced twice before I turned thirty. Do you believe that?"

"It happens," Amanda replies when she can find her voice.

"I guess. You married?"

"No."

"No, you're smart. I can see that. Too focused on your career to waste time on incidentals. I never had a career. When I was fourteen, I had dreams about being a doctor. Oh, well, at least I finished high school." Rachel tries to smile, but her lips form a stubborn purse and refuse to cooperate. "Johnny dropped out as soon as he turned sixteen. He started running with a bad crowd, drinking, doing drugs, the usual crap. Couldn't hold a job. In and out of trouble. Got arrested at least half a dozen times, although the police could never make anything stick. Anyway, the last time I saw him, he was boasting about this great guy he'd just met, and how this man was taking him under his wing, how everything was gonna be different, and . . ."

"And?"

"And then he disappeared off the face of the earth."

"What do you mean, he disappeared?"

"I mean I never saw him again."

"Did you go to the police?"

"Of course. Just how interested do you think they were in finding him?" Rachel shakes her head. "About as interested as they are in speaking to me now."

Amanda tries to make sense of everything Rachel has told her. "But why should the police be interested in speaking to you if you say the John Mallins who was murdered isn't your brother?"

"Because the man who was murdered isn't John Mallins," the woman states simply.

Amanda says nothing. Instead she nods as if everything she has heard makes perfect sense, then resumes her seat on the sofa, and waits to hear more.

SIXTEEN

I could use a drink," Rachel announces, slapping her hands against her thighs. "How about you?"

"Sounds good to me," Amanda agrees, watching the woman cross back to the kitchen and kneel in front of the cabinet beside the fridge, her knees cracking loudly in protest.

"That's the problem with being short and fat," the woman says, rummaging through several bottles of wine. "You can't store your booze on a high shelf 'cause you can't reach it, and it kills you every time you bend down. I should just line the bottles up along the counter. Except that's what my parents used to do. I think they considered it sculpture. Red wine okay?"

"Perfect."

Rachel smiles her most engaging smile and reaches into the top drawer for a corkscrew.

"When I first moved out on my own, away from my parents, both of whom have moved on to that great saloon in the sky, incidentally, I wouldn't even consider keeping liquor in my apartment. Oh, I was such a goody-goody. Wouldn't drink or smoke. Still don't smoke." She expertly uncorks a bottle of what Amanda realizes is a very good bottle of wine. "So, anyway, one night I had a date, some guy I'd been hoping to impress, and I'd invited him over for dinner. God only knows what I was thinking, since the only thing I knew how to make was shepherd's pie. Good thing he liked shepherd's pie." She laughs, reaches for two wineglasses. "Anyway, this guy brought a bottle of wine, but we couldn't open it because I didn't have a corkscrew." She shakes her head, obviously playing the scene out in her mind as she pours the wine into the glasses. "I had to knock on my neighbor's door and ask if they had one I could borrow." She crosses back into the living room, hands Amanda her wine. "I don't have a drinking problem, by the way. In case you're worrying that I'm some old lush who lured you here under false pretenses."

"I'm not worried," Amanda says, although that very thought has just crossed her mind.

"No, I made a solemn vow to myself many years ago that I was never going to be like my mother."

Amanda nods. At last—**something** she understands.

"So I'm very careful about how much alcohol I allow myself. A glass of wine here and there under special circumstances. I'd say this qualifies, wouldn't you?"

"I don't know. What circumstances are we talking about?"

Rachel raises her glass. "The man calling himself John Mallins finally getting what he deserved. Cheers."

"Cheers." They click glasses. Silence fills the small space between them. Amanda waits for the older woman to continue, but she says nothing. "Why do you say that he got what he deserved?"

"Because the bastard obviously killed my brother."

How is that obvious? Amanda wonders, taking several sips of wine before asking the question out loud.

"I told you that right before my brother disappeared, he told me he'd met some guy who was going to turn his life around. Well, I think it's pretty clear this guy killed him. And

now, twenty-five years later, your client killed
him."

Amanda tries to follow the woman's convo-
luted logic. "That's quite a stretch," she says finally.

"Why? How is it a stretch? You don't think
it's more than a little suspicious that twenty-
five years after my brother disappears, a man
calling himself John Mallins, who just happens
to be the exact same age as my brother would
have been, and who even looks a little bit like
him, suddenly shows up in the same city where
he used to live. You don't find that just a little
bit strange?"

"A coincidence maybe."

"A coincidence, my ass. That man killed my
brother and stole his identity."

"Whoa. Hold on a minute. Just because the
man has the same name as your brother doesn't
mean he killed him. You don't think it's possible there's more than one John Mallins?"

"No, I don't think it's possible. You're the
one who looked us up in the phone book.
There were only six listings in a city of almost
three million people."

"That doesn't mean there's only one John
Mallins in the entire world. The John Mallins
who was shot and killed was from a little town

in England, north of Nottingham," Amanda says, recalling her earlier geography lesson from the man's widow.

"And he came back to settle his mother's estate, that's what you said, right?"

"Yes."

"How much do you want to bet that if you check the death notices for the past few weeks, you won't find any mention of anyone named Mallins? Hell, check the last year."

"Even if that's true, it wouldn't necessarily prove anything."

Rachel throws her hands up in the air, the wine sloshing around in her glass. "Shit, are you always this stubborn?"

"I'm just trying to tell you that . . ." Amanda stops. What **is** she trying to tell her? "If you really believe John Mallins is not only an impostor, but a murderer, why haven't you gone to the police?"

"And tell them what exactly?"

"Exactly what you've told me."

Rachel Mallins shakes her head. "The police are even more stubborn than you are. Hell, I went to the bastards twenty-five years ago, right after Johnny disappeared. I begged and pleaded with them to find my brother, and you know what they said? 'Don't worry about Johnny.

He'll turn up. Bad pennies always do.' " She gulps at her wine. "They wouldn't help me then. Why would I help them now? Besides, it won't bring Johnny back. It's twenty-five years too late for that."

Amanda finishes the last of the wine in her glass, accepts Rachel's offer of more. "Isn't it possible, just possible," Amanda begins slowly, "that the man who was shot is, in fact, your brother?" She hurries on before Rachel can object. "You said it yourself—it's been twenty-five years. People can change a lot in a quarter of a century. They get older, they gain weight, they grow a mustache."

"They don't disappear for no reason."

"Maybe he **had** a reason. You said he was always in and out of trouble. Maybe he got in over his head and had to leave town in a hurry. Maybe he decided it was best not to tell you. Maybe he decided to start over. Maybe he eventually moved to England, opened a little shop, got married, had a family . . ."

"He didn't get married and have a family."

"How can you be so sure?"

"Because my brother was gay," Rachel says, pouring herself a second glass of wine. "And please don't tell me that gay men often get married and have families, because I know that. But I also know the man your client shot isn't my brother."

"Then it's another man named John Mallins." Amanda feels a sudden rush of dizziness. No wonder, she thinks, lowering her wineglass to the floor. They were going around in circles.

A long pause. "How much do you want to bet that John Mallins's passport lists his birthday as July fourteenth?"

Amanda says nothing. A gnawing sensation in the pit of her stomach is telling her if she takes that bet, she'll lose.

"Look, you said you're representing the woman who killed that bastard. Why don't you just ask her who she thought she was pumping bullets into?"

You think I'm stubborn? Amanda wants to shout. "What about this guy your brother was involved with? Did Johnny ever mention his name?"

Rachel shakes her head. "He called him Turk. Apparently it was a nickname of some sort."

"I hate nicknames," Amanda mutters.

"Me too. But I do like this wine. Would you like another drink?"

Amanda lifts up her empty wineglass, holds

it out for more. "Thanks," she says, taking several quick swallows. "I should probably get going, let you pack."

"Oh, I'm not going anywhere. I just said I was leaving to get you to move your ass." Rachel walks to the closet, retrieves Amanda's coat. "You warm enough in this thing? It's kind of flimsy."

Amanda is thinking this is as good a description as any of her life at the moment as she slips her arms inside the coat's sleeves. "I'm fine, thanks." She opens the door, steps into the hall. "Thanks again for the wine."

"Amanda," Rachel calls as she heads for the elevators at the end of the hall. The word tugs at Amanda's back, like a fishhook. "You'll let me know if I'm right about July fourteenth, won't you?"

An elevator door opens. Amanda steps inside.

Two things Amanda feels grateful for: (1) the hotel's housekeeping staff has mopped up her bathroom floor, replaced the towels, and generally returned the room to its original pristine condition, and (2) they have not taken away her glass of wine.

She gulps at the latter while admiring the

former, debating whether to call Ben. He won't be happy when she tells him about her latest escapade. **You did what?** she can almost hear him yell. **You did what?** It was bad enough she'd gone to see Hayley Mallins without his permission, but this latest stunt, going out alone to interview some woman who, in all probability, was nothing but a delusional drunk, well, that took the cake. Where was her common sense? She could have gotten herself killed, for God's sake. Hadn't he told her to order room service, take a bath, and get into bed? "I tried," she offers weakly, finishing her wine while sitting on the side of the bathtub, and reaching for the hot-water tap. "If at first you don't succeed." She giggles, a large puddle of wine settling between her ears, upsetting her already delicate balance, as she pulls her sweater over her head and walks into the bedroom. Soon she is naked, and standing by the phone. She is also, she recognizes, very drunk.

"This is Ben Myers. I'm not home right now, but if you'll leave your name and number after the beep, I'll get back to you as soon as possible. Thank you, and remember to wait for the beep."

Isn't that just like Ben to assume she

doesn't know how voice mail works, as if everyone doesn't know you're supposed to wait for the beep. "Well, hello there, Ben Myers," Amanda says, speaking before the beep has a chance to sound. "Oops. Not a very good listener, am I?" She laughs, waits for the beep. "Well, hello there, Ben Myers," she says again. "I'm calling—why am I calling?—oh, yes, I'm calling to apologize because it seems I was a bad girl and didn't do what you told me to do. Whatever that was. I can't remember. But hopefully I'll figure it out by the time you get this message and call me back. Did you hear me? Call me back. It's important. I think." She laughs again as the beep cuts her off in the middle of her last word. "Well, that was rather rude," she says as she replaces the receiver. "Didn't even have time to tell him to give Jennifer my love. Give Jennifer my love," she shouts in the direction of the phone, hearing the muffled sound of water from the bathroom. "Oh, no!"

Amanda trips over her feet as she races into the bathroom and throws herself at the tub, the water just about to spill over the top as she plunges her hand into the boiling water and pulls up the plug. "Shit! That's hot!" The water level begins receding immediately.

Amanda waves her arm, red from the elbow down, into the air in an effort to cool it down, then waits till the water level is at a suitable level before replacing the plug and adding cold water to the mix. "I think somebody's had a bit too much to drink," she says, climbing inside the bathtub and pushing away the little voice telling her this is becoming an all-too-frequent occurrence of late. "These are special circumstances," she says, recalling Rachel's words. "The man calling himself John Mallins got what he deserved."

The man calling himself John Mallins, she repeats silently, reaching for the bar of soap and running it across her breasts before she realizes the soap is still wrapped. "Oops." She laughs again, the sound becoming noticeably shrill, as she pulls the paper from the bar of soap, watching the paper float along the top of the water even as the soap sinks to the bottom. Is it possible that any of what Rachel Mallins told her is true? That the man calling himself John Mallins isn't? That's he's an impostor who killed the real John Mallins twenty-five years ago, to steal his identity?

And so what if he did? Does it really matter if the man her mother shot is named John Mallins or not? Facts are facts, and the fact is this: her mother killed a man, a man who might be someone named John Mallins, or he might not. "Whoever he was, he isn't anymore," Amanda pronounces, reclaiming the soap and running it haphazardly across her body.

Except if he wasn't John Mallins, who was he?

And wouldn't the answer to that question go a long way to clearing up a lot of other questions?

Such as why her mother shot him?

He called him Turk. Apparently it was some sort of nickname.

"I hate nicknames," Amanda whispers into the washcloth she spreads across her face. The wet terry cloth burrows into her mouth and nostrils, like a death mask.

Puppet, she hears someone call. **Puppet. Puppet.**

Amanda pulls the washcloth roughly from her face, struggling to her feet and climbing out of the tub. She proceeds, dripping wet, into the main room, where she picks up the phone. "The Metro Convention Center hotel," she directs the operator. "Jerrod Sugar," she tells the voice at reception. "Jerrod Sugar," she informs the man who answers on the second ring. "This is Amanda Travis. And this is your lucky night."

* * *

A knock on the door wakes her up at two in the morning.

Amanda hears the knocking as part of a dream in which she is alone in the middle of a rickety, old rowboat that is rapidly sinking into the ocean. As she frantically bails water, she can see sharks circling beneath her, one shark disappearing under the boat to hammer against its fragile bottom. One knock. Two knocks . . .

Amanda sits up in bed, the pounding in her head echoing the pounding on the door. She checks the clock on the nightstand, wondering who the hell could be knocking on her door at two in the morning. Is there a fire? Has she slept through the fire alarm? Is someone trying to warn her to evacuate the building before it's too late?

She climbs out of bed, wrapping herself in her terry-cloth robe as she hurries to the door, her head throbbing painfully with each step. "Hello?" she whispers hoarsely, securing the chain across the door and opening it just a crack.

"Amanda, what the hell is going on?"

"Ben?" Amanda unfastens the chain and steps quickly into the hallway. "What are you doing here? Has something happened?"

"You tell me."

Amanda stares hard at the handsome young man who was her first husband. She sees that he is dressed in jeans and a heavy Irish knit sweater, that his hair is uncombed and sprinkled with snow, and that his face is contorted with a mixture of worry and fatigue. And something new, she realizes, trying to focus on his eyes. Anger, she realizes, gripping the door handle behind her back.

"What was with that message you left on my voice mail?"

"The message . . . ?"

"You don't remember?"

Amanda struggles to regroup. "I don't remember my exact words. I'm half-asleep. You woke me up."

"Have you been drinking?"

"No. I was sound asleep."

"I've been working all night on this case I have in the morning. I'm dead tired. I'm just about to crawl into bed when I decide I better check my messages—"

"You weren't out with Jennifer?"

"And there you are, sounding so . . . I don't know . . ."

"What?"

"Desperate," he says finally, and Amanda pulls back, the word hitting her like a slap across the face. "You scared the hell out of me."

"I assure you I'm not at all desperate."

"Okay, listen, I think we' getting off the point here."

Unexpected tears fill Amanda's eyes. Immediately, she lowers her head, looking toward her bare toes, and struggling to control her voice. "I'm sorry I scared you. That wasn't my intention. Look, I'm really sorry. Why don't you go home, get some sleep, and I'll see you in the morning."

Ben brushes the hair from his forehead, closes his eyes in frustration. "Are you all right?"

"I'm fine."

"Why did you call me?"

"What?"

"You said it was important."

"It's nothing that can't wait until tomorrow."

"You said you'd been a bad girl, whatever the hell that means, and you didn't do what I told you to do. What **did** you do?"

Amanda glances over her shoulder toward her room, the pounding in her head increasing with each subtle shift in position. What's the matter with me? she wonders. What am I doing to myself?

"Let's take this inside," Ben is saying. "There's no point arguing out here in the hallway."

"No. Really. I think you should go," Amanda protests, but Ben's hand is already pushing her door open, and his hand is on the light switch on the wall before she can stop him.

"What happened tonight, Amanda?" Ben asks as, all over the room, lights snap on.

Shuffling noises. The sound of sheets crumpling. A ghostly figure, pale and befuddled, stirs in the middle of the bed. "Jesus," Jerrod Sugar says, pushing his head off the pillow and shielding his eyes from the unexpected spotlight. "What's going on here?"

Amanda watches Ben's cheeks stain bright pink, as if frostbitten. She feels the clenching of his jaw, the coiling of his fists. "Okay. Well. Okay," he says, his body swaying uneasily from one foot to the other. "Sorry about the interruption. My mistake." He switches off the lights and walks from the room.

Amanda doesn't move.

"What was that all about?" Jerrod Sugar asks as the door slams shut.

Amanda stands absolutely still for several seconds before climbing back into bed, the sharp crack of the slamming door echoing, like a whip, inside her brain. "Nothing," she says, gathering the covers around her ears in an effort to block the sound, and closing her eyes.

SEVENTEEN

The Toronto courthouse—referred to as the **new** courthouse, despite its being more than thirty years old—is located at the corner of University and Armoury. It's called the **new** courthouse to distinguish it from the **old** courthouse, which is located in **old** City Hall, at the intersection of Bay and Queen. **New** City Hall, whose construction was completed in 1965, stands just across the street and consists of two crescent-shaped buildings of towering gray granite, curving in toward one another. New City Hall boasts a large, once-controversial outdoor sculpture by Henry Moore that looks a bit like a bronze chicken without its head, and a large, public skating rink, where people are already showing off their moves at eleven o'clock in the morning.

Amanda is reminded of these facts the next

morning when the taxi driver takes her to the wrong address.

"You say new City Hall," the cabbie insists in heavily accented English.

"I said the new courthouse."

"Courthouse in old City Hall."

"That's the **old** courthouse. I want the **new** courthouse."

"New courthouse not here," the man replies. He makes an illegal U-turn on Bay, heads back in the direction from which they came.

It's my fault, Amanda thinks, leaning her still-throbbing forehead against the cab's dirty side window, watching the dull parade of downtown buildings as they fade into the sickly gray sky. I should have been paying closer attention.

To a lot of things, she decides ruefully, thinking back on last night's disaster. "How could I let that happen?"

"Something wrong, Mrs.?" the cabdriver asks warily. His dark, liquid eyes in the rearview mirror have narrowed, as if he suspects she is about to change her mind again.

Well, let's see, Amanda thinks. My mother's in jail. I have a horrible hangover. I slept with a virtual stranger. And my former husband thinks

I'm a slut. Make that my **old** former husband, she thinks, stifling a laugh. As opposed to my **new** former husband. Who cares what he thinks anyway? "No," she tells the cabbie. "No problem."

She pulls back her shoulders and sits up straight, the dark green vinyl of the seat making noises of protest beneath her black coat. What right has Ben to judge her anyway? Doesn't she have enough to deal with at the moment? So she was drunk. She's entitled. Just as she's entitled to sleep with whomever she wants. Even if she doesn't really want to.

Damn you anyway, Ben Myers. Why'd you have to come over last night, like some white knight riding to the rescue on his antique steed? Who said I need rescuing anyway? "Do I look like I need rescuing?" she demands out loud, spooking the cabbie, who makes a sharp left turn, causing Amanda to lose her balance and tumble over onto her side.

"New courthouse," the driver says, pulling up in front of an attractive gray-stone building.

Amanda takes a moment to steady herself before climbing out of the car. "What am I doing here?" she asks, her words disappearing inside the collar of her coat. She wonders how Ben is going to react when he sees her and hopes it's better than the way he reacted last night. Taking a deep gulp of bitterly cold air, she enters the building, checking the piece of paper in her purse for the number of the correct courtroom. "Courtroom 204," she whispers under her breath, passing through the metal detector and mounting the escalator just inside the entrance, watching as the main floor recedes beneath her.

Stepping off the escalator, she walks right into the path of an icily attractive blonde wearing the flowing black robes that lawyers in Canada wear when arguing a case in court. Jennifer? she wonders, seeing flashes of the woman's shapely calves beneath her robe as she strides confidently into Room 201. Is that you? And why weren't you with Ben last night?

At least that way I wouldn't feel so damn guilty about Jerrod Sugar. Although why I should feel guilty about Jerrod Sugar is a mystery to me. I can sleep with whomever I please. You can hardly accuse me of cheating on a man who hasn't been my husband for eight years.

Okay. Well. Okay, she hears Ben say, the door slamming behind him.

Amanda notices a middle-aged man looking lost and inconsolable on a bench outside one of

the courtrooms and can't help but remember
the hapless look that overwhelmed Jerrod
Sugar's face when he saw Ben standing at the
foot of the bed. Her hand still pulsates with
the beat of his heart as it raced against her open
palm when she tried to hold him after Ben's
departure. He'd left minutes later, claiming he
was too shook up to get back to sleep, and not
even the promise of another round of lovemak-
ing was enough of an enticement to persuade
him to stay. He was sorry, he demurred, scrambling into his clothes, but he had a really full
week ahead of him, he'd try to call her before
he left town, maybe they could arrange to meet
back in Florida, good-bye, it was great, thanks
for thinking of me.

My pleasure, Amanda thinks, stomping
some invisible snow off her boots and walking
down the long corridor. Except it hadn't been.
Not really. Amanda tries to think of the last
time she really enjoyed sex, stops when an
image of Ben pushes itself back into her line of
vision. "Oh, no. You are definitely not going
down **that** road," she castigates herself, pulling
open the door to Courtroom 204 and stepping
inside.

The courtroom is modern but unexceptional.
A robed judge sits at the head of the room, sur-

rounded by numerous court clerks, all looking
somewhat bored with the proceedings. A policeman sits in the witness box, looking toward the
empty jury box on his left. Several spectators sit
on rows of wooden benches behind the lawyers'
tables. The assistant crown attorney, a dumpy
young woman whose sallow complexion is
framed by a bramble of unruly dark hair, makes
an obvious show of rifling through a stack of papers. She wears the constipated expression on her
face almost proudly, like a diamond necklace she
never intends to take off. Amanda shakes her
head knowingly and sits down beside a middle-
aged woman twisting a string of rosary beads
through her shaking fingers. Amanda cranes her
neck around the people in front of her, sees Ben
whispering to a pretty young girl sitting beside
him at the defense table. He pats the girl's hand,
then stretches, looking casually over his shoulder, his eyes stopping on Amanda.

What are you doing here? his eyes say.

I have something to tell you, Amanda answers silently, but Ben has already turned his
attention back to the front of the courtroom
where the prosecutor has risen to argue a point
of law.

Her voice is nasal and unpleasant, and every
time she glances at the pretty young woman

who is the defendant, her eyes narrow with barely contained fury. What she is really saying beneath all her high-sounding legal phrases is **I'm going to show you. You, with your long, shiny hair and your expensive little dress on your perfect little body. You** spoiled child of privilege who thinks life is nothing but a big bowl of ice cream to be devoured without consequence. Well, I'm here to burst that little bubble once and for all. I'm here to show you what life is really like.

Amanda tries to pay attention, but gives up after ten minutes of the prosecutor's hopeless posturing, only snapping back to attention when Ben rises to make an objection. He looks almost as good in his lawyer's robes as he did in that Irish knit sweater, she is thinking, as the judge sustains Ben's objection. What might have happened between them had Jerrod Sugar not been in her bed last night?

What did she want to happen?

Nothing.

Been there, done that. Remember?

Amanda assures herself she is just feeling vulnerable because of the fact she is back in her hometown after a prolonged absence, forced by crazy circumstance into spending time with a man she once loved, into remembering long-repressed details of their shared past. Under such circumstances, it's difficult not to feel familiar stirrings. Probably he's feeling them too, and that's why he rushed over last night when he could easily have phoned in his concern. Amanda closes her eyes, tries not to picture the look of shock and dismay on Ben's face when he flipped on the light and saw Jerrod Sugar in her bed.

The judge announces an hour break for lunch, and Amanda glances at her watch, surprised to see it's almost half past twelve. She rises as the judge sweeps dramatically from the courtroom, watching as Ben leaves the defendant's side to approach the crown attorney. "Come on, Nancy," she hears him cajole in his best Ben voice. "Why are you being so stubborn? She's a good kid who got involved with the wrong guy. It's a first offense. Let her do some community service."

"You're wasting your breath, Counsel," comes the retort from dry, pinched lips.

"Community service, and everybody gets something out of the deal."

The prosecutor's response is to arch one bushy eyebrow and gather her papers together, then walk from the room.

"She's a charmer," Amanda states, listening to the clunk of the woman's heavy shoes as they reverberate down the hall.

"What are you doing here?" Ben asks without looking at her.

"Your secretary said this is where you'd be."

"Mr. Myers?" A woman approaches, clutching her rosary beads. "Is it all right if I take Selena out for lunch?"

"Mom, for God's sake, put the beads away."

"Make sure you have her back in an hour," Ben tells her as the woman surrounds her daughter with her arms and leads her from the room.

"That's got to be so hard," Amanda says, watching them leave.

Ben says nothing.

"How about you?" Amanda ventures. "Can I take you to lunch?"

"I'm not very hungry. Thanks anyway."

"Ben . . ."

He looks at her for the first time since he saw her come in. "Look, if this is about last night, you don't have to apologize. What you do with your life is your own business."

"I couldn't agree more. I'm not here to apologize."

He looks surprised, maybe even a little disappointed. "Why **are** you here?"

"Can you find out for me if John Mallins's birthday is July the fourteenth?"

"Why would you want to know that?"

"Just a hunch."

"That's a pretty strange hunch, even for you."

"It's just that I was talking to this woman last night, and she said——"

"What woman last night?" His eyes narrow. Was there a woman in your bed too last night? they seem to ask.

Amanda quickly recounts the details of her meeting with Rachel Mallins, watching the expression on Ben's face ricochet between curiosity and disbelief, admiration and anger.

"Please tell me this is your idea of a joke," he says when she's through.

"I know I shouldn't have gone there on my own. You don't have to tell me that. But I really don't think she was bullshitting me. I went to the reference library first thing this morning," she continues before he can interject. "I spent almost an hour going through the records of everyone who died in Toronto in the last month, and there was nobody on that list by the name of Mallins."

"Why should there be?"

"Because Hayley Mallins told me her husband was here to settle his mother's estate."

"Hayley Mallins? When were you talking to Hayley Mallins?"

"I went to see her after you dropped me off at the hotel."

Ben shakes his head, trying to keep up with the steady barrage of information. "You had a very busy night."

"I didn't plan any of it. Believe me. It just kind of evolved."

"Exactly what evolved?"

Amanda describes her visit with Hayley Mallins.

"I can't believe she agreed to talk to you."

"I think I took her by surprise."

"Yes, you have a way of doing that to people." They stand facing one another for several seconds. "All right," he says finally. "You can buy me lunch."

They sit slurping hot cream of broccoli soup in the coffee shop of a nearby hotel. "That prosecutor seems like a real bitch on wheels," Amanda says, then laughs out loud, a distant memory jumping in front of her line of vision, like a pedestrian darting out from between two parked cars.

"What's so funny?"

Amanda shakes her head, as if trying to shake the memory away, but it digs in its heels, refuses to budge. "When I was a little girl," she begins reluctantly, "I remember my mother referring to one of the neighbors as a real 'bitch on wheels.' And from then on, I was absolutely terrified of the woman. I used to go to great lengths to avoid walking past her house, even if it meant I had to go all the way around the block. I mean, not only was this woman a bitch, but she was **on wheels.**" Amanda laughs at her childish naïveté.

Ben grins. "Nancy's not that bad really."

"She isn't?"

"She's just doing her job. You know prosecutors."

Not as well as you do, Amanda thinks, trying to picture his friend Jennifer.

"They love nothing better than to see convictions on their records," he continues.

"Convictions without convictions," Amanda muses. "Is your client guilty?"

"Guilty of being young and stupid. It would be to everyone's benefit to let her do fifty hours of community service instead of saddling her with a prison record."

"That doesn't seem to be an option."

"Only because the powers-that-be are even more stupid than she is."

"Think you have a chance?"

Ben laughs, bites into a warm roll. "It's a slam dunk. I have them on a technicality. As soon as I get the chance to present my case, she walks."

"Ah, justice."

"That's what happens when people get greedy."

Does Jennifer get greedy? Amanda wonders. "You look very attractive in your robe, by the way," she says.

"So did you." He smiles, the gentle curve of his lips dissipating any tension that remained between them. "Sorry about barging in on you that way last night. I guess it seemed rather proprietary."

"Just a little. Anyway, I'm probably the one who should be apologizing to you."

"I thought you weren't here to apologize."

"I'm not," Amanda says. "I said I probably **should** be."

He laughs. "I guess you just caught me off guard. I didn't realize you knew anyone in the city anymore."

"I don't."

"He's someone else you met last night?"

"Actually I met him on the plane."

Ben digests this latest tidbit along with the rest of his bun. "A little old for you, isn't he?"

"I like older men."

"I hadn't realized that."

"My second husband was an older man."

"And what was he like?"

It's Amanda's turn to laugh. "I don't know. I never really got to know him very well."

"Why is that?"

Amanda rolls her eyes. She hadn't meant to get into all this. "I guess I really didn't want to. I mean, he was—**is**—a very handsome man. Wealthy. Cultured. Even nice. I guess that was enough for me at the time."

"When did it stop being enough?"

"When he started talking about having babies."

"Babies don't appeal to you?"

"Hell, no. **I** wanted to be his baby. Why else does a woman marry a man twenty-five years her senior?" She pauses, looks around the crowded room, wonders if any of the other women present is talking to her first husband about her second. "Everything was fine in the beginning, as things usually are. He put me through law school, bought me anything my little heart desired, took me everywhere I wanted to go. Didn't give me a hard time. Showed me off. I liked that. But then suddenly he started talking about how now that I was finished school, maybe we should be thinking about starting a family, and I'm going, whoa, hold on a minute here. Who said anything about starting a family? 'I don't know nothing about birthing babies,' I kept joking. But it turned out he was deadly serious. He wanted kids. I didn't. I believe he said something about it being time to resolve my 'issues' with my mother, that until I was able to do that, I'd be stuck in this kind of prolonged adolescence. I countered with a terribly mature 'Fuck you, Charlie Brown.' . . . Oh, hell. It doesn't really matter what either of us said at that point. The marriage was over."

"And yet you kept his name," Ben observes.

"Whose name was I going to use?" Amanda frowns. "I'd never been very happy as Amanda Price. And I couldn't very well go back to being Amanda Myers, now could I?" She finishes her soup, signals the waiter for a refill of her coffee. "Besides, Sean was a good man. It wasn't his fault I had 'issues.' " She lifts her freshly filled coffee cup to her lips, blows at the rising steam. "So what about you and Miss Jennifer? Think there's a baby carriage lurking in your future?"

Ben shrugs. "Anything's possible, I guess."

Wrong answer, Amanda thinks, stabbing at the butter with her knife, then smearing it across the top of a bun she grabs from the bread basket. "Ever come up against her in court?"

"It's happened a few times."

"Who wins?"

"I think the record's tied."

"That means she's, what, two up on you?"

"Three." They laugh. "This is nice," he says.

"Yes, it is."

"It doesn't mean I'm still not pissed at you for going off half-cocked last night."

Amanda smiles, restrains herself from adding, **So to speak,** although she can tell by the glint in his eyes, he's thinking the same thing. "You think I might be onto something?"

"Like what?"

"I wish I knew." Again they laugh, something Amanda notices gets easier each time it happens. "Maybe if we do a recap . . ."

Ben puts down his soupspoon, gives her his full attention.

"Okay, so last week, my mother meets her friend, Corinne Nash, for tea in the lobby of the Four Seasons. She sees John Mallins and his family returning to the hotel, and according to Corinne, she looks like she's seen a ghost. So, John Mallins is obviously someone my mother thinks she recognizes. Okay so far?"

Ben nods.

"The next day, she returns to the hotel, waits for John Mallins to show up, and pumps him full of bullets. So John Mallins is not only someone she recognizes but someone she hates enough to kill." Amanda pauses, trying to corral her thoughts, put them in some form of cohesive order. "Now, according to **Hayley** Mallins, her husband was here to settle his mother's estate. But the death notices in the local papers show nobody by the name of Mallins having died recently, which lends credence to **Rachel** Mallins's theory that the man calling himself John Mallins is really an impostor, a man she knew only as 'Turk,' who may, or may not, have murdered her brother, the **real** John Mallins, twenty-five years ago, in order to steal his identity. Still with me?"

"Hanging by a thread," Ben admits. "But Hayley Mallins told you her husband was brought to England as a child by his father after his parents divorced."

"That may be what he told her."

"Or it may be the truth."

Amanda nods. "Which would mean that my mother either shot the wrong man or that she's as crazy as everyone seems to think."

"What do you think?"

"I think we need to find out who this man calling himself Turk really was."

EIGHTEEN

Amanda accompanies Ben back to court after their lunch, watches him succeed in having the case dismissed on a technicality, and derives more pleasure than she probably should from the pout of dismay that renders the crown attorney's face even less attractive than it already is. "Way to go, Mr. Myers," Amanda says, watching both Selena and her mother throw their arms around Ben's neck in a congratulatory hug, and fighting the urge to do the same.

"Piece of cake."

Amanda smiles, finding his arrogance even more alarmingly attractive than she had a decade earlier. "So what now?"

"Hopefully she manages to stay out of trouble."

"I meant, with us?" A nervous laugh, an unnecessary clearing of the throat. "I meant, with our plans for the rest of the afternoon."

"Well, I don't know about your plans, but I have to get back to the office." Ben thrusts a fistful of papers into his briefcase and starts walking toward the escalator. His pace is brisk and Amanda struggles to catch up.

"What about my mother?"

"What about her?"

"I thought we were going to see her."

"Can't today."

"But aren't we due in court tomorrow?"

"There'll be plenty of time to talk to her in the morning." They ride in silence down the escalator. Amanda is about to ask why the rush to get back to the office all of a sudden, when Ben points toward the corridor on his left. "Room 102. Try to get here by eight forty-five, if you can."

"Wait!" Amanda runs to catch up with him as he steps off the escalator and marches toward the side exit. A splash of cold air whips against her cheek as he pushes open the door, causing her to cry out with equal measures of shock and pain.

Ben stops. "You all right?"

"Do you think you could do something about the weather?"

"What's the matter—you don't like minus ten degrees?"

"Why do you think I moved to Florida?"

"I can't answer that," he says simply. "Can you?"

Amanda ignores both the question and its implication. "I was thinking I should probably stay in town a few more days."

"I think that's probably a good idea," he concurs, his voice as crisp as the outside air. His lawyer's voice, she thinks, the one he uses to talk to clients.

"Look, how about dinner tonight?" She tries to make the invitation sound casual and spur-of-the-moment and is grateful her teeth are chattering loud enough to hide the tremble in her voice.

"Can't tonight." He offers no further explanation as he strides south along University Avenue.

"Ben, we really need to talk about my mother," Amanda says quickly, as if her mother is the reason for the dinner invitation.

"What's to talk about?"

Amanda grabs Ben's arm, forces him to a stop at the corner of University and Queen. "You're not really going to let her plead guilty tomorrow, are you?"

"Of course not."

"How are you going to stop her?"

"It's a bail hearing, Amanda. She doesn't get the opportunity to enter a plea until Friday."

Amanda feels something akin to relief, then puzzlement as to why. "Okay. Well, at least that buys us a little time."

"You might think of buying something else if you're planning on sticking around," he says.

"What's that?"

"A new coat." He smiles, then hurries across the street before the light changes, waving good-bye over his shoulder without looking back.

Amanda spends the next several hours navigating the stores in the Eaton Center, a huge, indoor, three-story shopping mall and office tower located in the heart of downtown Toronto. She remembers when Eaton's was the number one store in the country, but that all changed sometime in her absence, and the once venerable department store chain went into receivership and was taken over by its chief rival. Can't leave you alone for a minute, she thinks, spotting a black parka in the window of a small shop on the main level and going inside.

"Can I help you?" a young woman, whose name tag identifies her as Monica, asks before Amanda even has a chance to browse. Monica has frizzy blond curls and a bare midriff that protrudes over a pair of low-slung designer jeans.

"Aren't you cold?" Amanda can't help but ask. Even though the girl can't be more than five years her junior, Amanda is starting to feel as if she belongs to another generation entirely. When did I start to feel so old? she wonders.

Monica shakes her head, frizzy blond ringlets bouncing across her forehead and into close-set, gray-blue eyes. "Gets pretty hot in here. You looking for anything in particular?"

"That coat in the window . . ."

"The black parka?"

Amanda nods as the salesgirl leads her through the crowded racks of merchandise to the fleece-lined parkas at the rear of the store. She quickly removes her coat and drops it to the floor, allowing Monica to help her into one of the black parkas, then appraising herself in the full-length mirror against the back wall.

"Have you considered red?" Monica asks.

"Red?"

"The black's nice and everything—don't get me wrong, it looks great on you—but the red is fabulous. You should try it."

"I don't think so."

"Trust me," Monica says, and Amanda

smiles. Since when have frizzy blond ringlets and a pair of low-slung jeans ever served as a shortcut to trust? However, in the next instant, she is willingly exchanging the black parka for the red one. "I knew it," Monica says. "You look gorgeous. The red really suits you."

Amanda studies herself in the mirror, surprisingly pleased with what she sees. Gone is the dejected little waif, waving after her former husband on a cold and windy street corner. Here instead is a true scarlet woman, the famed lady in red. "I'll take it."

"Great." Monica claps her hands together in girlish enthusiasm. "Will there be anything else?"

"I don't know. You have any ideas?"

"There's this to-die-for purple sweater."

"Purple?"

"Trust me," Monica says.

Half an hour later, Amanda watches in bemused wonderment as the girl rings up her various purchases, thinking, What am I going to do with all these winter clothes in Florida?

"Let's see. One purple mohair sweater, one blue cashmere turtleneck, a pair of navy pants, some black leather gloves, and of course, one fabulous red parka. How would you like to pay for these things?"

Amanda pulls out her credit card, hands it to Monica. "Is it all right if I wear the coat now?"

"It's your coat," Monica says with a smile that reveals two rows of perfect teeth. "Here. Just let me get the tags off." She expertly removes the various tags, then slides the shiny red parka across the counter. "I can put your old coat in a bag for you, if you'd like."

"No, that's all right. Keep it."

"What?"

"Give it to someone who needs it."

"You're sure?"

"Positive."

"Well, that's very nice of you . . . Amanda," she says, reading the name on the credit card and ringing up the sale. "You bought some wonderful things. Wear them well."

"Thank you." Amanda slides her arms into her new coat and wraps it around her torso, luxuriating in its comforting warmth. Who needs Ben Myers? she is thinking as she pulls the parka's fleece-lined hood up over her head and walks from the store.

"Amanda?" the salesgirl calls after her. "Excuse me, Ms. Travis?"

Amanda stops and turns around, hugging the coat tighter to her chest, in case Monica tries to pry it from her. **There's been a mistake,** she hears the salesgirl apologizing. **I'm afraid this coat has already been sold. You'll have to give it back.**

"You wouldn't want to forget this," Monica is saying, holding out her hand. Amanda sees a bankbook and a small key resting in the salesgirl's open palm. "Looks like a key to a safety-deposit box."

"My God." Amanda realizes she'd forgotten all about the key and the passbook she took from the shoe box in her mother's closet.

"Good thing I checked the pockets."

"Good thing," Amanda repeats.

"You're sure about leaving the coat?"

"Positive."

"Okay. Thanks again."

"Thank **you.**"

"Have a good day."

I don't know about **good,** Amanda is thinking as she leaves the store. But the day just got a lot more interesting.

It is almost four o'clock when Amanda arrives at the address on the bank's passbook, a thirty-five-minute drive from downtown. "Where are we?" she asks the driver, noting that the meter reads $14.75, $7 more than the balance on her mother's account. She pulls a $20 bill from her purse and dangles it over the front seat. This trip is proving to be expensive.

"North York," the man replies in a heavy Eastern European accent.

Why would her mother have chosen a bank all the way up here, when there are TD banks all over the city?

"Should hurry," the man advises. "Bank close in two minutes."

Shit, Amanda thinks, watching several people exit the establishment, wondering if they'll even let her in. "Keep the change," she tells the cabbie, pulling open the car door and making a beeline for the bank's entrance, seeing a bank employee walking toward her with a heavy set of keys, about to lock up for the day.

"I won't be long," she tells the skinny young woman whose helmet of curly black hair adds at least three inches to her height.

"Take your time," the woman drawls in a soft Jamaican lilt, locking the front door after her.

Amanda takes a quick look around the bank's interior, trying to plot her next move. She is relieved to see that the bank is relatively large and modern, and that half a dozen other customers are still milling about. Perhaps the fact it's closing time will work to her advantage. The tellers are preoccupied with closing up and balancing. They are therefore less likely to pay too close attention to a stranger in their midst, to look too carefully at the signature she offers to gain entry to the safety-deposit box in the vault at the rear of the bank. Not that she couldn't fool them. Years of forging her mother's signature to high school report cards has made her something of an expert.

So now you're forging your mother's signature and breaking into safety-deposit boxes, she hears Ben whisper disapprovingly. **You know you could get disbarred for this.**

Amanda pulls off her new black leather gloves, noting the nervous trembling in her fingers, as she walks past the row of tellers along the bank's mauve west wall. "I need to get into my safety-desposit box," she says to a woman rifling through a stack of checks on the other side of the counter.

"Be with you in half a second," the woman answers without looking up.

Good, Amanda thinks. I like your attitude. Don't smile or ask how I am. Don't tell me to have a good day. Just saunter over here as if you're doing me a great big favor by letting me do business with you, and let me inside the goddamn vault.

The woman sighs with obvious frustration, runs an impatient hand through short-cropped brown hair. "Why can't I figure this out?" she mutters to herself.

I know how you feel, Amanda sympathizes, shifting her weight from one foot to the other, and feeling snug and warm inside her new parka. She hears an angry voice beside her and looks toward the sound.

"What do you mean you have to put a hold on my check?" an indignant customer is demanding.

"It's an out-of-town check, Mrs. Newton," the teller explains. "I'm afraid it's bank policy."

"I've been a customer at this bank for more than thirty years. Since before you were born."

"Yes, and I'm so sorry, but—"

"I'd like to talk to the manager."

Amanda stares at the intersecting trails of wet footprints that crisscross the dark slate floor. My mother's been a customer at this bank for the same amount of time, she is thinking, fighting the urge to flee. I might be able to forge her signature, but there's no way I'm going to convince anyone that I'm Gwen Price. Suppose one of these tellers knows my mother beyond a casual hello. Suppose she's been following the newspaper accounts of the shooting and, at the very least, recognizes her name. She'll know I'm an impostor. And then what will she do? Throw me out? Call the police? Ben will be furious when he finds out, that's for damn sure.

The exasperated teller drops the stack of checks to the counter and looks up with a weary smile. "You want to get into the vault?" she acknowledges, pushing a card across the counter for Amanda's signature.

Something else that's for damn sure: it's too late to turn back now.

Amanda signs her mother's name to the card, holds her breath while the teller compares it to the one she has on file. "This way," she says, offering not even a flicker of recognition and ushering Amanda around the counter toward the imposing steel vault at the back of the room. Then she stops abruptly, turns, stares hard at Amanda. "Oh," she says.

Amanda feels her breath stop in her throat, as if the woman's hands are around her neck. Tell the woman it's all a big mistake, that you haven't been yourself lately. She thinks of John Mallins, or the man calling himself John Mallins. Haven't been yourself lately, she thinks again, and almost laughs. Must be contagious.

"Your coat," the teller is saying.

"My coat?"

"Yes. It's gorgeous. I love it. Where'd you get it?"

"Uh. A little store in the Eaton Center."

"It's fabulous. I absolutely love the color." She opens the vault, stands back to let Amanda enter first.

"Thank you."

"I can't wear red. Wish I could. But it washes me right out." She uses her key, and then Amanda's, to release the safety-deposit box. "You can take it in there." She points to a small, curtained-off area. "Well, you know the routine."

The long, rectangular steel box feels heavy in Amanda's hands. "Thank you. I shouldn't be long."

"No problem."

That's what you think, Amanda says silently, watching the woman leave before pulling back the mauve velvet curtain and stepping inside the womblike space. She stares for several long seconds at the dull gray box, as if the force of her gaze will be enough for her to make out its contents. "Come on. What are you waiting for?"

I'm waiting for the cops to come bursting in here to arrest me.

Then you might as well give them something to arrest you for, she decides, pulling open the box and staring inside.

Whatever she was expecting to see, it wasn't this.

Amanda gasps and falls back against the curtain, feeling hot and cold, light-headed and lead-footed, all at the same time. "Dear God," she says, reaching into the long box and running her fingers along the neat stacks of $100 bills. "What the hell is going on here?" What is her mother doing with all this money? At least $100,000, Amanda calculates quickly. In cash. As compared to the $7.75 in her account. "What the hell is going on?"

Amanda stares at the money until she hears a shuffling of feet, followed by a discreet cough, on the other side of the curtain. "Excuse me, but is everything okay?" a voice asks.

Amanda slams the safety-deposit box closed, then takes several seconds to compose herself before pulling back the curtain and forcing a stiff smile onto her lips.

"I'm sorry," the teller apologizes. "Normally we don't like to interrupt our customers, but you've been in there a long time, and . . ."

Amanda checks her watch, is startled to see that more than twenty minutes have passed. "I'm sorry. I had no idea it was so late."

"It's just that we're trying to close up."

"I understand." She hands the heavy box back to the teller and watches as the woman slides it carefully back into its slot, thinking, Please don't let me faint until I'm out of here.

"Will there be anything else we can do for you today?" the teller asks, leading Amanda back into the main area, all of Amanda's concentration going to putting one foot in front of the other.

"No. I think that's quite enough for one afternoon."

The young woman with the keys is waiting to accompany Amanda to the front of the bank. "Great coat," she says, unlocking the door.

Amanda waits until she hears the door lock again behind her before lowering herself to the curb and covering her face with her hands.

"What do you mean, I have to check out to-morrow?" Amanda demands of the clerk at the reception desk at the Four Seasons hotel.

The young man smiles patiently. "Well, technically, you were supposed to check out this morning."

"But I've decided to stay until the week-end."

"And I wish we could help you. I really do.

But our records show that you only reserved until last night. Now we can accommodate you for tonight, but I'm afraid that, as of tomorrow at noon, we're fully booked."

"You don't have **anything** available?"

"I'm afraid not. I can call some of the other hotels in the area . . ."

"No, that's okay. Thank you." Amanda backs away from the reception desk.

Some of the things Amanda is thinking as she steps into a waiting elevator: her mother has $100,000 in $100 bills sitting in a safety-deposit box in a bank on the other side of town; she should call Ben, tell him of her discovery; her mother has $100,000 in $100 bills sitting in a safety-deposit box in a bank on the other side of town; she should call her office, tell them she won't be back in town until next week; her mother has $100,000 in $100 bills sitting in a safety-deposit box in a bank on the other side of town; she needs to find a new hotel room; her new coat is toasty warm; red is definitely her new favorite color; her mother has $100,000 in $100 bills sitting in a safety-deposit box in a bank on the other side of town.

NINETEEN

Amanda arrives back at the new court-house at precisely eight forty-five the next morning. Already the corridors are crowded with visitors: harassed-looking lawyer-types in dull, ill-fitting suits scurrying purposefully back and forth from one end of the hall to the other, stopping to chat briefly with colleagues or confer with clients; uniformed police officers gathered in small blue clusters, suspiciously eyeing the young men who slouch past them clothed in baggy jeans and attitude; nervous parents sitting on uncomfortable-looking wooden benches propped against the high walls, holding back tears and trying to reassure each other that everything will be all right.

Amanda feels all eyes on her as she walks up and down the corridor, looking for Ben. I stand out like a sore thumb, she is thinking as she un-

zips her bright red parka and adjusts the
overnight bag that weighs heavily on her shoulder. Make that a ripe tomato, she amends, suc-
cumbing to the lure of an empty bench and sitting down, lowering her overnight bag to the
floor, and closing her eyes. She didn't sleep well
last night, which isn't surprising. Her head was
a war zone of conflicting ideas. One minute, she
was trying to convince herself that there was
nothing unreasonable about her mother having
all that money stashed away in a safety-deposit
box in a bank halfway out of town because, after
all, her mother was nothing if not eccentric,
and the next minute, she was reminding herself
that crazy was several huge degrees away from
eccentric, and it was definitely crazy for her
mother to have all this money hidden away, and
besides, what was she doing with $100,000 in
$100 bills, and what, if anything, was her con-
nection to John Mallins, if John Mallins really
was John Mallins, and if not, then who the hell
was he, and did it really matter, when what
really mattered was where she was going to stay
for the next several days? "What the hell am I
still doing here?" she whispers into the hood of
her new parka, thinking of the plane reservation
she canceled first thing this morning, and hearing the almost audible shiver of delight in her

secretary's voice when she phoned to tell her she wouldn't be back in the office until next week.

"So what was it like seeing him again?" Kelly asked, her voice a conspiratorial whisper.

"What was it like seeing **whom** again?" Amanda replied flatly, hoping her imperious tone would be enough to silence the curious young woman.

"Ben Myers," Kelly said, stubbornly refusing to take the hint.

"It was strange." But even as Amanda spoke the word, she knew it was the wrong one. While the situation in which she and Ben found themselves might rightly be deemed strange, seeing Ben again, actually spending time with him, was anything but. Their initial awkwardness had dissolved into an easy comfort born of familiarity and a mutual, if reluctant, respect. Simply put, it felt good to be around Ben, she realized. It felt like home. "I'll be home this weekend," Amanda told her secretary, brushing the distinctly uncomfortable feeling aside with a swat of her hand.

What's the matter with me? Amanda wonders now, opening her eyes when she hears footsteps approaching, then closing them again when she realizes the man about to plop down on the far end of the bench isn't Ben. What am I doing obsessing over a man I walked out on eight years ago? she berates herself. You can be damn sure he isn't wasting his time thinking about me. No, sir. He has his office and his caseload and his Jennifer. **Can't tonight,** he'd responded to her dinner invitation, without even bothering to offer an explanation. And yet, there was something about the way he looked at her . . . "Oh, no. You are not going there."

"Sorry?" the man asks from the other side of the bench. "Are you talking to me?"

"What? Oh, no. No. Sorry."

The man nods, his head continuing to bob up and down nervously even after he turns away. Seconds later, they are joined on the bench by a woman in a heavy down jacket, who squeezes in between them, glancing over at Amanda. "Nice coat," she says.

Amanda smiles her thanks, then checks her watch. It's already five minutes to nine, and Ben still isn't here. She should have called him when she got back to the hotel last night, told him of her trip to the bank, and her shocking discovery. Why didn't she? Because she knew he'd be angry? Because she'd neglected to tell him about finding the key to the safety-deposit box in the first place? Beause she'd gone to the bank without him? Because she'd forged her mother's signature and opened her safety-deposit box under false pretenses? Because of the disapproval she knew she'd hear in his voice?

Or because she was afraid she wouldn't hear his voice at all?

Because he already had plans for last night, she reminds herself again. Plans that didn't involve her.

Is that why she didn't call?

"What's with the suitcase?" a voice is asking from somewhere above her, and Amanda opens her eyes to see Ben, wearing a charcoal gray overcoat over a dark blue suit, his own eyes directed at the overnight bag at her feet. "I thought you'd decided to stay till the end of the week."

Instantly Amanda clambers to her feet. "Got kicked out of my hotel. You're late."

"Sorry," he says without explanation. "New coat?"

"You like it?"

"Great color." He grabs her overnight bag, takes her elbow, and starts leading her down the hall. "Your mother's in a holding cell downstairs." He points toward a set of doors at the far end of the corridor. "They should be bringing her up those stairs in a few minutes."

"There's something I need to tell you before we see her," Amanda begins as a middle-aged man with thinning gray hair and a worried scowl brushes past.

"Sam," Ben calls after him. "Everything all right?"

The man shakes his head, continues walking backward as he speaks. "Seems my esteemed client went berserk last night and almost killed the poor sucker sharing his holding cell. The usual crap. You?"

"The usual crap," Ben agrees, before turning his attention back to Amanda.

"Well, that was flattering."

He smiles, his eyes crinkling. "You were saying?"

Amanda hesitates. "Where do you think I should stay for the next few days? I've already called a few hotels. Seems they're all filled up."

"I don't see a problem."

"You don't?"

"I would think the solution's pretty obvious."

"Tell me." I've never been very good with the obvious, she thinks, hearing the silent invitation to stay at his place, and immediately wondering if this would really be such a good idea. She doesn't want to start something she has no intention of finishing. A casual fling is one thing, but Ben has proved himself less than adept at casual.

"You already have the key," he tells her, interrupting her inner dialogue.

"What?" How does he know about the key? "How do you know?"

"What do you mean, how do I know? I was there when she handed it to you."

"What are you talking about?"

"Corinne Nash."

"Corinne Nash?"

"Amanda, are you okay?"

The truth slams against Amanda's brain like a surprise left hook. "You're talking about the key to my mother's house?"

"What other key would I be talking about?"

"I can't stay there."

"What other key would I be talking about?" Ben repeats, the pressure of his hand on her elbow increasing, directing her to a stop. "Amanda, what are you talking about?"

"I found a key to my mother's safety-deposit box," Amanda admits.

"What? Where?"

"In a shoe box in my mother's closet."

Ben's face registers confusion, understanding, confusion. "And you didn't tell me about it because . . ."

"Because I put it in my pocket and forgot all about it." Not quite a lie, Amanda decides. She **had** put it in her pocket. She **did** forget about it.

"Why do I think there's more to this story?"

"Because I went to the bank yesterday. And I opened the safety-deposit box."

"Please tell me you're kidding."

"And you won't believe what I found."

"What I don't believe is that you did anything this stupid."

"I found money, Ben."

"You broke the law, Amanda."

"A hundred thousand dollars, Ben."

"What!"

"A hundred thousand dollars in hundred-dollar bills. What do you think it means?" she asks the silence that follows.

Ben shakes his head. "I haven't got a clue."

"There she is." Amanda points with her chin as her mother comes into view at the top of the stairs. Gwen Price is standing in the middle of a small group of women prisoners, all wearing the same ugly dark green sweat suits with the hot pink trim. The female police officer in charge carefully removes the handcuffs from each of the prisoner's wrists. "Can you believe it?" Amanda murmurs, watching the scene as if it were part of an unpleasant dream. "She's smiling."

"She's rich," Ben reminds her, guiding Amanda through the beveled-glass doors to the area where the prisoners are gathered and waiting. "Ben Myers," he announces to the attending officer, offering the woman his identification. "I'm Gwen Price's attorney. This is Amanda Travis. We'd like a few minutes alone with our client."

Not quite a lie, Amanda thinks again, as the officer directs them to a private area within her viewing range. Ben **is** Gwen Price's attorney. She **is** Amanda Travis.

"You look lovely," her mother tells her, brightening noticeably when she sees her. "That's a wonderful color on you."

Amanda opens her mouth to speak, but no words emerge. Who **is** this woman? she is thinking.

"How are you today, Mrs. Price?" Ben asks.

Gwen Price rubs her wrists, still red with the imprint of her handcuffs. "I'm fine, thank you, Ben. Although it's a good thing I'm not claustrophobic. That paddy wagon, or whatever it is they call it, has no air whatsoever, and we're all so squished together, it's hard to breathe. Is something wrong, dear?" she asks Amanda.

"Wrong? What could possibly be wrong?" Amanda's voice registers her incredulity. She's thinking of the old movie **Invasion of the Body Snatchers,** where creatures from outer space take over the bodies of human beings while they sleep. You're too late, she is thinking, directing her thoughts to the alien behind her mother's eyes. You came too late.

"We have to go over a few things, Mrs. Price."

"I really have nothing more to say, Ben. Other than to enter my plea."

"This is a bail hearing," Ben tries to explain. "We're here to try to get you out of prison, at least until the trial."

"But there isn't going to be a trial. I intend to plead guilty."

"Which is just one of the things we have to talk about."

"Then we have **nothing** to talk about," Gwen Price says stubbornly.

"Mother," Amanda interrupts.

"Yes, dear?"

Dear?! Who is this woman? "What are

you doing with a hundred thousand dollars in a safety-deposit box in North York?"

Her mother's skin turns ashen against the dark green of her prison uniform. "What?"

"I found the money, Mother."

"I don't have a clue what you're talking about."

"I don't believe you."

"I don't give a damn."

At last, Amanda thinks. The woman I know and loathe.

"I found the key in the shoe box you keep in your closet. The same shoe box, incidentally, where I found—"

"What were you doing going through my closet?" her mother interrupts angrily.

"What are you doing with that kind of cash?"

Her mother's response is to turn toward the window at the end of the hall, fluff out the back of her hair with her hand.

"What's all that money doing hidden in a bank vault halfway out of the city?"

Amanda feels the pressure of Ben's hand on her shoulder, a silent warning to keep her voice down.

"I believe I'm entitled to keep my money anywhere I please," her mother says.

"And what do you think the police will do when they find out about that money, Mother?"

"That money is none of their business," her mother says evenly. "Or yours."

"Where did you get it?"

"What difference does it make?"

"Does it have anything to do with why you shot John Mallins?"

"Ben," her mother says, ignoring Amanda, "shouldn't we be going inside?"

"Did someone pay you to shoot that man?" The question shocks Amanda almost as much as it shocks her mother. Is she seriously suggesting her mother is a contract killer?

"Of course not," Gwen replies with a laugh. "That's ridiculous."

"Not as ridiculous as shooting a man for no reason at all."

"No one paid me to shoot John Mallins."

"Then where did you get the money?"

Her mother sighs, says nothing.

Amanda looks toward the high ceiling, throws her arms into the air in a gesture of defeat. "You're unbelievable."

"And you're getting yourself all worked up over nothing. Please, can we just go inside and get this over with?"

"They'll call us when they're ready," Ben tells Gwen.

"Who's Turk, Mother?" Amanda asks.

Her mother's complexion goes from ashen to deathly white, as if she is being rapidly drained of blood. Her eyes widen, her chin drops, then quivers. Her lips open, as if to speak, remaining open even when no words emerge.

"Who is he, Mother?"

Her mother's eyes suddenly snap back into focus. She takes a deep breath, then another, before bringing her lips together, forcing them into a smile. "I'm sorry. What was that name again?"

"Turk," Amanda repeats wearily, understanding further conversation is futile, that she has played all her cards, showed her hand, exhausted all elements of surprise. After a momentary shock, her mother is now firmly back in control. There'll be no startling revelations here.

"I don't think I know anyone by that name."

"I think you do."

Her mother's eyes narrow in mock concentration. "I don't believe so, dear."

If she calls me "dear" one more time . . . , Amanda thinks, her fists clenching at her sides. "I don't believe you."

"I guess that's your prerogative."

"Not only do I think you know who Turk is," Amanda continues, her voice a hoarse whisper, "I think he's the man you shot in the lobby of the Four Seasons hotel."

Her mother tries to laugh, but a catch in her throat turns the laugh into more of a howl. "And I think you must have read too many Nancy Drew novels as a child."

"How would you know **what** I did as a child?" The sudden, unleashed rage in Amanda's voice bounces off the walls and echoes down the hallways.

"Amanda . . . ," Ben warns.

"How dare you," Amanda stammers, tears filling her eyes and dropping down her cheeks, disappearing into the powder blue turtleneck of her new cashmere sweater. "How dare you presume to know anything about me?"

"I'm sorry," her mother offers, her gaze dropping to the floor.

"Amanda," Ben says gently, "this isn't the time or place."

"Trouble here?" the attending officer asks, approaching cautiously, signaling for a nearby colleague to join her.

"Everything's fine, Officers," Ben says.

"Everything's a fucking mess," Amanda counters under her breath.

"You're sure there's no problem?" The police-woman looks from Ben to Amanda to her mother and back again.

"I think we're finished here," Gwen says.

"I think we're just getting started," Amanda counters.

"Just a few more minutes," Ben instructs the officers, who back away, making no secret of their continuing surveillance.

"She's a very pretty girl, don't you think?" Gwen says, as if this were the most natural of follow-ups.

"What are you talking about, Mother?"

"The police officer. Her name is Kolleen, with a **K**. You'd never guess she was a cop if she weren't in uniform."

"Mrs. Price . . ."

"You always have this picture of police officers being these big, burly guys with big, thick necks, and then you meet someone like Kolleen, who's not nearly as tall as you are, Amanda," Gwen continues without looking at her daughter, "and she's this skinny little thing, not very muscular at all, although you can tell she's strong. She probably has a black belt in karate, or some such thing."

"I don't give a shit about Kolleen," Amanda interrupts, furious at herself for being unable to stop the steady flow of tears falling down her cheeks.

"And I don't give a shit about some guy named Turk," her mother says.

"But you **do** know who he is."

Gwen Price spins slowly toward her daughter, smiling sadly, and taking several steps toward her. Gentle fingers reach out to wipe the tears from Amanda's face. "I'm sorry I was such a bad mother to you, Amanda," she says softly, her own eyes welling up with tears.

Amanda pushes her mother's hand abruptly aside, falls backward, as if she's been punched. "Who the hell are you?" she asks.

The door to Courtroom 102 opens and a large man with a surprisingly high-pitched voice steps into the hall, craning his neck in their direction. "Gwen Price," he calls out, his gaze skipping across the various prisoners.

Gwen nods in his direction. "That's me," she answers cheerily, turning toward Ben. "Well, now. Shall we go inside?"

TWENTY

The courtroom is much like the one she was in yesterday, Amanda thinks, as she follows her mother and Ben inside. Maybe a little smaller, a little less crowded. The same serious faces, the same serious lack of air. "Are you going to call me to testify?" Amanda asks Ben as they take their seats in the front row of the spectator benches.

"Are you kidding?" comes the reply out of the side of his mouth. "You said it yourself—I put you on that stand, the next thing I know, they'll be bringing back capital punishment."

"I'll be good," Amanda assures him. "Put me up there."

"What are you two whispering about?" her mother asks as, once again, her name is announced. Ben leads Gwen toward the defense table at the front of the room, pulling out her chair and waiting while she sits down.

"Proceed, Counsel," the judge directs. Amanda makes a mental note of his large head, his receding hairline, and that his features are all squished together in the middle of his face, as if he were permanently trapped inside closing elevator doors.

"Your Honor," Ben begins.

"I plead guilty," Gwen states, rising to her feet.

"Excuse me?" The judge's eyebrows arch toward the bridge of his bulbous nose. He regards Gwen with a mixture of amusement and disbelief.

"Sit down," Ben tells his client.

Gwen remains stubbornly on her feet. "I want to plead guilty, Your Honor."

"Be that as it may," the judge informs her, "this is not a venue for entering pleas, but rather a bail review hearing to determine whether you—"

"I'm not interested in bail, Your Honor," Gwen insists.

"Counsel, perhaps you'd like a minute to consult with your client?"

"That won't be necessary, Your Honor," Gwen tells the judge. "I don't want bail. I'm guilty, and I should be in prison."

"Your Honor," Ben pleads. "With the

court's indulgence. If I could request a five-minute recess—"

"I don't want a recess," Gwen says. "I demand to be put back in jail."

"Seems like your client already has her mind made up, Mr. Myers."

"Your Honor, my client is going through a very difficult time."

"That's a lie," Gwen says.

"Sit down, Gwen." Ben's voice is gruff, bursting with frustration.

Gwen shrugs and reluctantly resumes her seat.

"Counsel, your client is charged with murder. She says she's guilty. I say if she wants to go back to jail, let her."

"Your Honor, despite the heinous nature of the crime with which she's charged," Ben interjects quickly, "Mrs. Price is not a flight risk, nor is she a threat to society—"

"I shot a total stranger," Gwen interrupts. "You don't think that makes me a threat to society?"

"Mother, for God's sake—" Amanda is out of her seat and marching toward the front of the courtroom as the judge bangs on his gavel and an officer of the court moves to restrain her.

"This is the defendant's daughter, Your Honor," Ben says. "She practices law in the state of Florida, and she's put that practice on hold in order to be with her mother until everything can be resolved. She's prepared to stay and look after her—"

"I don't need looking after." Gwen's face reddens with alarm.

"You need to be quiet," the judge tells her. "You're not helping your case any with these antics."

"That's just the point, Your Honor. I don't want to help my case. I want to plead guilty. I want to go to jail."

"Fine with me." The judge bangs decisively on his gavel. "Bail is denied. Bailiff, please remove the prisoner."

"Thank you, Your Honor." Gwen Price smiles as the officer approaches to lead her from the courtroom.

"I'll be up later to talk to you," Ben tells her.

"Not necessary," Gwen says over her shoulder. "Nice to see you again, Amanda. Have a safe trip back to Florida."

"Shit," Amanda swears into the palm of her hand.

The judge shakes his head, as if to say, Now

I've seen everything. Then he laughs. "Good luck, Mr. Myers," he tells Ben before instructing the bailiff to call the next case.

"Now what?" Amanda asks as she follows Ben out of the courtroom and down the long hall.

"I think we may have just run out of options."

"We're onto something, Ben," Amanda tells him, feeling it in her gut. "That's why she's so eager to wrap this whole thing up. You saw her face when I mentioned the name Turk. That name means something to her, Ben."

Ben stops before they reach the side exit. "So what?" he says plainly.

"So what?"

"John Mallins, Turk, William Shakespeare. What difference does it make? A man is dead, and your mother is only too happy to take the credit. You saw her in front of that judge. She's bound and determined to go to jail, and frankly, I don't see that there's much we can do to stop her. She doesn't want our help. Her little performance today proved that."

"So what do we do?"

"Amanda, I don't think you're listening."

"I'm listening. I'm just not agreeing."

"I don't see where we have any choice."

"There's always a choice."

"Yes, and sometimes somebody else makes it."

"So, what are you saying?" Amanda asks stubbornly.

"You know what I'm saying. I'm saying that maybe it's time for you to cash in that return ticket and go back to Florida. You didn't want to come here in the first place. I practically had to drag you down here."

"Yes, and now I'm here, and—what?— you're just going to throw in the towel? You're prepared to let my mother rot in jail for the rest of her life?"

"A few days ago, you were looking forward to letting that happen."

"A lot's changed in the last few days."

"What's changed, Amanda?"

I don't think I've ever told you how beautiful you are.

"I don't know."

You look lovely. That's a wonderful color on you.

"It's just that nothing makes any sense."

I'm sorry I was such a bad mother to you, Amanda.

"I can't go back to Florida, Ben. I just bought all these clothes. Where am I going to wear them in Florida?"

"What?!"

Amanda begins spinning around in helpless circles. "There's something wrong with my mother, Ben. She's different, and you know it."

"She shot a man, Amanda. That can do strange things to your head."

"Or maybe there's already something strange in her head. Maybe she has a brain tumor. We didn't think of that. Can we arrange for an MRI?"

Ben sighs, looking longingly toward the exit. Why did I ever get involved in this mess? the sigh asks. "I can petition the court, but I doubt your mother would agree, and without her permission—"

"Which you know she won't give."

"—our hands are tied."

"Shit." The epithet, louder than she'd intended, ricochets off the walls, races down the corridors.

Ben looks nervously around. "Okay, look. Why don't we grab a cup of coffee." He doesn't wait for her response, his hand already on her elbow as he leads her out the side exit and across the street to the coffee shop where they had lunch the previous day.

"We have to find out who this guy Turk is," Amanda is saying moments later, ripping into a cranberry muffin and blowing the steam from her coffee. "He's the key to this whole thing."

"How do you propose we do that?"

"I have no idea." Amanda stares across the table at her former husband, feels a slow grin tugging at her lips.

"What are you smiling about?"

"Just that I'm not used to seeing you in a suit."

"And what's the verdict?"

"That suits suit you," Amanda says, her grin widening, stretching across her face.

Ben shakes his head. "Who'd have thought," he says, a now-familiar refrain.

"Who'd have thought," she echoes. "What made you decide to become a lawyer anyway?"

"Truthfully?"

"If you think I can handle it."

"I always wanted to be a lawyer."

"What? You never told me that."

He shrugs. "Too embarrassed. I mean, here I was, the classic angry young man with that whole 'rebel without a cause' thing going, no way I'm going to be a lawyer like my father. Perish the thought. And what do I really want to be, deep down?"

"A lawyer like your father," Amanda answers.

"Exactly."

"How **is** your father?"

"Great. He's in Paris right now. On his honeymoon, actually."

"His honeymoon?"

"My mother died five years ago," Ben explains. "Cancer."

"I'm so sorry. I had no idea."

"How would you? We haven't exactly stayed in touch over the years."

Amanda takes a sip of her coffee, feels it burn the roof of her mouth, and wishes the numbness in her palate would spread to the rest of her body. "Were you close to your mother?"

He nods. "We got closer as time went on."

"You mean, you got closer after I left town?"

"Something like that," he acknowledges.

"She didn't exactly approve of me, as I recall."

"She just thought we were too young."

"Mother knows best," Amanda says, shaking her head in wonderment. "I can't believe I said that."

"Maybe she **does** know best," Ben says, effortlessly shifting the focus from his mother to Amanda's. "Maybe the best thing is to leave bad enough alone."

"I can't do that."

"It could get worse, Amanda."

Amanda laughs, a painful sound that hacks at the air like a machete. "So, who'd your dad marry? Anyone I know?"

"Believe it or not, yes." Ben finishes the coffee in his cup and signals the waitress for a refill. "Remember Mrs. MacMahon? Grade eleven history?"

"You're kidding."

"Her husband passed away around the same time as my mother. Some mutual friends fixed them up about a year ago, and what can I say? The rest is—"

"Don't say it."

They laugh, this time easily.

"Can I stay at your place?" The question is out of Amanda's mouth before she has time to consider either its ramifications or repercussions.

"What?"

"It would only be for a few days. Till we know what's happening. I don't know, Ben. It just seems to make sense."

"It makes no sense at all."

"I'm not suggesting we sleep together," Amanda continues quickly. "Obviously, I'd sleep on the couch. And I'd try to stay out of your way if Jennifer—"

"You can't stay with me, Amanda."

Amanda nods her head in silent acquiescence. He's right. Of course he's right.

"I can have one of the secretaries at my office call around, see if they can find you a hotel room. There might even be something here," Ben adds, looking past the coffee shop doors toward the lobby of the adjoining hotel.

"No, that's all right. I'm a big girl. I'm sure I'll be able to find something on my own."

"I just don't think it would be wise for you to stay with me."

"Of course. I understand. You're absolutely right. It was a lousy idea."

"An interesting one though," he admits after a pause.

"I thought so."

"Maybe we—"

"Ben!" a woman's voice exclaims.

Amanda feels a swoosh of fabric beside her, smells the overpowering scent of lemon-based perfume, and turns to see an attractive woman in a dark green overcoat bending over to kiss Ben's cheek, her chin-length brown hair falling across cheekbones that are high and well-defined.

"You finished in court already?" the woman asks, her voice husky and low.

"I'm finished all right."

"The judge denied bail?"

"The judge never had a chance."

The woman smiles as if she understands and turns her penetrating gaze on Amanda. Her eyes are the same color as my coffee, Amanda thinks, knowing this is Jennifer even before Ben introduces her.

"Jennifer Grimes, I'd like you to meet Amanda Travis," she hears him say as she casually absorbs the details of the woman's face—the dark eyes, the long, aquiline nose, the coral-colored lips. "Gwen Price's daughter."

"And Ben's ex-wife." Amanda extends her hand. "In case he forgot to mention it."

Disappointingly, Jennifer takes her hand, gives it a vigorous shake. "He didn't forget. I'm so sorry we had to meet under these circumstances."

"It's a difficult time," Amanda says. "Would you like to join us?"

Jennifer Grimes waves to two colleagues waiting by the door. "I'll see you over there in a few minutes," she tells them, pulling up a chair from a nearby table and squeezing it up against the table for two. "Actually it's good I ran into you. I was able to find out some of the things you asked me about last night." She casts a sidelong glance at Amanda. "We were at the most boring party. Did he tell you?"

"Said it was too boring to talk about," Amanda says with a smile.

Jennifer's dark eyes widen. She turns her attention back to Ben. "Seems they got back the initial autopsy reports on John Mallins."

"And?" Ben and Amanda ask together.

"And there are a number of interesting results."

"How so?" Ben asks.

"What do you mean, 'interesting'?" Amanda asks at the same time.

"Well, they're inconclusive, and so, of course, they have to do further testing."

"What do you mean, 'interesting'?" Amanda asks again.

"Well, for one thing, it seems our Mr. Mallins is older than first thought."

"How much older?"

"Ten, maybe even fifteen years, if his internal organs are to be believed."

Ben looks at Amanda. "Which would make him about—"

"—the same age as my mother," Amanda says, finishing the thought.

"Is that significant?" Jennifer asks.

They shrug.

"There's more."

"Go on."

"Well, it seems our Mr. Mallins has had some plastic surgery."

"What kind of plastic surgery?"

"A nose job. And a face-lift. Apparently both done some time ago."

Amanda puts her elbows on the table, balances her head in her hands. What does all this mean? That John Mallins was a desperate man, or merely a vain one? That he was trying to keep up appearances or disguise his appearance altogether? "He was trying to look the age on his passport," Amanda realizes out loud. A passport he stole from the real John Mallins, after he killed him and assumed his identity. Dear God, who was this man?

"That's the other thing," Jennifer says.

"What other thing?" Ben and Amanda ask, their words overlapping.

Jennifer looks a bit taken aback. "You asked about his date of birth."

"Yes?" comes their joint response.

"Well, you were right. According to his passport, it's July fourteenth."

"Shit," says Amanda, her hands dropping into her lap.

"Shit," echoes Ben, leaning back in his chair.

"How'd you know that anyway?"

Neither Ben nor Amanda says a word.

"What's going on here?"

Again, only silence.

"Well, I'd love to sit and chat . . . ," Jennifer says, dark eyes flitting between the two. After a lengthy pause, she pushes back her chair, stands up.

Immediately Ben is on his feet. "Thanks," he says simply.

"For what exactly?"

"I'm not sure."

Jennifer touches his cheek with a tenderness that makes Amanda wince. Then she extends that same hand toward Amanda. "Nice meeting you, Amanda. I hope everything works out."

"Me too."

Amanda watches Jennifer stretch onto her tiptoes to brush her lips against Ben's. "Call me later?"

"Absolutely."

Then she walks to the door, leaving only the scent of lemons behind.

TWENTY-ONE

Right here. This is fine," Amanda says as the taxi pulls to a stop at the corner of Bloor and Palmerston. She hands the driver a crisp, purple $10 bill, tells him to keep the almost $4 in change. What the hell, she thinks, climbing out of the cab into about three inches of freshly fallen snow. It all looks like play money anyway. Blue five-dollar bills, purple tens, green twenties, rose-colored fifties, brown hundreds. Not to mention the one- and two-dollar coins, referred to respectively as loonies and toonies. It's Looney Tunes, all right, she thinks, deciding the coins provide an apt metaphor for her life.

Throwing her purse over one shoulder and her overnight bag over the other, she proceeds down the wide street, lined with giant oak trees and dotted with wonderful, old-fashioned gas lamplights. Snow coats the branches of the trees like a heavy syrup, causing them to droop like the branches of a weeping willow. She pictures those same branches in spring, crowded with new buds just waiting to burst, and feels her face relax into a smile.

Spring was always her favorite time of year: the gradual transition from frigid to more temperate climes as winter grudgingly relinquished its hold on the land; that first tantalizing tease of warm air that appeared in late March only to be pummeled into oblivion by an early-April snowstorm; the snow ultimately washed away by rain, the rain falling on bright yellow daffodils and brilliant red tulips that push their thin, yet surprisingly sturdy, stalks out of the wet ground, demanding their time in the sun.

This changing of the seasons is probably the only thing Amanda misses, living in Florida, where the threat of hurricanes is the only thing that differentiates one season from the next. The palm trees are always full of fronds; the sun shines with monotonous regularity. It might be a little more humid in July, a little chillier in January, but by and large, Florida is a land of constant summer.

Which is why she moved there in the first place, Amanda reminds herself, deliberately hammering her boot heel into a patch of thin ice, watching it crack like glass, then shatter. What is she doing? Who gives a shit about the change in seasons? Yes, at one time she might have enjoyed that first invigorating rush of cool air blowing away the stifling August heat, and, yes, at one time she might have marveled at a sudden November storm that carpeted the city in soft white snow, but experience had taught her that cool breezes had a nasty habit of turning into biting winds, and pure virgin snow too quickly degenerated into slush. The seasons had a way of getting old quickly.

No, Florida is her home now, and she wouldn't have it any other way. It has everything, Amanda tells herself, slipping her overnight bag off her shoulder and stretching the muscles in her neck before repositioning the bag and continuing down the street. It has sun, even though she avoids it with almost religious fervor; the ocean, although she rarely goes to the beach and certainly never swims in the dangerous water—think of the sharks and the sea lice and the invisible undertow, not to mention the occasional oil spills that pollute the sand and tar the bottoms of your feet; shopping malls, even though they're filled with the same stores you can find anywhere, one shop looking pretty much the same as the next—hell, the Eaton Center is as impressive as any of them; culture—just think of the Kravis Center and the Royal Poincianna Playhouse—all right, so Toronto's theater district is second only to New York's, so what?; art—yes, there's the wonderful Norton gallery, and some truly fabulous art shows and lots of charming little galleries, but if she sees one more ceramic frog, she just might scream, I mean, really, how can they call that art? "What am I doing?" Amanda demands, the words sliding out of her mouth into the cold air, like children on a sled, so that she can almost see them written on her breath. "I love ceramic frogs."

Besides:

What Florida doesn't have: her mother.

What Florida also doesn't have: Ben.

Isn't that why she went there in the first place?

Amanda continues south along Palmerston toward Harbord, wondering why she didn't tell the cabbie to let her off directly in front of her mother's house. "Because some things you have to lead up to gradually," she says into the collar of her coat. "Some things you have to take nice and slow. Fools rush in," she whispers, smiling at an elderly man gingerly making his way along the icy sidewalk.

"Damn winter," the man grouses audibly as he passes.

"Damn right," Amanda agrees, soldiering on. And while we're at it—damn Ben, damn her mother, and damn Jennifer. Where did that woman get off, anyway? With her sleek, modern hairdo and flawless complexion. Planting a pre-emptory kiss hello on Ben's cheek. Not to mention that totally unnecessary kiss on the lips as she was leaving, as if to say, He's mine now. **Call me later?** Whose benefit was that for? Certainly not Ben's. And Ben's response? **Absolutely.** Was he really so easily fooled? Couldn't he see that behind Jennifer's calm, competent exterior was . . . what? A calm, competent interior? So what? Who needs calm and competent when you can have competent and chaotic? What's more fun anyway? Damn it. Ben couldn't be in love with this woman.

Unless he was.

Amanda kicks at a mound of snow, watching it disperse like baby powder. And so what if he's in love with Jennifer? What possible difference does that make to her? The fact that they were once husband and wife—briefly, when they were way too young, when they had

no idea what they wanted to do with their
lives, let alone whom they wanted to spend
them with—doesn't give her any residual
claim to his affections. Nor is she interested
in staking any such claim. She's only feeling
this way—what way exactly is she feeling?—
because of circumstance. As soon as she gets
back to Florida, these feelings for her former
husband—what feelings exactly?—will disappear. She's only feeling this way—what way?—
because she's confused and vulnerable and not
used to men who say no. **You can't stay with
me, Amanda,** he'd told her. Although it was
possible he'd been about to change his mind.
Maybe, he was saying, just as calm, competent
Jennifer appeared on the scene.

Maybe what?

"Guess we'll never know." Amanda stops in
front of the brown brick house with the bright
yellow door. We may never know a lot of
things, she thinks, walking toward the front
steps that are all but buried beneath a small
mountain of snow. She treads carefully, feeling
for the concrete with the toes of her boots. We
may never know who John Mallins really is, or
why he had plastic surgery, or who this guy
Turk is, even if it's obvious that her mother
knows.

I'm sorry I was such a bad mother to you, Amanda.

What the hell does **that** mean?

Amanda shuffles through the snow on the landing, stopping at the front door, as if waiting to be admitted. It's not too late, she is thinking. She can still turn around, hail another taxi, hightail it back to the downtown core, find a hotel, **any** hotel, even the Metro Convention Center, maybe call Jerrod Sugar again, ask him if he'd like the pleasure of her company for a night or two.

Sure, she thinks, shrugging off the memory of their last encounter, although in truth, she remembers little of that night except for the way it ended. She was too drunk; he was too eager; the whole thing was over too fast. Or maybe not fast enough, she amends, smiling at the memory of Ben's unscheduled visit, the way he came knocking on her door in the middle of the night, pushing himself into her hotel room over her objections, then flipping on the lights. And then—the startled look on his face when he realized she wasn't alone, the surprise in his eyes giving way to . . . what? Anger? Disappointment? Regret?

What might have happened that night had Jerrod Sugar not been in her bed?

"Guess we'll never know," she says again, fumbling inside her purse for the key to her mother's house. Why did she let Ben talk her into staying here? Yes, it was silly to spend money on a hotel when her mother's house sat empty, and, yes, it would give her another opportunity to search through her mother's things at a more leisurely pace. After all, their previous search had been rather perfunctory, and in light of everything they'd discovered in the last twenty-four hours, it probably wouldn't be a bad idea to go through the house again more carefully. **You never know. You might find something else,** Ben had said before putting her in the taxi and telling her he'd speak to her later.

Call me later?

Absolutely.

"Abso-fucking-lutely," Amanda mutters as she unlocks the front door, pushes it open, and teeters over the threshold, as if she were standing on the edge of a dangerous precipice.

Well, what are you waiting for? she hears her mother shout from upstairs. **Either come in or stay out. Don't stand there letting all the cold air inside.**

The cold air was always inside, Amanda thinks, carrying her overnight bag into the front hall, and kicking the door closed with the heel of her boot.

Suddenly her father is walking toward her, his index finger held tight against his lips, urging her to keep her voice down. **What are you doing?** he whispers. **You know your mother is resting.**

"She's always resting," Amanda says now, as she protested then, her eyes following the memory of her father as he turns his back on her, leaving her to tend to her mother. "That is, when she isn't killing people." Amanda laughs, the giddy sound spiraling through the empty house, bringing another shout from her mother, another plea from her dad.

She kicks off her boots and hangs her new parka in the hall closet, then walks into the living room, absently running her hands across the yellow-and-gray-print sofa that occupies much of the small room. Tiny little dots inside tiny little triangles inside tiny little squares, the pattern repeated again in the trim of the two yellow chairs on either side of the fireplace. A fireplace that was rarely used, Amanda remembers, admiring the towering plant in the far corner of the living room, recalling Corinne Nash's admonition that someone should probably water the plants.

She plops down in one of the chairs, stares through the delicate white sheers drawn across the front windows to the street beyond. As a child, she was never permitted to sit in this room, let alone play in it. No, if she wanted to play, she was supposed to go down to the basement, where any noise she might make wouldn't disturb her mother. Amanda never liked the basement. It was cold and damp and dreary, even with all the lights on. And sometimes there were shadows that scared her, even though her father told her there was nothing to be afraid of.

Once, when she was down there, she'd found a bunch of old hand puppets. Someone had tossed them in a box behind the furnace, and their faces and clothes were so dusty they made Amanda sneeze when she fitted them over her hands. So she brought them upstairs and washed them carefully in the sink. But that made the sink filthy, and she knew her mother would get angry when she saw the mess, and it was important not to make Mommy angry or upset her in any way—wasn't Daddy always telling her that? But Daddy was at work, and Mommy was sleeping, and the puppets looked so much prettier now that they were all cleaned up, surely her mother would see that. Although their hair was still a mess, it could use a good cutting. And she knew where her mother kept her scissors, although she couldn't trim their hair here, not in the kitchen, where her mother might hear her moving around, and it was too dingy in the basement to do the job properly. But the living room was just right. There was carpeting to muffle her footsteps, and the light from the windows so that she could see, and besides, she wouldn't be very long. And maybe when she showed her mother how nicely she'd cleaned up the old puppets, her mother would stop being so sad, and maybe she'd smile and be happy, and then Amanda might even put on a show for her with the puppets, and her mother would laugh the way Amanda remembered she used to laugh. Yes, there was a time when her mother used to laugh, she reminded herself as she carried the puppets into the living room and set up a little impromptu hairdressing salon, and proceeded to cut the dolls' hair, watching the yellow threads scatter across the gray carpet, like flecks of gold dust. And now she'd make her mother laugh again.

Except that her mother wasn't laughing. She was crying, and yelling, and hurling the dolls across the room with such fury that the plastic head of one of the puppets was completely severed, its freshly cut hair spraying out in all directions. **What have you done?** her mother was sobbing, over and over and over again. **What have you done? What have you done?**

I just wanted to make them pretty, the child Amanda whimpered in response, grabbing her stomach and turning away from her mother, doubling over at the waist, as if she'd been punched.

What have you done? came her mother's only response. **What have you done?**

"What have I done?" Amanda asks now, jumping to her feet. "What have I done? Goddamn it, I was six years old. I was a child."

Not for long, she thinks, deciding she can't stay here after all. She marches back into the foyer and pulls on her boots, then retrieves her coat from the closet, the back of her hand brushing up against something cold and hard. Pushing aside several of her mother's coats and jackets, she finds a brand-new shovel with a bright red handle, the price tag still dangling from its thin, wooden neck. Never been used, Amanda thinks, pulling it out of the closet and examining it. No—her mother was too busy shooting people to have time to shovel snow off her front steps.

"What the hell? Might as well do something useful with my time." Amanda removes the price tag—$19.95 from Home Hardware—and steps onto the front porch, leaving the door open behind her as she slides the shovel under the snow and drags it across the concrete, before tossing the snow toward the front lawn. She works steadily, one shovelful of snow quickly replaced by another. Within minutes the landing is clear, and she moves on to the stairs, scraping the shovel along each step until they are free of snow. The walkway is more difficult, the snow more compact, and several times she almost slips on the ice. By the time she reaches the sidewalk, her face is wet with perspiration and her back is filling with unpleasant twinges. What she needs is a hot bath, she decides, remembering Ben's earlier admonition: **Take a hot bath, order room service, and get some sleep.** Sure thing. "What the hell am I doing here?"

"Excuse me," a voice calls from across the street.

Amanda looks toward the sound. What Amanda sees: a young woman in a raccoon coat and black, fur-trimmed hat standing in the middle of the sidewalk on the other side of the street, looking at her expectantly. "I'm sorry? Did you say something?"

The woman looks both ways before crossing the street. Amanda estimates that they're about the same age, although it's impossible to make out exactly what the woman looks like beyond her full cheeks and small, turned-up nose, the tip of which is glowing bright red, like Rudolph's. "I'm sorry to bother you, but my grandmother saw you from across the street and got very agitated. She insisted I come over here to find out 'who's the woman shoveling Gwen Price's snow?'" She nods toward the house behind her.

Amanda looks at the house across the street, then back at the young woman standing in front of her, watching the years fall away from the woman's face, until she disappears into a slightly pudgy, apple-cheeked little girl with big brown eyes and an eager smile. "Sally?"

Wariness replaces curiosity. "Do I know you?"

"It's Amanda. Amanda Tra— Amanda Price." The name feels foreign on her lips, as if it belongs to someone else.

"Amanda! Amanda, oh my God. Amanda. How are you?"

"I'm fine. I mean, considering . . . I assume you've heard about my mother . . ."

"Yes. I can't believe it. How is she?"

"Holding up okay," Amanda says. Better than okay, she thinks. "How are you?"

"I'm good."

"And your grandmother?"

"Not so great."

"What's wrong?"

"What isn't?"

Amanda pictures old Mrs. MacGiver, with her gray hair and blue-veined hands. She always seemed ancient, even when Amanda was a child. "I'm sorry to hear that."

"Well, what can you do? She's eighty-six."

"Does she still bake?" Amanda remembers the lemon cake Mrs. MacGiver brought over after her father's death.

"Not so much anymore. Mostly she just sits in her room and watches TV. But will she consider selling the house and moving into an assisted-living community, which would make life easier on everybody?" The question hangs in the air without completion, the ensuing silence all the answer necessary.

"Do you live with her?"

"Oh, no. I just stopped by to see if she needs anything. Then she saw you, and she insisted I come over immediately."

"I'm glad. It's nice to see you again."

"Nice to see you too. And I'm really sorry about your mother. Did she have some kind of breakdown or something?"

Or something, Amanda thinks, spotting a stooped figure in a long, white flannelette nightgown and a pair of fuzzy blue slippers rapidly descending the steps of the house across the street. "Oh, my God. Sally, your grandmother . . . Mrs. MacGiver, wait. There are cars—"

An approaching driver blasts his horn as old Mrs. MacGiver steps off the curb without looking, her slippers disappearing under the snow. "What the hell!" the driver yells out the window.

"Oh, hold your horses," Mrs. MacGiver shouts in return, thumping on the car's front fender and swatting away her granddaughter's restraining arms, squinting through the cold sun at Amanda. "Who are you?"

"Grandma, for God's sake. You have to get back in the house. You'll freeze to death out here."

"I know you," Mrs. MacGiver says, her watery blue eyes focusing solely on Amanda.

"Grandma, you have to get back inside." Sally tries to surround her with her arms, but her grandmother wriggles away from her.

"I'm Amanda Price," Amanda tells her, the name sounding no less strange for having repeated it. "Gwen's daughter."

Sally quickly removes her coat, throws it across her grandmother's shoulders. "At least put this on."

"I hate raccoon coats," the woman grouses.

"Please, Grandma, raccoons are hardly an endangered species."

"Hah! As far as I'm concerned, they aren't nearly endangered enough. I hate the damn things."

Amanda bursts out laughing, wondering whether life could possibly get any more absurd. "It's nice to see you again, Mrs. MacGiver, but I think Sally's right. It's way too cold to be out here in just a nightgown and slippers."

"I'm freezing," Sally concurs, her teeth already chattering.

Mrs. MacGiver takes several tiny steps forward, her spindly fingers reaching for Amanda's cheek. "Puppet?" she asks.

Amanda takes a sharp intake of breath, feels the air freeze in her lungs as Mrs. MacGiver's fingers brush across her face.

"Puppet," Mrs. MacGiver repeats, now wiggling her fingers in the air, as if operating the strings of a marionette. "Puppet," she says with a giggle. "Puppet, puppet. Who's my little puppet?"

"Okay, that's enough. You're kind of freaking me out here, Grandma," Sally tells her, spinning the old woman around. "She drifts in and out," she offers by way of a parting explanation, leading her grandmother back across the street toward her house. "Nice to see you again, Amanda," Sally says with a wave, before gently pushing her grandmother inside the house and closing the front door behind her.

Amanda tries not to replay the scene in her mind. But even after the two women have disappeared, and even after Amanda has returned to her mother's house, closing first the front door and then the door to her old bedroom, where she takes refuge under the covers, she can still hear the words echoing in the stillness. **Puppet,** the walls whisper as she presses the frilly, pink comforter against her ears.

Puppet. Puppet. Who's my little puppet?

TWENTY-TWO

Amazingly, Amanda falls asleep, not waking up until almost eight o'clock that night. "This can't be right," she marvels, pushing herself out of bed and squinting through the darkness at her watch, tapping impatiently on its round face before lifting it to her ear to hear it tick. "Something's obviously screwy. This can't be right." She flips on the delicate white-and-pink-flowered lamp beside the bed and checks the time again. "No, this isn't right." Except that it's dark outside the window, and the moon is a high, luminous crescent amidst a smattering of bright stars. Can it really be eight o'clock? **At night?** Can she really have slept away an entire afternoon?

Amanda makes her way down the stairs to the kitchen, flipping on the lights as she goes, and compares the big, white clock on the wall beside the stove to the stainless-steel watch on her wrist, noting a discrepancy of only three minutes. "I can't believe it," she tells the empty room, hearing her stomach growl to announce its lack of recent nourishment. She opens the fridge and peers inside, sees a large carton of orange juice and a smaller container of skim milk, as well as some eggs, a couple of Granny Smith apples, and an old, withered lettuce that she quickly discards in the garbage bin underneath the sink. "Nothing to eat. Why am I not surprised?"

She checks the freezer, rifling through several bags of frozen peas and corn, before finding a package of Stouffer's macaroni and cheese behind a large bag of frozen bagels. "Thank you, God," she says out loud, hearing her stomach rumble its appreciation, as she pops the package into the microwave oven. Minutes later, she stands in front of the oven, gobbling the creamy, cheese-covered noodles straight from the container, shoveling one forkful after another of the steaming macaroni into her mouth, and scraping the bottom of the small package until not a speck of sauce remains. "All gone," she says proudly, washing dinner down with a glass of water, then deciding now was as good a time as any to water the plants. Nothing more depressing than a houseful of dead plants, she tells her-

self, finding a pitcher and filling it with luke-
warm water, then balancing on a chair to sprin-
kle the row of leafy plants that line the tops of
the counters. She moves on dutifully to the dining and living rooms and does the same with the
plants there.

It's funny, she is thinking as she returns to
the kitchen to refill the pitcher. She wouldn't
have thought her mother had such a green
thumb. But the plants are all doing miracu-
lously well, their branches full of lush, green
leaves, uniformly shiny and healthy, so perfect
as to be almost fake. They **are** fake, Amanda
realizes minutes later, watching the water she's
pouring spill over the side of a dark blue china
pot on the mantel over the fireplace. "My God,
they're all fake. I don't believe this." She runs
back to the kitchen and grabs some paper tow-
eling, quickly wiping up the spill from the
mantel before it has time to leave a stain, then
retraces her steps, checking the leaves of all the
counterfeit plants she's already watered, and
careful to clean up any mess she might have
made. She repeatedly looks over her shoulder as
she wipes away unsightly spills, as if afraid her
mother might descend the stairs at any moment to berate her for her carelessness and
stupidity.

Her task completed, Amanda lowers herself to the living room floor and sits cross-legged on the gray carpet, wondering when she stopped being able to distinguish between what is real and what is not. Truth is stranger than fiction—isn't that what they say? But when did it get so hard to differentiate between the two?

Probably around the same time her mother started shooting total strangers in hotel lobbies.

Although the man calling himself John Mallins was no stranger to her mother. Amanda is certain of that.

She looks toward the tiny front hall, deciding she should probably call Ben. He's undoubtedly wondering what happened to her. Didn't she promise to call him as soon as she settled in? She sidles over to where her purse is propped up against her overnight bag in the middle of the foyer floor where she dropped them more than eight hours earlier and retrieves her cell phone, staring at it for several long seconds before finally tossing it back inside her purse. Hell, he knows her number. Let **him** call if he wants to speak to her. Which he obviously doesn't, she decides, pulling out her phone again to check for messages, finding none.

So what now?

She's already slept away an entire afternoon, eaten her frozen dinner, and watered the fake plants. What's left? "How about an after-dinner drink?" she asks, crawling toward the liquor cabinet in the dining room, finding nothing inside it but a dozen old crystal glasses and a couple of large fruit platters. "You didn't even keep any liqueurs?" she demands of the empty house, returning to the kitchen and searching through the cupboards there. When had her mother stopped drinking anyway? And couldn't she have kept a little something around in case company dropped in? What's with all this herbal tea crap she keeps finding? "Oh, well, why not?" She's probably been drinking a little too much herself lately, she decides, filling the electric kettle with water, then plugging it in, and waiting for the water to boil.

She sips the surprisingly good, peach-and-raspberry tea while rifling through the various kitchen drawers, finding a desultory collection of old newspaper recipes, now yellowed with age, and stained with grease, in the first drawer she opens. There's a recipe for a cold cream of avocado soup that makes her mouth water, and another one for a cranberry-and-orange soufflé that sounds divine, as well as a whole stack of other recipes for creative things to do with chicken. Amanda reads through all of them, trying to connect these obviously much-used recipes to her mother, a woman who rarely cooked anything other than frozen dinners, and whose idea of dessert was to open a can of fruit cocktail, if she remembered dessert at all.

The next two drawers are filled with ordinary kitchen items: stainless-steel cutlery; colorful, cotton dish towels; round, plastic place mats covered with pictures of succulent purple and red berries; white paper napkins, trimmed in blue and pink swirls. There's a drawer filled to bursting with instructions for operating the various kitchen appliances, along with their accompanying warrantees, and another drawer weighted down with saved wooden chopsticks and plastic cutlery from various take-out restaurants. A telephone-address book sits on top of a large manila folder in the drawer directly underneath the phone, and Amanda flips through the book's pages, not surprised to find most of the pages blank. Nothing under **M** for Mallins. Nothing under **T** for Turk. Although Corinne Nash is listed under both **C** and **N**. On impulse, she checks the **A**'s, and gasps when she sees **AMANDA** printed large across the middle of two pages, **AMA** on one side, **NDA** on the other. Beneath both halves of her name is a list of all the phone numbers she's had since she moved away, as if her mother has been following her from place to place, and from man to man, up to and including her current home and office numbers in Florida, although her mother has never called her at any of these numbers. Amanda makes a dismissive clicking noise with her tongue, then tosses the book back inside the drawer, about to close it when she decides to check inside the large manila folder.

"I'm wasting my time," she says, remembering that Ben has already searched through these very drawers and come up empty-handed. Still, that was before she'd spoken to Rachel Mallins, before they'd heard of a man named Turk, before the puzzling autopsy report had come back. It's entirely possible that Ben, having no idea what he was looking for, might have missed something. She opens the folder, turns it sideways to get a better look at the papers inside.

Report cards, she realizes, lowering herself to the bench along the wall of the little breakfast nook, and spreading the report cards across the laminated tabletop. PALMERSTON

PUBLIC SCHOOL. Name: Amanda Price. Key to Grading: A = excellent, B = good, C = average, D = unsatisfactory, NA = not applicable. And then a list of marks: A's in reading, creative writing, handwriting, spelling, and math. A's in School Citizenship and Study Skills, although only C's for Participation in Class Discussion.

Amanda is a quiet and conscientious student, always a pleasure to have in the class. Again this term, she has produced excellent written work, and her stories are both fanciful and well told. However, I wish she would speak up more in class.

I am very pleased with Amanda's progress. Her homework is always done and presented on time, and her book reports are done with care, although she needs to proofread her work so that unnecessary errors could be avoided. She's very quiet in class, although she seems to get along well with the other children.

Amanda is a quiet, pleasant, hardworking individual and I very much enjoy having her in my grade five class. Her project on Japan was well researched and interestingly presented.

"What the hell?" Amanda asks out loud,

scanning the seemingly endless supply of reports, from junior kindergarten on up. "She saved them all? No, of course she didn't," she says, answering her own question. "It was my father who saved them. She just couldn't be bothered throwing them away."

Once again, I was simply too much of an effort, she thinks, perusing the rest of the report cards, noting the concern in the teachers' comments that started to appear when she transferred into junior high—**Even though her grades are good, I'm a little worried about Amanda's attitude**—and the impatience that was evident in their comments by the time she reached high school. **Amanda would benefit from a stronger work ethic. She prefers to coast on her natural ability and lacks discipline. Her attendance in class also leaves something to be desired.**

"Passed, didn't I?" Amanda demands, slapping the folder shut and jumping to her feet, then dumping the folder with all its report cards into the garbage bin underneath the sink. "Made it into law school, didn't I? Near perfect LSATs. Hah!" What the hell am I doing? she wonders, quickly retrieving the report cards from the garbage and picking off several wilted lettuce leaves before returning the folder to its former resting place in the drawer. I'm going crazy, that's what I'm doing. And why not? "It runs in the family," she announces to the empty house. She returns to the foyer, throws her purse over one shoulder and her overnight bag over the other, and totes them up the stairs, pushing one weary leg in front of the other, hearing her muscles groan, as if she is navigating a steep mountain. Might as well go back to bed, she decides, suddenly over-whelmed with fatigue.

Maybe I'm coming down with something, she thinks. Maybe I picked something up on the plane. Everyone knows planes are hotbeds for germs. All that stale air. People cramped together in a narrow, confined space, coughing and sneezing. And then the extreme change in the weather, the cold air she's no longer used to. Not to mention the circumstances that have brought her here, the reunion with her mother and former husband, the unpleasant reminders of a past she thought she'd put behind her. It was enough to make anyone tired. Plus all that damn snow she shoveled. No wonder her arms ache and her back is stiff. No wonder she's ex-hausted. No wonder all she wants to do is climb into bed and go back to sleep.

The light is still on in her old bedroom. She

moves directly to the window and stares out at the driveway that runs between her mother's house and the house next door, thinking of poor old Mr. Walsh and trying to recall the details of his face. But beyond the wrinkles that drooped across his face like heavy curtains, and the limp strings of white hair that fell across the top of his mostly bald head, all she can see is the massive stomach that strained at the buttons of his short-sleeved shirts and poured over the tops of his perpetually stained Bermuda shorts in summer. While the setting is clear, the man's features are fuzzy and indistinct, like a photograph in which the background is in focus but the main subject is a frustrating blur. Amanda can picture a dark green sedan pulling to a stop in the middle of their mutual driveway; she can see a giant walrus of a man pushing himself out of the car; she can make out the sweat dripping off his forehead as he casts a furtive glance over his shoulder toward her mother's house and hears his derisive snort. For an instant, Amanda even thinks she sees a sneer playing with the corners of his lips. "Why, you miserable son of a bitch," she says out loud. "You parked there on purpose." No wonder my mother put a curse on you.

"Please don't tell me I'm actually sympathizing with my mother," Amanda moans loudly, unpacking her few belongings and spreading them across the bed. "Now I know I'm sick." Certainly I must have been suffering from some sort of delirium when I bought this, she thinks, holding her new purple sweater out in front of her. Purple, for God's sake. And mohair. When is she ever going to wear it? "I'll wear it to bed," she decides, stripping off her clothes and pulling the sweater over her head, feeling it toasty and warm against her bare skin.

She grabs her toothbrush and walks into the bathroom, stares at herself in the mirror over the sink, surprised to see how good the purple sweater looks on her, how nicely it meshes with her blond hair and compliments the delicate blush in her cheeks.

I don't think I've ever told you how beautiful you are.

I certainly don't look very beautiful now, Amanda thinks, brushing her teeth and washing her face, then pushing her face close to the glass, examining her skin for tiny lines. "You're never too young to start moisturizing," she tells her reflection, opening the medicine cabinet and staring in openmouthed amazement at the rows of pill bottles that line the shelves.

Scattered among the usual over-the-counter medications, she finds numerous bottles of Tylenol 3 and Percodan, as well as prescriptions for a host of well-known antidepressants, several of which have lately been found to induce psychosis in an alarming number of people. Is her mother one of those people? Was she under the influence of one or more of these powerful narcotics when she shot and killed John Mallins? Amanda checks the dates on the various bottles, noting that each has long since expired. Is it possible her mother had been taking these drugs for a long time, then stopped cold turkey, resulting in a chemical imbalance that rendered her incapable of rational thought, thus making her a victim of diminished capacity and clearly not responsible for her actions?

Amanda races back into her bedroom, grabs her cell phone from her purse, about to call Ben and share with him her latest discovery and apologize profusely for having failed to check the medicine cabinet the last time they were here. What was the matter with her? How could she have missed anything so obvious?

Except:

What difference does it make that her mother might have been abusing prescription drugs, if her mother persists in claiming she knew what she was doing and knew it to be wrong? What difference does it make if her mother went off the drugs cold turkey, or that she was taking drugs that had long since passed their expiry date, if her mother refused to consider a plea of diminished capacity, which she undoubtedly would?

Still . . .

Amanda presses in Ben's telephone number, listens to its repeated rings, and hangs up before Ben's voice mail can click on. No point in leaving a message. She'll probably be asleep by the time he gets home. With Jennifer undoubtedly glued to his side. And why not? Why shouldn't they be together? Jennifer is attractive and smart, and it's unlikely her mother goes around shooting people in hotel lobbies. Clearly, she's a much saner choice, a much safer bet. Undoubtedly, Ben's mother would have approved. And his father, she thinks, picturing the handsome, senior Mr. Myers, now on his honeymoon with her former history teacher.

So funny how things work out.

Ben's father is about the same age as her ex-husband, Sean, she realizes, grimacing at the disconcerting thought as she wanders into her mother's bedroom and flips on the light.

Whatever had possessed her to marry Sean any-way? More to the point, what had possessed Sean to marry her? True, she was young and pretty, but Florida was full of young and pretty women, and smart and sophisticated men like Sean weren't easily impressed. So what had he seen in her? And how could he love her—how could any man really love her?—when her own father had been so indifferent? When her own mother had looked at her and seen right through her, deemed her unfit to love?

Amanda walks toward the alcove beside her mother's bed, her eyes scanning the miniature crystal knickknacks sitting on the shelf, her fingers gently caressing a small glass poodle with tiny black beads that serve as its eyes and nose. "Okay, enough of this. This is getting us nowhere." She marches over to her mother's dresser, begins rummaging impatiently through the drawers. "Same stuff that was here last time I looked," she mutters, closing the last of the drawers and glancing out the window, staring at Mrs. MacGiver's house across the street.

Someone is standing in the upstairs window, Amanda realizes, taking a step back even as her body leans forward to catch a better glimpse. "Mrs. MacGiver, is that you?" she whispers, inching back toward the window, leaning her forehead against the cold pane of glass. The figure in the opposite window retreats, disappearing behind layers of curtains. Seconds later, the lights in the room go out.

Amanda stands for several minutes staring into the darkness, wondering how many of her old neighbors are still around, if any of them is watching her now. Maybe she should canvass the street tomorrow, talk to people who know her mother. It's possible someone might be able to shed some light on the situation. People often know more than they think they do. Although experience has taught her they generally know less.

"Okay, enough of this," she says to anyone who might be watching. "For all those who are interested, I'm going to bed now. How does everyone like my new sweater, by the way? You like the color? Don't think purple's too much? Good. Okay. Well, sleep tight, and pleasant dreams." She flips off the light, returns to her old room, and crawls into bed. "Who am I kidding? I'll never fall asleep," she says, the words barely out of her mouth before she drifts into unconsciousness.

Amanda?

Amanda opens her eyes to see a skinny boy

with a big wooden head and a high pompadour of black painted-on hair walking toward her. He is wearing a crisp white shirt tucked inside a pair of stiff denim jeans, and his eyes are as green as his smile is wide.

Dance with me, he says, his hands jerking into position in front of him.

Amanda climbs out of bed and curtsies, the boy responding with a low bow. Seconds later, she is securely fastened inside the boy's wooden arms, and he is spinning her around a tall stage.

I like your new sweater, he tells her as a gust of cold air blows against her face, freezing her smile, and causing her skin to harden, like ice. Her arms and legs begin moving in careless abandon, without thought or grace. First her right knee lifts into the air, then her left hand, then both legs together. Then her right arm shoots out to one side, her mouth opening and closing, although the voice that emerges is no longer her own.

Puppet, puppet, the unfamiliar voice chants, the muscles in her back starting to twitch, as if a fishhook were lodged between her shoulder blades. **Who's my little puppet?**

"Shit," Amanda says, jumping up and reaching for the lamp beside the bed, watching the

dream evaporate in a burst of bright light. She
runs her hand through her hair and tries to
calm the wild beating of her heart, every muscle in her body starting to ache. "Should never
have shoveled all that damn snow." Despite the
fact she's now wide-awake, the strange voice
continues to reverberate in the recesses of her
mind. Whose voice? she wonders, pushing herself out of bed, and walking into the hall, shaking her shoulders in an effort to free herself
from the uncomfortable feeling that someone is
still pulling her strings.

TWENTY-THREE

Amanda shuffles into the bathroom, where she turns on the tap and splashes several handfuls of cold water across her face, a face that she is startled to realize is already wet with tears. "What the hell am I crying about?" she asks her reflection impatiently, watching the familiar shake of her head in the glass, her head continuing to twist feverishly back and forth until her hair wraps itself around her eyes, like a surprise pair of hands—"Guess who?"—and the offending image disappears. She stands this way for several seconds, her head bowed, her hair clinging to her damp skin, her breathing punctuated by a rhythmic series of stillborn cries that threaten to burst from her body, like the final ticks of a bomb strapped uncomfortably around her chest. Her left hand reaches blindly toward the towel rack, her veiled eyes noting the time on the watch she forgot to remove when she crawled into bed. She's surprised to realize it's just past eleven o'clock. "Not even midnight," she grouses, drying her face with a scratchy white towel, and filling the pink plastic glass at the side of the sink with water, drinking it down in one long gulp. "What am I supposed to do till morning?"

She thinks of going downstairs and getting something to eat, but then she remembers the state of her mother's fridge and decides that Granny Smith apples don't exactly cut it as comfort food. Too healthy. Too good for you to be of any good to you in times of crises, when what you crave is something rich and gooey and overflowing with calories, like the macaroni and cheese she has already dispensed with. Of course, she could get dressed and try to find an all-night grocery store, although she's not sure Toronto even has such things. Or she could simply order a pizza. Surely there are restaurants that are still open and prepared to deliver at this hour. It's hardly the middle of the night. Or better yet, she could call Swiss Chalet. How long has it been since she had one of their half-chicken dinners with french fries smothered in tangy barbecue sauce? Much too long, she decides, returning to the bedroom and reaching inside her purse for her cell phone, already feeling her mouth watering in anticipation. She flips open her phone, is about to call information for the restaurant chain's number, when she sees she has a message waiting.

"Hi. It's me. Ben," his recorded message states without emotion, although the fact he deemed it necessary to add his name carries an inherent hint of recrimination. "I just wondered how you were doing, but since you're out and about, I guess you're fine." A slight pause, then: "Call me in the morning."

"Out and about," Amanda repeats in Ben's Canadian twang, so that the words emerge as **oot** and **aboot**. "Yes, I'm oot and aboot all right." Oot and aboot in nothing but my new mohair sweater, wandering the upstairs halls of my mother's house, like some big purple ghost, she continues silently. Salivating over the thought of a greasy fast-food dinner, my second of the night, incidentally, so quite obviously, there's nothing wrong with my appetite, which I guess means I'm doing fine, thank you so much for your concern.

She replays Ben's message three times before erasing it. "When did you call anyway?" she asks the tiny phone, angry at herself for going to bed so early, for not taking the damn thing out of her purse, for not hearing it ring. She checks her watch again, decides it's not too late to call him back. Surely he doesn't go to bed before midnight.

Call me later?

Absolutely.

Amanda presses in Ben's number, her finger poised to disconnect should his answering machine pick up.

"Hello?" Ben asks before the first ring is completed. His voice is warm, welcoming. She wants to curl up inside it.

"It's me." Unlike her former husband, she doesn't bother to clarify who "me" is. "I just got your message."

"Where are you?"

"Home," she says, the word teetering awkwardly on her tongue. "My mother's," she corrects instantly. "When did you call?"

"A few hours ago."

"I fell asleep. I didn't hear my phone ring."

"You feeling all right?"

"Yeah. A little hungry."

He laughs.

"I don't suppose you feel like going out for something to eat?"

"Can't," he says without further explanation.

An annoying habit, Amanda decides, picturing Jennifer gazing at him from the other side of the room, her head tilted quizzically in his direction, as if to ask, Who's calling at this time of night? She swats the unpleasant image aside with a flick of her wrist, watching Jennifer fly into the air and explode, like cheap fireworks, before being swallowed by the dark night sky.

"So, have you had a chance to look around?" he asks as Amanda struggles to recall the details of her day. "You find anything we missed last time?"

"Yes," she says, her voice rising with excitement as the contents of her mother's medicine cabinet pop clearly into view. "I found pills."

"Pills?"

"At least ten bottles of them. Antidepressants, painkillers—you name them, they're in her medicine cabinet. Most of them expired years ago, but that doesn't mean she hasn't been taking them. Did she ever say anything to you about being on medication?"

"The only pills I've ever heard your mother mention are her calcium," Ben says, and Amanda can almost see him shaking his head in wonderment.

"Do you think we have a shot at diminished capacity?"

"It's certainly something to consider. You find anything else?"

"Nothing," Amanda says. "Except that all the plants in her house are plastic."

He laughs again, the hearty sound reaching through the phone wires to caress her cheek.

Amanda suddenly fears that he is about to hang up, that she has exhausted her usefulness and has nothing of interest left to offer. "You have plants?" she asks, tightly gripping the phone, as if trying to hold on to him.

"A few. But they're not doing very well. Too much sun, I think."

Amanda tries to picture Ben's condominium at Harborside, with its floor-to-ceiling windows overlooking the lake, but all she can see is the tiny, second-floor, one-bedroom apartment on Vaughan Road they once shared. The apartment was located in an old yellow-brick building that had even then seen better days. No elevator. No air-conditioning. No dishwasher. The bedroom barely big enough for a double bed, the two of them unable to move about the room at the same time, the living room not much bigger, barely large enough to accommodate the creaky old sofa they'd picked up at Goodwill, their downstairs neighbor forever banging on his ceiling with a broom, his way of telling them they were playing their stereo—the only household item they owned that was actually worth anything—too loud. "You remember our apartment on Vaughan Road?" she hears herself ask.

A slight pause before he answers. "Who could forget?"

"It was pretty awful."

"That it was."

"I liked it though."

"I liked it too."

Another pause. Longer than the first. For a moment Amanda fears they've been disconnected. "Ben?"

"Yes?"

"Nothing." She shakes her head, as if he can see her. "I was just afraid you weren't there."

"I'm here."

Amanda smiles sadly. She's made such a mess of things, she thinks, wanting to apologize to him for running out on him the way she did, for all the disruptions she's brought to his life, for all the pain she's caused. "So, what do we do now?" she asks instead.

"I'm in court first thing in the morning," he answers, oblivious to the question's larger implications. "But we should probably drive up to see your mother in the afternoon, if that's convenient for you. I'd like to find out about this pill business."

"What time?"

"Can you be at my office at two o'clock?"

"Of course."

"Good. I'll see you then."

"See you then," Amanda repeats, reluctant to end the conversation.

"Sleep well, Amanda."

"You too."

And then that awful stillness when someone disconnects. Amanda listens to the unwelcome silence for several seconds, straining to hear Ben's breathing on the other end of the line, before reluctantly accepting his absence and snapping her cell phone shut, then dropping it back inside her purse. Almost immediately, she retrieves it, deciding to leave it on the night table beside the bed in case he calls back.

She lowers herself onto the narrow bed and sits staring at the Renoir print on the opposite wall. How many nights had she lain in this bed staring at that painting, with its joyous depiction of a carefree young woman in a long, frilly dress, balancing on a swing in the middle of a crowded park, her body leaning into the sunlight, her round face glowing pink with serenity, completely at ease with her privileged existence, as if such happiness was somehow her due? How she'd envied this girl who wore her entitlement as proudly and easily as the dark blue bows that decorated the front of her creamy white dress, a girl with the confidence to **stand** on a swing. How many times had she prayed to trade places with her, to be the girl in the sunlight surrounded by admirers, and not the child shivering alone beneath her covers night after night?

When she was little, she'd actually imagined that if she got close enough to the picture, she might actually be absorbed inside it, and so one night she'd climbed up on the desk and knelt before the painting, pressing her nose against it until it started to hurt and the glass covering the picture fogged with her breath. The girl on the swing remained blissfully unaware of her presence, and Amanda silently cursed the young woman her selfishness. "I hope you fall off and break your neck," she'd hissed at the wall before crying herself to sleep. But the next morning, the girl was still standing on the swing, looking as contented and peaceful as ever. Clearly, Amanda's powers of destruction weren't as great as her mother's.

"Want to bet?" Amanda asks now, visually pushing the young woman off her comfortable perch and watching her fall to the ground, dirt soiling her frilly dress, a deep gash opening on her forehead, bathing the soft impressionist palette in bright red blood. Amanda lies down on her bed, closing her eyes in satisfaction. Just ask Ben whose powers are greater. Ask Sean. Ask her father.

Amanda groans audibly and turns over onto her stomach, trying to find a comfortable position. But guilt, like a lover who takes up more than his fair share of the bed, keeps nuzzling up against her, and after ten minutes of restlessly flipping from one side to the other, trying to stay out of his reach, she abandons any notion of sleep. Maybe she'll watch some television. There must be a hockey game on somewhere, she thinks, climbing out of bed and walking back into the hall.

She has no intention of going into the middle bedroom, and so she is surprised to find herself lingering in its doorway. She has no intention of proceeding to the closet, so she is startled to find herself standing in front of it, her hand hovering over the doorknob. She certainly has no intention of picking up the puppet stage and carrying it into the center of the room, so she is amazed to find herself sitting on the floor, separating the strings of the marionettes, then dangling them over the stage's tall, wooden backdrop. "Hi, guys," she says, watching the puppets bow and curtsy in turn.

Hi, yourself, cutie, the boy puppet replies with a slight cock of his wooden head.

Where've you been? the girl puppet asks politely.

Amanda shrugs, twirls the puppets around the stage.

They move together easily, sailing gracefully through the air, the girl's head resting on the boy's shoulder, the boy's arm draped protectively across the girl's shoulder, their limbs gradually overlapping, their strings becoming entwined, wrapping around one another like vines around the trunk of a tree, until the two puppets become one, impossible to separate without causing irreparable damage. True love, Amanda thinks wistfully, picturing herself in Ben's arms, feeling his cheek against hers, his arm pressing into the small of her back.

Nobody before or since has ever been able to make her feel the way Ben did, as if by touching her, he was reaching clear into her soul.

Except she doesn't want anyone reaching that far inside her. Because if he does, he'll find out there's nothing there. Nobody worth knowing. Certainly nobody worth loving. Because if your own mother didn't love you . . .

"What am I doing?" Amanda demands in the voice of someone waking up from a prolonged trance. "What the hell am I doing?" She tears the strings from her fingers, causing the puppets to jerk and pull apart. In disgust, she throws them across the room, watching them bounce off the wall and collapse on the bed, one on top of the other, as if determined to complete what she has started. She spins around in helpless circles, her agitation increasing with each turn. "Damn it. What's wrong with you?" She bends down and scoops up the wooden stage, then takes a final spin around and hurls it toward the window, like an athlete throwing a shot put. The stage misses the window by mere inches, crashing instead against the wall and taking a chip out of its pale pink surface before shattering. Pieces of wood fly into the air, like debris after an explosion.

Amanda stares at the mess. Tiny wooden planks litter the top of the desk, looking like the Popsicle sticks she used to collect as a child. The floor of the stage has separated from its sides and hovers precariously over the edge of the desk, swaying in anticipation of its imminent fall. Jagged slivers of wood are everywhere. "Great," Amanda mutters. "I've made another mess." She backs out of the room and heads down the stairs to the kitchen to retrieve the Dustbuster. First the plants, and now this. "I'm just a walking disaster area." Maybe her mother had been right to keep her distance.

By the time she returns to the room, the Dustbuster and green garbage bag in hand, the stage floor has already tumbled off the desk and now lies upside down on the gray broadloom, sawdust leaking from its broken form, like blood. "Sorry about that," Amanda apologizes, about to toss the large piece of wood into the garbage bag when she notices the corner of what appears to be a business card sticking out from a long crack in the wood. "What's this?" Slowly and carefully, she extricates the card from its hiding place.

AAA Water Purification Systems, the card announces in bold black letters. **Walter Turofsky, Sales Manager.**

"What the hell is this?" Amanda shakes the piece of wood, watches as several more business cards fall to the floor. She drops to her knees, examining one card, then the next, and the next.

AAA Property Management Inc. George Turgov, President.

AAA Flooring Company. Milton Turlington, Sales Representative.

AAA Waterproofing Inc. Rodney Tureck, Senior Vice President.

"What's going on here?" Amanda's eyes dart from one business card to the other. What are all these companies? And who are all these men? Turofsky, Turgov, Turlington, Tureck? "Turk," Amanda states, the name rising from the pit of her stomach. "Turk," she says again, this time the name exploding on her tongue. "Goddammit, I know it's you." The man the real John Mallins had been involved with before he disappeared. "What are you doing here?"

Amanda tries peering between the narrow slats of the stage floor to see if there is anything else secreted inside. But the space is too thin and dark for her to know for sure. Shaking the piece of wood as hard as she can brings no results. "What the hell," she decides, slamming the piece of wood against the side of the desk, watching it break in two. The corner of a shiny piece of paper instantly pops into view, peeking out from inside what is left of the puppet stage. Amanda slides the paper out, careful not to tear it, then flips it over. "Dear God, what the hell is this?" she gasps, falling back on the splinter-laden broadloom.

What Amanda sees: a photograph.

And while the picture is faded, scratched, and crinkled, the image is unmistakable. It is a photograph of a man holding a young girl on his lap. Both are smiling and happy, sharing a private joke. The man is the man her mother shot and killed. The girl is his daughter, Hope.

What is her mother doing with this picture? How did she get it? Why does she have it? How long has she been hiding it?

By the look of it, the picture is at least three or four years old. Hope looks to be about nine or ten, although she still has essentially the same face she had when Amanda saw her several days ago, the same dark hair, the same piercing eyes. Her father is thinner, handsomer than the passport picture that ran in the newspapers, although a thin crease in the paper cuts across his cheek like a scar. "Turk?" Amanda asks his smiling face. "It's you, isn't it?"

The man's smile in the photograph seems to widen, as if he is taunting her.

What's wrong with this picture? Amanda thinks.

"I'm going to find out, you know," she tells him, searching the picture for clues, finding none. It is what it is: a father and his daughter sit underneath a large tree in what appears to be someone's backyard; their clothing is summery, but otherwise nondescript; there are no telltale buildings in the background, no rare flowers growing at their feet; a generic blue sky fills the background. "I'm going to find out if you're George Turgov or Rodney Tureck or Milton Turlington or Walter Turofsky, or whoever else you might have called yourself. I'm going to find out what you did with John Mallins. And I'm going to find out how my mother got this picture," she says with a determination that surprises and astounds her. "Even if it kills me."

TWENTY-FOUR

Less than five minutes later, Amanda has pulled on a pair of black pants under her purple sweater and is running down the stairs, her purse flung over one shoulder, her cell phone pressed against her ear. "Pick up, dammit," she mutters, reaching the foyer and fumbling with her boots. "Come on, Ben. I haven't got all night."

The call is answered at the start of its fourth ring. "Hello?" a sleepy voice says. A woman's voice, Amanda realizes, a rush of fresh adrenaline pushing an unwanted twinge of disappointment out of the way.

"Jennifer, hi. I'm sorry to be calling so late. I need to speak to Ben."

"Who is this?"

"It's Amanda," she answers, not bothering to hide her annoyance. What's the matter with this woman? Who else would be calling Ben at this hour of the night?

"Who?"

"Jennifer, just put Ben on the goddamn phone. This is an emergency."

"You're looking for Ben and Jennifer? Are you kidding me?" the woman says just before the line goes dead in Amanda's hand.

"Ben and Jennifer—shit!" Amanda shouts at the ensuing silence, unwanted images of the infamous Hollywood duo dancing around her head. "Oh, that's perfect. Perfect." She chases the images away with a swat of her hand and makes the call again, taking extra care to punch in the correct numerals, this time forgetting to include the area code—she didn't need an area code for a local call eight years ago—and listening as an annoying recorded message tells her to try her call again. "I don't want to try the call again." Amanda drops the phone back inside her purse, careful not to disturb the photograph and business cards she has tucked inside a flower-trimmed pink envelope—the stationery in the bottom drawer of her old dresser having proved very handy. She pushes her bare feet inside her boots, the thick lining feeling soft and warm on her toes, then reaches inside the closet for her coat, throwing it over her shoulders as she opens the front door and steps outside, shoving her arms through the sleeves just as a bitter wind whips snow into her eyes. "Could we please do something about the weather?" she shouts at the black sky before hurrying down the steps and along the path she shoveled earlier to the street. There should be plenty of cabs on Bloor, she thinks, deciding against calling Ben again. Better to just show up at his door, present him with her discovery firsthand. If Jennifer is with him, well, so what? What difference does it make? By Friday, this whole mess will be over one way or the other, and she'll be on the first plane back to Florida. And she won't see Ben ever again, no matter how many strangers her mother guns down.

In fact, it will be good if Jennifer is with Ben, Amanda decides, reaching the corner of Palmerston and Bloor, her eyes searching both sides of the road for a taxi, finding none. It will put an end to all this silly romanticizing once and for all. She's never had much patience for romance.

Amanda sees the crest of a taxi behind an approaching car, and she waves her hands over her head in an effort to attract the driver's attention, but either he doesn't see her or he deliberately ignores her. Either way, he doesn't stop. Neither does the next cabbie who, she notices as he speeds past, already has a passenger in his backseat. "Damn it," she mutters, tapping the toes of her boots together, her bare feet already growing cold inside their fleece lining. Should have put on socks, she thinks, walking east along Bloor. "Come on," she wails as a series of cars whiz past. "Where are all the damn taxis?"

She finally spots one on the other side of the street, about to head north. "No," she shouts, running across the road and waving her arms frantically in front of her. "Not that way. Over here. Over here." The taxi stops, and she slides toward the car on a frozen stream of slush. "Thank you," she whispers hoarsely, climbing inside, automatically checking the driver's name on his ID, thinking, Wouldn't it be funny if his name turned out to be Walter Turofsky or George Turgov or Milton Turlington or Rodney Tureck?—and almost laughing out loud when she sees his name is Igor Lavinsky.

"Where to?" the man asks over his shoulder. His skin is pasty and deeply lined. Thick brown hair falls across his forehead into preternaturally dark eyes. A half-smoked cigarette dangles from his lips despite a prominent sign on the dashboard advising passengers to refrain from smoking.

"Harborside," Amanda says, wiggling her toes inside her boots in an effort to warm them. She leans back in her seat and exhales a deep breath, watching it take shape and rise into the air, like a genie released from a bottle.

"You okay?" the driver asks, his eyes narrowing in his rearview mirror. "You no going to be sick inside my cab, I hope."

"No. Oh, no. I'm not going to be sick. I'm just cold."

"Cold. Yes, is very cold. But coat look very warm."

"Yes," Amanda agrees, unconsciously assuming the man's thick Russian accent as she draws the coat's collar tight against her neck. "Coat is very warm."

"Nice coat," the taxi driver says before turning up the melancholy wail of a saxophone on the radio, signaling an end to the conversation.

Five minutes later, Amanda exits the cab and runs for the large glass door of Ben's condominium. The wind from the lake turns her hair into hundreds of tiny whips, lashing at her face. It fights her efforts to open the already heavy door, then pushes past her into the marble foyer, as if it too is desperate to escape the cold. Amanda shivers as she pushes the hair away from her eyes to scan the list of occupants, finally locating Ben's name, and pressing in his code.

"Come on up. Ten twelve, in case you forgot," he announces over the intercom, not even bothering to ask who it is. Did he see her taxi pull up from his window? Does his apartment wrap around the corner of the building, affording him a look at both Lake Ontario and Lake Shore Boulevard? The buzzer sounds to unlock the inner door, and Amanda hurries into the large, marble lobby, taking scant notice of the tastefully muted furniture and bright modern tapestry that hangs on the wall beside the elevators. Luckily, an elevator is waiting, its door already open, and she steps inside, pressing the button for the tenth floor.

By the time she reaches Ben's apartment, Amanda is almost starting to feel her toes again. What she needs is a nice cup of hot peach-and-raspberry tea, she thinks, knocking gingerly on Ben's door.

"What took you so long?" he asks as he opens the door, then stops, his face freezing in surprise. "Amanda!"

"Don't you know it's dangerous to let people

into the building without even asking who they are?"

"I assumed I knew who it was." He looks up and down the hall.

"Never assume. Didn't they teach you that in law school? Are you going to invite me in or what?"

Ben takes another look down the hall, as if considering the "or what?" part of the question, then steps aside to let her enter. "What are you doing here?" he asks, watching as she leans against the high black table that sits underneath the oval mirror in his small foyer and pulls off her boots. "Good God—you went out in this weather without any socks?"

"I was in a hurry." She pulls off her coat. "Can we hang this up?"

"Can you tell me what you're doing here?"

"I have something to show you."

"Aside from your purple toes?"

"They match my sweater," Amanda jokes, proceeding into the living room, feeling strangely at ease, considering the circumstances. After all, she's freezing, it's closing in on midnight, and she's standing in the middle of her ex-husband's apartment in her bare feet, her toes are numb, and said ex-husband is obviously and anxiously awaiting the arrival of his new girlfriend. Not to mention, she's clutching a purse that is heavy with bewildering new information. And yet, she feels . . . what? Happy. Peaceful. Even serene. Like Renoir's girl on a swing, she realizes, leaning forward into an imaginary ray of sunlight.

"Have you been drinking?" Ben asks, following her into the living room.

"No, although that sounds like a wonderful idea."

He shrugs, as if realizing he is no longer master of his own domain. "What'll it be?"

"A cup of tea?"

"You want tea?"

"Peach-raspberry, if that's possible."

"Peach-raspberry," he mutters, shaking his head as he walks toward the kitchen.

Amanda's eyes sweep across the casually furnished living and dining areas. The walls are cream-colored, the sofa a soft, butterscotch-colored suede that doesn't quite go with the black leather lounger across from it. Six smoky-gray plastic chairs are grouped around a rectangular glass table in the dining area, and several geometrically abstract paintings hang on the walls across from the floor-to-ceiling windows overlooking the lake. Amanda walks to the window, leans her head against it, and peers into the darkness, thinking she can almost hear the waves rustling through the icy waters of Lake Ontario.

"I don't have any peach-raspberry tea," Ben announces from the kitchen. "I only have Red Rose."

"Red Rose it is." Amanda approaches the kitchen, watches from the doorway as Ben fills a kettle with water and drops a tea bag into a mug whose sides are decorated with sunflowers. "I like your place," she tells him, sitting down at the small glass kitchen table.

"Why are you here?"

"I know who Turk is."

"What? How?"

"I found something. In my mother's house."

Ben lowers himself to the chair across from her, leans forward on his elbows, giving her his full attention. He is wearing jeans and a blue shirt, open at the collar. Amanda thinks she has never seen him look so handsome. "What did you find?"

"These." Amanda pulls the pink envelope from her purse, extricates the business cards, and spreads them around the table.

"What's this?"

"See for yourself."

" 'Triple A Water Purification Systems,

Walter Turofsky, Sales Manager,' " Ben reads, his eyes moving warily from card to card. " 'Triple A Flooring Company, Milton Turlington, Sales Representative . . . Rodney Tureck . . . George Turgov.' " Ben lifts his face to Amanda's.

"Turk," she says as their eyes connect.

"Where did you find these?"

"In the spare bedroom," Amanda says simply, deciding to spare him the gory details of exactly how she came to find them. "I must have missed them the first time around."

"Anything else?"

Amanda pushes the photograph she found in front of Ben. "That's our man with his daughter, Hope. Probably taken about four years ago."

"How did your mother get it?"

"I don't know."

"Do you think she took the picture?"

"I don't know."

"So what exactly do we know?"

"I don't know."

He smiles. "Okay, then. Good. Well, there you go." A whistle sounds, signaling the water is ready. Ben rises from his chair, pours the boiling water into the waiting mug. "Milk and sugar?"

Amanda nods. "So, what do you think this means?" She wraps her hands around the mug he hands her, feeling the sunflowers glow against her palms.

"It means we have something else to ask your mother about."

"You think she'll tell us anything?"

"Probably not." He sneaks a glance at his watch. "Drink your tea."

"Trying to get rid of me?"

A long pause, tempered only by his smile. "Truthfully, I'm still not sure what you're doing here."

Amanda motions toward her findings on the table. "You don't think this was worth a trip?"

"I think it could have waited till tomorrow."

Amanda feels his gentle rebuke with the same force as a violent shaking of her shoulders. He's right, of course. This could easily have waited until morning. There was no need for her to rush over at midnight. He's obviously misinterpreted her enthusiasm for something else entirely, assumed her being here is really about him, and not her mother. She's made a fool of herself, she realizes, suddenly seeing herself through his eyes, finding the image disdainful, even—what was the word he once used?—desperate. She has to get out of here. She gulps at her tea, feels it burn the tip of her tongue as the steam rises to her eyes, causing them to tear. "Dammit. I burned my tongue."

"I told you to drink your tea, not swallow it whole."

"Can't do anything right, can I?"

"That's not what I said."

"Look, it's obvious you want me out of here. So, fine. I'm out of here." She jumps to her feet, her hands shaking with anger, and tries unsuccessfully to maneuver the photograph and the business cards back into their pretty pink envelope. After several seconds, she gives up, tossing the items loose into her purse. "Thanks for the tea. Sorry I bothered you." She marches into the dining area, slamming her hip against the corner of the glass table. "Shit!" she hollers, picturing a nice purple bruise and picking up her pace.

Ben is right behind her, his hand grazing her elbow. "Amanda, wait. What are you doing?"

"I'm leaving before the next shift arrives." She shrugs away his arm and continues through the living room to the foyer. "Isn't that what you're afraid of? That Jennifer might see us together and jump to the wrong conclusions?" She pushes her foot inside one still-freezing boot, begins struggling with the other.

"Amanda, wait," he says again.

"What?" She looks up at him, her right foot half-in, half-out of the stubborn boot.

"Would her conclusions really be so wrong?" he asks simply.

For a moment, the only sound is their breathing. "What are you talking about?"

"Look. I've obviously never been very good at reading you. So maybe I'm all wet here."

"You're all wet," Amanda agrees.

"It's just that you show up at my apartment in the middle of the night—"

"Midnight is hardly the middle of the night."

"—with some information that, however intriguing it might be—"

"I'm sorry I disturbed you. I thought you'd be interested."

"—could have waited until morning."

"The last time I withheld information from you, you got angry."

"I got angry because you went off half-cocked on your own. I got angry because you put yourself in danger."

"I'm not in danger now," Amanda says.

"And I'm not the one who's angry."

Amanda kicks off the boot dangling from her right foot. "Okay, this is getting us nowhere. And I've never been very good at subtleties, so spit it out. What are you saying exactly? That you think I came over here to seduce you?"

"Did you?"

"I came over here because I found something I thought might be important. And maybe it could have waited till tomorrow, I don't know. But I couldn't. And maybe that was selfish, but I was excited and confused and I knew I'd never get back to sleep. And I tried to call you, but I got the wrong number, and then I tried again, but I forgot to use the area code, and I just couldn't stay in that house another minute. It was making me crazy. I had to get out of there. And where else was I going to go but here? And I'm really sorry. Sorry I bothered you. Sorry you got the wrong idea. Sorry for every awful thing I've ever done to you."

"Sorry you married me?"

The question catches her off guard, momentarily takes her breath away. She shakes her head. "No. I'm not sorry about that."

He smiles. "In that case, your apology is accepted."

Amanda tries to smile in return, settles for a slight twitch of her lips. "Thank you."

"I'm sorry too."

"What for?"

"For being so off base and egotistical." He shrugs, his hands lifting from his sides, then lingering in the space between them, as if unsure where to go next. "Probably just a case of wishful thinking."

Again Amanda feels her breath being sucked from her lungs. "What are you saying?"

"What do you think?"

"I don't know what to think anymore. You'd better tell me."

"Tell you what? That I want to hold you so badly, I can hardly see straight? That I've been wanting to rip that stupid purple sweater off you ever since you walked in the door?"

"You don't like purple?" Amanda reaches down and pulls the mohair sweater up over her head, tossing it toward the high black table against the wall of the foyer. She stands in front of her former husband, one foot inside a heavy black leather boot, the other bare, her naked breasts rising and falling in anticipation. "Can I seduce you now?"

And suddenly she is in his arms, his lips pressing against hers, her mouth opening to receive his gentle tongue, and it feels just like the first time they kissed, each kiss bursting with that same tender urgency, except now it's even better because the hands that are caressing her body are practiced and knowing, as if they have never stopped touching her, as if the two of them have never been apart, as if they have been this way forever, will **be** this way forever.

The buzzer sounds.

They break apart.

Forever is over.

"Shit," he says, looking toward the floor.

"Shit," she agrees, looking at him.

They stand this way until the buzzer sounds a second time.

"You don't have to answer it," she says.

"If I don't answer it, she goes away."

"That's the general idea."

"And you?" he asks, looking up from the floor, staring directly into her eyes. "When do you go away?"

Amanda takes a deep breath. What she wants to say is **never.** What she says is, "Friday. Saturday at the latest."

Ben reaches over to scoop her sweater off the floor. "That's what I thought," he says as the buzzer sounds a third time.

"Saved by the proverbial bell." Amanda

takes the sweater from his hands and pulls it down over her head as he stretches his hand toward the intercom.

"Jennifer?" she hears him say as she buries her head inside the thick mohair, like a turtle inside its shell. The soft hairs fill her nostrils, make the tip of her nose itch.

Jennifer's voice fills the foyer. "There you are. You had me worried."

"Sorry. I was in the bathroom. Come on up. Apartment 1012."

"I'm on my way."

"She's on her way," Amanda mimics, poking her head out of the sweater and spitting a few stray woolen hairs out of her mouth. Grabbing her boot from the floor and her coat from the closet, she opens the door to the apartment and steps into the hall. "Don't worry. I'll make sure she doesn't see me."

"Where will you go?"

"Oh, I'm sure I can find somebody who wants to sleep with me."

"Amanda . . ."

"I'm fine, Ben. It was a whim. It didn't work out. No big deal. Honestly."

He nods understanding. "See you tomorrow?"

"Two o'clock sharp." Amanda walks away without saying good-bye. She stands in the corridor on the other side of the elevators until she hears an elevator pull up and its doors open. Soft footsteps quickly disappear down the carpeted hall. A door opens in the distance.

"Hey, you," a female voice says lovingly.

"Hey, you," Ben's voice echoes back.

The voices disappear inside Ben's apartment as Amanda presses the button for the elevator. Doors open almost immediately, and Amanda steps into an elevator redolent of lemons.

Twenty-Five

Amanda wakes up with a jolt at nine thirty the next morning, wondering (a) what day it is, (b) where she is, and (c) **who** she is. The first two questions are by far the easiest of the three to answer. It's Wednesday, and she's in her mother's living room, where she's spent the hours since midnight lying on the uncomfortable sofa, staring at the plastic plant on the mantel over the fireplace and thinking about last night's fiasco with Ben. "That was definitely not me last night," she states emphatically, pushing herself to her feet and stumbling toward the window, pulling back the dusty white sheers and shielding her eyes from the surprisingly bright sun.

What she sees: a deserted street that seems frozen in time, like a picture on a Christmas card. The white snow covering the front lawns of the houses on either side of the road glistens like hard metal. Huge clumps of frozen slush have been shoveled haphazardly from the middle of the road to the curbside and now stand, leaning like drunken sentries, at irregularly spaced intervals, making parking almost impossible. Several cars have been abandoned almost in the middle of the street, their tail ends sticking away from the sidewalk precariously. "It looks cold," Amanda mutters, wrapping her arms around her body, feeling the soft tickle of mohair against her hands, trying not to feel Ben's fingers digging at her flesh through the delicate wool.

Whatever had possessed her?

"I need a shower," Amanda announces to the empty house, heading for the stairs she was both too tired and too frightened to climb last night, although what exactly she was so frightened of is a mystery to her now. Did she think the puppets might attack her in her bed, payback for her having so thoughtlessly gutted their own resting place? Or was she afraid she might find something else hidden in unlikely places? "Like my heart?" she scoffs, avoiding the bedrooms and proceeding directly to the bathroom. "Not bloody likely." She turns on the shower, extending her hand beneath the old-fashioned nozzle. It used to take forever for

the water in this shower to heat up, she remembers, smiling as a torrent of cold water
splashes down on her waiting hand, strangely
comforted by the fact that some things, at
least, haven't changed. She makes a face at her
reflection in the mirror over the sink, noting
how the purple of the sweater brings out the
blue in her eyes. Then she pulls her sweater up
over her head and tosses it toward the hall, the
move mimicking her action of the night before.

"Oh, God," she groans, lifting her face to
the ceiling, reliving the touch of Ben's lips on
hers, his hands at her breasts and buttocks,
his fingers fumbling with the zipper of her
pants. "Damn it," she says, roughly pulling
off her slacks, and standing naked in the middle of her mother's bathroom. It was a bless-
ing that Jennifer had showed up when she
did. There was enough confusion in her life at
the moment. The last thing she needed was to
compound that confusion by sleeping with
her ex-husband.

Still, she couldn't remember the last time a
man had turned her down.

So why hadn't she simply taken a cab to the
Metro Convention Center hotel and surprised
Jerrod Sugar with another late-night treat?

"Been there, done that," she says with a shrug, as the small bathroom fills with steam. Besides, any more late-night surprises and Jerrod Sugar might go into cardiac arrest. She smiles as she steps inside the tub and pulls the shower curtain closed, recalling the stunned look on the poor man's face when Ben showed up unexpectedly at her door in the middle of the night. "Which makes us even," she decides, pushing her head underneath the water's spray, the now hot water running into her open mouth. "One unexpected late-night visit from you, one unexpected late-night visit from me."

All square. Finished. Over. Done.

Except they aren't. And she knows it.

She grabs the shampoo from the side of the tub and washes her hair, letting the soap stream into her eyes, giving them the excuse they need to tear. "This is just stupid. You are being so stupid," she repeats, angry fingers massaging her scalp. "I can't believe you are obsessing over a man you dumped years ago." The shampoo slides off her hair and over her shoulders, like a silk scarf, then clings to the tips of her breasts. She feels Ben's fingers at her nipples and grabs the bar of soap from its dish, impatiently rubs his hands away. "Been there, done that. Remember?"

Amanda finishes her shower and dries herself with a thin white towel, then searches for a hair-dryer in the cabinet underneath the sink. It's just her competitive juices that have been aroused, she tells herself, not any latent feelings of love. She simply doesn't like letting another woman win. That's all there is to it.

She locates an ancient dryer buried underneath an unopened bag of cotton balls, at least half a dozen shower caps, and several rolls of white toilet paper. Nothing else of significance. "Thank you, God," she whispers, aiming the blow-dryer at her head, pushing the ON button as if it were a trigger, and feeling a blast of hot air at the side of her temple. Wet hair immediately whips up and around her face. Just like last night outside Ben's building, she thinks. "Oh, no. I am not going back there."

Instead, she finishes drying her hair, purposefully blocking out everything but the whir of the motor, then gets dressed in her new navy pants and blue sweater. She knows she should finish cleaning up the guest bedroom, that there are still pieces of the shattered puppet stage scattered across the floor, not to mention the puppets themselves, who have been lying facedown on the bed all night and need to be returned to the safety of their closet hiding place, assured that everything is all right. "Later," she says, heading for the kitchen, making herself a three-egg omelet, and chewing on a Granny Smith apple as she ferrets around inside her purse for the business cards she discovered last night. She spreads them across the kitchen table, examining each one in turn. Walter Turofsky, Milton Turlington, Rodney Tureck, George Turgov. Bogus business cards obviously, the useful props of a man who called himself Turk. So, which one was he really? Or was he none of the above, someone else entirely? And was there any way of finding out? "Think," she tells herself forcefully. "You're a smart girl. You can figure this one out."

A woman, her round face framed by a soft mop of auburn curls, winks at her playfully from across the room.

"Rachel Mallins," Amanda says, leaving the table to flip through the phone book. "Malcolm, Malia, Mallinos . . . Mallins, A. . . . Mallins, L. . . . Mallins, R."

The phone is answered on the first ring, almost as if Rachel has been expecting her call. "Hello?"

"Rachel, this is Amanda Travis."

"I was right, wasn't I?" Rachel asks immediately.

"I checked the death notices for the past month. There was no listing for John Mallins's mother."

"And the man himself? Were you able to find out when he was born?"

"His passport lists his date of birth as July fourteenth. You were right about that too." Silence. "Rachel? Are you still there?"

"I'm here," she says, her voice heavy with the threat of tears. "Anything else?"

"Apparently the autopsy revealed that the victim was ten to fifteen years older than his passport claimed, and that he'd had a face-lift, maybe a nose job."

"So that bastard really did murder my brother."

"Rachel, did your brother ever mention anybody named Walter Turofsky?"

"Walter Turofsky? No, I don't think so."

"How about Milton Turlington?"

"No."

"Rodney Tureck . . . George Turgov?"

"No. Who are these men?"

"Think," Amanda says. "Turofsky, Turlington, Tureck, Turgov . . ."

"Turk," Rachel says, her voice a whisper. "You think they're aliases?"

"Criminals are generally lazy, as well as

unimaginative. They tend to stick with what they know."

"Where did you find those names?"

"I found a bunch of bogus business cards hidden in my mother's house."

"Your mother?" Shock resonates through Rachel's voice. "What's your mother got to do with this?"

The shock transfers to Amanda. "My mother?" What is Rachel talking about? "What are you talking about?"

"You said you found a bunch of bogus business cards in your mother's house."

"My mother? No. I said my client."

Silence. "Oh, sorry. My mistake. So what now? Back to the death notices?"

"What?" Amanda hears the quiver in her voice. Is it really possible she'd said **mother?** "Why would I recheck the death notices?"

"Think," Rachel instructs, as Amanda had instructed earlier. "Last time you were checking for a woman named Mallins. But if anybody's mother really died, her name would be Turlington or Turgov or whatever those other names were."

"Tureck or Turofsky."

"Tur-something, anyway."

Amanda sighs, not particularly anxious to return to the Reference Library.

"Want some help?" Rachel asks, understanding the sigh.

"No," Amanda tells her quickly. This is something she needs to do alone. Besides, she's already said too much. Could she really have misspoken, said **mother** instead of **client?** It was a good thing that Rachel, like most people, was so willing to ignore the evidence of her own ears.

"You'll keep me informed?"

"Of course."

"Thanks. Oh, and Amanda?" she adds as Amanda is about to disconnect.

"Yes?"

"Next time you see your mother, give her a big hug from me, will you?"

And then she is gone.

"Shit." Amanda hangs up the phone. "Shit." She sits for a few seconds without moving. "Give my mother a big hug," she repeats wondrously. "That'll be the day." In the stillness, she feels her mother's arms reach out to encircle her.

I don't think I've ever told you how beautiful you are.

"Whoa! Enough of this crap." Once again she grabs the phone book, turning to the blue-bordered government section in the middle, locating the listing for City Hall. There has to be an easier way than plowing through all the death notices again, she thinks, blocking out all unwanted thoughts and images. Surely there must be some central listing. Amanda dials the number and waits, bracing herself for a recorded message advising her of the many choices available to her.

"City Hall. Davia speaking."

"Davia? You mean you're real?"

"In the flesh," the woman responds, as another unwanted image, this one of Ben, instantly materializes before Amanda's eyes. Amanda promptly replaces this image with one she conjures up of Davia, who she decides is a tall, willowy brunette with a high forehead and large, pendulum-shaped breasts. "How can I direct your call?" Davia asks.

Amanda hesitates, her mind so full of uninvited guests, it's almost impossible to remember why she phoned in the first place.

"Hello? Are you still there?"

"Do you have some sort of death registrar?" The question pops from Amanda's mouth, like a pellet from a gun.

"No, I'm afraid we don't," Davia answers, as if this is a question she hears every day.

"So how would I find out if someone has died in this city in the last month?"

"Probably the best thing to do is check the death notices in the papers," Davia says, as Amanda knew she would. "The Reference Library has a wonderful newspaper morgue."

Amanda almost laughs at the term. "What if no one put a notice in the papers?"

"Well, in that case, I guess you could forward a request for the information to the province, although they require a period of seventy years since the person died."

"Seventy years? No, this person died very recently. Look, I don't understand why this is so difficult. Isn't death a public record?"

"No, actually. It isn't."

"It's a secret?"

"No. It's just not public."

"Oh."

"Sorry I can't help you."

"Thank you," Amanda says instead of good-bye. "Reference Library, here I come." She thinks of calling Ben as she is pulling on her boots and slipping into her coat, but he's in court, and besides, what is there to say to him really? **Idiot—you missed your chance?** "I don't think so," she says, shivering even before she opens the front door, lowering her head and shielding her face from the biting wind.

Except the wind isn't biting. It isn't even blowing. And while it is far from balmy, the temperature is substantially warmer than the day before. A good omen, she hopes, walking down the front path, about to turn toward Bloor, when she sees old Mrs. MacGiver staring at her from her front window. "Just ignore her," she whispers into the upturned collar of her coat. "Keep walking."

In spite of her admonitions, Amanda finds herself negotiating the front steps of Mrs. Mac-Giver's home, and ringing the bell. What the hell am I doing now? she wonders, looking toward the living room window when no one comes to the door, seeing nothing. Maybe I scared her, Amanda thinks. Maybe the poor old woman saw me walking over here and died of fright. And what then? Would her family, who already think she's lived too long, bother putting a notice of her death in the newspapers?

The sound of locks jiggling, and then the door opens. Just a crack. An ancient head peeks through, crowned by a thin halo of white hair that sprouts like weeds from patches of dry, pink scalp.

"It's me. Amanda. Gwen Price's daughter," Amanda tells the woman. "I'm going out for a few hours, and I just wondered if there was anything you needed I could pick up for you."

"I need a pair of red shoes," the woman replies.

"What?"

"There's a dance at the Royal York this weekend," Mrs. MacGiver says, her face becoming quite animated as she flings open the door. She's wearing an old, coffee-stained, yellow housecoat and heavy, gray-and-white gym socks. "It's my senior prom, you know, and this year they're holding it at the Royal York. I've been so looking forward to it."

"Mrs. MacGiver . . ."

"My father wasn't going to let me go at first. He's very strict. Very strict," she repeats with a shake of her head, seemingly oblivious to the cold. "He doesn't like Marshall MacGiver. But my mother thinks he's a very nice young man, and she talked him into letting me go. She even bought me a new dress." She looks down at her feet. "But how can I go to the prom without matching shoes?"

"I'm afraid I can't go to the shoe store today, Mrs. MacGiver. Maybe tomorrow," Amanda offers, trying to back away.

"Then where are you going?" Mrs. Mac-Giver's tone is harsh, almost accusatory.

"To the library."

"I don't need any books."

"Yes, I know that. I just thought you might need some orange juice or milk or maybe some tea."

The woman smiles, revealing several missing upper teeth. "Tea would be nice."

Amanda breathes a sigh of relief. "Okay, then. I'll bring you some tea."

"Yes, tea would be very nice. Red Rose, if they have it."

Amanda feels the burn of last night's tea on the tip of her tongue. "Red Rose it is."

"I didn't know they sold groceries at the library," Mrs. MacGiver marvels.

"You should go back inside the house now. You'll catch cold."

"Yes, it **is** cold," the old woman says. "Well, thanks for stopping by. You're a good girl, Puppet."

The door shuts in Amanda's face.

The Reference Library is a stunning glass and redbrick structure located at 789 Yonge Street, a block north of Bloor. Designed by award-winning architect Raymond Moriyama in the late 1970s, it contains almost 4.5 million items that are readily accessible to over a million visitors annually. Amanda discovered these facts during her last visit two days ago, and she is reminded of them as she pushes through the glass doors into the huge entrance hall that looks and functions like a public square. She strides through the light-filled, five-story atrium, around the clear, decorative pool that occupies most of the center of the floor, which is surrounded, she is pleased to note, by **real** plants, heading for the staircase to the lower level. Water trickles soothingly along stones and concrete into the pool's shallow surface, and the smell of coffee wafts from a small snack bar to her left, although a sign at the entrance to the turnstiles advises her that no food or beverages are allowed beyond this point.

The information desk is straight ahead, but Amanda already knows where to go. She follows the beige carpet past the two circular glass elevators to the winding, purple-carpeted staircase, amazed to see that the more than one hundred computers on the library's main level are all occupied, and there is already a line of people waiting to access the free Internet service.

How could she have lived in this city for so

many years and not set foot inside this magnif-
icent building? How ironic that she has found
out more about the city of her birth in the last
few days than in all the twenty years she lived
here. Why is it we never appreciate the things
we have until we lose them? she wonders,
shaking away the unpleasant cliché with a toss
of her hair, trying not to see Ben's face in the
face of a young man passing her on the stairs.

The Toronto Star Newspaper Centre—**Centre** spelled with an **re**—is located at the bottom of the stairs. It is a vast, open area, en-
closed by glass, and full of light, despite its
basement location. An abstract, wire-mesh
sculpture of newspapers being swept into the
air by an imaginery gust of wind stands in
front of the glass doors. Amanda pushes her
way inside, her eyes scanning the casual sitting
area to her left, furnished with fourteen gold-
and-purple leather chairs in front of a curved
wall lined with newspapers from all over the
world. The main room, carpeted in oddly subtle gold-and-purple berber and punctuated by
huge glass panels etched with copies of histori-
cal front pages, is filled with glass lecterns that
rest like open books atop steel stands, in front
of modern wooden chairs. These lecterns are
arranged in clusters of six, three to a side, and

are large enough to accommodate an entire newspaper, spread out to its full height and width. Computers run along the glass walls of the main room, behind which is another room for newspapers consigned to microfilm. Amanda doesn't need to access the microfilm. She discovered the last time she was here that the library keeps actual copies of the Toronto dailies for the previous three months. Of course the last time she was here, she was checking the death notices for anyone named Mallins. This morning she'll be looking for Turlingtons, Turecks, Turgovs, or Turofskys. Only the names have been changed, she thinks, approaching the plump, middle-aged woman behind the main desk. To protect the innocent or the guilty?

"Hi. I'm back," she tells the woman, wondering if she recognizes her from her last visit. "I need a month's worth of **Globes** and **Stars**, dating from last week. Again," she adds, hoping for some small sign of recognition.

"We can only give you two weeks at a time," says the woman, the same thing she said last time.

"Of course. Sorry. I forgot."

The woman, Wendy Kearns by the nameplate on her desk, smiles blankly and leaves her desk to retrieve the requested papers from the storage area at the back, returning moments later with a stack of newspapers whose spines are neatly bound in plastic wrap. She hands them across the desk to Amanda. "Have fun."

"Thanks." Amanda balances the neat stack of papers underneath her chin, carrying them over to the closest vacant spot, and dropping them to the heavy glass as softly as she can manage, which isn't as softly as the man next to her would like. "Sorry about that," she whispers, but his nose is already back in his newspaper. Literally. Obviously very nearsighted, Amanda decides, throwing her coat over the back of her chair and sitting down, then taking a few deep breaths before opening the paper on the top of the pile. "Okay, so let's get started." Beside her, the nearsighted man makes a great show of clearing his throat. "Sorry," Amanda apologizes again quickly. "I'll try to keep it down."

She flips to the birth and death notices at the back of the sports section in the **Globe,** thinking somebody has a strange sense of humor, and scanning through the names. Avison, Laura; Danylkiw, Dimitri; Parnass, Sylvia; Ramone, Ricardo; Torrey, Catherine; Tyrrell, Stanley. Not a Turlington, Turgov, Tureck, or

Turofsky in the bunch. "Of course not," she mumbles under her breath. "Did I really think it was going to be that simple?" She checks the **Star,** finds the same names and more, the **Star** clearly the paper of choice for the dearly departed. Amanda goes through each of the papers in turn, finding nothing, then returns to the main desk for another two weeks' worth of dailies, back and forth, up and down, deciding, what the hell, might as well go for broke, and looking through the library's complete collection, three months' worth of dead people passing before her tired eyes. Taggart, Timmons, Toolsie, Trent, Vintner, Young. The closest she comes to what she's looking for is Margaret Tulle, who died on December 2, after a courageous battle with cancer, at age fifty-one.

Not the woman she's looking for.

"Any success?" Wendy Kearns asks as Amanda drops the last of the newspapers back onto her desk.

"It was a long shot." Amanda shrugs. "Do you have a copy of the yellow pages?"

Wendy Kearns stretches for the phone book on a low shelf beside her desk.

"Is it okay if I take it in there?" Amanda motions toward the room with the gold-and-purple chairs.

The woman nods and hands over the heavy tome. Amanda carries it into the adjoining room, settling into a chair against the end wall, beneath two framed newspaper clippings. She opens the phone book, laughs when she sees she's turned to the page headed **Lawyers**. "Don't want any of those nasty people," she whispers, glancing toward the four other occupants of the room. But they're either engrossed in their newspapers or napping. Not a bad idea, she thinks, sleep tugging at her tired eyes. "Later," she says, flipping through **Maids, Mufflers,** and **Naturopaths,** to **Office & Desk Space**. "Uh-oh. Missed it." She turns back several pages. **Nuts and Bolts**. "See Bolts and Nuts." Figures. **Nutritionists, Nutrition Consultants, Nursing Homes**. "Here we go," she says, retrieving her cell phone from her purse, punching in the phone number at the top of almost two columns of such numbers, wondering what the hell she's planning to say.

"Extendicare Bayview," a woman answers promptly.

"Excuse me, but who would I speak to about a possible former resident?" Amanda ventures.

"I'm sorry. I'm not sure I understand what you mean." The woman's thick Eastern European accent grows wary.

"I'm trying to find out about a woman who may have been a resident at your place until very recently."

"What is her name?"

"It's either Turlington or Turgov or Tureck or Turofsky. Something that starts with **Tur**. Hello?" she asks when no answer is forthcoming.

"Is this a joke?"

"No. Trust me. I'm not joking."

"Who is speaking, please?"

"Look. I know it's a rather peculiar request, but it's really important. If you could just tell me whether you had a woman living there who died in the last month or so, whose last name is either Turlington or Turgov or—"

The line goes dead in her hands.

"This is going to be fun." Amanda takes a deep breath, then calls the next number on the list.

And then the next one after that, and then the next, and the next.

TWENTY-SIX

Her name was Rose Tureck and she died of congestive heart failure at age ninety-two on January thirty-first," Amanda says, strolling into Ben's office on the twenty-fourth floor of the Royal Bank Tower at precisely two o'clock that afternoon. Her tone is brisk, almost breezy, something she's been working on ever since she left the library. The tone says, Nothing of consequence happened last night. The tone says, Don't worry about me—I am neither hurt nor wounded. The tone says, It's business as usual.

Ben jumps to his feet behind his desk, knocking the file he's working on to the floor. "What are you talking about?"

"Rose Tureck, mother of Rodney Tureck, aka Turk. Do you think I could trouble your secretary for a cup of coffee before we head out to see my mother?"

Ben looks as if he's just been mowed down

by a truck. "Sandy," he calls through the open doorway. "Could you bring Ms. Travis a cup of coffee, please. Cream and sugar."

"Sure thing," Sandy calls back.

"Do you want to tell me what's going on here?" Ben motions toward the chair in front of his cherry-oak desk.

Amanda flops down on the chair, pushes her hair away from her face, stares Ben straight in the eye. This is also something she's been practicing since she left the library. The full-on stare, the one that informs her first ex-husband that he's of little or no consequence to her, that what he does with his life is of no real concern to her, and that what happened between them last night, what **almost** happened, what **should have** happened, has already been forgotten. "I made another trip to the library this morning," she begins.

"Are you all right?" he interrupts unexpectedly.

Amanda's shoulders stiffen. Is it possible he missed the professional tone in her voice, the look of indifference on her face? "Of course I'm all right. Why wouldn't I be all right?"

"Last night—"

"—is over. Case closed. Move on, Counselor." She smiles. The smile says, Get over yourself. You take things much too seriously. You always did.

Ben's smile in return is tenuous and doesn't last long. "Okay, so you went to the library," he repeats, sitting back down and waiting for her to continue.

Amanda leans back in her chair, crosses one leg over the other. "I went back to the library because I thought I might be able to find a listing in the death notices for either Turlington, Turgov, Tureck, or Turofsky."

"And you found Rose Tureck?"

"I found bugger-all," Amanda contradicts quickly. "I spent over an hour going through every goddamn Toronto paper for the last three months, and do you think I could find even one bloody Turlington, Turgov, Tureck, or Turofsky?" She almost laughs. She's been rhyming these names off for so long, they're starting to sound like a rock group.

Ben's secretary appears in the doorway. The petite young woman in a brown leather miniskirt crosses the small room in two easy strides and hands Amanda a mug of steaming coffee. "I hope it's not too sweet."

"I'm sure it's perfect. Thank you." Amanda takes a long sip, several thousand grains of sugar immediately congregating on her tongue, like sawdust. She closes her eyes, partly from fatigue, partly because she's afraid that if she has to keep looking Ben straight in his gorgeous face much longer, she'll end up flinging herself across his desk and into his arms, giving lie to her earlier protestations and embarrassing them both. Damn him anyway. Does he have to look as handsome in a pin-striped suit as he does in jeans? "How much do you charge anyway?" she asks.

"What?"

"Your hourly rate. What is it?"

"Two hundred dollars. Why?"

She shrugs, opens her eyes. "Just wondered." She even makes more money than he does, she thinks, taking another sip of the sickly sweet coffee and trying not to shudder.

"Well, you obviously found **something**," Ben says, encouraging her to continue.

"Not in the death notices, I didn't."

"Are you going to tell me or do I have to beg?"

"I'd love it if you begged."

He laughs. "Okay, I'm begging."

This time Amanda's smile is genuine. Once again they've managed to break the ice, establish an easy rapport, almost in spite of themselves. "Okay, well, when I didn't have any

luck with the newspapers, on impulse I decided to try the nursing homes. Hayley
Mallins said her husband came back here to
settle his mother's estate. So I figured his
mother had to be pretty elderly, and she probably lived alone, since no one bothered to put
a notice of her death in the papers. I thought
there was a chance she might have lived in a
nursing home or an assisted-living community. Anyway, I figured it was worth a shot, so
I started calling around. Started with the A's.
Well, no, actually, I started with Extendicare
because they had this big ad, but then I went
back to the A's and kept going until I reached
the K's. Kensington Gardens, to be precise.
Thank God I didn't have to call the million
Leisureworlds that were next on the list. Anyway, guess what? Kensington Gardens told me
that a woman named Rose Tureck had lived
there for the past two years, and lo and behold,
she had a son named Rodney who lived in England, and whom they'd been instructed to
contact at the time of her death. Rodney
Tureck, aka Turk, aka—"

"John Mallins," Ben states, the glint in his
eye betraying the calm of his voice.

"Certainly looks that way."

Ben rises from his seat, comes around the

front of his desk, takes the mug from Amanda's hands, and deposits it on his secretary's desk as they walk past. "Let's say we go talk to your mother."

Half an hour later, they pull into the parking lot of the Metro West Detention Center. "Careful," Ben says as Amanda opens her car door, the first words either has spoken since getting into his car and strapping on their seat belts. "It's slippery," he reminds her, and she responds with an exaggerated yawn, as if to tell him she isn't quite awake yet from the nap she pretended to be taking on the drive over.

It was easier that way, she decided. Spared them both the effort of small talk, or worse, of having to rehash the unfortunate events of last night. So instead she'd simply closed her eyes and feigned sleep, going so far as to produce a small, counterfeit snore, and trying not to imagine what went on in Ben's apartment last night after she'd left.

Amanda also pretends not to notice the elbow Ben offers for support as they walk through the parking lot. They proffer their identification to the official on duty, who makes a great show of studying their driver's licenses before permitting them to sign in, then continue through the familiar routine of metal detectors and searches through bags and briefcases, before being led down the long, airless corridor to the small, windowless room that serves as a conference room for prisoners and their attorneys.

"You all right?" Ben asks, as he asked earlier.

Why does he keep asking me that? Amanda wonders testily. Do I look unwell? Does his ego require that I be a quivering mass of jelly in his presence? "I'm fine." She removes her coat, throws it over the back of one of the chairs, begins pacing back and forth across the concrete floor. What's the matter with him anyway? "Why?"

"Why what?"

"Why do you keep asking if I'm all right?"

The question seems to catch him off guard. "No reason."

"No reason?"

He shakes his head. "Try not to be confrontational," he says.

"You think I'm being confrontational?"

"I don't mean with me."

"What **do** you mean?"

"I'm talking about when you see your mother."

"I have no intention of being confrontational with my mother."

"Good."

"Why would you say such a thing?"

"Amanda . . ."

"I mean it, Ben. What makes you think I'd be confrontational?"

"I don't think that necessarily."

"Then why say it?"

"Because I'm detecting a slight edge," he admits after a pause.

"You're detecting an edge?"

"Maybe I'm wrong."

"You think?"

"Okay, then. I'm wrong. I apologize. My mistake."

"What's with you anyway?"

"I guess I'm just being a lawyer."

"You're being an asshole."

Ben winces, as if he's been slapped. "Okay. Do you think we could rein it in a few notches?"

"Rein what in?"

"Whatever the hell it is we're doing."

"You started it."

"Fine, then I'm finishing it."

"Fine."

"Good."

"Good."

They stare at each other from opposite sides of the room.

"What just happened?" Ben asks.

Amanda takes a deep breath, exhales slowly. "I think we had our first fight."

"About?"

"I have no idea." They laugh, although the laugh is muted, tempered by embarrassment. "Think we could kiss and make up?"

He smiles. "Cost you a dollar."

"A dollar? That's pretty cheap. You charge more as a lawyer than a lover?"

"I'm a bigger prick as a lawyer," he says.

This time Amanda's laugh is both genuine and hearty. "Sorry for before. It was entirely my fault."

"No. I shouldn't have said what I did."

"It was good advice."

"It was provocative."

She nods. "Okay. So you were provocative and I was confrontational."

"We make a good team."

Yes, we do, Amanda thinks, looking away.

The sound of footsteps. The door to the small room opens. Gwen Price steps inside.

"Hello, Ben. Amanda." Her lips flex into a questioning smile. "To what do I owe this unexpected treat?" The guard closes the door as Gwen straightens her shoulders inside her awful green sweat suit and approaches the table in the middle of the room. Ben immediately pulls out a chair for her, and she sits down, folding her hands in front of her and eyeing them both warily, waiting for a reply.

"We have a few questions to ask you," Ben says.

"Shoot," Gwen says, then laughs. "Sorry. A rather unfortunate choice of words."

"You think this is funny?" Amanda asks.

"Amanda . . . ," Ben warns.

"What is it you want to ask me?"

Amanda pulls three of the bogus business cards out of her purse, slaps them on the table in front of her mother.

Gwen looks briefly down at the cards, then up again. "What's this?"

"Looks like a bunch of fake business cards," Amanda tells her, sliding into the chair across from her mother, straining to detect even the slightest crack in the other woman's steely facade.

"Are they supposed to mean something?"

"You tell me."

"I don't know what you want me to say."

"Walter Turofsky, George Turgov, Milton

Turlington," Amanda recites slowly. "These names mean anything to you?"

"No. Nothing."

Amanda drops the last card onto the table. "How about this one?"

Gwen Price turns ashen, although not a muscle in her face so much as twitches.

"Rodney Tureck," Amanda pronounces carefully. "Name ring a bell?"

"No."

"I don't believe you."

"I don't much care."

"Tell me who he is, Mother."

"I don't know who he is."

"The hell you don't."

"Amanda . . . ," Ben cautions.

"Rodney Tureck, also known as John Mallins. Ringing any bells now?"

"Didn't I shoot someone named John Mallins?"

"John Mallins, also known as Rodney Tureck, also known as Turk," Amanda persists, ignoring her mother's sarcasm. "Son of Rose Tureck."

"Son of a bitch," Gwen swears under her breath, just loud enough to be heard.

Amanda eyes Ben without moving her head. "Who is he, Mother?"

"Where did you get these cards?"

"I found them in the house."

"My house?"

"Yes. I lived there once too. Although you probably don't remember. . . ."

"Amanda . . . ," Ben warns again.

"You have no business going through my things."

"You have no business shooting people!"

Gwen Price struggles to her feet. "This conversation is over."

"She's dead, you know."

"What? Who?"

"Rose Tureck. She died a few weeks ago. Congestive heart failure. Age ninety-two."

Gwen digests this latest bit of information, says nothing.

"It's the reason her son came back here. To settle her estate."

"I don't see what any of this has to do with me," Gwen maintains stubbornly.

"You killed the man, Mother."

"So I did. At last, something we agree on. Can I go now?"

Amanda makes a great show of reaching back into her purse. "Not until you tell us how you got this." She drops the photograph of Rodney Tureck and his daughter onto the table.

Tears spring to Gwen's eyes as she lifts the picture into her now-trembling hands. Surprisingly, she makes no move to wipe them away. "Where did you find this?"

"What difference does it make?"

"You have to stop this," her mother warns.

"Stop what?"

"Stop snooping where you don't belong."

"And you have to start leveling with us or we can't help you."

"I don't want your help," Gwen shouts. "Can't you understand that? I want you to go away and leave me alone."

"Of course you do," Amanda shouts back, her own eyes filling with tears. "That's all you've ever wanted from me."

"No." Her mother shakes her head vigorously back and forth. "No, that's not true."

"Of course it's true. And trust me, as soon as you start giving me some straight answers, I'm on the first plane out of here. You never have to see me again."

"You think that's what I want?"

"I don't know **what** you want."

"Please," her mother says, crying now. "I know you think you're helping me, and I appreciate it, I really do—"

"I don't need your appreciation."

"—but you're only making things worse."

"How can things possibly get any worse?"

"Because they can."

Amanda pulls at her hair in helpless frustration, bringing the back of her head over the top of her spine, thrusting her chin high into the air. "Okay, Mother. This is what we know. We know that the man you shot isn't really John Mallins. We know that the real John Mallins disappeared twenty-five years ago after becoming friendly with a man who called himself Turk. We know that Turk's real name is Rodney Tureck, and that he probably killed John Mallins and assumed his identity. We know from the autopsy report that he had plastic surgery, possibly to impress his young wife, but more probably to make himself look younger, since John Mallins's passport gives his age as forty-seven. That's what we know." She takes a breath before continuing. "What we don't know is where you fit in to this mess."

"Maybe I don't fit in. Maybe it doesn't matter whether he's John Mallins or Rodney Tureck or George W. Bush. The fact is, whoever he was, he was still a stranger to me."

"The fact is you had this picture of him in your home. Which kind of shoots your story about him being a total stranger straight to hell."

"Which is exactly where he deserves to be," Gwen says, pushing away her tears and staring at the wall ahead.

Silence.

"You're admitting you knew him?" Ben asks quietly.

"I'm admitting nothing except I killed him."

"What about the pills you were taking?" Amanda asks.

"Pills?"

"I found bottles of antidepressants in your medicine cabinet."

"I haven't taken any of those pills in years."

"Why were you taking them at all?"

"That's none of your business."

"Oh, for God's sake—"

"Mrs. Price," Ben interrupts calmly. "You know that everything you say to us here is confidential."

"That's very reassuring. But I've said everything I'm going to say."

"Fine." Amanda throws her hands into the air in a gesture that manages to combine defiance with defeat. "If you won't talk to us, maybe Hayley Mallins can shed some light on who her husband really was." She grabs her coat, strides toward the door. "Come on, Ben. We've wasted enough time."

"No," her mother calls out as Amanda is reaching for the door handle. "Wait."

Amanda holds her breath, unable to move or turn around.

"There's no need to involve Mrs. Mallins. I doubt she knows anything about her husband's extracurricular activities."

Slowly, Amanda turns to face her mother. "And you do?"

"I should," her mother answers. "I was married to the man for more than ten years."

Amanda inches back into the room, drops into the empty chair. She doesn't know what she'd been expecting to hear, but whatever it was, it wasn't this. "What did you just say?"

Gwen Price smiles sadly, lowers herself into the other chair. "I believe I just handed you a motive for murder."

TWENTY-SEVEN

Amanda glances at Ben, who, mercifully, is looking as stunned as she is. "I think you better explain," Amanda says, reluctantly bringing her eyes back to her mother.

"Yes, I guess I should," her mother agrees, although she volunteers nothing further.

"You were married to John Mallins?" Ben asks quietly, as if leading a reluctant witness.

"John Mallins, Walter Turofsky, Milton Turlington, George Turgov, Rodney Tureck," Gwen Price rhymes off listlessly. "Rodney Tureck was his real name. At least I think it was."

"So you knew about his various aliases?" Again the person asking the question is Ben. Amanda acknowledges him with a grateful nod, her own voice stuck in the middle of her throat, like a lump of unchewed meat.

"Not when I first married him, no."

"And when was that?" Amanda asks, forcing the question out of her mouth with a harsh clearing of her throat. The voice that emerges is bruised and scratchy.

"A long time ago."

"How long?"

"I was nineteen when I married him." She smiles at Amanda. The smile says, The same age as when you married Ben.

Amanda shudders, looks away.

"I suppose I should have known better," Gwen says. "But what can I say? He was a very charming, charismatic man, as con artists usually are. They know instinctively what buttons to push, what words to say. I found him enormously appealing. Everyone did. Even my mother thought he was wonderful. Until he cheated my father out of his life savings, of course."

Amanda has slowly been zeroing in on her mother's mouth as she speaks, focusing on the tiny lines that run along her prominent upper lip, like a series of quotation marks. She takes note of the deep creases pulling at the bottom corners of her mouth, giving her pale skin the appearance of parched earth that has cracked under a relentlessly cruel sun. Minuscule blond hairs, like peach fuzz, grow along the underside of her chin, and her flesh is soft and translucent with age. For the first time, Gwen Price looks every one of her almost sixty-two years. Still, there are traces of the beautiful young woman she once was, especially in the ferocious intensity of her light blue eyes. Amanda feels the scrutiny of those eyes even as she keeps her attention riveted to her mother's mouth. "I don't remember your parents," Amanda says, trying to pull their faces out of her distant past.

"No, you wouldn't. They died before you were born."

"How did Rod Tureck cheat your father out of his life savings?" Ben asks, circling the periphery of Amanda's vision.

"The same way he cheated everyone. Phony companies, fake investment schemes. He talked my father into putting up money for a new waterproofing business he claimed to be starting up, said the return on his investment would more than cover my mother's medical bills. My mother was undergoing chemo at the time, so my father probably wasn't as prudent or careful as he normally would have been."

"How much did he lose?"

"Pretty much everything. Over a hundred thousand dollars."

"The same amount of money that's in your safety-deposit box," Amanda states, picturing the neat stacks of $100 bills.

"That was pretty much the nail in the coffin, as far as our marriage was concerned," Gwen Price continues, ignoring Amanda's inference and folding her hands across her chest, chewing angrily on her bottom lip. "He'd been cheating on me for years, of course. Getting more brazen all the time. I learned later that he always had at least two other women on the side, that he seemed to get some sort of sick satisfaction out of taking them to places where we'd been together. He even had an affair with a rather emotionally disturbed young woman who lived in our apartment building. It was her frantic phone calls to him in the middle of the night that finally persuaded me to pack my bags. By then, of course, my mother was dead. And a few months later, so was my father. He just keeled over one afternoon on the street and died before the ambulance arrived."

"So you lost a husband and both your parents in a relatively short period of time. That's a lot to deal with," Ben says sympathetically. "No wonder you were depressed."

"I got through it."

"But you blamed Rodney Tureck for your father's death," Amanda states rather than asks. "Why didn't you just put a curse on him, like you did with old Mr. Walsh?"

"I put a curse on Mr. Walsh?" her mother asks with a smile. "I don't remember that."

Amanda thinks, Sure—one of the pivotal events of my childhood, and she has no memory of it.

Figures, she thinks.

"And the money in your safety-deposit box?" she hears herself ask.

"What about it?"

"Where did you get it?"

"I like to think of it as my divorce settlement."

"And was it?"

"In a manner of speaking."

"And what manner would that be exactly?" Amanda presses.

"Rod Tureck was a crook," her mother says after a long pause in which she twists her lips, pats her hair, and shifts her position several times. "He stole that money from my father and I simply reclaimed it."

"What do you mean, you reclaimed it?"

Another twist of her lips, another pat of her hair. "Rod was always wheeling and dealing. He insisted on being paid in cash, and we paid for everything the same way. Assuming we actually paid for anything. I don't know. There were always collection agencies after us. Rod kept assuring me it was all a mistake, that I shouldn't worry, he'd take care of everything. And he did. Problems would suddenly erupt; just as suddenly they'd go away. We never had bank accounts like normal people. He gave me an allowance every week. He was very generous, and I was very stupid. What can I say? The times, they hadn't changed yet."

"Go on," Ben prompts as Amanda rolls her eyes in exasperation.

"Rod had cash stashed all over the city. Obviously we never stayed in one place for any length of time because of creditors and other unsavory characters who occasionally showed up on our doorstep. Rod, of course, had a perfectly plausible explanation for everything. He had a restless nature, he'd say. He'd get antsy if he had to stay too long in one place. What was the matter with me? Had I no sense of adventure? Didn't I like meeting new people, making new friends? Except every time we made new friends, he'd pull one of his crazy stunts, and we'd have to move. Of course, he claimed nothing was ever his fault. He never did anything wrong; he never cheated anyone. If we didn't have any friends, it was because they were all envious of his success. The few friends I did manage to make were few and far between, and I learned to keep them to myself."

"The money, Mother," Amanda says, steering the other woman back on course, refusing to feel sorry for her.

"Yes. Well, I'm getting to that," Gwen Price continues reluctantly. "I realized it was only a matter of time before my marriage was over, and I'd better take steps to protect myself. So I opened a bank account of my own and started slowly socking money away. Not a lot, of course. Nothing to make Rod suspicious. Just a couple hundred dollars here and there. Eventually, I had five thousand dollars saved up, and I'd become quite friendly with one of the tellers at the bank, a woman who was having marital problems of her own. She told me Rod kept a safety-deposit box at the bank. So one night when he was out of town, supposedly on business, I did some sneaking around, and I found his cigar box where he kept his various safety-deposit-box keys. It was at the back of his sweater drawer, the keys all neatly labeled, and I simply helped myself to the one I wanted. My friend let me into the vault. I walked out with the money."

"You're saying you stole a hundred thousand dollars from your ex-husband?" Amanda asks, her head starting to spin.

"It was my father's money," Gwen says unapologetically.

Amanda is almost afraid to ask another question, for fear of what her mother might say.

"And then what?" Ben asks in her stead.

"Then I opened my own safety-deposit box in a different bank, put the money inside, and returned the original key to Rod's cigar box. I never so much as looked at the money again. That wasn't the point."

"Tell me again," Amanda says. "Exactly what **was** the point?"

"The point was getting some of my own back," her mother says.

"And how did Rodney Tureck feel about that?"

Her mother waves a dismissive hand in front of her face. "By the time he discovered the money was missing, it was too late. We were already divorced, my friend at the bank had moved to Chicago, and he couldn't very well report it to the police, now, could he?"

"He didn't confront you?"

"Of course he confronted me. But I pleaded

ignorance. Told him I had no idea what he was talking about. What safety-deposit box? What money? Do I look like I'm living high off the hog? I asked. I was working as a secretary, barely making enough to scrape by. But that didn't matter. He said he knew I took the money, and that one way or the other, I was going to pay for it."

"He threatened you?"

Gwen looks toward the door, says nothing.

"Is that why you shot him, Mother?" Amanda asks. "Because you were afraid for your life?"

"I shot him because he was a miserable son of a bitch who deserved to die for all the misery he'd caused everyone."

"No," Amanda says steadily, the defense attorney in her taking charge of the situation, running with it. "Listen to me. You shot him because the last time you saw him he threatened your life, and when you saw him in the lobby of the Four Seasons hotel, you were convinced he'd come back to make good on those threats." She tries not to look too self-satisfied. "That sounds like a pretty decent argument for self-defense, doesn't it, Ben?" She looks at Ben for support.

"That all happened a very long time ago,"

her mother says before Ben can formulate a response. "I don't think a jury is going to be persuaded—"

"Let Ben worry about persuading a jury," Amanda says.

"No one is going to buy—"

"Buy what? That you were married to a man so amoral he thought nothing of stealing from his own father-in-law? That the theft of your father's life savings led directly to his premature death? That you spent years on antidepressants as a result of Rod Tureck's emotionally abusive behavior, both during your marriage and after your divorce? That he threatened you? That you spent your life looking over your shoulder, always afraid one day he'd return to make good on his threats? Why wouldn't a jury believe that you panicked when you saw him again? That you shot him with the gun you'd been keeping all these years for your own protection? Don't tell me a jury wouldn't buy it," Amanda says with a sudden rush of exhilaration. "They'll buy it all right."

"Do you?" her mother asks.

Amanda leans back in her chair, her exhilaration rapidly dissipating. "Why not? It makes sense."

"That's not what I asked."

"It doesn't matter whether I buy it or not," Amanda says finally. "All that matters is whether we can convince a jury to buy it."

Her mother shakes her head. "No."

"What do you mean, no?"

"I mean I won't go along with it."

"What do you mean, you won't go along with it?"

"It's not entirely truthful."

"What the hell is?" Amanda snaps.

"Amanda . . . ," Ben interjects.

"Let me get this straight: you have no problem with stealing or killing, but you're squeamish about not telling the truth. Is that what you're trying to tell me?"

"Look, we now have something we can take to the crown attorney," Ben argues calmly. "There are enough mitigating circumstances here to make them think twice about going to trial. At least they may be willing to talk to us about a deal."

"You'd have to tell them the things I just told you?"

"Yes, of course."

"The things you assured me were confidential."

"They have to know the facts, Mother."

"No."

"No?"

"As far as the police are concerned, I'm a crazy woman who shot a stranger in a hotel lobby. That suits me fine." Her mother looks toward the door, as if she is considering calling for the guard.

"Well, at least the police have it half-right," Amanda says. "You're crazy all right."

"Amanda . . ."

"Will you please talk some sense into this lunatic?" Amanda jumps out of her chair and resumes her earlier pacing.

"Mrs. Price," Ben begins, sliding into Amanda's now-vacant seat. "Do you mind telling us why you're so adamant about not letting us mount any kind of defense?"

Gwen smiles sweetly at her former son-in-law. "Because I'm guilty," she says. "I shot a man. Not because of any mitigating circumstances. Not because I was abusing antidepressant drugs. Not because I feared for my life. But because I wanted to shoot him. Because he was a bad man who deserved to die. It's as simple as that."

"There's nothing simple about any of this," Amanda says.

"Only because you insist on complicating everything."

"I complicate everything?"

"I know you mean well, sweetheart—"

"Sweetheart?"

"Amanda . . ."

"You don't know anything about me."

"That's probably true," her mother admits, managing to sound genuinely contrite. "But I do know I shot a man in cold blood and I should go to prison. Can't we leave it at that?"

"There's something you're not telling us," Amanda says, swooping toward her mother, like an eagle chasing its prey.

Her mother shakes her head. "I've told you everything."

"How long after your divorce until you met my father?" Amanda asks, trying a different tack.

"About a year. Why? What does it matter?"

"Tell me about it."

"About what?"

"About my father," Amanda says, leaning against the wall of the small room, hoping it will keep her upright, prevent her from sliding to the floor.

"I'm not sure I understand the point."

"Please," Amanda says, unable to say more.

Her mother sighs her acquiescence, as her

lips tremble into a smile. "Your father was a wonderful man. I loved him very much."

"He knew you'd been married before?"

"Of course. I would never have kept that from him."

"Did he know about the money?"

"No."

"So he didn't know about Rod Tureck's threats?"

"He knew I was afraid of Rod."

"And where was I during all this?"

"You? You were just a toddler. Not more than two years old."

"Is that when you started taking antidepressants?"

Again her mother looks away, says nothing.

"Mother?"

"I don't remember."

"Why were you so depressed, Mother?"

"I don't remember."

"Suppose I tell you what I remember," Amanda says, once again shifting gears. "I remember laughing." She pauses, allowing the memory to unfold, the irony to sink in. "That's the first memory I have. I'm actually laughing. Amazing, isn't it? We're playing, and you're waving some sort of finger puppet in my face, tapping on my nose. And we're laughing."

Amanda stops, wondering for an instant if this memory is real or something she only imagined. "And another time, I remember you holding my hands above my head and making me dance, calling me your little puppet. 'Who's my little puppet?' you'd tease, and I'd laugh and say, 'I am. I am.' And we were happy. I **know** we were happy. And then suddenly, everything changed. And the only memories I have after that are of people crying. Why is that, Mother?"

"I don't know."

"The hell you don't."

"Amanda . . . ," Ben cautions.

"What happened, Mother?"

"What can I say?" Gwen Price asks. "The laughter stopped."

"Why did it stop?"

"What difference does it make?"

"Why did it stop?"

Her mother sighs, looks toward Ben for help, but his gaze is focused on Amanda, and he says nothing. "I was on those damn pills," she says after a long pause. "They turned me into a goddamned zombie. When I tried to go off them, it only made things worse. I alternated between stupor and rage. It was a nightmare."

"Why were you on antidepressants, Mother?"

Another sigh. Another lengthy pause. "It was like you said. I'd been through a lot. I'd lost both my parents, divorced my husband . . ."

"You were remarried. To a wonderful man you loved very much. You had a little girl."

"I suffered from postpartum depression."

"Well, isn't that convenient," Amanda scoffs.

"It was anything but convenient, I assure you."

"Interesting you've never mentioned it before."

"Times were different then. It wasn't something we discussed. Not like today."

"The times, they hadn't changed yet," Amanda says, repeating her mother's phrase.

Gwen nods. "And then Rod tracked me down, and he threatened me, and it was just too much, I guess."

Amanda stares at her mother in open-mouthed disbelief. "Too much bullshit, you mean."

"Amanda . . . ," Ben pleads.

"Who the hell do you think you're talking to, Mother? The police? You seriously expect us to believe this crap?"

Her mother turns away, says nothing.

"You want to know why we don't believe it?" Amanda bangs her fist on the table, reclaiming her mother's attention. "Because it doesn't make any sense."

"I'm sorry you feel that way."

"Not only doesn't it make any sense, it doesn't explain what you were doing with this." Amanda holds up the photograph of Rodney Tureck and his daughter, waves it in front of her mother's face. "What were you doing with this picture, Mother? How did you get it?"

In response, her mother rises slowly to her feet. "I'm afraid I'm feeling very tired. You'll have to excuse me." She walks to the door and knocks for the guard.

"This isn't over," Amanda says to her mother's back, watching it stiffen.

Then the door opens, and the guard leads her mother from the room.

TWENTY-EIGHT

Do you believe that?" Amanda whispers between clenched teeth as she charges down the prison corridor, Ben at her side. "Not only did she know the man, she was married to him! For ten fucking years! Do you believe that?"

"I think we should wait to discuss this until we're in the car." Ben nods toward the guard watching them from behind the glass partition near the front entrance.

"She stole a hundred thousand dollars from the man!"

"I really think we should wait—"

"She was a goddamned drug addict!"

"Amanda—"

"First we have no motive for the shooting. Now we have nothing **but** motives."

"Is there a problem here?" A guard materializes, attracted by the commotion. He emerges from a distant wall as if by magic, ambling toward them, one hand hovering above the gun in his holster.

"No, Officer." Ben's fingers dig right through Amanda's parka into the flesh of her arm as he maneuvers her toward the front door. "No problem."

"She called me **sweetheart!**" Amanda pushes open the door to the parking lot and marches through. Then she stops, spins around on her heels, and bursts into a flood of angry tears. "Who the hell is this woman?"

Ben nods understanding, although his eyes are a mirror of her own confusion.

I could really use your arms around me right now, Amanda thinks, swaying toward him.

His right hand reaches for her. But instead of drawing her into a comforting embrace, he merely takes her elbow and guides her through the thick slush of the parking lot, as if they are wading through potentially treacherous ocean waves, the keys to his white Corvette already extended between his fingers. "Are you all right?" he asks, once they are settled inside the front seat, the engine of the old car spewing streamers of noxious fumes into the already gray air.

"I guess."

"What did you think of her story?"

"I think that for a psychopath, she's a surprisingly bad liar."

"You think everything she said was a lie?"

Amanda shakes her head. "I think she was married to Rodney Tureck. I think he was a con man who cheated on her and stole from her father. I think she might even have stolen that money back. After that, it gets kind of murky."

"There's definitely a lot she's not telling us."

"So how do we find out what it is?"

Ben takes a moment to deliberate. Amanda watches his eyes dart back and forth across the car's front windshield, as if he were reading from an invisible list of options. "We do exactly what you told your mother we'd do if she didn't level with us." He pauses, waits for her mind to catch up.

"We pay a visit to Hayley Mallins," Amanda says quietly, then buckles her seat belt and settles in for the ride.

There is an accident on the Gardiner Expressway—a trailer-truck has jackknifed and is taking up all the eastbound lanes—and as a result, it takes Ben and Amanda almost two hours to return to the downtown core. This is worse than I-95, Amanda thinks, but doesn't say, be-

cause in truth **nothing** is worse than I-95. And
besides, to say anything at all would be difficult, considering how loudly Ben is playing the
car radio. A familiar signal, she recognizes with
a nod of her head. It means he doesn't want to
talk. It means he wants to be alone with his
thoughts, or possibly that he doesn't want to
think at all. Amanda remembers this about
Ben from their years together, and she smiles,
wishing she could block everything out so easily. For a while she tries, silently repeating a
mantra she learned from her friend Ellie, who
once paid over $1,000 for a four-day course in
Transcendental Meditation. **Kir-rell, kir-rell,
kir-rell.** But either because she is too impatient, or because it is Ellie's mantra and not her
own, and Ellie has betrayed some kind of oath
by divulging it, the mantra doesn't work. **Kir-
rell, kir-rell.** After only half a minute,
Amanda is back in that awful, airless little
room with her mother, and her mother is
telling her she was married to Rodney Tureck,
aka John Mallins, for more than a decade—**kir-
rell, kir-rell**—that he'd cheated her father out
of his life savings—**kir-rell, kir-ell!**—that
she'd stolen it back—**kir-rell, kir-rell**—that
he'd threatened her—**kir-rell, kir-rell!**—and
that her subsequent depression threw her into

the nightmare world of anti-depressant drugs. **Kir-rell, kir-rell, kir-rell!!!**

Fucking hell is more like it.

Amanda abandons the mantra. It floats, like a sigh, on her breath, forming a cloud on the windshield. Somewhere along the way, her mother's story loses the ring of truth.

The truth, the whole truth, and nothing but the truth, Amanda thinks wearily. "**Anything** but the truth," she says out loud, glancing over at Ben when she realizes she's said these words out loud. But either he hasn't heard her or he's pretending not to, having listened to enough of her frustrated ramblings during the first hour of the drive back into the city. Now he sits staring straight ahead, calmly advancing when he can, and tapping his fingers against the steering wheel to the ferocious beat of the rock music on the radio. Coldplay, she thinks, but isn't sure. In truth, she's lost touch with most of the music of her generation.

Don't tell me you actually like this stuff? she remembers Sean demanding, before switching the channel on her car radio from rock to classical without even asking. At least it was better than the awful country music he liked to listen to. **This is America,** he'd say over her vociferous protestations, singing along with a chorus that invariably had something to do with cheating women and pickup trucks. **This is the heartland.**

This is crap, she'd think. But four years into their marriage and she was singing the chorus right along with him. "There's hope for you yet," Sean had joked. Maybe that's why she'd felt such a pressing need to leave. Country music ruined my second marriage, she decides now with a chuckle. Somebody should write a country song about **that.**

Except ultimately, of course, it wasn't the truth, the whole truth, and nothing but. Their marriage had failed not because of conflicting tastes in music or movies, the difference in their ages, or even their opposing ideas with regard to starting a family. No, their marriage was doomed from the moment she said **I do.** Because the simple truth, the whole truth, and nothing but the truth was that she **didn't.**

Amanda closes her eyes, sees her mother's face. **I was married to the man for more than ten years.** Obviously, multiple marriages run in the family, she thinks, laughing out loud.

"Something funny?" Ben asks, lowering the volume on the radio.

"Not really."

He nods as if this makes perfect sense.

By the time they arrive at the Four Seasons hotel, the late-afternoon sky is already sour with the threat of night. "You really think this is a good idea?" Amanda asks, feeling strangely reluctant, even a little squeamish, about confronting Hayley Mallins.

Ben hands his car keys to the valet as they enter the lobby. "You have any better ones?"

Amanda glances toward the crowded lobby bar to their left. "I could use a drink."

"Definitely a better idea." They pass the comfortable enclave where her mother sat waiting to gun down her former husband, then climb the few steps leading to the bar proper, where they settle into a small table by the window. "What'll it be?" Ben asks.

"Some peach-raspberry tea," Amanda says as a waiter approaches.

Ben laughs. "One peach-raspberry tea and one glass of very dry red wine," he tells the young man before turning his attention back to Amanda. "You never cease to amaze me."

"Is that a good thing?"

He shrugs, ignores the question. "Sure you don't want anything stronger?"

"I think I should probably keep a clear head."

He nods. "Not a bad idea."

"What exactly are we planning to say to Hayley Mallins anyway?"

"Well, for starters, we'll tell her her husband's real name. See what kind of reaction that generates."

"And if my mother is right? If Hayley Mallins doesn't know anything about her husband's past?"

"Do you really believe there's any chance of that?"

"I don't know what to believe anymore. Nothing makes any sense."

"It all makes sense," Ben corrects. "We just haven't figured it out yet."

The waiter returns several minutes later with their drinks, lowering them to the small round table between them. The subtle aroma of warm fruit wafts toward Amanda's nose. "Yum. Doesn't that smell wonderful?"

Ben buries his nose inside the delicate lip of his wineglass, inhales deeply. "That it does." He lifts his glass toward her teacup. "Cheers."

"Cheers." Amanda clicks her china cup against the curve of his glass, wondering what it is they're cheering. "And after we burst Hayley Mallins's bubble, then what?"

"That will depend on what Hayley Mallins has to say."

"What if she doesn't say anything?"

"We show her the photograph."

"Thus proving the old adage—a picture is worth a thousand words?"

Ben nods, takes a long sip of his drink.

"And if she doesn't know anything about that either? If she has no idea how my mother got ahold of that picture or what she was doing with it? What if all we accomplish by our visit is to traumatize the poor woman even more than she's already been traumatized? I mean, maybe my mother is right. Is there really any point in upsetting the applecart?"

"Are you sure you're all right?" Ben asks, as he asked earlier, peering at her from over the top of his glass.

"Yes. Why?"

"It's not like you to be concerned about upsetting applecarts."

"You're right," Amanda agrees. What's the matter with her? Had she really said her mother might be right—about anything? "I think it's the tea."

"Look," Ben says. "Even if we don't find out anything of consequence, think of it as a public service."

"A public service?"

"At least this way Hayley Mallins learns

about her mother-in-law's estate. She could go back to England a very wealthy woman."

"You think?"

"I think you should finish your tea." He downs the rest of his wine, then stands up. "Let's get this show on the road."

Minutes later, they step out of the elevator onto the twenty-fourth floor. "This way," Amanda says, already halfway down the hall.

"Amanda, wait," Ben calls after her. "Promise me you won't go flying off the handle."

She glances back over her shoulder without stopping. "I won't be confrontational. I promise."

"Just take things slow and easy."

Amanda approaches the door to the Mallinses' suite. "Don't I always?"

"Shit," she hears Ben mutter as she raises her hand to knock on the door.

"Mom," a boy's voice calls out from inside seconds later. "Someone's here."

Footsteps—halting, tentative. A woman's voice—guarded, fearful. "Who is it?"

"It's Amanda Travis, Mrs. Mallins. We talked the other day. . . ."

The door, secured by a brass chain, cracks open. A dark eye peers into the hallway, widens when it discovers Amanda isn't alone. "Who's this?"

"This is Ben Myers. He's—"

"—representing the woman who shot my husband," Hayley Mallins acknowledges.

"Could we come inside for a few minutes, Mrs. Mallins?" Amanda asks. "There are some things we need to discuss with you."

"Such as?" The chain remains stubbornly in place.

"Such as this." Amanda reaches into the pocket of her red parka, pulls out the picture of father and daughter, and holds it up to the crack in the door. The exposed eye widens further, fills with alarm. The door shuts in Amanda's face.

"So much for taking things slow and easy," Ben says.

"Sorry. I couldn't help myself." Amanda raises her hand, knocks determinedly on the door.

"Go away," comes the immediate response.

"Mrs. Mallins . . . Hayley. Please . . ."

"Go away or I'll call the police."

"That's fine," Ben says loudly. "I think the police might be very interested in seeing this picture."

A pause in which no one seems to breathe.

Then the sound of a chain sliding out of its lock, a knob turning, a door opening. Hayley Mallins stands back to permit them entry.

"Way to go," Amanda whispers admiringly to Ben as she steps over the threshold and takes a furtive glance around the room. The first thing she notices is that Hayley's normally pale skin is now a ghostly white, as if she's just emerged from a vat of bleach, and that the sleeves of her oversize, moss-green sweater cover all but the tips of her trembling fingers, the sweater hanging loose over a pair of baggy, brown corduroy pants, her hair falling like anemic dark threads around her chin. Everything about her looks tenuous. Even her features appear fluid, ready to slide from her face, as if she is melting. Amanda watches the woman as her eyes dart nervously toward the closed bedroom door to her left. **Don't you think Victor deserves to know the truth?** a woman is demanding on the other side of the door. **Please,** another woman begs in return. **You don't know what you're doing.**

Amanda recognizes the familiar voices from her once-favorite soap and finds fleeting reassurance that some things, at least, never change. Women have been keeping secrets from Victor from the beginning of time. In the end, he always discovers the truth, and everybody pays dearly for their deceit. You'd think they'd learn. "How are the kids holding up?" she asks.

"They're very anxious to get back to England." Hayley's fists clench and unclench inside the cuffs of her sweater. "What is it you want with me?"

"We found this picture in my client's house. Do you have any idea what she might have been doing with it?" Ben asks, taking the photograph from Amanda and offering it to the other woman.

For a second, Hayley Mallins looks as if she might faint. She grabs on to the side of the nearest gold-and-red-striped chair and sinks into it slowly.

"Are you all right, Mrs. Mallins? Would you like some water?"

Hayley shakes her head, a hint of color slowly returning to her cheeks as she glances toward the picture, although her eyes refuse to linger. "What does it mean?"

"We were hoping you could tell us."

Hayley stares into her lap, says nothing.

"We found something else," Amanda says. "A number of bogus business cards."

"I don't understand."

"Does the name Rodney Tureck mean anything to you?"

An audible intake of breath. The slight blush that had returned to Hayley's cheeks quickly vanishes. "No. Nothing."

"Let us tell you what we know," Amanda says.

"I'm really not interested in what you **think** you know," Hayley protests.

"We know that your husband's name wasn't John Mallins."

"You're wrong."

"We know it was Rodney Tureck."

"This is absurd."

"You were right about your husband coming back to settle his mother's estate," Amanda continues, "but his mother's name was Tureck, not Mallins."

"Maybe she remarried. Did you think of that?"

"Did you know that your husband's autopsy revealed he was ten to fifteen years older than he claimed, and that he'd had some cosmetic surgery on his face?"

"You're lying."

"Call the police. Ask them yourself."

"I think you should leave now."

"There's something else we know," Amanda says quickly.

"Something else you're wrong about," Hayley insists.

"We know your husband was no stranger to Gwen Price. In fact, we know they were once married."

Hayley scrambles to her feet, her head shaking violently from side to side. "You're out of your minds."

"It's the truth."

"Is that what that woman told you? Because she's either lying or she's crazy. How could you possibly believe anything she says?"

"It'll be easy enough to prove," Ben tells her.

"I want you out of here. I want you out of here right now."

The door to the bedroom opens. A young boy steps into the room, followed by his older sister, her hands resting nervously on his shoulders. They're similarly dressed in gray sweatshirts and jeans, and their eyes flit fearfully between their mother and her visitors. In the background, angry voices continue. **I can't believe you let that woman into our home after everything she's done.**

"Hello, Hope, Spenser," Amanda says.

"You remember Amanda Travis," Hayley says politely, as if she's reintroducing an old friend.

"This is Ben Myers, my—"

"—associate," Ben says quickly, offering his hand. "How are you holding up?"

"Is something wrong?" Hope asks her mother, ignoring both Ben and Amanda. "We could hear you arguing above the telly."

"Everything's fine, darling. These people were just leaving."

"We just need a few more minutes of your mother's time," Ben says.

"It doesn't look like she wants to give you any more minutes," Spenser tells him, breaking away from his sister to stand between his mother and her unwelcome guests.

"Spenser . . . ," Amanda begins.

"Go away or we shall be forced to contact the authorities."

Amanda almost smiles, wondering if it's the young boy's clipped British accent or the formality of his phrasing that makes him sound so mature.

"It's all right, Spenser." Hayley's smile is filled with motherly pride. "I can handle this. You and Hope go back to your program."

Hope's body sways toward the bedroom.

Victor's responsible for this, and you know it. "You're sure you'll be all right?"

"Positive. I'll be in straightaway."

Hope nods, signaling for her brother to follow her with a cock of her head. Spenser crosses one arm over the other, widens his stance, refuses to budge.

"I'm fine," Hayley Mallins assures her son again. "I can manage here. Go on now, Puppet."

And then the blood rushes into Amanda's ears, and the room explodes into silence.

TWENTY-NINE

What did you say?" Amanda says when she can find her voice.

Spenser takes a step back, clearly frightened by Amanda's tone.

"What's the matter?" Hayley asks, sensing a shift in the air, looking warily toward Ben.

"Spenser," Ben says. "Why don't you go with your sister." This is an obvious directive and not a request.

"Go on, love," his mother urges.

"I don't want to go."

"Please, darling. It's all right. I promise."

Still the boy hesitates. "You'll scream if you need help?"

"I assure you that won't be necessary," Ben says as Amanda fights the urge to start screaming herself.

Reluctantly the boy sways from his mother's side and creeps toward the bedroom door.

"What did you call him?" Amanda asks, walking briskly after him and closing the door behind him.

"I don't understand," Hayley stammers, her eyes appealing to Ben for help.

"You called him Puppet."

"Yes. I suppose. Why?"

"You tell me."

"I don't understand. It's just a nickname."

"Not just a nickname."

"I'm afraid I'm not following."

Amanda takes a few seconds to regain her composure. Is it possible that Puppet is a more common nickname than she thought? That it is on a par with Pumpkin and Sweetie? That it transcends countries and cultures? That Hayley's easy use of it is merely a remarkable coincidence? Is that possible? "My mother used to call me that," Amanda says, "when I was a toddler."

"Really?" Hayley's voice is so low in her throat it's barely audible. "Well, I suppose it's not that uncommon."

"I think it is," Amanda says, answering her own earlier questions.

"Well . . . ," Hayley says, then offers nothing further.

"When I was little, I used to love puppets . . . marionettes . . . whatever you want to call them.

And my mother used to hold my hands and dangle me from her fingertips, and she'd say, 'Puppet, Puppet . . .' "

Hayley's skin goes from pale to cadaverous. " 'Who's my little puppet?' " she whispers, as the two women lock eyes, the shallowness of their breathing echoing one another's. It fills the room like the shuffling noises of a drum. "Who **are** you?"

"My name is Amanda Travis," Amanda says slowly, carefully measuring out each word. She pauses, not for dramatic effect, but because she finds herself dangerously short of breath. "Gwen Price is my mother."

Hayley stumbles back against the nearest chair, her hand reaching for her chest. "Mandy?" The word emerges as a gasp for air.

Amanda feels every hair lift from her body, as if she just stepped on a live wire.

"My God." Hayley's eyes widen to take in every detail of Amanda's face. "I can't believe I didn't make the connection."

Amanda inches forward. "What connection?"

Hayley takes a few seconds to respond, her glance darting between Amanda and the door to the hallway, as if she is considering trying to escape. "I only knew you as Mandy. My God. You don't remember me?"

"Should I?"

Hayley shakes her head, her eyes refusing to settle. "No, of course you wouldn't. You were just a baby the last time I saw you."

"Who the hell are **you**?" Amanda asks, throwing the other woman's question back at her.

"Your mother didn't tell you?"

Amanda shakes her head. "Who **are** you?" she asks again.

Hayley hesitates, looks toward the window, as if searching for answers in the bright lights of the surrounding city. Then, quietly, haltingly: "My name was Hayley Walsh."

"Walsh?"

"I lived next door to you on Palmerston."

Amanda sees a giant walrus of a man smirking at her from the middle of the shared driveway between the two homes. "Old Mr. Walsh's daughter?"

"I used to babysit you when you were little. I called you my little puppet because you were so crazy about those damn dolls."

"That was you who carried me around the house?"

" 'Puppet, puppet. Who's my little puppet?' " Hayley repeats, tears suddenly spilling from her eyes to stain her ashen cheeks. She stares at

Amanda as if she is preparing to swallow her whole.

Amanda walks over to the sofa, sinks into its soft pillows, fighting the desire to lie down, fall into a deep sleep. It occurs to her that everything that is happening is a dream, and that if she simply brings her feet up and closes her eyes, this whole surreal episode will vanish as soon as she reopens them. Slowly, she allows her eyes to close. When she reopens them seconds later, Hayley Mallins is still there, lowering herself into the nearest chair, her knuckles growing white as she grips the armrest. "I don't remember Mr. Walsh having a daughter," Amanda says finally, reluctantly accepting the reality of her situation, and trying to make sense of these latest revelations.

"No, of course you wouldn't. You were so young when I left."

"Left?"

"Ran off," Hayley corrects.

"You ran off? Why? Where did you go?"

Hayley lowers her head, stares into her lap. "To England." Her breath quivers into the stillness of the room. "With Rodney Tureck."

It takes Amanda several seconds to absorb what she has just heard. "I don't understand," she says finally, looking toward Ben. "How would you have met Rodney Tureck? My mother wasn't married to him when she lived on Palmerston. She was married to my father."

"Mr. Price, yes," Hayley agrees, a small smile tugging at the corners of her mouth. "He was a lovely man."

"He died eleven years ago." Amanda struggles to contain the tears that have rushed to her eyes.

"Yes. I read in the paper that your mother was a widow. I'm really very sorry for your loss."

"Why should you be sorry?"

"Because I liked your father very much. He was always exceptionally kind to me."

"None of which explains how you met Rodney Tureck," Amanda says, surprised by the impatience in her voice.

"Does it matter?"

"It definitely matters."

Hayley nods, takes a moment to compose her thoughts. "I met him when I was coming home from school one afternoon. I was carrying all these books, and I tripped over a crack in the sidewalk in front of your house, and the books went flying off in all directions, and suddenly there he was, on his hands and knees, picking up everything for me." She stops, as if trying to recall the precise order of the events. "Anyway, he was on his way to see your mother, and I mentioned I often babysat for her, and we chatted a bit, and he cracked some jokes, and I laughed, and I don't know, we just kind of connected." She tucks her hair behind her right ear, smiles sheepishly. "I was in my rebellious teenage phase. The idea of an older man—one who listened to me and took my opinions seriously—well, that was very appealing. And he was very charming," she continues, the same word Gwen Price had used earlier. "I was quite flattered by the attention."

Amanda thinks of Sean Travis, sympathizes with what Hayley is saying in spite of herself. "You obviously saw him again after that afternoon."

"He'd call when I was babysitting. At first, he pretended to be phoning to speak to your mother, but after a while, he admitted he was calling to speak to me. He said he enjoyed our little talks, that I was refreshing and sweet and delightful, all the things I was desperate to hear. We started meeting, secretly of course. He said people wouldn't understand, and he was right."

"What else did he tell you?"

"That I was beautiful, that I was wise beyond my years, that I was an old soul who made him feel young, that we were destined to be together. Stuff like that."

"He convinced you to run away with him?"

"He didn't have to do much convincing. By that time, I was crazy mad in love with him." Hayley shakes her head. "It's funny because he wasn't much to look at. Not really. But when he looked into your eyes, he made you feel as if you were the most beautiful woman on earth, the only person in the world who mattered."

"So you ran off to England."

"Yes. It was terribly romantic. And surprisingly easy."

"Did he ever say anything about my mother?" Amanda asks.

The question seems to catch the other woman off guard. "Like what?"

"Like what he was doing coming to visit her, why he was calling?"

Hayley takes a deep breath, releases it with deliberate slowness, as if she is blowing smoke from a cigarette. She seems reticent about answering the question. "He said he had business with her."

"What kind of business?"

"The unfinished kind," Hayley says after another deep exhalation.

"Meaning?"

"Look, I really don't think you want to get into this."

"I think I do."

"It's not going to help your mother."

"What kind of unfinished business?" Amanda repeats.

Hayley rises from the chair, walks to the window, stares into the darkening sky. "He said your mother was a thief, that she'd stolen a great deal of money from him. He asked me to have a look around the house when I was babysitting, see if I could find anything."

Amanda feels a sharp stab of pain to her chest, realizes she is holding her breath. "Like what?"

"Bank books, safety-deposit-box keys, stuff like that."

"And did you?"

"No. I didn't feel right about it. I told him I couldn't do it."

"And what was his response?"

"He said it just proved how sweet and lovely a girl I was, and that it made him love me even more."

"What a guy." Amanda buries her head in her hands, trying to push away the headache gnawing at her temples.

"What happened after you got to England?" Ben asks.

"Rodney Tureck became John Mallins," Hayley answers. "We moved around for a few years. Eventually we settled in Sutton."

"North of Nottingham," Amanda says quietly, massaging the bridge of her nose.

"He bought a small shop, we got married, started a family."

"Lived happily ever after," Amanda says, louder than she'd intended.

"Pretty much," Hayley says.

Amanda looks over at Ben. He looks back at her. "Why didn't you tell any of this to the police?" they ask together.

"How could I?"

"How could you not?" Amanda asks.

"Think about it," Hayley tells her. "What was I supposed to tell them? That twenty-five years ago, when I was still a minor, I ran off with my neighbor's ex-husband, that we changed our names and spent years hiding from the authorities, that my husband's real name was Rodney Tureck, and that he was probably wanted by the police? Why would I tell them that?"

"I don't know. Because it's the truth?" Amanda asks in return. The truth, she thinks. What a concept.

"When the police first told me that John had been killed, I was too stunned to say anything. John had gone out first thing that morning. The children and I had been waiting for him to come back to the hotel. There was a knock on the door, and I remember thinking, 'That's strange, I guess John forgot his key.' So I asked, 'Who's there?' Because John was a stickler for never opening the door unless you were absolutely sure who was on the other side. And this very deep voice answered, 'Mrs. Mallins, it's the police.' Well, my first thought was that John had been arrested, that they'd discovered his real identity, that they'd come to arrest me too. A million thoughts. But none of them the right one. Have you ever noticed that? That you project ahead a million possibilities, and none of them is ever right? That the reality is always the one thing you haven't thought of?"

Amanda nods. She knows exactly what Hayley is talking about.

"When the police told me that John was dead, that he'd been gunned down in the hotel lobby, I insisted they'd made a mistake. They asked me a million questions, what we were doing in Toronto, if we knew anyone in the city, if I could think of any reason why someone might have targeted my husband. I just kept repeating what John had told me to say if anyone ever asked why we were here: that we were here on holiday."

"And when you found out the woman who shot your husband was Gwen Price?"

"I'm not sure what I thought. I guess I assumed she'd tell them the whole story."

"And when she didn't?"

Hayley swallows, pushes several lifeless strands of hair away from her face. "Well, it was too late then, really. What was I going to do? Tell the police I'd been lying? That my whole life was a lie? Think about my children," she says, lowering her voice to a whisper, looking toward the closed door of the bedroom. "They'd just lost their father. To learn that he wasn't the man they thought he was, that the woman who shot him was his ex-wife, a woman I used to babysit for. I was so afraid."

"Afraid of what?"

"That the police would take my children away from me."

"Nobody is going to take your children away from you," Ben assures her.

"They're all I've got," Hayley says, wiping away a fresh parade of tears.

"Nobody's going to take them away from you," Ben says again.

"After we got married, I got pregnant straightaway," Hayley says, speaking more to herself than to either Ben or Amanda. "But then, four months into the pregnancy, I suffered a miscarriage. And then several more in the years that followed. And then there were two stillbirths. That was the worst. To carry a child full term, for it to be so perfectly formed, for it not to be breathing. I can't begin to describe . . . I'm so anxious to take my children back to England."

"Why do you think Gwen Price hasn't told the police the truth?" Amanda asks, interrupting the other woman's reverie.

"I don't know. Maybe **why** she shot him isn't really very important."

"And you're not at all curious?"

Hayley shakes her head. "They shared a past," she says, as if this is reason enough. For several seconds, the ramifications of that simple sentence ricochet off the walls like tiny stones. "I'd like you to go now," she says. "Please. My children will be beside themselves with worry."

"I guess we've said enough for one night," Ben agrees, as slowly, reluctantly, Amanda pushes herself to her feet.

"You're not going to tell anyone about any

of this, are you?" Hayley asks, following them to the door. "I mean, it would just open up a whole can of worms, and it wouldn't do anybody any good. Clearly your mother feels the same way. Please," she says, reaching out, her hand closing over Amanda's as she reaches for the door. "Please, Mandy."

The name drops from the other woman's lips onto Amanda's skin, like acid. It burns through her flesh and into her brain, the accompanying hiss obliterating all other sounds. Somewhere in the distance, Amanda hears Ben's voice. "We'll be in touch," she thinks she hears him say.

Please, Mandy.

Somewhere far away, a door closes. Another one opens.

Please, Mandy.

"Are you okay?" someone is asking.

"Fine," someone answers back.

"You're sure?" The voice is louder, closer.

"What?"

Please, Mandy.

"I asked if you're okay," Ben says.

Amanda snaps back into the present, as if propelled there by an elastic band. "Why wouldn't I be okay?" she says, stepping inside a newly arrived elevator and pushing the button for the lobby. "Just because I find out that the one nice memory I have of my mother isn't about my mother at all? That it's about the babysitter! The fucking girl next door. Except that this girl next door was fucking my mother's ex-husband."

"You're not okay," Ben says.

"I'm fine."

"Fucking fine or just fine?"

She smiles. "I'm fine, Ben. Or I will be once I get something to eat."

"Okay. Why don't we go grab some dinner? Try to figure out our next move."

"You think we have any?"

He shrugs, his cell phone ringing inside his jacket.

"They share a past," Amanda repeats wondrously as he answers it. "I guess that's as good a motive for murder as any."

"Hi," Ben says into the phone, angling his body slightly away from her, so that she knows it's Jennifer on the other end even before she hears echoes of the other woman's voice. "What? When was this?"

"What is it?" Amanda asks, alarmed by the change in his voice.

"Is she all right?"

"Is who all right?"

"Okay. . . . Yeah. Thanks. I appreciate it. . . . Of course. I'll call you later."

"What was that about?" Amanda asks as Ben returns the phone to the inside pocket of his leather jacket.

"Your mother tried to kill herself," he says quietly, without further adornment.

"What? How?"

"Apparently she swallowed a bunch of pills."

"Pills? Where would she get pills?"

"I don't know. They've taken her to Etobicoke General."

"Can we see her?"

The elevator doors open and Ben leads Amanda through the lobby. "We can try."

THIRTY

By now the drive to the west end of the city is getting so familiar, Amanda thinks she could do it in her sleep, although she doubts she'll ever sleep again. Her head feels like a glass jar full of old coins—cumbersome and heavy, in danger of cracking, of dubious value. Thoughts, like pennies, rattle through her brain, roll across her line of vision: her mother is crazy/her mother is dying; her mother shot a total stranger/she shot her ex-husband; Hayley Mallins is the proverbial girl next door/the girl next door has been lying to everyone since day one.

So what makes Amanda think she's telling the truth now?

Amanda keeps her eyes peeled out the window, staring through the darkness, and concentrating all her energy on the host of new condominiums sprouting up like mushrooms along the lakeshore. So much has happened to the city in the last eight years, she thinks, in a concerted effort not to think anything else. If she lets her guard down, allows anything other than the dark sky, the bright lights, the traffic, the seemingly endless construction, into her thoughts for even one minute, her head will surely implode.

Her mother swallowed a bunch of pills. Why? Where did she get them? What made her do it?

"Lots of new buildings," she says, her voice unnaturally loud, as if trying to scare away unwanted musings.

"The city just keeps growing," Ben says in the same booming tones, as if his head is similarly afflicted.

Do you think my mother will be all right? "Do you think all this growth is a good thing?" **Do you think there's a chance my mother might die?**

"I guess you can't stop progress," Ben says.

It was the babysitter, and not her mother, who dangled her like a puppet from her arms.

"I was never a big fan of suburbs," Amanda says.

"Which is funny, don't you think?" Ben says, half-statement, half-question.

Did her mother even know that her former husband had run off with the babysitter? Would she have cared?

"What's funny?"

"Well, isn't Florida pretty much one suburb after another?"

Amanda pictures the southeastern coast of the aptly named Sunshine State, sees one small oceanside community melding effortlessly into the next: Hobe Sound, Jupiter, Juno Beach, Palm Beach Gardens, Palm Beach proper, Hypoluxo, Manalapan, Delray . . . "I guess."

Puppet, puppet. Who's my little puppet?

Not her mother.

The babysitter.

Amanda grabs her head, presses the sides of her temples. Talk about false memories.

"Headache?"

"A doozy."

"You have anything for it in your purse?"

Amanda shakes her head. A mistake. It shakes back.

"Maybe they can give you something for it at the hospital."

"Maybe I could borrow something from my mother." Amanda covers her eyes with her hands. "God, I don't believe I said that."

"She'll be all right, Amanda."

"I know," Amanda agrees. Her mother is a force of nature. It will take more than a handful of pills to finish her off. "Did your girlfriend say what kind of pills my mother took?"

"I don't think she knew."

"Did she know where she got them?"

"Apparently she stole them from one of her cellmates."

"The druggie who likes to clean, no doubt."

"That would be my guess."

"Any guesses as to why she'd do such a stupid thing?" Amanda realizes she is both angry and scared. Scared that her mother might die, and angry at herself for being scared. So what if her mother succeeds in killing herself? The truth is she's been dead to Amanda for years. "Do you think she did it because of our visit? Because she realized how close we were to finding out the truth?"

"This isn't your fault, Amanda. Don't start blaming yourself."

"I'm not blaming myself," Amanda snaps, exchanging her anger at herself for anger at her former husband, finding it a far more comfortable fit. "Let's get one thing straight here, shall we? Whatever my mother does is entirely up to her. If she wants to kill herself, that's fine with me. Please don't labor under the mistaken impression that I actually give a shit."

"Don't you?"

"I couldn't care less that my mother tried to kill herself. I'd just like to know **why**. And I don't need or appreciate the cheap psychoanalyzing. I am not blaming myself for anything. You're a lawyer, not a therapist. You're certainly not my husband anymore."

"You're absolutely right," he tells her after a pause, refusing to take the bait, to give her the fight she craves. The tight clenching of his jaw is the only sign she might have gone too far.

"Dammit, can't you make this thing go any faster?"

"I'm already going twenty kilometers over the limit."

"Try twenty-five."

"This is fast enough."

"Look, if she's really on her deathbed and we can get there before she croaks, maybe we can convince her to tell us the truth."

Ben glances at her sideways. "Those are pretty tough words."

"Yeah, well, I'm a pretty tough girl."

"I don't think that's true."

"Then you have a pretty short memory."

Ben nods knowingly, grips tightly on the wheel. "Hang on."

Ten minutes later, they pull into the parking lot of Etobicoke General. Amanda follows Ben through the front doors of the hospital into the main lobby and toward the information desk on the left. She tries not to take in too much of her surroundings, never having felt too comfortable around hospitals, and concentrating her focus on the wet footprints of the other visitors that run along the floor. Even still, she can't help but notice the gift shop, the pharmacy, the mini food court. As if she's stumbled into a mall and not a hospital. Only the smell gives it away, she thinks, trying to ignore the potent mix of rubbing alcohol and flowers, of blood and perfume, of disinfectant and medication. Of disease. Fear. Loss of control.

The fleeting aroma of one's own mortality.

"Fourth floor," Ben tells her, walking briskly toward the elevators, not bothering to take her elbow or slow down for her to catch up.

He's hurt, she realizes. Although he'd never admit it. She's opened up old wounds, ripped the bandage off a scar that was only just starting to heal. There he was, trying to be sympathetic and understanding and **there** for her, and her immediate reaction was to get away from him as fast as possible. To be anywhere but there. Just as she did eight years ago when she walked out on their marriage. **This isn't working,** she'd told him one night. They were lying in bed, having just finished making love.

What isn't?

This whole marriage thing.

What are you talking about?

I want out.

I don't understand. Did I do something wrong?

No.

Then why? Can we at least talk about it?

Nothing to talk about. It's over. I want out.

That was it. He didn't argue. He didn't fight to make her stay. He did what he'd always done—he took her at her word. And so, with a few simple sentences, her marriage to Ben was over and done, over and out. She'd stuck to pretty much the same script when she'd ended her marriage to Sean. **This isn't working,** she'd said as they were getting ready to go out for dinner with friends. Hell, might as well stick with what you know.

And so it goes, Amanda thinks, watching

Ben disappear around a corner, wondering when **his** feelings became **her** responsibility. She has no time to cater to bruised male egos, no interest in making nice or playing fair. Besides, Ben's the one who volunteered for this mess. It wasn't her idea. She never told him to get involved. Just because they "shared a past" doesn't mean she owes him anything. And just because she snapped at him in the car doesn't give him the right to try to make her feel guilty now. She has absolutely nothing to feel guilty about. Not his hurt feelings. Not her mother's pathetic attempt at suicide. None of it is her fault. She isn't to blame for any of this.

Isn't that exactly what he said?

This isn't your fault, Amanda. Don't start blaming yourself.

Goddammit, did he always have to be so right?

"I'm sorry," she apologizes, joining him at the bank of elevators. "I was a bitch."

He shrugs, says nothing. But when the elevator arrives, she feels the gentle, reassuring pressure of his hand on her elbow as he ushers her inside. The elevator quickly fills with people of various shapes and hues. Gloved hands reach across her as if she doesn't exist to press the buttons on the side panel. Not one floor is missed, Amanda notes, her body pushed against Ben's as the occupants of the elevator juggle for position. She folds in against his side, his arm reaching protectively around her shoulders as she inhales the strangely comforting damp leather of his jacket.

They exit the elevator at the fourth floor and follow the corridor around to the nurses' station. "Room 426?" Ben asks the small gathering of nurses chatting behind a tall counter lined with recently delivered floral arrangements.

The nurses turn toward them in one graceful swoop. One of the nurses, a middle-aged woman with shiny brown skin and black, curly hair, extricates herself from the group. "You're looking for Gwen Price?"

"Is she all right?" Amanda asks, holding her breath.

"You family?"

"I'm her daughter."

The nurse glances at Ben. "You?"

"Her lawyer."

"Other side, turn left, last room on the right."

Amanda shoots from Ben's side, vaults to the other side of the nurses' station.

"I'm not sure they're allowing visitors," the nurse calls after them.

They spot the guard sitting outside her door as soon as they turn the corner. He has light brown skin and short-cropped hair. Not too tall, Amanda notes as he pushes himself off his chair, but muscular beneath his neat blue police uniform, and the eyes in his handsome face are dark and wary. His expression is a warning. It says, Come closer only if you dare. "Something I can do for you folks?" he asks in a voice that says they better not be wasting his time.

"I'm Ben Myers, Gwen Price's attorney," Ben tells him, proffering his identification. "This is Amanda Travis, her daughter. We'd like to see Mrs. Price."

Amanda hands the officer her driver's license, glancing toward the closed door of her mother's hospital room as the policeman takes a moment to examine it. Her mother is inside that room, she thinks. Lying in bed. Possibly dying.

Why?

"Excuse me a minute," the officer says, walking a few steps away from them and talking into his cell phone discreetly.

Why would her mother want to kill herself? Why would she rather die than tell the truth?

Amanda rocks back and forth on her heels. Because she's my mother, that's why. When has she ever done anything that makes sense?

"All right," the police officer says, returning his phone to the holder on his belt. "You can go in. But just for a few minutes."

"How is she?" Ben asks.

"She'll be all right. But I should warn you . . ."

"Warn us about what?" Amanda asks.

"She's got a lot of bruises."

"Bruises? Why does she have bruises? Did she fall?"

"From what I understand, her roommate didn't take too kindly to the theft of her drugs. She went a little ballistic." He makes a sound that is something more than a sneer, something less than a laugh. "The commotion probably saved your mother's life."

Amanda tries to picture her mother trading punches with another woman. She sees her being wrestled to the ground, pummeled about her head and shoulders, imagines her delicate skin awash in bruises. The image causes Amanda's legs to buckle at the knees, and she crumples toward the floor. Ben catches her before she hits the ground. "It just keeps getting better and better," she says, pushing herself back to her feet and maneuvering out of his protective reach.

"Everything okay?" the officer asks.

"Are you all right to go in there?" Ben asks her.

"I'm fine."

"Everything's fine," Ben says, turning from the officer back to Amanda. "You're sure?"

In response, Amanda pushes open the door to her mother's hospital room and steps inside.

What Amanda sees: a small woman tucked inside the stiff folds of the white hospital sheets, her face an angry palette of red and purple splotches. A series of tubes are attached to her arms, and fluid drips slowly from an IV bag into her veins.

A figure sitting at the foot of the bed suddenly stirs, makes its presence felt.

What are you doing in here? Amanda's father asks.

"This is Gwen Price's daughter and her attorney," the police officer tells the attending nurse, who lowers the paperback book she's been reading to the chair.

Why is Mommy in bed?

"How is my mother doing?" Amanda asks the nurse.

She's resting.

"She looks worse than she is because of the beating," the nurse replies.

Why is she resting? Is she sick?

"We had to pump her stomach, of course," the nurse continues. "But she's lucky. The pills weren't in her system very long. She'll be fine by morning."

She'll be better in the morning.

"How long will you keep her here?"

Run along now, Mandy. You don't want to wake her up.

"Just overnight."

Yes, I do. I want her to play with me.

"Can we have a few minutes alone with her?"

Not now, Amanda. Maybe when she's feeling better.

"I'm afraid that's not possible," the police officer states.

You'd think I'd be used to seeing my mother in bed, Amanda thinks, banishing the images of her childhood with a wave of her hand. Although she suspects it's something you never get used to, no matter how old you get, no matter how estranged from one another you are. Mothers are supposed to be the caregivers. They aren't supposed to get sick. They certainly aren't supposed to try to kill themselves. "Why'd you do it?" she whispers, her fingers clasping the steel railing of the bed as she stares into her mother's battered face.

Then again, mothers aren't supposed to go around shooting people either.

"What's that?" Amanda zeroes in on a horrifying mark on the inside of her mother's left wrist. She draws a sharp intake of breath, waits for confirmation of what she already knows.

"I'm afraid that during the fight with her cellmate, she sustained several rather nasty bites," the officer says.

Amanda's entire body grows tense. "There are more?"

"There's another one on her left shoulder, not quite as big," the nurse tells her. "We cleaned them out and gave her a tetanus shot. Human bites are very tricky. They can be more dangerous than those pills she swallowed."

Amanda pictures the bite marks Derek Clemens left on Caroline Fletcher's back. How I hate bite marks, she thinks. "How long has she been sleeping?"

"On and off for the last hour."

"And tomorrow you send her back to jail?"

"There's no reason to keep her here."

"She'll be placed in a different cell, of course," Amanda says, directing her remark to the officer, who is positioned just inside the door and has been closely monitoring their visit.

"That would be my assumption," the officer says. Then: "I'm afraid I can only allow you a few more minutes."

Amanda turns back to her mother, pulls a chair up to the bed. "I'll say one thing for you, Mom—you sure know how to get people's attention. God knows you got mine." She tries to laugh, but the sound that emerges is harsh and strained. "Amazing, isn't it? We don't have anything to do with one another for the better part of a decade, and then we see each other almost every day. And in such interesting places too. Especially for a woman who rarely left her house the whole time I was growing up." She draws her chair closer to her mother's head. "We went to see Hayley Mallins," she whispers, pretending to be stroking her mother's forehead, although her fingers only inadvertently brush up against her skin. She scans her mother's face for a flicker of recognition, some sign that she has heard her. She gets nothing. "She told us all sorts of interesting things."

"I'm afraid I'll have to ask you to back away from the bed a bit," the officer directs.

"She told us everything," Amanda says, reluctantly pushing her chair away from the bed, then standing up, closely monitoring her mother for any reaction at all, seeing none. "Okay. Let's get out of here." She walks to the doorway, glances back at the woman asleep in the bed. She can't be sure from this distance, but she thinks she sees a lone tear escape her mother's closed eyes to trickle down the side of her face and disappear under the curve of her pillow.

THIRTY-ONE

As soon as they get back to the house on Palmerston Avenue, Amanda orders a pizza and Ben lights a fire in the living room fireplace. "I don't think it's been used since I was a child," Amanda marvels, warming herself in front of the flames, recalling the image of her mother sitting on the sofa, oblivious to the dangerous sparks shooting toward her feet.

"Seems to be working fine." Ben smiles, walks out of the room.

"Where are you going?"

"To get a corkscrew."

"What for? There's no wine."

"Oh, but there is." He returns carrying a corkscrew in one hand and a bottle of expensive Bordeaux in the other. "I have a case in the car," he explains before she can ask. "I keep forgetting to take it up to the apartment."

It occurs to Amanda that this is a ruse, that

he's been planning this evening all along, and that the wine and the roaring fire are all part of a master plan to seduce her. At least she finds herself hoping as much as he uncorks the bottle and she retrieves some glasses from the kitchen. It's been a long, trying day, full of unpleasant surprises. She could use a pair of strong and tender arms around her. Tender enough to rekindle pleasant memories, strong enough to keep the unpleasant ones at bay. She lowers her chin while lifting her eyes and smiling shyly. Remember how good we used to be together, the smile says.

He pours them each a full glass of wine, lifts his glass to hers in a silent toast. He smiles. I remember, the smile says.

Forty minutes later, they are sitting on the living room floor in front of the fire, their backs against the sofa, devouring a large, thin-crust pizza with double cheese and tomato slices, and finishing off a second bottle of wine. "This is nice," she says, enjoying the pleasant buzz that has settled in around the top of her spine. "I needed this."

"It's been a long day."

"That it has."

"Your mother—"

"Let's not talk about my mother."

"Let's not," Ben echoes.

"Or Hayley Mallins or Rodney Tureck or any of those silly people."

"Sounds good to me."

"And not Jennifer either."

Ben clicks his glass against Amanda's in agreement. Jennifer is summarily dismissed.

Their eyes meet, lock, linger. She giggles, knowing she isn't quite as inebriated as she is pretending to be, wondering if Ben is pretending the same thing. Being even slightly drunk permits them a greater range of options. They can say things to one another that might normally be considered off-limits. They can do things that might be regarded as ill-advised. They can cross invisible lines, then giggle and step back. They can throw caution to the biting wind, give in to the temptation that's been pulling at them like a magnet since she stepped off the plane, and make mad passionate love in front of a romantic fire. **It was the wine,** they can say in the morning, pulling themselves out of their respective fantasies, going back to their lives. "So what will we talk about?" she asks, giving him three minutes before he kisses her.

"Why don't we talk about you?"

"Oh, God, not her. She's so boring."

"She's many things," Ben corrects. "Boring isn't one of them."

"Only because you don't know her very well."

"Only because she never sticks around long enough."

"Consider yourself lucky."

Ben stares into his glass. "Ever think about moving back here?" he asks after a pause.

The question catches her off guard. Amanda feels an involuntary arch of her back, like a cat whose defenses are suddenly on high alert. "Why would I do that?"

"Because it's your home."

"Not for a long time."

"Because it would give you a chance to get to know your mother," he offers.

"I repeat, why would I want to do that?"

"Because she's your mother."

"We aren't talking about my mother, re-member?" Amanda finishes the wine in her glass, reaches for the bottle.

"Sorry. I forgot."

Her fingers brush against the back of his hand. He makes no move to pull his hand away. Two minutes, she thinks.

"What would I do back here anyway?" she asks.

"The same thing you do in Florida."

"Except I'd be colder."

"Only in winter."

"Which lasts six bloody months."

"Three," he corrects, holding out his glass for her to fill.

"Only according to the calendar."

"I thought you loved the change in seasons," he says.

She nods, picturing the first miraculous appearance of buds in the spring. "I don't have a license to practice law in Canada," she reminds him, the buds bursting, the image scattering, like pollen, as she divides what's left in the bottle between their two glasses.

"You got more than I did," he points out.

"Did not."

"Did too."

Amanda takes a quick swallow. "There. Now we're even."

He laughs. "So you go back to school for a year. Pass the bar here."

"Pass a bar?" She takes another gulp of wine. "I'd rather go in it."

One minute.

"We could even open up a practice together," he says with a laugh, as if he knows how ridiculous this suggestion is. "God knows there's plenty of lowlife to go around," he adds, leaving room for the possibility he doesn't consider his suggestion quite as far-fetched as it seems.

"God knows that's true," Amanda says, avoiding both interpretations altogether, and staring into the empty box on the floor between them. "What happened to the pizza?"

"I guess we ate it."

"So fast?"

Ben finishes his wine, lowers his glass to the floor, and leans toward her. "There's another reason for you to come back," he says quietly.

Thirty seconds, Amanda thinks, downing the rest of her wine in a single gulp. This is it, she is thinking. And not a moment too soon. Her heart is beating so fast, she's in danger of going into cardiac arrest. "And what would that be?" She reaches across him, careful to let her breast brush up against his arm as she deposits her empty glass next to his, then looks into his eyes expectantly. And it's about time, she is thinking, her body swaying toward his. Ten seconds . . . nine . . . eight . . .

"Well, there's this house," he says, his tone suddenly all business as he leans back against the sofa and stares at the fire. "If your mother goes to jail, which seems increasingly likely, you'll probably have to sell it."

"What?"

"I said—"

"I heard what you said." Amanda pulls back angrily. "I thought we weren't going to talk about my mother."

"You're right. I'm sorry."

"The hell you are. What's going on here?"

"What are you talking about?"

"You know what I'm talking about. You set me up."

"Set you up for what?"

"Don't play dumb with me. You did this on purpose."

"Did what on purpose?"

"It was payback for the things I said to you in the car, wasn't it?"

"I'm sorry, but I'm having trouble remembering that far back."

"I don't believe you."

"I don't know what you're talking about," he insists.

"Yeah, well, I'm going to bed." She clambers unsteadily to her feet. Is it possible she's mistaken? That Ben really has no clue what she's so upset about? That she let her fantasies and her ego get the better of her? No, Amanda decides, catching the sly smile behind his seeming confusion. He knows exactly what's going on.

You're a lawyer, not a therapist, she told him in the car. You're certainly not my husband anymore.

You're absolutely right.

Amanda storms into the hall, stops, returns to the living room, her fury building with each step. "You were wrong, you know."

"Wrong? About what?"

"You aren't a bigger prick as a lawyer." She pivots around on her heels, runs up the stairs. "You can show yourself out," she calls from the top of the landing. "Son of a bitch," she cries as she slams her bedroom door behind her and falls on her bed, using her pillow as a silencer, not wanting to give Ben the satisfaction of her tears. How long has he been waiting to humiliate her? she wonders. Since this afternoon? Since she arrived back in Toronto? Since she left?

She hears the front door open and close, and she goes to the window. Ben is trying to force his keys into the lock of the white Corvette. "You're too drunk to drive, asshole," she mutters, returning to the bed, hoping he gets stopped by the police, charged with drunken

driving, thrown into jail. Or better yet, maybe
he'll crash his car into a tree. . . . "No," she
says, quickly withdrawing her silent curse. "I
don't want you to get stopped by the police. I
don't want you to get hurt. I don't want anything bad to happen to you. Ever. Do you hear
me? I take it back. I take it back." She returns
to the window, but his car is already gone. "I
take it back," she is crying as she pulls back
the covers of her bed and collapses inside. "I
take it all back. Everything. Do you hear me?
I take it back."

She wakes up at two o'clock in the morning
with a pounding headache. "I thought this
wasn't supposed to happen with good wine,"
she says, debating whether to get out of bed
and take something for it. Ultimately she opts
to do nothing. She has the headache she deserves. It would be an injustice to dilute it.

Ben is right to hate her. She humiliated
him when she walked out eight years ago
without either apology or explanation, and
she's been using him shamelessly ever since
she got back to town. If he managed to get
back even a little of his own tonight, well,
more power to him. She asked for it. At any
rate, everything that happened today and

everything that **didn't** happen tonight have made one thing crystal clear: there's nothing to be gained by sticking around town any longer. Ben doesn't need her. Her mother doesn't want her. What is she doing here except making everyone, including herself, miserable? She'll call the airlines in the morning, book the first available flight home.

Amanda crawls out of bed, walks to the window, stares down at the now-empty driveway between her house and the house next door. "I really hope you got home all right," she whispers, debating whether to call Ben. But her cell phone is in her purse, and her purse is downstairs, and she hasn't got the energy to go down there, although there's a phone in her mother's room, she remembers, traversing the small hallway. "I'll just be waking him up," she says into the receiver, as she sits down on her mother's bed, pressing in Ben's number. She hangs up when the recorded voice reminds her she's forgotten to include the area code. He's probably with Jennifer anyway, she thinks, watching Sean Travis emerge from the shadows flickering across the wall, his arm around his pregnant wife, also named Jennifer. So many Jennifers, she thinks, as their images are absorbed by a shadow from a nearby tree. "I

wasn't very nice to you either," she acknowledges, once more reaching for the phone, this
time remembering to include the area code.

The phone is answered after two rings.
"Hello?" The familiar voice is muffled, husky
with sleep.

"Sean?" She pictures her former husband sitting up in bed, securing a blue cotton blanket
around his naked torso.

"Who is this?"

"It's Amanda."

A pause. "Amanda?"

"I'm sorry to be phoning you so late."

"Has something happened? Are you hurt?"

"No. I'm okay."

"Are you in some sort of trouble?"

"No."

"Are you drunk?"

"No."

"Then I don't understand. Why are you
calling?"

"Is there a problem?" she hears Jennifer ask
from somewhere beside him.

"I'm in Toronto," Amanda says.

"Toronto?"

"Remember how you once told me that
until I worked things out with my mother, I
would never really grow up?"

"I remember how angry you got," he says gently, after a pause.

"Yeah, well, sometimes it's hard to hear the truth."

Another pause. "So, how's it going?"

She laughs. "It ain't easy."

"I'm sure it isn't. But I'm also sure you can do it."

Amanda's eyes fill with grateful tears. "Sean?"

"Yeah?"

"I just want to apologize."

"It's all right. I was only half-asleep."

"Not for waking you up. Although I guess you can add that to the list."

"There is no list, Amanda."

"No? There should be."

Silence.

"Sean?"

"You don't have to apologize."

Amanda shakes her head. "I was a lousy wife to you."

"We were just a bad fit," Sean allows graciously.

"You never stood a chance."

Another silence. Then: "Well, it all worked out in the end. I'm very happy now."

"The baby's due this summer?"

"July eighteenth."

Amanda nods. "You know that I wish nothing but good things for you."

"I know. I wish the same for you."

"Good luck, Sean."

"Good-bye, Amanda."

Amanda remains on her mother's bed for several minutes cradling the receiver, now damp with her tears. The apology she gave Sean was long overdue. As is the apology she owes Ben, although that apology will have to wait till morning, she decides, returning to the hall, feeling the warmth from the fireplace rising to embrace her. Had they replaced the screen? Or were sparks even now shooting toward the carpet? She races down the stairs and into the living room, already seeing the headlines in the morning paper: **Lawyer Burns to Death in Murderer's House.** And just how many people would be upset about that?

Amanda runs into the living room, immediately sees that the screen is in place. She pulls it aside and pushes at the dying embers with a nearby poker.

"What are you doing?" a voice asks from behind her.

Amanda screams and drops the poker, spinning toward the sound.

"Careful," Ben says, getting up from the sofa

and retrieving the poker from the floor, returning it to its stand beside the fireplace.

"What are you doing here?"

"Trying to sleep." Ben points to the rumpled pillows of the sofa.

"I thought you left."

"I'm sorry, Amanda. I was in no condition to drive."

"Where's the car?"

"I put it in the garage." He stretches, smooths down his hair. "I'm probably sober enough now. I'll get out of your hair."

"No," Amanda says quickly. "I don't want you to leave. Please—don't go."

The light from the fire dances across Ben's face, illuminating his confusion. "I'm not sure I understand."

"I think you do."

A long pause, then, "You were right," he admits. "About my setting you up."

"I know."

"I honestly didn't plan it in advance. It just kind of played itself out."

"It doesn't matter."

"What do you mean, it doesn't matter?" They take small, tentative steps toward one another.

"I don't know what I mean," she tells him.

"I just know what I want. I want **you**. And it doesn't have to mean anything. It can be for revenge, if that makes you feel better."

"For revenge," he repeats, leaning over to smooth some stray hairs away from her face.

"Or for old times' sake."

"For old times' sake."

"Or just something to get out of our systems once and for all," she says as he bends his head to kiss the side of her mouth.

"Something to get out of our systems," he says, kissing her full on the lips.

"Once and for all," she repeats.

And then nobody says anything.

When Amanda wakes up at seven o'clock the next morning, Ben is gone.

"Damn," she says, wrapping herself in the pink blanket he obviously placed over her before he left, and pushing herself off the floor. "Damn." She pushes some hair away from her face, recalling the softness of Ben's touch, the hardness of his body, the effortless way in which their bodies reconnected, as if they'd never been apart. Even now she feels him pounding away between her legs, and she has to grab the side of the sofa to remain upright.

What has she done?

Wasn't she the one who told him it didn't have to mean anything, that it could be for revenge, for old times' sake, something to get out of their systems once and for all? Was she crazy? Dammit, did he always have to take her at her word? "Damn you, Ben," she whispers, hearing a loud banging on the front door. "Ben?" She runs to the door and throws it open.

Mrs. MacGiver, wearing a green tweed coat and knee-length, red vinyl boots, stands on the other side of the threshold. "I came for my tea," she says, not seeming to notice that Amanda is wearing nothing but a large pink blanket.

"Mrs. MacGiver . . ."

"Aren't you going to invite me inside?"

Amanda steps back to let the old woman enter. Immediately she hears water coming from the upstairs bathroom, realizes the shower is running. "Ben," she gasps, fighting the urge to throw off her blanket and run up the stairs to join him. He's here. He didn't leave. "I'm so sorry, Mrs. MacGiver," she says, fighting to contain a smile that is rapidly spreading across her face. "I forgot all about your tea."

"You forgot it?"

"Yesterday didn't go exactly as I planned."

"You forgot my tea," Mrs. MacGiver repeats incredulously.

The events of the previous day unfold in reverse order across Amanda's mind, like a videotape being rewound. She sees her mother lying in her hospital bed, the miles of construction along the Gardiner Expressway, the lobby of the Four Seasons hotel, Hayley Mallins standing in front of the window of her hotel suite. No, not Hayley Mallins. Hayley Walsh.

"I saw someone yesterday you might remember," Amanda tells Mrs. MacGiver, a way of making polite conversation as she tries ushering the old woman out the door. "Hayley Walsh. Mr. Walsh's daughter. Do you remember him? He lived next door."

"That miserable bastard," Mrs. MacGiver says with surprising strength. "Of course I remember him. He was one mean son of a bitch, that one."

"Yes, my mother wasn't too fond of him either."

"Rumor had it he used to beat his wife. And his sons. Until they got big enough to hit him back."

No wonder his daughter ran away to England, Amanda thinks. Obviously she wanted to get as far away from the man as possible.

"You said you saw his wife?" Mrs. MacGiver asks. "I thought she was dead."

"I saw his daughter," Amanda corrects.

"No." Mrs. MacGiver shakes her head. "Mr. Walsh didn't have a daughter."

Upstairs, the shower shudders to a halt.

"Yes, he did. She used to babysit me when I was little. She called me her puppet." Amanda's hands bounce up and down as if manipulating the strings of a marionette. "You remember—'Puppet, puppet, who's my little puppet?' "

Mrs. MacGiver stares at Amanda as if she has taken complete leave of her senses. "That wasn't Mr. Walsh's daughter."

"What do you mean?"

Mrs. MacGiver laughs, shakes her finger into Amanda's face, as if Amanda has been trying to put something over on her. "That was Lucy."

"Lucy? Who the hell is Lucy?"

Ben suddenly materializes at the top of the stairs, a towel wrapped around his wet torso. "What's going on?"

"Who are you?" Mrs. MacGiver asks, a sudden twinkle in her eye. "Is that you, Marshall MacGiver?"

"Who is Lucy?" Amanda repeats.

"You know."

"I don't know."

Old Mrs. MacGiver waves at Ben, her fingers fluttering with girlish grace.

"Who. Is. Lucy?" Amanda repeats a third time, each word its own sentence, as Ben slowly makes his way down the stairs to stand behind her.

Mrs. MacGiver sighs coquettishly. "Why, Marshall MacGiver. You know you're not supposed to be here. What will my parents say if they find out you've been sneaking around?"

"Mrs. MacGiver . . ."

"You're being very naughty."

"Who is Lucy, Mrs. MacGiver?"

"Lucy?" Mrs. MacGiver looks confused. Tears threaten her already watery eyes. "You must mean Sally."

"Mrs. MacGiver . . ."

"You're not Sally." Mrs. MacGiver begins spinning around in awkward circles, like a top winding down, about to fall over on its side. "What have you done with my granddaughter? Where is she?"

"Mrs. MacGiver, if you'd just calm down—"

Mrs. MacGiver vaults toward the doorway. "I want to go home. Now." Gathering the bottom of her nightgown up around the tops of her red vinyl boots, she throws open the door and hurries across the street. Amanda and Ben, wrapped in a pink blanket and white towel respectively, watch helplessly as the old woman's front door opens, then slams shut, a clump of snow from an overhead windowsill landing, like an exclamation point, behind her.

THIRTY-TWO

Where are you going?" Ben asks, trudging through the snow after Amanda.

Amanda marches up the walkway of the house next door, rings the doorbell three times. "There has to be someone on this street who isn't nuts, and who lived here when I was little. Hopefully they'll be able to tell us something."

"What exactly are you hoping to find out?"

"For one thing, if Mr. Walsh had a daughter."

"And for another?"

Amanda rings the doorbell again. "Who the hell this Lucy is."

"*If* she is," Ben stresses. "The old woman was obviously confused."

"Not that confused."

"She was wearing a nightgown and red vinyl boots," he points out, as if this clarifies everything.

Amanda rings the doorbell a fifth and final

time. "Doesn't look like anyone's home." She cuts across the snow-covered lawn to the house next door and is about to ring the bell when the front door opens.

"Oh," says a young woman, clearly surprised to find anyone on the other side. She balances a squirming baby awkwardly in her arms, while a toddler sways restlessly at her feet. All three are wearing heavy blue snowsuits and expressions of barely suppressed hysteria. "Who are you?"

"My name is Amanda Travis. I live—"

"I'm sorry," the woman interrupts, the toddler at her feet pulling on her jacket as the baby in her arms begins stretching toward the ceiling. "Now isn't a great time. As you can see, we're just on our way out, and we're pretty tapped out from Christmas anyway, so it's probably not the best time to come asking for donations."

"We're not looking for donations."

The woman manages to look confused, harassed, and anxious with one arching of her overly plucked eyebrows.

"I think we have the wrong house," Amanda allows.

The woman nods gratefully as she lifts her now-squealing toddler into her free arm, then carries both struggling children down the front steps toward the street.

"She obviously wasn't here twenty-five years ago," Amanda says, walking toward the house next door.

The story at the next five houses is essentially the same. The residents assume Amanda is either trying to sell them something or exhort money from them, and the reception she gets is as frosty as the outside air. One man, loudly proclaiming that he's sick and tired of Jehovah's Witnesses disturbing him when he's in the bathroom, slams the door in their faces before Amanda has a chance to open her mouth. None of the people they actually talk to has lived on the street for more than ten years. No one looks even vaguely familiar.

"How many houses do you want to try?" Ben asks patiently as they approach a large brick house framed by tall, white pillars.

"A few more on this side," she tells him. "Maybe a few across the road."

Ben offers his arm to help her navigate a patch of sidewalk that hasn't been shoveled. Amanda doesn't move. "Something wrong?"

Amanda stares at the old house, no less foreboding now than it was when she was a child. She tries picturing the woman who lives inside,

but all she can hear is her mother's harsh as-
sessment— **She's a real bitch on wheels.**

"Amanda?"

Amanda sucks in a breath of fresh resolve
and trudges up the unshoveled front walkway.
Her mother is hardly the world's best judge of
character. And besides, the house, like most of
the others on the street, has probably changed
ownership many times in the last several
decades. She takes another deep breath as she
reaches the front door, then rings the bell.

"Who is it?" a woman's voice calls from inside.

"My name is Amanda Travis," Amanda calls
back. "I live down the street. I was wondering
if I could talk to you for a few minutes."

The door opens. A woman, stylishly dressed
in black pants and a bright coral sweater, stands
in front of her, jeweled fingers resting on slim
hips. She is between sixty and seventy, and a
wide streak of white cuts through her chin-
length ebony hair, like the dividing line on a
highway. Or a skunk, Amanda thinks, vaguely
recognizing the cool green eyes and thin patri-
cian nose. She glances surreptitiously toward the
woman's feet, checking for wheels.

"Mrs. Thompson?" she asks, pulling the
name out of the past with surprising ease, then

taking an involuntary step backward, feeling Ben at her back.

"Yes? Who are you?"

"Amanda Travis," Amanda repeats. "This is Ben Myers." Mrs. Thompson's eyes flit back and forth between them. "My mother lives down the street." Amanda waves in the general direction of her mother's house. "I guess you don't remember me."

"Should I?"

"Well, no. I guess not. I haven't lived with my mother in some time, and I've changed considerably."

"What is it you want?"

Amanda clears her throat. "Just to ask you a few questions."

"About what?"

"Maybe we could come inside?"

"What is it you want?" the woman asks again, ignoring the request.

Amanda gulps at the cold air. She smells coffee emanating from inside the house and longs for a cup. "Mrs. Thompson, my mother is Gwen Price."

Silence. The woman's eyes blink recognition of the name. Then: "I still don't understand what you want with me."

Neither do I, Amanda agrees. Aloud she

says, "Do you remember Mr. Walsh, by any chance. He lived in the house next door to my mother."

"Mr. Walsh? No. I've never heard of him."

"Then you don't remember if he had a daughter?" Silly question, Amanda thinks, as the woman purses her lips and rolls her eyes.

"If I don't remember **him,** how would I remember if he had a daughter?" If possible, the woman's tone is even icier than the sidewalk.

Amanda nods. Her mother was right.

"What about Mrs. MacGiver?" Ben asks. "She lives across the road . . ."

"That crazy old coot? The one who runs around the street in her nightgown?"

"That's the one."

"What about her?"

"She mentioned someone named Lucy," Amanda continues. "I was wondering if—"

Mrs. Thompson becomes quite agitated. Her shoulders twitch back and forth as if she is about to sprout wings. "What are you trying to pull?" she demands angrily.

"I'm sorry?"

"I don't have time for this." She tries to shut the door, but Ben's hand stops her.

"I don't understand," he says. "What just happened?"

"Who's Lucy?" Amanda asks.

"You really don't know?" Mrs. Thompson mutters in obvious disbelief.

"No." Amanda feels a sharp poke in the center of her chest and realizes she is holding her breath.

"You're trying to tell me you don't know your own sister," the woman states.

"What?"

The door slams in Amanda's face.

The white Corvette races along Bloor Street toward the Four Seasons hotel. "What the hell is going on here, Ben?"

"Take it easy, Amanda," Ben cautions, as he has been cautioning ever since Mrs. Thompson's startling announcement.

"It doesn't make any sense." Amanda taps her feet with impatience as the traffic light at Bloor and Spadina turns from orange to red. "Just go through it," she urges. Ben ignores her, bringing the car to a full stop. "Come on," Amanda directs the stubborn traffic light, tapping her feet in growing frustration. "What's the matter with the damn thing? You think it's stuck?"

"It's only been a few seconds."

"Just go through the damn thing. Nobody's coming."

"Take it easy, Amanda. We want to get there in one piece."

Is it possible that old Mrs. MacGiver is right? That Mr. Walsh didn't have a daughter? That the person who used to dangle her from her arms, like a real live marionette, was someone named Lucy?

The light goes from red to green. "Go," Amanda instructs before Ben has a chance to react.

Is it possible that what Mrs. Thompson said is true? That Lucy is her sister?

"Hayley Mallins better have some answers for us." Amanda stares out the front window, chagrined by the number of cars that have suddenly materialized, as if for the express purpose of slowing her down. "I'm not leaving her room until she starts telling us the truth."

And if Hayley Mallins isn't Mr. Walsh's daughter, but someone named Lucy, and Lucy is her sister . . .

"Just remember you catch more flies with honey than with vinegar," Ben says.

"What?"

"I'm just saying—"

"I know what you're saying, and if I wanted advice from Ann Landers I'd ask for it."

. . . then that means Hayley Mallins is her sister.

Ben's fingers grip tightly on the wheel. "We'll be there in two minutes," he says, staring straight ahead.

Which is impossible.

It doesn't make any sense. So why is she snapping at Ben when he's the only thing in her life that does?

Does what happened between them last night make any sense at all?

"Sorry," Amanda apologizes, recalling the softness of his lips as they brushed against hers, the sureness of his touch. She shakes the unwanted memory aside. How can she be thinking about such things now?

"It's okay," he says, his hands relaxing their grip on the wheel. "And just for the record, I'm pretty sure Ann Landers passed away. We have **Dear Ellie** to advise us now."

Amanda nods. "I'll be sure to write."

Dear Ellie, I'm having a wee bit of a problem. You see, my mother, from whom I've been long estranged, has been charged with killing a total stranger in a hotel lobby. Except she now claims that this total stranger was actually her ex-husband, from whom she stole vast sums of money. As

well, the possibility has just been raised that the dead man's widow might actually be my sister. Added to my woes is the fact that I seem to be falling in love with my very own first ex-husband, who just happens to be my mother's attorney. What should I do? Follow my heart or follow my mother's example and simply shoot everyone involved? Signed, In Trouble in Toronto.

A minor logjam slows them down to a crawl. "Where are all these cars coming from?" Amanda asks between tightly gritted teeth.

"It's rush hour," he reminds her.

If only she hadn't offered to buy Mrs. Mac-Giver that stupid tea. If only she hadn't answered her knock on the door. If only she hadn't mentioned damn Mr. Walsh. She and Ben could still be rolling around in front of the fireplace, instead of stuck on Bloor Street in the middle of rush-hour traffic. Amanda checks her watch. Barely eight o'clock. "It's always rush hour," she says as the light they're approaching at the corner of Bloor and St. George turns from green to orange. "Step on it, Ben. We can make it."

Ben steps on the gas, plowing right into the back of the dark blue Toyota in front of him. "Shit," he says over the sound of metal colliding.

"I don't believe this," Amanda mutters.

"Are you all right?" Ben asks Amanda as the driver of the Toyota jumps out of his car and marches angrily toward them, arms flailing wildly in the frigid air.

"I don't believe this," she repeats, as behind them cars start honking their displeasure.

"Where the hell do you think you're going in such a damn hurry?" the Toyota driver demands. He is about forty, wearing a black suede coat and a black hat with sheepskin flaps that cover his ears. Only his nose is clearly visible. It is large, and already turning red with the cold. He paces back and forth beside their car, flapping his arms like a giant crow.

Ben gets out of the car. "I'm sorry. I thought you were going through."

"It's a fucking red light."

"It was my fault," Amanda admits, climbing out of the car, and surveying the damage to the two cars. She sees only a few scratches, all of them on the bumper of Ben's white Corvette. Thank God, she thinks. This means we don't have to involve the police or the insurance companies. We can just apologize and get the hell out of here. "It looks like your car's okay," she tells the Toyota driver. "You got lucky."

"I got lucky? I've got news for you, lady. I've got a bad back. God only knows what this has done to it."

He can't be serious, Amanda thinks, fighting to keep her temper in check. "You seem to be moving around pretty good for a man with a bad back," she tells him dismissively. She doesn't have time for this. She has to get to the Four Seasons hotel. She has to see Hayley Mallins, also known as Hayley Walsh, also known as Lucy, also known as . . .

Who the hell is she?

"There's nothing wrong with your car, and there's nothing wrong with your back," Amanda tells the man flatly.

"Oh, really? Are you a doctor?"

"No, I'm a lawyer. We both are. So if you're thinking of suing, which is the feeling I'm getting here, I'd seriously consider thinking again."

"Is that some kind of threat?"

"Amanda . . ."

"I don't have time for this crap, Ben. You want to stay here and argue with this jerk, fine. That's up to you. I'm out of here."

"Lady, you're a real wack-job," the man says.

"Yeah? You should meet the rest of my family."

"Amanda. Just calm down. I'll call the police. They'll be here in a few minutes."

"I don't have a few minutes." She is already running down the street.

"Amanda . . ."

"You know where to find me," she calls back without slowing down.

The elevator comes to a stop on the twenty-fourth floor of the Four Seasons hotel. Amanda vaults out, stopped only by the imaginary touch of Ben's hand on her shoulder. **You catch more flies with honey than with vinegar,** she hears him say.

She stops, takes one deep breath, then another. "Okay, listen to Ben. Slow down. Take it easy." She then proceeds briskly down the corridor, where she takes another deep breath before knocking gently on the door to Suite 2416. No one answers. After a pause, Amanda knocks again. This time the knock is slightly more insistent.

It's still early, she reminds herself. They could be asleep. Give them a minute to wake up, to realize someone is at the door. "Come on," she whispers, the gentle knocking growing louder, losing its hold on civility. "Come on. I haven't got all day."

No response.

"Hayley," Amanda shouts. "Hayley, it's Amanda Travis. Open up." She kicks at the door with her foot.

Still nothing.

"I'm not leaving till I talk to you." Amanda presses her ear against the door, waiting to pick up even the tiniest of sounds. But after several minutes, she is forced to the realization that no one is there. Is it possible the grieving family went out for breakfast? And if so, where?

Amanda runs back to the elevators, holding her finger down on the call button until an elevator finally arrives. Then she pushes through the doors before they're fully open, stumbling into the arms of two men standing in the center of the car. Normally she would have cracked a vaguely risqué joke and walked out with at least one invitation for breakfast, but this morning is far from normal. "Sorry," she says simply to the two men, not quite looking at either of them, and pressing the button for the Studio Café on the second floor.

The Studio Café is a long, narrow space, with lots of windows overlooking the shops along fashionable Yorkville Avenue. The furniture is modern, as is the decorative art hanging from the walls, and brightly colored glasswork occupies prominent positions throughout the room. Perhaps a dozen people are already seated, reading the morning paper and enjoying breakfast. The smell of food reminds Amanda she hasn't had anything to eat.

"Good morning, miss." The maître d' gathers several large menus into his hands. "Will someone be joining you for breakfast this morning?"

"Actually, I'm just looking for someone." Amanda's eyes flit from one end of the room to the other. "A woman and two children. A boy, around ten, and a girl, maybe thirteen."

"Looks like you're the first one here," the maître d' proclaims. "I can seat you, if you'd like."

"No, that's okay. I'll check downstairs first."

"Certainly," he says, as if his approval were required.

Amanda hops on the escalator that runs from the second floor to the lobby. A second restaurant is located at the foot of the escalator, but a quick glance reveals Hayley and her children aren't there either. "God, don't tell me she took them to McDonald's," Amanda whispers into the collar of her coat. She just passed one on Bloor Street. Is it possible she'd run right past them? That they were enjoying Egg Mc-Muffins and hash brown potatoes while she was fleeing the scene of an accident?

She pictures Ben standing beside his beloved Corvette. He'd always taken such good care of that car. Never an accident, never even a dent. Until now. And it was all her fault. She was the reason he'd driven his car into the back of that stupid Toyota, that he was forced to make nice to that odious little man. And what had she done? She'd announced she didn't have time for such nonsense and run off. Something Ben should be used to by now, she thinks, wondering what to do next.

There are dozens of restaurants in the area. She can't very well check them all out. It's hopeless. She'll just have to make herself comfortable in the lobby, relax, and wait for them to come back. Just like her mother, she realizes with an audible groan, deciding to check with the front desk instead. It's possible someone might have seen them leave, noted the direction they took. Perhaps Hayley even spoke to one of the clerks, told him where she'd be. Admittedly a long shot, but then, it never hurts to ask.

Sometimes it does, Amanda corrects, thinking of all the questions she'd asked her mother, the questions she has yet to ask Hayley Mallins. Sometimes it does hurt to ask.

She takes off for the lobby, practically pouncing on an unsuspecting clerk behind the reception desk. "This is an emergency," she tells the startled young woman, who takes a wary step back. "I'm trying to locate Hayley Mallins. I know she's staying in Suite 2416, but I've just been up to her room, and she's not there, and it's urgent I get in touch with her. Did you see her?"

The young woman quickly types something into her computer. "I'm sorry, but Mrs. Mallins has checked out."

"What do you mean, she checked out? That's impossible."

"It appears she checked out last night."

"Did she say where she was going?"

"I'm afraid not."

Amanda feels sick to her stomach. Is it possible she took her children and returned to England? "Shit. Shit," she says again, louder the second time.

"Is there a problem here?" a man asks, coming up beside the young woman and glancing at the computer screen. The name tag on his lapel identifies him as William Granick, Hotel Manager. "Can I help you with something?"

"I'm trying to locate Hayley Mallins. It's urgent that I speak to her."

"I'm afraid Mrs. Mallins has checked out."

"Yes, so I've been told. But surely she left a number where she can be reached."

"I'm afraid I can't help you." The tone of William Granick's voice says he wouldn't help her even if he could.

"I don't think you understand—"

"Amanda!" Ben's voice suddenly calls out from somewhere behind her.

She spins around to see him walking toward her. His face is very red, an indication he's been standing outside in the cold for some time. "Ben, thank God."

"What's happening?"

"They checked out last night."

"I was afraid of that."

"What happened with your car?"

"Guy decided he didn't want to involve the police after all. I think you scared him."

Amanda smiles, the smile immediately flipping into a frown. "Do you think they went back to England?"

"It's a good possibility."

"Can we find out?"

"Let's get some coffee." Ben leads Amanda toward the lobby bar. "Two coffees," he orders, pulling his cell phone from his pocket, and checking his watch as he punches in a series of numbers. "Hi. It's me," he says, his voice unnaturally low. She can tell by the guilty hunch of his shoulders that he's speaking to Jennifer. "Yeah, I'm sorry about that. I didn't get home till really late. . . . Actually, I didn't get home at all," he admits after an uncomfortable pause. Then: "Yeah, she's still here. Yes, I'm with her now." Another pause, this one even more uncomfortable than the first. Amanda wonders if it's as uncomfortable for Jennifer as it is for Ben. She watches his face, sees the sadness in his eyes, hears the regret in his voice. Is he having second thoughts? About Jennifer? About her? "Can we talk about this later?"

"Is there really anything to say?" Amanda hears the other woman ask.

"It's a complicated situation," he tells her. Then: "Look, I need to ask you for another favor."

Certainly not what the other woman was hoping to hear, Amanda knows, holding her breath and saying a silent prayer that Jennifer will be curious enough to listen to his request.

"Can you find out if Hayley Mallins has gone back to England? We're at the hotel now, and apparently she checked out last night." Ben waits for several seconds before dropping the phone to the small round table between them. "She hung up."

The waiter brings their coffee, asks if they'd like anything else.

Ben stares out the side window.

"No, thanks. That's everything," Amanda tells the waiter. "I'm sorry," she says to Ben.

"Don't worry. I have a few other connections. At nine o'clock, I'll start calling around."

"I meant about Jennifer."

He shrugs. The shrug says, I'm sorry too.

"You didn't have to tell her you were with me."

"Yeah, I did." He takes a sip of his coffee. "Besides, she had it pretty much figured out for herself."

"I'm sorry," Amanda says again.

The air around them grows heavy with the silence of regret. "You're still planning on leaving, aren't you?" he says, a leading question. Like any good attorney, he already knows the answer.

What have I done? Amanda wonders. She satisfied an itch, and now everybody's bleeding. "As soon as this is over." Is that all she can think of to say? "I think it's for the best."

He nods, glances back out the window. "And last night?"

"Last night was—"

"—something to get out of our systems once and for all," he says.

More like temporary insanity, Amanda thinks. "She loves you, Ben," she says, thinking of Jennifer. "You'll call her in a couple of days, explain the circumstances . . ."

As if on cue, Ben's cell phone rings. "Hello?"

"Okay, don't ask me why I'm doing this," she hears Jennifer say.

So maybe he won't even have to wait a couple of days, Amanda thinks, watching as Ben listens, his eyes narrowing in concentration. "Okay, thanks. I'll call you later. . . . Okay, yeah. Bye."

"Okay, yeah, what?"

"Apparently we freaked Hayley out yesterday. She got permission from the police to return to England."

"Oh, no."

"It's all right. We got lucky. She couldn't get a flight back to England until tonight."

"She's still here?"

"At the Airport Hilton."

"Let's go."

THIRTY-THREE

The Airport Hilton can be summed up in two words: Hilton and airport. That tells you pretty much everything you need to know about the hotel, Amanda thinks as she and Ben cut across the lobby to the elevators at the back. Functionally attractive in shades of beige and green, it is situated a short distance from the airport, in the middle of a strip of such hotels that cater predominantly to businesspeople with neither the time nor inclination for sightseeing, or to travelers connecting with early-morning flights. The lobby is rife with women in smartly tailored suits and men toting heavy briefcases, everyone looking terribly purposeful, Amanda thinks, stepping aside to allow a newly arrived elevator to disgorge its passengers.

"What if she's not here?" Amanda asks as Ben presses the button for the third floor.

"She's here."

The elevator bumps to an unexpected stop on the second floor, and the doors open to reveal a couple locked in a lovers' embrace, and surrounded by suitcases. So tightly are the two people welded together that Amanda can almost see the young man's tongue jammed down his companion's throat. She turns discreetly aside, trying not to remember the feel of Ben's tongue as it played gently with the corners of her mouth only hours earlier. She brings her fingers to her lips, feels Ben lingering, but she can't bring herself to wipe him away. Only a few hours ago he was inside her. Now he stands a careful distance away, the hands that caressed her limp at his sides.

Which is exactly as it should be.

Did he really expect anything different?

Did she?

Amanda coughs into her hand, and the couple breaks apart, the young woman's mouth and chin red with the imprint of the man's pronounced morning stubble.

"Just married," the young man says, grinning sheepishly, as he carries the assorted bags inside the elevator. His face is the shape of an inverted triangle, and black, curly hair falls across his flat, wide forehead.

"We're going to the Bahamas." The girl giggles, leans into her husband's side. Her long, honey-blond hair falls around a heart-shaped face that is dominated by huge brown eyes.

She looks barely out of her teens, Amanda thinks. Barely older than I was when Ben and I eloped. Of course she and Ben hadn't been able to afford a honeymoon in the Bahamas, or anywhere else for that matter, and they'd spent their wedding night on a mattress in the middle of the floor of Ben's tiny, one-room apartment. Even now she can recall the joy of waking up in the morning to find him beside her. This is it, she remembers thinking. I've come home. I'm never leaving.

And yet, that's exactly what she did.

That's what she's still doing.

The new groom presses the button for the lobby. "Oh," Amanda tells him apologetically. "I'm sorry. We're going up."

The young man shrugs. "Guess we are too."

"What time's your flight?" Amanda asks in an effort to still the voices in her head.

The bride grabs her new husband's wrist, checks his watch, and groans audibly. "Not for another couple of hours. We have **so** much time."

"I just think it's smarter to be a little early

than to rush around at the last minute getting all uptight," the young man says defensively.

It's clear to Amanda that they've already had this discussion several times since the wedding, and that they will probably be having variations of this argument throughout their married lives. She wonders whose patience will be the first to run out, who will be the first one to bolt for the door. "Good luck," she wishes them as the elevator doors open onto the third floor.

"You too," the newlyweds say together.

Amanda looks back before the doors are fully closed, catches a brief glimpse of two forms swaying toward one another, their hands reaching for each other, their fingers almost clawing at the air, as if it's physically painful for their bodies to be apart. It **is** painful, she decides, feeling an ache growing in the pit of her stomach, then metastasizing like a particularly virulent cancer and spreading throughout her body. She fights the urge to shout after Ben as he walks down the hall, to yell at him to stop, slow down, turn around, come back to her. This can wait, she wants to tell him. Everything can wait.

Except it can't.

And she doesn't.

And he doesn't.

"What room?" she says instead, catching up to him.

"Right here." He stops in front of Room 312, knocks with quiet authority on the door. "Hotel manager," he announces before the occupants of the room have time to ask who it is.

The voice from inside is tentative. "Is something wrong?" Hayley Mallins opens the door a tiny crack, her eyes widening in alarm when she sees who's on the other side. She tries to shut the door, but Ben has grown used to people slamming doors in his face, and his foot is already wedged inside, acting as a doorstop. "No," Hayley hisses, slamming her shoulder against the door. "Go away. Go away."

"Please," Amanda urges the woman. "Just let us talk to you."

"Spenser, call downstairs," comes the immediate response. "Tell them to send security."

"I don't think you want to do that," Ben advises, pushing so hard against the door that Hayley has no choice but to step aside and let them enter.

The room is clean and nondescript, taken up almost entirely by two queen-size beds. Ben moves quickly toward Spenser, who is standing at the small desk in front of the third-floor window, cradling the phone and fighting back tears. The boy, still in his faded blue pajamas, drops the receiver as Ben draws near and runs to his mother's side.

"It's okay, Spenser," Ben tells him. "We're not going to hurt you."

"What do you want with us?" another voice asks, and both Ben and Amanda turn toward the sound.

Hope is sitting in the middle of the second bed, also in her pajamas. She stares at Ben and Amanda with cold defiance.

"Go away," the young boy shouts at the intruders, emboldened by his mother's protective arms. "Go away and leave us alone."

"We can't do that," Amanda says.

"I don't have to talk to you, you know," Hayley tells them. "The police said I'm under no obligation to talk to you."

"Then suppose you just listen."

"And if I'm not interested in anything you have to say?"

"You'll listen anyway."

"Please," Hayley pleads. "You'll only make things worse."

"Your husband is dead and my mother is in jail," Amanda tells her. "How can things possibly get any worse?"

"Because they can," Hayley replies simply, sinking to the foot of the nearest bed, Spenser seemingly glued to her side. She is wearing the same moss green sweater she had on the day before, and her hair is pinned away from her face by two large bobby pins. She wears no makeup at all, and her skin is ashen, verging on outright gray. She nods, giving in. "I don't want my children to be present," she says softly.

"Why don't I take them downstairs for something to eat?" Ben offers.

"No," Spenser wails, clinging tightly to his mother's waist.

"We're not leaving you," Hope says.

"Breakfast sounds like a very good idea," Hayley says calmly. "You were just saying how hungry you are, Spenser. That you fancied a big plate of blueberry pancakes."

"I want you to come too," the boy cries.

"And I want you and your sister to get dressed and go with Mr. Myers."

"Ben," Ben says.

"You go with Ben, and I'll be there as quickly as I can. I promise." Hayley smiles, although the smile is forced and wobbly. "Please, sweetheart. There's nothing to worry about. I promise you. Obviously this lady has something very important she wants to say, and she isn't going to go away until she says it. So let's just get this over with, shall we?" She appeals to Hope with her eyes. "Please, love. Go get dressed."

With great reluctance Hope climbs out of bed. She grabs her clothes from the closet and disappears inside the bathroom.

"Get your things together, Pup— Spenser," his mother directs.

"I don't know what to wear."

"Wear what you wore yesterday."

"Don't want to."

"How about your new brown sweater? You look so handsome in it."

Spenser slides off the bed and retrieves his sweater from a drawer, pulling it over his head, and only then removing his pajama top. He pushes his arms into the sweater and smooths down his hair, staring at Amanda with a look that tells her exactly what he's thinking. Which is that he wishes she were dead.

Amanda looks toward Ben. "Thank you," she mouths, as reluctant to let him leave as Hayley's children are to leave their mother.

After several minutes, Hope emerges from

the bathroom, neatly dressed in jeans and a pale pink sweater, her long, dark hair swept into a high ponytail.

"You look lovely," Amanda tells the young girl sincerely, reminded that pink was always her mother's favorite color. Hope ignores the compliment as she assumes Spenser's former position on the bed beside her mother. Hayley takes her daughter in her arms and kisses her forehead. They all have variations of the same face, Amanda thinks as Spenser brushes past her into the bathroom. The same high cheekbones, the same full lower lip, the same piercingly sad eyes.

"I'm not very hungry," Hope tells her mother when Spenser reemerges.

"You'll eat what you can," Hayley says.

"I hear they have a great buffet table," Ben says.

"Go on now," their mother cajoles. "I'll join you straightaway."

"If you're not down in twenty minutes," Spenser warns, "I'll scream for the police."

"Twenty minutes then," Hayley says, looking to Amanda for confirmation.

"Twenty minutes it is," Amanda agrees.

Ben opens the door and watches as Spenser

and Hope walk through, Hope stopping in the doorway, turning back just as he is about to close the door. "See you in twenty minutes," she repeats, the intensity of her gaze remaining even after she is gone.

"They're lovely children," Amanda says.

Hayley's eyes fill with tears. "How did you find us?"

"Does it really matter?"

"I suppose not. What is it you want?"

"I think you know."

"I think you should stop beating around the bush and get to the bloody point," Hayley snaps, losing her temper for the first time, and slapping her hands against her sides in frustration.

"I know you're not Mr. Walsh's daughter," Amanda tells her. "Mr. Walsh didn't have a daughter."

"Is that what your mother told you?"

"My mother hasn't told me anything. She's in the hospital."

"The hospital?"

"She tried to kill herself."

"What?" Hayley looks stricken. "Oh, God. Is she all right?"

"She will be," Amanda says, startled by the other woman's unexpected concern. "Why would

she do something like that, Hayley? What secret would she be willing to protect with her
life?"

"How would I know?"

"I don't know, but you do."

Hayley becomes agitated, starts pacing back
and forth in front of the bed. "You have to
leave. Now. Before more people get hurt."

"Tell me who you are."

"I can't."

"I'm not leaving till you do."

Tears fill Hayley's eyes. "You don't know?
You really don't know?" The same question
Mrs. Thompson asked earlier.

"I know your name isn't Hayley."

"No. You're wrong."

"I know your real name is Lucy."

"No, please. You don't know what you're
talking about."

"I know you're my sister," Amanda ventures,
bracing herself for more of the woman's vehe-
ment denials.

There are none.

"Oh, God," the woman moans, clutching
her stomach. "Oh, God. Oh, God."

"You're my sister," Amanda repeats incredulously as the other woman bolts past her into
the bathroom. Seconds later, the room fills

with the sounds of violent retching. Amanda wills herself to be calm, to think nothing at all until Hayley returns. She assures herself this is all a mistake, that Hayley is playing with her head. Payback for all the trouble she's caused. "I don't understand," Amanda says when Hayley reenters the room, perspiration dotting her forehead, a washcloth at her mouth. "How is that possible?"

Hayley sinks to the bed, stares toward the window. "You still haven't figured it out," she marvels.

"Tell me."

Hayley shakes her head. "I can't. Please. I can't."

"How can we be sisters?" Amanda presses. "I'm twenty-eight. You're . . . what?"

"Forty-one next month," Hayley says, her voice a monotone.

"That's a difference of more than twelve years. My parents were only married a few years before I was born, so obviously we can't have the same father."

Hayley nods, says nothing.

"And before that my mother was married to—"

"—my husband."

"So what are you saying, that my mother has

another ex-husband I don't know anything about?" Like mother, like daughter, she is thinking.

"No, that's not what I'm saying."

"Then I don't understand. Who is your father?"

"My father," Hayley repeats, as if she doesn't understand the word.

"Yes. Who is your father?"

A pause that lasts a lifetime, followed by a voice that is barely a whisper. "My husband," Hayley says as she said only seconds ago.

For a second Amanda thinks that Hayley has misunderstood the question. What other explanation can there be for her strange response? Surely she can't be suggesting . . . Amanda stops, her breath freezing in her lungs. No. It can't be. It's impossible. Beyond impossible. Trembling fingers reach into the pocket of her new winter coat. They withdraw the picture she found hidden in her mother's house. She raises it to her disbelieving eyes.

What Amanda sees: John Mallins, also known as Rodney Tureck, the man her mother shot and killed, holding his young daughter on his lap. The girl is about eight or nine, with dark hair and piercing eyes. "Oh, my God." Amanda staggers back against the desk, as if she's been pushed. The young girl isn't Hope. She's the woman sitting in front of her.

"John Mallins was your father?" Amanda says, her voice so low it seems to be coming from the floor.

"John Mallins was my husband," the other woman corrects, shaking from head to toe. "Before that, he was Rodney Tureck." A sharp cry escapes her throat to stab at the air. "My father."

Amanda's mouth opens, though no sound emerges. She tries to move, but her arms and legs have disappeared. She hangs suspended in the air as Hayley crumples to the floor.

"Please don't let them take my children away from me," Hayley begs, rocking back and forth. "You can't let them take my children away from me."

The full horror of the situation only now begins sinking in. "Your children? Oh, my God. His children."

"He told me if anyone ever found out, they'd take them away from me."

Amanda drops to the floor beside the other woman's feet. "Nobody is going to take your children away from you. Do you hear me?"

Hayley nods her head, although the look on her face says she's far from convinced.

"You have to tell me what happened. Please, Lucy," Amanda says, using the woman's real name for the first time, watching the years fall away from her face, as if a horrible burden has suddenly been removed. "Please tell me what happened."

"He was my father and I loved him. You loved your father, didn't you?" Lucy asks plaintively.

"Very much."

"Yes, your father was a lovely man. He was so wonderful to me."

Amanda nods, conjuring up her father's kind face.

"But he wasn't my father. And I missed my dad so much. He'd always been my hero, always taken my side whenever I was having problems with Mom. She'd say I couldn't have something, and he'd run right out and buy it for me. She'd say I couldn't do something, and he'd tell me I could. Of course, I thought he was the best father on earth. And then he and Mom got a divorce, and he disappeared from my life. All of a sudden, he was just . . . gone. And after a while Mom married Mr. Price, and then, pretty soon, you were born. And it made me miss my father even more.

"And then suddenly, there he was, standing

in front of the house as I was coming home from school. My mother forbade me to see him, of course, so we had to sneak around. He said Mom was an evil woman who'd stolen a lot of money from him, and he asked me to help him find it. I tried, but when I couldn't find anything, he said he had to go away again. The thought of losing him a second time was unbearable, and I begged him to take me with him. He said we'd have to change our names and go into hiding. I thought it sounded terribly exciting, a big adventure. We went to England, and we moved from town to town, and it was okay at first. But after a while, I started missing my mother, and my friends, and especially you. He said we could never go back home, that he'd be charged with kidnapping, and I'd be responsible for him spending the rest of his life in jail. Then he said he'd give me a baby of my own one day."

Amanda buries her head in her hands, unable to hide her growing revulsion.

"You have to understand how isolated I was. We'd spent two years moving from place to place. I had no friends. No one but him. We were never apart. He was everything to me. My father, my teacher, my best friend. Eventually even my lover. Then my husband. We settled in Sutton. He bought a small shop. After a while it started to feel almost . . . normal. I had a string of miscarriages, and then two still-births. God's punishment, I told myself, and then I got pregnant with Hope. And she was all right. Better than all right—she was perfect. And then Spenser came along. And then, well, what was I supposed to do? I'd married my own father. I'd had children with him. Surely he was right—they'd take away my children as soon as anyone found out."

"Nobody is going to take away your children," Amanda assures her again.

"And then John's mother died. And John insisted we come back to settle her estate. He said there was a lot of money involved, and that it would be safe after all this time. The kids were pretty excited. They'd never been anywhere outside of Sutton. And so we came to Toronto, to the Four Seasons hotel."

"And my . . . **our** mother was in the lobby, having tea."

"Yes. Can you imagine? She was having tea with a friend." Lucy laughs through her tears. "Call it what you will—coincidence, fate, divine intervention. Whatever. There she was—having tea."

"And she saw you with the children . . ."

"And she knew immediately what had happened."

"And she came back the next day and killed him."

"The minute the policeman showed up at my door and told me John had been shot," Lucy says, "I knew it was her."

"How did you know?"

"Because I would have done the same thing." Lucy releases another deep breath of air, as if she's been holding her breath for twenty-five years.

And maybe she has, Amanda thinks, taking her sister in her arms. "Any mother would," she tells her, drawing her close. "Any mother would."

THIRTY-FOUR

Some of the crazy thoughts racing through Amanda's mind when she sees her mother on Friday morning: that her mother looks surprisingly beautiful for a battered sixty-one-year-old woman who recently had her stomach pumped; that the awful green of her prison uniform actually complements the color of the bruises on her face; that behind those bruises she can make out faint traces of the sister she only just discovered she has; that she wants to take her mother in her arms and magically kiss away those bruises, and tell her that she understands.

"That was one hell of a stupid stunt you pulled," she says instead, stubbornly refusing to feel sorry for the woman, to allow the small measure of insight she has gleaned into her mother's behavior to sway her sympathies. Sympathy can't erase guilt. Understanding can bridge only so many gaps. And she has been

angry with her mother for far too long to simply let it go. Her anger has fueled her since she
was a child. It has defined her. If she relin-
quishes it, who will be left standing in her
stead? Who will she be?

"Yes, it was very stupid," her mother agrees,
glancing from Amanda to Ben. They are standing in the hallway of the new courthouse, in
roughly the same spot where they'd convened
earlier in the week. Several guards watch from
a discreet distance away. Court has yet to be
called into session.

"How are you feeling, Mrs. Price?" Ben asks.

"Much better, thank you. Eager to get this
over with."

"We have to talk, Mother."

"I know."

Did the fact her mother had lost one daughter justify her neglect of the other? Did it give
her the right to drink herself into oblivion and
medicate herself into psychosis? Did it give her
permission to take the law into her own hands?

"Why don't we sit down?" Ben motions toward a bench against the far wall.

Amanda braces herself for an argument, is
amazed when none is forthcoming. She finds
herself standing alone in the middle of the hall
as Ben leads her mother toward the long

wooden seat, and she glances around self-consciously before following after them. She is trembling, she realizes, as she lowers herself slowly to the seat beside her mother, Ben perching on the other end of the bench. "We talked to Hayley Mallins," she begins. "We know—"

"—everything," Gwen Price says softly. "Yes, I believe you mentioned that in the hospital."

"Why didn't you tell me?"

"What exactly was I supposed to tell you?"

"Everything," Amanda says, using her mother's word, the only word that seems appropriate under the circumstances.

"What was I going to say? Where was I going to start?"

"How about with the fact that Hayley Mallins is my sister?"

Gwen Price nods, tears immediately filling her eyes and spilling down her cheeks. "How is she?"

"Obviously she's very upset."

"She must hate me."

"She doesn't hate you."

"Really? Is that true?"

Amanda shrugs, wondering, Who knows what's true anymore?

"And the children? How are they?"

"They're holding up. They still don't know the whole truth."

Again Gwen nods. "No, they're far too young to understand."

"We're all too young to understand," Amanda says. "I know I can't comprehend it, no matter how many times I repeat it, no matter how hard I try to force the words to make sense. So you tell me, Mother, how could something like this have happened? And how could you have kept it from me all these years?"

"When was I supposed to have told you?" her mother asks. "When you were a baby and your sister disappeared off the face of the earth? When days became weeks and weeks became months and then years, and the police had long since moved on to other, more pressing cases? When I was lost in a maze of booze and antidepressant drugs? When I was too zonked out to get out of bed, or too drunk to see straight? When every time I looked at you, I saw your sister?"

"And so you stopped looking at me? Is that it?"

Her mother bows her head. "I'm so sorry."

"Oh, well, I guess that makes everything all right," Amanda snaps.

"I don't expect you to understand."

"You never gave me a chance to understand."

"You were a child."

"Not for long, I wasn't. You made sure of that."

"I'm so sorry," her mother says again.

Amanda isn't about to let her mother off the hook with anything as simple as an apology. "What about later? When I was all grown-up. Why didn't you tell me then? Why didn't Daddy?"

"He wanted to," her mother says simply. "I wouldn't let him. I made him promise . . ." Her voice sputters to a halt. "Besides, by then it was too late. I was a bitter, angry woman with a bitter, angry daughter who wanted nothing to do with me."

"You're saying it was my fault you didn't tell me?"

"No. God, no," her mother says quickly, reaching for Amanda's hands. "How could it be your fault? It was my fault. Everything was my fault. He warned me. He said if I didn't give him back the money I stole from him, he'd get even. He told me, but I didn't listen. I didn't imagine even he could be so heartless. So evil."

Amanda feels the touch of her mother's fingers like an electric shock, and she jumps to her feet, burying her hands in the pockets of her blue pants. "And so . . . what? I'm supposed to feel sorry for you? I'm supposed to forgive you? Is that it?"

"I don't expect you to forgive me."

"Good. Because it's not going to happen. Trust me—it's never going to happen."

"Tell us about that afternoon when you saw Rodney Tureck with your daughter in the hotel," Ben advises calmly from his seat.

Gwen Price leans back, resting her head against the ivory-colored wall behind her and closing her eyes. "I'd been to a movie with my friend, Corinne. And then we'd gone to the Four Seasons for tea, something we did every week. And we were finishing up, I believe we were just about to leave, it's hard now to remember exactly what happened. But I remember hearing the sound of children laughing, and looking toward the middle of the lobby. And there they were."

"You recognized them after all these years?"

Gwen opens her eyes, stares at the opposite wall as if the scene is being replayed across its smooth surface. "I saw the young girl first. It was like seeing a ghost. She looks just like her mother did at her age. Well, you've seen the photograph. You know. For a second, I actually thought it **was** Lucy, and then I realized that was impossible. Twenty-five years had passed. It couldn't be Lucy." Gwen's eyes shoot from side to side. "I thought my mind was playing horrible tricks on me, like when I was drinking, and I was about to turn away, get the hell out of there, when I saw Rod. And, yes, I recognized him immediately. It's like when you bump into someone you haven't seen since grade school, and it's been decades, and yet you think they haven't changed a bit. Besides, there was no mistaking that face, no matter what he tried to do to it." She rubs her forehead, as if trying to rub the unpleasant image away. "And then I saw the little boy, and then the woman holding on to his hand. His mother. My daughter. And suddenly I knew. It was all so horribly, terribly clear."

"Why didn't you confront them?"

"You have to understand that the whole episode took place in a split second. I was too stunned to do anything," her mother admits. "And then in the next instant, they were gone. I was a complete mess. I don't know how I even made it home. But next thing I knew I was standing in front of my medicine cabinet, with all my pill bottles in my hands, those awful pills I'd saved to remind me how low I'd sunk and how far I'd come, and all I could think of was that I was right back where I'd started, that I was sinking faster than ever, and that if anything, things were far worse than I'd ever imagined. And I thought of swallowing all those pills, of putting an end to my pain once and for all." She laughs, a sharp bark that snaps at the air. "But then I realized they'd all expired, and they'd probably just make me sick. And what would be the point in that?"

"So you decided to kill him instead?"

"I don't remember deciding anything. I don't remember finding the gun or holding it in my hand. His gun, incidentally. One he'd bought for his protection when we were married. Ironic, isn't it? Anyway, all I remember is sitting in that hotel lobby the next day, waiting. And then seeing him push through those revolving doors, and me getting up and walking over to him. And the look of casual dismissal on his face when he saw me. Just some old lady getting in his way, he was thinking. And then that click of recognition in his eyes when it suddenly dawned on him who I was. As clear as the cocking of a trigger." She takes a deep breath before continuing in one long rush. "And then several loud bangs and he was on the floor, and people were screaming, and he was bleeding all over that beautiful carpet, and, well, you know the rest."

"Why didn't you tell the police the truth?"

"How could I do that?" Gwen Price asks her daughter. "How could I do that to Lucy? It was my fault he took her. Everything that happened to her—my fault. Can't you see I had to protect her, that at the very least, I owed her my silence?"

"And you just assumed if you confessed, nobody would bother investigating further?"

"Nobody did," her mother states. "The police had all they needed. Nobody really cared why I did it. Except you." She smiles. "I'd forgotten how stubborn you can be."

"How would you know anything about me?" Amanda asks, her anger returning to resonate through her voice. "All this time I've been away, you never once tried to contact me. You never once tried to see me."

"It took me years to get my act together," her mother says. "When I finally got clean and sober, I hired a private detective. He found you in Florida. I bought a ticket, and then another, and another. But I could never bring myself to get on that plane. I told myself it was because you were doing so well without me, and what was the point in reopening old wounds? And I consoled myself with the knowledge that, unlike your sister, at least I knew where you were. I could watch you from a distance. But the truth was I was scared. I knew what a horrible mess I'd made of everything. I knew how awful I'd been to you, especially after your father died. I knew no amount of apologizing could make that right."

Her mother's harsh judgment, never far from her ear, comes hurtling toward Amanda, like a lance aimed directly at her soul. **Well, with a daughter like you, no wonder your father had a heart attack.**

"You told me I was responsible for Daddy's death."

"Oh, God. That was so unfair. And so untrue. Sweetheart, if anyone was responsible for your father's heart attack, it was me, not you."

Amanda shakes her head. "I was a nightmare."

"You were a teenager. **I** was the nightmare."

Tears fill Amanda's eyes. "I let him down. Every day, one way or another, I let him down."

"No, darling," her mother says adamantly. "He let **you** down."

"What?"

"He was so busy taking care of me that he forgot his most important job was to take care of you. No matter how independent you were, no matter how strong you seemed, no matter what attitude you projected. No matter what. You were his little girl and his first duty was to protect you. Even if the person he had to protect you from was me." She reaches out her hand, returns it to her side when Amanda refuses to acknowledge it. "It wasn't your fault, Mandy. It was never your fault."

The words spin gently around Amanda, wrapping her in a warm cocoon. Like a prisoner wrongly convicted and pardoned after a lifetime in jail, she's been completely and unexpectedly exonerated of all wrongdoing. She's free.

It wasn't your fault, Mandy. It was never your fault.

Amanda collapses back onto the bench. She is not guilty.

"I'm so sorry, darling," her mother continues. "Sorry for everything I put you through, sorry for all the terrible things I said. If there is anything I can say or do to make up for all the pain I've caused you . . ."

Amanda stares into her mother's bruise-covered face. How beautiful she looks, she is thinking. "There is something," she hears herself say.

"What?"

"You can plead not guilty."

"What?" her mother says again.

"You were in an obvious state of disassociation. No jury in the world is going to convict you once they hear your story."

Her mother shakes her head vehemently from side to side. "No jury is ever going to hear that story. **No one else** is ever going to hear that story."

"It's too late," Amanda tells her.

"What? What do you mean?"

"The police have already heard it."

"What are you talking about?" Her mother suddenly becomes agitated, her fingers pulling at the folds of her sweatpants. "You had no right. You had no right to tell them anything."

"She didn't," Ben says.

"What? Then how . . . ?"

"Lucy went to the police last night."

"Lucy went to the police?"

"She told them the truth."

"No. You're lying. You're trying to trick me."

"No, Mother," Amanda says. "No more lies."

"Oh, God. My poor sweet girl. Is she all right?"

"Why don't you ask her yourself?" Amanda says, as Ben stands up and walks toward the doors to the adjoining corridor.

And suddenly there she is, standing in the doorway, framed by the sunlight that pours in from tall, nearby windows. Hayley Mallins, a grown woman who was once a young girl named Lucy Tureck.

Her mother's daughter.

And my sister, Amanda thinks as the woman cautiously approaches. She is wearing a pale pink sweater over a pair of charcoal gray pants, and her dark hair is pushed neatly behind her ears. Although her eyes are slightly puffy from crying and her lips are noticeably trembling, there is an aura of calm about her, Amanda realizes. Serenity surrounds her. Like the girl in Renoir's painting, the one standing on a swing.

Her mother rises slowly to her feet. She teeters there unsteadily, as if held upright by delicate strings, as the stranger who is her daughter draws closer. Invisible wires pull her lips open and apart. "Lucy," she mouths, no sound emerging.

"Mother," comes the silent response.

The two women fall into each other's arms, her mother's hands digging into the soft wool of Lucy's sweater, Lucy's fists clutching at the harsh cotton of her mother's sweatshirt. After several minutes, they pull apart, slowly, reluctantly, their eyes searching each other's face for vestiges of the past, their fingers tracing each new, unfamiliar line. Amanda absorbs the scene from a distance, watching her mother plant at least a dozen kisses along her sister's cheeks, and trying not to imagine the feel of those lips against her own skin.

"I love you," she hears.

"I love you," someone whispers in return.

Amanda swats away an unwanted tear as the women fold effortlessly back into each other's arms, swaying together rhythmically on their invisible swing. She shakes her head impatiently. What the hell is happening? Surely she isn't jealous or upset. God knows she wants no part of such a maudlin display. So what's the matter with her? Why is she feeling so left out? Why is she tearing up over two women she barely knows, and doesn't want to know? Everything has worked out perfectly. Her mother and sister have been reunited. No doubt the crown attorney will be amenable to a deal. She can finally get the hell out of this miserable city once and for all. There you go. Everybody wins. Everything's fine.

Everything's fucking fine.

"Puppet?"

The word floats through the air toward her, beckoning her like a crooked finger. Amanda watches in wonder as the closed circle that is her mother and sister opens like a flower, their arms extending longingly toward her. No, she thinks. I don't want to go. There isn't enough room up there for me. I'll fall off. It's too scary. It's too dangerous.

Except that even as Amanda is shaking her head no, her body is propelling her forward. She feels her sister's arm reach out to grab her elbow. She feels her mother's hand encircling her back. The two women lift her up. Amanda steps onto the swing.

THIRTY-FIVE

They drive in silence to the airport. It is a beautiful, cloudless day, the sun a bold yellow ball in the middle of a dense blue sky. The kind of day that fools you into assuming it's warmer than it actually is, Amanda thinks, wrapping her arms around her new parka, wondering when she'll ever get to wear it in Florida. She was foolish to have spent so much money for something she has so little use for, she is thinking. And red, of all colors. What on earth possessed her?

Obviously, she wasn't herself. Her evil twin, she decides, with a silent chuckle. Or maybe her good one. It was surely this other self who'd agreed to let Ben drive her to the airport when he showed up at her mother's house at six thirty this morning, despite their already having said their good-byes the previous day. Hadn't they both agreed it would be easier that way for both of them, less gut-wrenching and certainly more adult, a fitting and calm conclusion to a surprising and tumultuous week? Hadn't they hugged chastely and wished each other well? Hadn't he promised to keep her apprised of her mother's progress? Hadn't she promised to stay in touch? Hadn't they congratulated one another on a job well done?

The crown attorney had postured stubbornly for several hours, but by yesterday's end, common sense had prevailed, and he and Ben had hammered out a deal, the end result of which would see her mother plead to temporary insanity and spend a minimum amount of time in a mental health facility. By the time she was released, likely in six months, Lucy would have settled up her affairs back in England and returned with her children to Toronto. Thanks to Rodney Tureck's recently deceased mother, she'd even have a bit of money in the bank. Not to mention the $100,000 still sitting in a safety-deposit box in North York.

So that was it. Case closed. Mission accomplished. Her work here was done.

"Are you okay?" Ben asks, breaking the prolonged silence, his voice steady and in control, as if he is comfortable with her decision to return to Florida, as if he has indeed gotten her out of his system once and for all.

Amanda nods, almost afraid to say anything out loud. The truth is she barely recognizes her own voice these days, and after the events of the last week, who knows what's liable to come popping out of her mouth? She arrived in this city a virtual orphan. She is leaving, somebody's daughter, somebody's sister, somebody's aunt. A former husband has become her closest friend. Is it any wonder she barely knows who she is anymore?

She needs time to digest everything that's happened. She needs distance. She needs to discover who Amanda Price Myers Travis really is.

Bullshit! she thinks impatiently, looking toward Ben. She knows exactly who she is. She doesn't need time. She doesn't need space. What she needs is sitting right beside her. What she needs is to bury her pride and tell Ben she's changed her mind, tell him that while Jennifer may be a perfectly competent crown attorney and a nice woman, she's definitely not the woman for him, that there's only one woman for him, and that woman wants another chance.

"So when are you taking the car in to be fixed?" she says instead.

"I thought I'd call the dealership on Monday," Ben answers, eyes on the road ahead. "Hopefully, the repairs won't cost too much."

Again Amanda nods. She thinks she should probably reiterate her apology, at least offer to pay for the damages—the accident was her fault after all. But her apology has already been accepted and her offer would only be rejected, so what's the point? Ben is as proud as he is stubborn.

I'd forgotten how stubborn you can be, she hears her mother say.

She and Ben are indeed very much alike.

Isn't that why you left? she hears him ask.

It was the right decision then, and it's the right decision now, she decides. You have to move forward, move on. You can't turn back time. It's a huge mistake to try.

The highway is less crowded than on previous trips, although there are still plenty of cars on the road. Amanda wonders where they're all going at barely seven o'clock in the morning. The old Corvette bounces over a large pothole. That's the problem with a car whose chassis is built so low to the ground, she thinks. You feel every bump in the road.

"Hungry?" Ben asks as they pass the Airport Hilton.

Amanda shakes her head, recalling the young couple kissing in front of the Hilton's elevators. She hopes they're enjoying their honeymoon in the Bahamas. She hopes they have a long and happy life together.

"We can grab something at the airport, if you'd like."

"No," she says, louder than she'd intended. "Sorry," she apologizes in the next breath.

"What for?"

"Can we make it one size fits all?"

Ben smiles. "You don't owe me any apologies, Amanda."

"I think I do."

"I'm a big boy. I knew what I was getting into."

Glad one of us did, she thinks, looking out the side window as Ben turns into the lane leading to Terminal 2. "You can just drop me off in front," she tells him. "There's no need for you to come inside."

"Yeah, right," he says, entering the parking lot. The car twists up a series of ramps and eventually finds a spot on the fifth floor near the skywalk to the departure level. Ben turns off the engine, removes the keys from the ignition, and turns toward her, a warm smile on his face. "Here we are."

"Here we are," she mimics.

He vaults out of the car, grabbing her overnight bag from the tiny backseat, and opening her door before she has a chance to unbuckle her seat belt.

"You're awfully chipper," she tells him, pushing herself to her feet, bidding a silent farewell to the old car as she follows after him. "Glad to be getting rid of me?"

He smiles. "All good things must come to an end."

Amanda fights the urge to push him down the nearest escalator. She follows him into the already crowded terminal. "God, where is everybody going?"

"Florida," Ben answers. He leads her toward the rows of automatic check-in machines. "You have a credit card?"

"I can do it." Amanda inserts her credit card into the designated slot, then types in the necessary information. They wait in silence for her boarding pass to be spit out. "So, I guess this is it," she says, forcing a smile onto her face.

"We have time," he tells her. "We could grab some coffee."

"No, I think I'd rather get settled. I still have to preclear U.S. customs and go through security. Who knows how long that'll take."

He glances down at the floor, then up again. "So, I guess this is it," he says, repeating her words.

"This is it," she agrees.

He leans in, his lips grazing the side of her cheek. "Take care of yourself, Amanda."

She resists the impulse to touch the spot he kissed, seal the kiss in. "You too."

"You'll call me if you need anything?"

"Absolutely. And you'll call me if there's any news about my mother?"

"You can visit her anytime, you know," he reminds her.

She nods. They've already been over all this. "I'll have to see when I can get some time off. It might not be for a while."

"Whenever," he says. They walk toward the entrance for U.S. customs. Already a lot of people are standing in line. "I think there are some forms you have to fill out." He points to a table of such forms just inside the doors.

"Oh, right. I better do that."

"Boarding pass, please," the uniformed guard says, holding out her hand.

"So, I guess this is **really** it," Amanda says with a laugh.

"This is really it."

"Good-bye, Ben."

"Good-bye, Puppet."

And then suddenly they are in each other's arms, and he is kissing her hair, her cheeks, her eyes, her lips. And she is kissing him back, and crying, and holding on to him for dear life. Don't let me leave, she is thinking. Please. Don't let me leave.

"You're blocking the way," the guard informs them curtly. "I'm afraid you'll have to step aside."

Amanda reluctantly pulls out of Ben's arms. She takes a long, deep breath, tries to regroup. It's time to move forward, she reminds herself. Time to move on. "That's all right. I'm ready." She offers the woman her boarding pass. The woman looks it over, then nods her inside. Amanda walks through the doors, then turns back to Ben. Tell me to stay, she appeals to him silently. "Call me sometime," she says out loud, watching him disappear into the crowd. So this is it, she is thinking. This is **really** it.

She fills out the necessary forms and takes her place in line. **Kir-rell,** she recites silently as a merciful numbness spreads from the top of her head to the tips of her toes. **Kir-rell. Kir-rell.** And then somebody's cell phone cuts into the hypnotic rhythm of her borrowed mantra.

Her cell phone, she realizes, snatching it from her purse.

"Too soon to call?" Ben's voice asks in her ear.

"Where are you?"

"In my car. And believe it or not, it's starting to snow again."

Amanda glances toward the long window at the front of the large room. It is indeed starting to snow.

"And I was thinking," he continues, "that I haven't had a vacation in some time, and I'd really like to get away somewhere warm for a few weeks."

"Florida's warm," she tells him, holding her breath.

"I don't know. It might be difficult to get a hotel. . . ."

"I know a great place you can stay. It's beautiful. Right on the ocean."

"Well, I'll have to arrange my schedule, see when I can get away. . . ."

"I think you should do that," Amanda tells him quickly, inching toward the front of the line. "And maybe, in the meantime, you could make some inquiries about what someone would have to do to pass the Canadian bar. I mean, I'll probably have to spend a fair bit of time there, making sure my mother doesn't kill anyone else."

"I think that's probably a good idea."

There is a long pause. What am I doing? she is thinking. "I love you," she says.

"I love you too," comes the simple reply.

"Next," the guard announces, directing Amanda to booth number 15.

"Bad time for you?" the customs agent asks sarcastically, motioning toward the phone in her hand.

"What? Oh, no." She drops the phone back into her purse and hands the man her passport, trying not to smile too hard. "It's a great time."

An hour later, she sits staring out the window of the crowded jet. The pilot has just announced they are flying at a cruising altitude of thirty-seven thousand feet. He has cautioned that although the sky is bright and clear, they can probably expect some pockets of turbulence along the way. Amanda lays her forehead against the small porthole, losing herself in the expanse of limitless blue.

What Amanda sees: the future.